Agent in th

Alex Gerlis was born in Lincolnshire and worked as a BBC journalist for nearly thirty years. His first novel, *The Best of Our Spies* (2012), is an Amazon bestseller and has been optioned for television serialisation.

Agent in the Shadows is his eleventh novel: he's written three series of espionage novels all set in Europe during the Second World War and all published by Canelo. There are four books in the *Spy Masters* series; four in the *Prince* series and three in the *Wolf Pack* series, of which *Agent in the Shadows* is the final book.

Alex lives in London, is married with two daughters and is represented by Gordon Wise at the Curtis Brown Literary Agency.

www.alexgerlis.com

Facebook: Alex Gerlis Author

Twitter: @alex_gerlis

www.canelo.co/authors/alex-gerlis/

Also by Alex Gerlis

Spy Masters

The Best of Our Spies
The Swiss Spy
Vienna Spies
The Berlin Spies

The Richard Prince Thrillers

Prince of Spies
Sea of Spies
Ring of Spies
End of Spies

The Wolf Pack Spies

Agent in Berlin
Agent in Peril
Agent in the Shadows

ALEX GERLIS

AGENT IN THE SHADOWS

CANELO

First published in the United Kingdom in 2023 by

Canelo
Unit 9, 5th Floor
Cargo Works, 1–2 Hatfields
London SE1 9PG
United Kingdom

A CIP catalogue record for this book is available from the British Library.

Print ISBN 978 1 80436 342 3
Ebook ISBN 978 1 80032 158 8

Cover design by Nick Venables

Look for more great books at www.canelo.co

Printed and bound in Great Britain by Clays Ltd, Elcograf S.p.A.

1

Main Characters

British (and US) Characters

Jack Miller American journalist and British agent

Barnaby Allen (Barney) MI6 officer, London

Piers Devereux Barney's boss at MI6

Roly Pearson British Intelligence chief

Basil Remington-Barber head of MI6 Berne

Noel Moore MI6 officer, Berne

Nicholas/Jeffrey Morgan British fascist

Tom Gilbey MI6 officer

Harold Dickson fascist recruit

Lawrence British radio operator, Switzerland

Stephen Summers solicitor, London

Cedric man at Hope pub

German Characters

Sophia von Naundorf British agent

Siegfried Schroth actor and British agent in Düsseldorf

Klaus Barbie Gestapo chief, Lyon

Konrad Busch SS officer, Berlin

Hannelore Busch wife of Konrad Busch

Heinz-Wilhelm Schütze man killed in Brandenburg

Klara Förster sister of Heinz-Wilhelm Schütze

Günther Förster husband of Klara

Johanna Brüderlin sister of Klara and Heinz-Wilhelm Schütze

Georg Lange Abwehr officer, Paris

Wagner Gestapo officer, Paris

Helmut Knochen SS commander, Paris

Luise Brunner secretary sent to work at Gestapo HQ, Lyon

Walter Möller Lyon Gestapo

Otto Winter Lyon Gestapo ADC to Barbie

Franz Boehm Lyon Gestapo

French Characters

Marcel Mars Resistance Network, Lyon

Maurice Mars Resistance Network, Lyon

Michel Mars Resistance Network, Lyon

Anna Rousseau Mars Resistance Network, Lyon

Madame Madelaine Mars Resistance Network, Lyon

René Dupont chef de centre adjoint, *milice*

Madame Faure café owner, Lyon

Doctor Hubert Mars Resistance Network, Lyon

Benoît Roux French Resistance in Geneva

Agnes Kléber office manager at Gestapo HQ, Lyon

Hugo Resistance, Strasbourg

Marie Resistance, Strasbourg

Georges Moreau traitor

Swiss Characters

Captain Gerber Berne police officer, contact of Basil

Harald Mettler clerk at Swiss Embassy, Berlin, British agent

Emile Jeanneret watch expert, Geneva

Rolf Eder MI6 agent Zürich

Russian Characters

A.I. Stepanov (Arkady) NKVD Commissar, Berne

Leytenant Mikhail Danielovich Marshak Red Army officer, Krakow

Polkovnik Krupkin NKGB officer, Krakow

Nikolai Soviet Legation, Berne

Polish Characters

Raisa Loszynski daughter of Roman Loszynski

Max Loszynski son of Roman Loszynski

The Wolf

In the closing hours of a wolf's life, as it approaches the end of its final journey, look into its eyes to understand the life it has led.

It will have been a hard life, always alert to danger, burdened by the strain of constant vigilance: not knowing who to trust and where the enemy lurks.

And as its final days approach, the wolf will leave the pack, knowing it is now vulnerable and hoping it can fade away in peace.

France was always dangerous territory for the wolf. It was hunted to extinction there in 1933, the same year Hitler came to power in Germany.

Yet for many years after, including during the Second World War, throughout rural France one would often see three words painted in large red letters on country walls and bridges.

Mort au loup.

Kill the wolf.

Introduction

The historical context of *Agent in the Shadows* is set out in more detail at the end of the book. However, I thought it would be helpful to mention some important elements of the story at the outset.

France fell to the Nazis in June 1940. From then until late 1942, Lyon – France's third largest city – was in the so-called Free Zone, the collaborationist Vichy regime. In reality, the city was under the Nazi yoke. It came directly under German control from November 1942 until its liberation at the beginning of September 1944.

On 14 September 1944 General de Gaulle, the leader of the Free French, visited the city and addressed the crowds on Place des Terreaux from the balcony of the Hôtel-de-Ville. Describing the city as '…*la capitale de la Résistance Française*…' he went on to say: 'How to tell Lyon all the emotion, all the gratitude I feel in this Gallic capital, which was the capital of the French Resistance and which is today a very large city in our France covered with wounds, shining in its honour and carried away by its hope.'

The question of the French Resistance is a complex one, not least because it tends to mask the significant collaboration – passive and otherwise – by large parts of the French population and officialdom. There is also no question that for a long period of the war the Resistance was little more than an annoyance for the German occupiers and limited in its effectiveness.

Having said that, as D–Day approached and thereafter, the Resistance was of considerable importance. Indeed, after the war, the Supreme Allied Commander in Europe, General Dwight

Eisenhower, famously described the French Resistance as having been worth 'an extra six divisions'. While this may have been an exaggeration, it would be wrong to underestimate the eventual scale of the Resistance and the enormous courage displayed by the *resistants*.

And finally, a brief mention of Klaus Barbie (there is more on him in the Author's Note at the end).

Barbie was just twenty-nine when he was sent to Lyon in November 1942, although by then he'd already acquired a reputation as a particularly brutal Gestapo officer. He soon became known as 'The Butcher of Lyon', a reputation based on his uncompromising brutality and effectiveness. Despite running the Gestapo in the city, he often personally carried out raids and tortured prisoners. It is estimated that he was personally responsible for the deaths of at least four thousand people and indirectly responsible for the deaths of at least twice as many more.

–

The story which follows is fiction, but based substantially on fact.

Chapter 1

'Abandon hope, all ye who enter here!'

The small landing at the top of the winding staircase was dark and fusty, with a pale shaft of light seeping out through the half-open doorway in front of him. He'd paused to catch his breath and the man who'd uttered these words was so short he'd not noticed him at first. He glanced down to spot him close to his elbow, just five foot if he was very lucky. He was craning his neck as he looked up, large eyes twinkling in the gloom.

'I beg your pardon?' Harold Dickson didn't want to sound rude, but he'd been in two minds about coming along to this place as it was and the last thing he needed was this odd little man talking nonsense.

'Dante – you've heard of Dante, I presume?'

He didn't reply: he wondered whether he'd got the date wrong. The monthly meeting of the Bloomsbury branch of the Lunatics Association, maybe. Perhaps he ought to leave now.

'Dante Alighieri, Italian poet, wrote *The Divine Comedy* in 1320: heard of him?'

'Who?'

'Dante!'

Harold Dickson said he was afraid he'd not and started to enter the room, but the man clutched his sleeve tightly with one hand and grabbed his right hand with the other and shook it vigorously and introduced himself as Cedric.

1

'In *The Divine Comedy* Dante describes being at the entrance to hell, with an inscription above the gates which translates as "Abandon hope, all ye who enter here!" Now perhaps you understand why I greeted you with that classical reference?'

Harold Dickson wasn't sure he did but nodded and tried to pull away from Cedric, who was still gripping his sleeve.

'Very apposite, wouldn't you say?'

'I'm not sure I understand, to be frank.'

'Not classically educated, are you? You sound northern to me! The reference to abandoning hope is apposite because of where we are – the Hope public house. Fancy that, eh?'

Harold Dickson said fancy that indeed and yes, he did now see what he meant and it was very good to meet him but he really didn't want to miss the start of the meeting so if Cedric didn't mind, he…

Harold Dickson freed himself from the little man's clutches and entered the room, which was oppressively warm and foul-smelling. The summer of 1933 was particularly unpleasant in London and when he'd set out from Whitehall a quarter of an hour earlier it had been a dry if humid early August evening. As he crossed Trafalgar Square a light drizzle started and by the time he'd reached The Hope in Kenton Street in Bloomsbury the drizzle had turned into a downpour.

This accounted for the atmosphere in the room, the fug hanging over it, the few people in there reeking of the unpleasant odour warm rain seems to release from clothes.

Again, he wondered how wise attending a meeting like this really was. What would happen if his employers found out? The encounter with Cedric had thrown him – what if they were all such oddballs?

But he was here now and maybe it would be fine, so he selected a chair towards the back of the room and looked around at the dozen other people, all sitting apart, all men, all in their forties or older, all looking slightly forlorn with sallow complexions and unhappy, angry eyes and evidently carrying the weight of the world on slumped shoulders.

He hoped he didn't look like any of them.

There were forty-eight chairs laid out for the audience and at the front of the room was a table facing the audience, a frayed Union Jack flag draped over it. Behind it sat a tense-looking couple, both short and rotund. Behind them was a banner tacked to the wall, drooping at one end.

The British Union of Fascists.

Taped to the front of the table was a large card.

For Britain!

The couple kept glancing at their watches and muttering to each other and then looking up anxiously at the door. At seven o'clock precisely a man entered the room, striding purposefully to the front. He was wearing a trilby and a raincoat and despite the time of year wore leather gloves, which he carefully removed – one finger at a time – as he surveyed the room. Only one or two more people had joined the audience, but if he was disappointed, he didn't show it.

He nodded to the couple and wished them a good evening and Dickson heard the woman apologise to the man and suggest that if they were to perhaps wait for a few more minutes she was sure the room would soon fill up, but the man said not to bother and he'd start and no, thank you, there was no need for them to introduce him and yes, please, a glass of water would be very much appreciated.

He spoke fluently, without notes, for the best part of three quarters of an hour. He wasn't a great orator like Oswald Mosley, who Dickson had heard speak the previous year. But he spoke in calm, measured tones with the occasional clever joke, which Dickson seemed to be one of the few in the audience to appreciate. He spoke in some detail – arguably in too much detail – about the economy: of Keynes and the need to tackle the scourge of unemployment and of how to spend more money to help people. There was a lengthy section on supply and demand and then something about the gold standard, which Dickson didn't understand but he nodded as if he did.

If he was honest, it was more of a lecture than an oration: too dry and academic. He found it interesting enough but then he made an effort to follow economics. He made a point of reading the office copy of the *Financial Times* in his lunch break.

Then the man stopped to drink some water. He paused for a while, as if gathering his thoughts, and then nodded, sure now of what he was going to say next. He swept his hand through his hair and his whole demeanour appeared to change and he began to speak more loudly, sounding angry and agitated as his voice rose and fell.

We all know who to blame for this mess we're in, do we not?

There was some nodding of heads in the sparse audience, though people seemed unsure how to react to this sudden change of mood, slightly taken aback by it.

Does one perhaps need to spell out precisely who is responsible for the crisis Christian Europe finds itself in today, just fifteen years after the end of the Great War?

He paused and looked directly at the audience, expecting an answer. His shoulders were thrust back, an orator's pose, as if in imitation of Mosley. There was more nodding of heads and mutterings of agreement.

Or is it not obvious – blindingly obvious – who is the cause of all our woes?

Someone started clapping, which Dickson thought didn't feel right but other members of the audience began to join in, though it sounded sporadic and discordant.

The speaker then spelt out – at length – precisely who was responsible.

There are in excess of half a million Jews in this country and a similar number of communists: which makes one million enemies of the state!

He'd shouted the words 'one million' and then paused at the end of the sentence, allowing his audience to absorb the enormity of what he'd just told them. Dickson nodded enthusiastically. He didn't doubt that these people – the Jews and the communists – were indeed the enemies of the state. That, after all, was the reason for his interest in this subject and for his attendance at the meeting. But he'd read up on this subject and his understanding was that there were considerably fewer than half a million Jews in the country and he very much doubted there were anything like half a million communists and many of them would be Jewish so were being double-counted.

But maybe a little exaggeration could be excused.

The point was still well made.

–

The meeting ended abruptly at eight o'clock. Harold Dickson assumed there'd be questions and had been making notes during the talk and had come up with what he considered were a couple of well-expressed questions.

But instead, the man said he had to leave now but he hoped it had been a useful talk and please could everyone ensure that they supplied their names and addresses to Cedric so they could be invited to future events. He pointed to the short man, now standing at the back of the room, grinning and raising himself on his toes so people could see him.

The man behind the table urged everyone to stay for a little longer. 'Just a few minutes and then we can repair downstairs for some liquid refreshment!' But Dickson didn't fancy the idea of Cedric or indeed anyone else in the room buttonholing him at the bar. Once on Kenton Street he was relieved to see the heavy rain was now a light drizzle. He headed towards Kings Cross from where he'd take the underground home.

He was on Tavistock Place when he became aware of someone walking alongside him. He glanced across and was surprised to see it was the speaker. He said nothing for a while as they walked along in step.

'I trust you found the talk interesting?'

Dickson said he had, very much so. The man continued walking silently next to him. By the time they came alongside

Regent Square Gardens it had stopped raining and the man suggested they find a bench and have a chat.

'I didn't pitch it right, did I?'

'I beg your pardon?' They'd found a bench that was more or less dry and were facing a strip of grass where some boys were playing football in defiance of a sign warning them not to.

'My talk: most of it was way above their heads. I tried to compensate for that towards the end, but I fear I ranted somewhat.'

'I actually found it most absorbing: what you said about the economy was most interesting. I'm no expert, of course, but I do take an interest.'

'So I could see: I always watch an audience most carefully and I can tell from their eyes how much they understand. You were the only member of the audience who seemed to comprehend what I was saying. I could tell you're an intelligent man.'

He said thank you very much and proffered his hand, introducing himself as Harold Dickson.

The man shook it and said Harold could call him Nicholas and Harold replied that his brother was called Nicholas and what a small world it was. He could have kicked himself as he said that: he had an infuriating habit when in the presence of someone more important of nervously making inconsequential and frankly inane remarks.

'And your line of work, Harold?'

'I'm with the Ministry of Labour, in Whitehall.'

Nicholas raised his eyebrows approvingly and then asked a series of questions: what was his job there, where was he from, how long had he been in London, his personal circumstances, how had he become interested in the British Union of Fascists, what did he think of Jews… and of Germany?

Harold Dickson couldn't make Nicholas out: he was clearly someone quite important, but what if he was a police agent? He'd heard about that, about how they were infiltrating various patriotic organisations.

6

Nevertheless, he answered as best he could. He was from Manchester, he'd been in London since 1931 – almost two years now – he was a senior clerical officer at the Ministry, he was single and lived in a bedsit in Finsbury Park and agreed with everything Nicholas had said about Jews – and communists, for that matter – and as for Germany he was a great admirer of the country, so much so that he'd enrolled in night-classes to learn German as part of a Civil Service staff education scheme. He was most heartened by recent developments there and if only this country was led by someone with the vision and determination of Herr Hitler and... what was the other question?

'How did you become interested in the British Union of Fascists?'

Nicholas was staring straight ahead, smoking a cigarette in a holder, which appeared to be made from ivory.

'I was handed a leaflet outside Charing Cross station and realised their views were very much in accord with my own. I joined the party a couple of months ago and now I subscribe to the *Blackshirt*. I find it speaks a good deal more sense than the Jewish-owned newspapers.'

Nicholas nodded and said 'indeed' but as he turned towards him it began to rain again and in the way of August weather it was soon very heavy and the two of them stood up and made to leave the small park.

'I suggest we meet again, Harold. I've enjoyed our brief chat but would appreciate a longer one. Perhaps in a week's time?'

Harold Dickson said yes, by all means – it would be a pleasure and...

'You have a lunch break, I presume?'

Harold said yes, Fridays were by far the best day because the senior officials left at lunchtime for their weekend in the country.

'A week on Friday then: head towards Northumberland Avenue and then walk in the direction of the river. I'll see you then.'

Harold Dickson did as Nicholas had instructed: he took a late lunch break and left the Ministry of Labour by the main entrance on Whitehall and headed north and just before Trafalgar Square turned into Northumberland Avenue.

It was a pleasant day, not as humid as it had been recently thanks to a light breeze from the river. It had occurred to him that he'd allowed himself to be charmed by a man he knew next to nothing about. It was one of his weaknesses, an excessive desire to court the approval of people, a tendency to be flattered and allow that to perhaps cloud his judgement. It was, he thought, down to his background: a working-class boy with a scholarship to a grammar school. Not quite fitting in, but always looking for someone who may allow him to do so.

It was at that moment that Nicholas appeared alongside, wishing him a good afternoon and asking how was he and without waiting for an answer suggesting maybe they should find a bench on the Victoria Embankment. They found an isolated one close to Hungerford Bridge.

'I see that you joined the party and subscribed to the *Blackshirt* in your own name. I wonder whether that was an altogether wise decision?'

'I didn't think it would be a problem.'

'You're a civil servant, Dickson. Not a terribly senior one, admittedly, but it could be a problem. How long did you say you've been with the Ministry of Labour?'

'Two years and—'

'Have you ever thought of applying for a transfer to another government department?'

Dickson said he hadn't, he was happy enough where he was, and he hoped he was in line for another promotion soon and after that, who knows?

'Who knows what, indeed. But let me come to the point. You're a bright chap and clearly one of us.'

He paused as he placed a cigarette in the ivory holder and Dickson wondered if Nicholas would elaborate on what exactly he meant by 'one of us' but got the impression that whatever it was, it was a compliment.

'You're the type of chap who could be most useful to us, but not in the Ministry of Labour. I would like you to consider applying for a transfer. There are two or three government departments where you could be of considerable help to us. I have some experience in this respect, but one needs to proceed with caution. I need you to listen carefully.'

–

Harold Dickson had listened carefully and found himself seduced by Nicholas's promise of greater things, of how invaluable he could be to the cause and of how he deserved a more important role.

His transfer duly came through that November and he was to start his new job at the beginning of 1934.

In the six weeks between getting his new job and starting it, he had – on Nicholas's instructions – changed his name. It had been surprisingly straightforward: Nicholas put him in touch with a solicitor who he said was also 'one of us' and who handled everything, all costs covered by Nicholas. He wrote on his client's behalf to the Personnel Department at his new department informing them of his new surname, explaining that he'd taken on his late mother's maiden name in her memory and no longer wished to use Harold, and from now his middle name would be his sole Christian name.

There was a change of address to inform them of too: a very pleasant small apartment in Highbury, somewhat beyond his budget, but Nicholas had been most helpful and generous in that respect.

All of which meant that by the time he began his new job Harold Dickson no longer existed.

On Nicholas's strict instructions he eschewed all interest in politics. He expressed no opinions. He was careful, discreet and very hard-working. He did nothing to give rise to the slightest suspicion and soon began to prosper in his new job as Nicholas promised he would. He continued his Civil Service German lessons and Nicholas arranged for him to have private lessons, which led to a noticeable improvement in that language, which in turn did his career no harm.

He met Nicholas once a month during 1934. Nicholas asked little of him at these carefully arranged meetings other than the names of people he worked with and their roles. These were more just friendly chats, constantly stressing the importance of keeping his head down and concentrating on his career. He also encouraged him to apply for an overseas posting.

Early in 1935 Nicholas confided in him that he and a number of others were coming to the view that Oswald Mosley was too moderate, unwilling to embrace the ideals of National Socialism. But for the time being, Nicholas told him, he was to carry on and keep his head down.

The time when they would call on his services was not now.

That time would come soon.

And then late in 1935 there was unexpected news. An overseas posting had come up and he'd obviously impressed his new bosses enough to be offered it. He barely had time to see Nicholas before he left and when he did, Nicholas seemed distracted.

He told him to keep his head down.

Maybe the time when Nicholas would call on his services would be sooner or later.

Chapter 2

Berne, Switzerland
August 1943

'You're going to need to snap out of it, I'm afraid.'

Sophia von Naundorf could sense Jack Miller bristling next to her on the sofa. Over the past few days Basil Remington-Barber had persisted in telling his two spies they needed to 'snap out of it' and Jack had sworn that if the Englishman said it one more time, the only thing that would snap was Basil's neck.

'You seem to forget, Basil, that we became very close to Roman. I smuggled him out of Austria into Switzerland and Jack and I then worked closely with him. His invention could have made an enormous contribution to the Allied war effort. And remember, Jack and I risked our lives going back into Germany. For us to be captured by the Gestapo and then escape only to be told that Roman had died in an explosion is—'

'He almost certainly blew himself up – deliberately. We need to understand that—'

'Whatever caused his death or led to it, Basil, that's not for us to judge. He was in despair about his family. He had to leave them behind in Poland and I don't think he ever got over that.'

'I know that, Sophia my dear. We have to accept that they're most probably dead now and—'

'Exactly, that's the point, isn't it, Basil?' Jack was speaking for the first time, the American's voice raised. 'He either found out his family were dead or had come to the conclusion there was nothing he could do to save them. We'll never know which it was, but I've no doubt he blamed himself. We –' at that point Jack paused and made a gesture which made it clear Basil was very much included in the 'we' '– we are all to blame. We ought to have done more to help him, to understand him.'

'There is a war on, you know, and—'

'For Christ's sake, Basil, if you say that one more time I'm finished, you can count me out of your games. I know there's a war on. My brother was killed in it and Sophia and I have spent enough time working for you as British agents inside Germany. Of all people we don't need telling there's a war on! We just think you ought to be more understanding. It's only six weeks since we escaped from Germany.'

Basil Remington-Barber was silent for a few moments and then said he was terribly sorry, perhaps he'd underestimated how long it would take them to get over everything and… There was another long pause and Sophia asked him what he was trying to say, and the Englishman said maybe they needed to get back in the saddle and Sophia said she wasn't sure what he meant.

'It's an English saying.' Jack placed his hand on Sophia's thigh and smiled and Basil shuffled around in his chair, as ever discomfited by their displays of affection. 'It means when you fall off a horse the best way to get over it is to get back on the horse again. Are you trying to say you have another mission in mind for us?'

They were in the library of the British Embassy safe house just outside Berne, where Sophia and Jack had been staying since returning from their last mission in Germany. Basil walked over to the far side of the room to face a large map of Europe, his back to his two spies. He nodded, as if satisfied all the countries were in their correct positions. Only then did he turn round, moving to one side of the mantelpiece, very much the schoolmaster about to start a lesson.

'Over the past six months the change in the course of the war has been most profound. Unlike the earlier part of the conflict, these changes have been almost entirely in the Allies' favour. At the beginning of February, the Germans surrendered at Stalingrad, which put pay to any ambitions the Nazis may have had of defeating the Soviet Union. At the same time, Tripoli – here – fell to the Allies. Then we saw the Allied bombing campaign on the Ruhr, which you know all about and which has undoubtedly been a success. Since then, the Nazis have been defeated in the Battle of Kursk; the Germans and Italians have been defeated in North Africa and in July we invaded Sicily and we're now on the verge of capturing the island, after which there's the Italian mainland.'

Basil surveyed the map for a while and then turned to Sophia and Jack, clearly taking some personal pride at the Allied success.

'It rather sounds as if we're redundant, Basil?'

'What do you mean, Jack?'

The American gestured towards the map. 'Sounds as if the war is almost over and maybe we're not needed any more.'

'I shall give you the benefit of the doubt, Jack, and assume you're teasing me. It is indeed tempting to take a view that victory is in our grasp but, in fact, there's still an awfully long way to go. Germany remains very strong and retains an iron grip on most of Europe. The war will not be won until we can open a second front and land somewhere around here – on the northern French coast – and move on from there to liberate Europe.

'All of which means France is the key to Allied success. We must be confident our invasion won't be repelled. We simply cannot risk failure. Were that to happen then the second front would be delayed for a year. Imagine, another year of this cursed war. And this is where you both come in.'

Basil outlined a series of rough circles over France with his pointer. 'We need to ensure that by the time the second front comes, the Nazi's hold on France is weakened. When our forces land, the German occupiers should be looking over their shoulders, worried about who else is fighting them inside France.

'I'm talking about the French Resistance: there is plenty of talk about them – brave chaps and girls, blowing up the occasional railway line or putting sugar in the fuel tanks of German military vehicles, slogans on walls, leaflets – all good for morale and whatever – but that isn't the point of the Resistance. Their real purpose should be for it to develop into a formidable fighting force by the time the second front arrives, whenever that is – most likely sometime next year. We need them to be a genuine underground movement by then – an army, if you like, one which will rise up and hit the Germans from every angle when our forces land on the northern coast. If they do their job properly then they'll be in a position to totally undermine the German defence. They'll be able to disrupt them, block their reinforcements, make them worry about being attacked from every angle.'

'And our role in this?'

Basil looked at Sophia, sitting in what his wife would describe as a demure manner. She really was the most remarkable woman: an SS officer's wife turned British spy and unquestionably one of the best they had. And such a contrast to Jack Miller, also a highly effective and brave British agent, but who was direct to the point of being rude. Yet the two opposites were clearly in love. He turned back to the map and placed the pointer close to the Swiss border.

'Lyon: not terribly far from here. Arguably as dramatic a city as Paris: wonderful food, home of French gastronomy. And more to the point, the heart of the French Resistance. You'll get a full briefing, of course, but the Resistance there has been severely wounded and if that proves to be fatal then so could be the outcome of the second front. We need to get into Lyon to sort it out, to help rebuild the Resistance, but it won't be easy. The Gestapo there is the most brutal and the most effective in all of France.'

The long silence that followed was broken only by the sound of a clock at the far end of the room and a dog barking in the distance. Basil Remington-Barber watched the two agents carefully: Sophia sitting quite still, the very faintest trace of a smile on her face but showing no reaction other than that. Jack Miller sighed, ran his hands through his hair, glanced at Sophia and then walked up to the map, as if checking Lyon really was there.

'Severely wounded, you say?'

'Yes, Jack: I'm afraid so.'

'And the most brutal Gestapo in all of France?'

'Young chap called Klaus Barbie runs it. Took over at the end of last year. Already acquired himself a dreadful reputation. The French call him *le boucher de Lyon* – the butcher of Lyon.'

'And you want us to go there?'

'As I say, Jack, you'll get a full briefing and we still have to work out cover stories and—'

'When were you thinking of sending us there, Basil?'

It was Sophia speaking. Basil had come to realise that while the American was more emotional, Sophia was much more practical. In a very Germanic way, she was good at taking orders, certainly less likely to question them.

'Not just yet because we need to work on your cover stories and liaise with what's left of the Resistance in Lyon. And there's another thing... someone else is going to be looking after you from now on.'

'Are you retiring, Basil?'

The Englishman laughed, not without a hint of bitterness. 'I was meant to retire in 1939 but this damned war put paid to that. Heaven knows when I'll be able to retire, but whereas the Swiss station was a bit of an outpost for MI6 before the war, now it's very much the centre of things, as you can imagine, and I'm afraid that the amount of work I have to do has become rather overwhelming. You are without doubt two of our most prized agents and you need more attention than I can give you.'

'Will it be Noel looking after us?'

'No, he's terribly busy too. You're so highly regarded they're sending someone over from London to run your operation.'

'And are you going to tell us who they are?'

Basil leaned back on the sofa and crossed his legs.

'You'll meet him very soon: but he's terribly senior. Outranks me!'

Chapter 3

Hanover, Germany
May 1941

By his thirty-eighth year Heinz-Wilhelm Schütze felt he'd reached an age where he no longer needed to crave the constant assurance and approval of others. Everything he'd done over the past year in particular had led him to the inescapable conclusion that he was indeed very bright and the description of genius – which had once been given to him by a teacher – was not an undeserved one.

He did sometimes wonder what would have happened had the tragedy of March 1937 not taken place, even though his mother had always told him there was nothing to be gained from always looking back and wishing life had turned out differently.

'We have to accept the life God has decided for us, Heinz-Wilhelm,' she'd say, a hint of bitterness in her voice, a sense that she herself hadn't quite accepted what God had decided for her. And in the same breath she'd use him as an example. It was God's will that he'd turned out so differently from other children, she'd say – and as a consequence had continued to live with his parents even though he was now in his thirties.

'Your father and I… it is our duty to care for you.' She never failed to make that sound like a punishment inflicted upon her. There was a conversation like this most weeks, invariably on the theme of the sacrifices Wilhelmine and Helmut Schütze had made for their son.

And then that bleak Sunday evening in March 1937 when his parents had gone for their usual drive in the countryside north-west of Berlin. He was never invited on these Sunday afternoon drives; it was understood this was his parents' time together.

They'd set off after lunch, the Daimler 15, which was his father's pride and joy, pulling out of the drive in Falkensee, the low sun glinting off the car's deep crimson paintwork.

He spent the afternoon working on his mathematical formulae and scribbling calculations in his notebook, the tiny, precise handwriting, intricately drawn diagrams on a facing page.

And as it began to get dark, he did wonder whether they should have returned by now but then remembered that since getting the new Daimler their Sunday afternoon drives had been longer, so he took out the envelope of stamps from his desk drawer and picked a Swiss one and set to work copying it. His technique was improving but he was some way from producing a perfect stamp, one indistinguishable from its original.

He was so absorbed that until he heard the doorbell, he had no idea that it was nearly seven-thirty, a good hour and a half after his parents should have returned.

After the police officer reassured a clearly panicked Heinz-Wilhelm that of course they weren't going to arrest him, he was quite blunt. He was sorry to say that his parents' car had come off the road just outside the town of Börnicke and...

The policeman had paused, obviously expecting Heinz-Wilhelm to understand from his tone that he was trying to impart terrible news, but Heinz-Wilhelm had smiled and said that was a shame because the Daimler 15 was his father's pride and joy and he'd be most annoyed if it was damaged in any way... and then the other police officer cottoned on that Heinz-Wilhelm was perhaps not all he seemed and asked if he had any close family in Berlin and Heinz-Wilhelm said he had two sisters, one in Berlin and the other in Zürich, which was in Switzerland.

His sister Klara came round soon after the policeman telephoned her. She and her husband, Günther, went into the sitting room with the police officers and then came out to talk with Heinz-Wilhelm alone, patiently explaining that his parents had been killed in the car crash. Heinz-Wilhelm had never especially liked his brother-in-law – he was wary of anyone in uniform – but Günther had been uncharacteristically pleasant and actually been rather reassuring, saying he wasn't to worry, he'd be looked after.

Except, of course, he wasn't.

He had no doubt that they started to watch the house that same evening, at least a dozen of them, hard to identify because their faces were usually covered and at any one time four or five of them were there, outside the house, in the garden and across the street.

He didn't say anything about them to either of his sisters until after the funeral and when he did raise the subject they gave him that look he was so used to and told him he was letting his imagination get the better of him yet again and he mustn't worry about things, and then his brother-in-law said he didn't think it was a good idea for him to stay on his own in such a big house and Heinz-Wilhelm replied and said he wasn't on his own, there was the housekeeper and the gardener and Günther said that really wasn't the point and in any case the house had to be sold but he wasn't to worry because some of the money would be used to look after him.

They sold the house in the summer of 1937. Heinz-Wilhelm had hoped to buy an apartment in the centre of Berlin, somewhere within walking distance of the Staats Bibliothek, the library between Dorotheen Strasse and the Unter de Linden, maybe close to the café on Gendarmen Markt which did the best sausages in Berlin and where he could eat every night because Günther had assured him money wouldn't be a problem.

But it turned out his monthly allowance was only enough to rent an apartment in Moabit – not quite as central as he'd have liked – and provide for his living costs. Every Tuesday he met Klara at Wertheim's department store on Leipziger Platz, where they'd lunch in the fifth-floor restaurant and then if he needed anything – socks, toiletries, for instance – Klara would help him because he was the first to admit he wasn't very good at shopping. He knew he spent too much on things his sisters said he didn't need.

Every month Klara would take him to the doctor on Leipzigerstrasse. The doctor – an overweight Bavarian called Braun – was nothing like Dr Sperling, the kindly doctor he'd seen regularly until 1935, when his parents announced that because Dr Sperling was Jewish it was not appropriate for him to continue to be treated by him. This was a shame because Dr Sperling was understanding and reassured Heinz-Wilhelm that there was nothing wrong with him other than that he was different to other people in the way he thought and acted. Nonetheless, said Dr Sperling, society expected people to behave in a certain way and the medication he was giving him would help control his behaviour.

Heinz-Wilhelm had the impression it was his parents who'd wanted him to be on the medication, because one day when his mother had to leave the room briefly Dr Sperling had told him he was actually on a much lower dose than his parents wanted him to be on.

But Dr Braun was totally lacking in empathy. He told Heinz-Wilhelm that the Jewish doctor had got it all wrong and he needed a weekly injection and he had to go to the surgery on Leipzigerstrasse every Thursday for a nurse to administer this. He dreaded the injections: they made him feel groggy and lethargic and by the time he began to feel normal it was time for the next injection. If he missed an appointment, then Dr Braun would threaten him with a stay in the clinic and that was something Heinz-Wilhelm couldn't even begin to think about, locked up with all those lunatics.

This life continued until September 1939 and the outbreak of war. His comfortable existence was shattered by the sound of the first air-raid siren and the realisation that Berlin was now a target. Everything about the war terrified him and he determined to move away. He thought about going to a village or a small town but that was no good because he took comfort from the bustle around him: he hated silence.

It took Heinz-Wilhelm Schütze until the beginning of 1940 to decide where to go. He wanted to be somewhere cultured, with a library and other places where he could improve his considerable knowledge. He mentioned it to Klara and his brother-in-law in the January and while his sister seemed to have considerable reservations Günther seemed to think it was a good idea and was all in favour, even making suggestions as to where he may wish to go.

If Heinz-Wilhelm hadn't been the type of person who liked to think the best of others he'd have thought that maybe Günther wanted to see the back of him. Günther even came up with a good suggestion: Hanover. The most cultured city in the Reich, he told him. He and Klara would help him find a place there.

Which they did, only too willingly, as it happened, Günther himself hiring a van to take Heinz-Wilhelm and his many possessions, including crates of books and boxes and cases stuffed with papers accumulated over the years.

His sisters had found him a pleasant apartment on the upper floor of a mansion block on Leine Strasse, overlooking the river and with the State Archive and the Provincial Library conveniently across the road. Just south of Leine Strasse lay a number of museums, including the Kestner, which had a fine collection of engravings from which he would learn so much. Also nearby was the Masch Park, which had a newly constructed artificial lake that he often swam in.

It took Heinz-Wilhelm a few months to adjust to life in Hanover, to get his bearings and to work out a routine that suited him. He knew that once he had a routine, he'd be more settled and by the April he was beginning to feel at home. He'd found a very pleasant café on Baring Strasse – just by the Reichsbank – where he had lunch every day, usually at around two-thirty in the afternoon when it was a bit quieter after the businessmen had gone back to work. The woman behind the counter soon got to know him and would sometimes even stop for a chat. He'd stop in Markt Platz on the way home to buy something for his supper and a roll to have with his coffee the following morning.

He had little trouble adjusting to the new rationing system and, even though it was something most people seemed to regard as an inconvenience, he liked the structure it imposed on him. Being told just how much he could buy appealed to him.

The biggest improvement to his life was his new doctor. His sisters had found a doctor recommended by Braun in Bern. Dr Köhler's surgery was on Artillerie Strasse, near the main railway station. He was an elderly man, brought out of retirement by the war, and clearly someone who wanted a quiet life. He agreed with his new patient that the injections seemed to be excessive. He was prepared to change his medication to tablets to be taken every other day as long as Heinz-Wilhelm promised to comply. If he noticed any deterioration in his behaviour, he'd have to revert to the injections.

The change was remarkable. Now he felt alert and alive and could make plans. He could set about his mission. He had no doubt that sooner or later the authorities would come for Heinz-Wilhelm Schütze to conscript him into the armed services and he had no intention of allowing that to happen. It wasn't that he was against the war – or for it, for that matter – but the idea of wearing a uniform and being surrounded by other people in uniform and then being shouted at and maybe even shot at, that was all too much to contemplate.

He knew he needed to stay in his own little world, where no one could criticise his eccentricities, as he saw them, or his strangeness, as his mother used to call it. At school they'd even called him mad and in the army they were bound to do the same.

And what saved Heinz-Wilhelm was the most wonderful shop in the world, which he found on Theater Strasse, just off Adolf Hitler Platz. It was an art materials shop and stationers, with a department full of everything a draughtsman would need. There were a few architects' offices nearby and they seemed to use the shop to buy their specialist pens and inks. The shop was divided into a series of rooms, set at different angles off a winding corridor and towards the rear was a room with the smell of a medieval library, the wide, deep shelves stacked with paper and card of every description.

There was a clinical feel to the shop: it was staffed by half a dozen men, all of a certain age, as his mother would have put it, her way of describing anyone over fifty. They all wore white coats and treated him and indeed the other customers as far as he could tell as if they were patients.

After a few weeks he'd built up a rapport with the staff. He explained he was a specialist artist and they believed him, never questioning why he was buying such a range of pens, inks and paper and always more than happy to answer his many questions on the best inks for different paper, the techniques he could use and how to fashion the blank stamps he bought.

Round the corner on Prinzen Strasse was a shop selling second-hand typewriters: there seemed to be no shortage of them. He bought two Erika typewriters and a printing set.

And as the spring of 1940 edged towards the summer Heinz-Wilhelm was ready to set to work. The art shop on Theater Strasse was beginning to run low on supplies with so much of what they normally sold now required for the armed forces. He'd bought a draughtman's board from the shop and also a special lamp, which was the last one they had in stock, and he turned the spare bedroom in his apartment into what he called his studio. He'd spent a good while making sure everything was arranged properly and then set to work.

It took him the rest of the year and into the early part of 1941, but certainly by the spring of 1941 he was coming to think that maybe he was indeed a genius.

His purpose was to protect himself by becoming someone else. He knew it was only a matter of time before he was conscripted and the prospect of that was unimaginable. And not far behind them in terms of having to worry about were the other authorities, the people who thought that because he was different there was something wrong with him and all the dreadful things they could do to him.

Heinz-Wilhelm Schütze decided he needed to create not one but five new identities, all of impeccable quality, all of which would withstand the most severe scrutiny. He came up with a plan to create these, operating to a set of rules to which he strictly adhered.

One of these rules was that none of his new identities would be from Hanover or Berlin. They'd all be places he'd been able to visit from Hanover in a day, being able to return well before the curfew.

He visited town halls, municipal archives, graveyards to get the details of children who'd died between thirty-five and forty-five years earlier, the addresses where their families may live, the local churches to study parish records. And once he had the beginnings of an identity he'd re-visit the city to create a life for his new personas: the libraries they were members of, their address, even the doctor they were registered with and the places they worked.

And by the May of 1941 he had his five identities.

Johann Neumann, a thirty-six-year-old teacher from Bielefeld.

Artur Jung, a hospital porter from Hildesheim, age forty.

Franz Förster – he liked the idea of using his brother-in-law's surname – a thirty-eight-year-old teacher from Wolfsburg.

And two residents of Bremen: Erhard Schröder, a forty-five-year-old clerk, and Friedrich Roth, ten years younger and an assistant in a menswear shop.

And then he decided that two of them would be married. Gretchen Förster was married to Franz from Wolfsburg and Franziska Roth was married to Friedrich from Bremen. He created their identities, using photographs of his own sisters.

All seven had their identity cards – the *kennkarten* – along with other incidental forms of identity, their ration cards and the ephemera which made up their mundane lives.

And Johann, Artur, Franz, Erhard and Friedrich all had something else. He'd taken an enormous risk in stealing everything he needed from Dr Köhler's surgery on Artillerie Strasse, but once he had it, he was able to fashion medical exemption letters for his five identities.

Heinz-Wilhelm Schütze was safe now. He could get on with his own life, not one the authorities or his family decided for him.

Chapter 4

Lyon, France
November 1942

A November morning in Lyon and an easterly wind whipping in from the not-too-distant Alps added a distinct sharpness to the air, though that was tempered by a strong sun. As the citizens of Lyon never tired of pointing out, the city was considerably closer to the Mediterranean than it was to Paris.

In more ways than one.

It was the third week of November in the fourth year of the war and just a week earlier France's third-largest city had moved. Until the 10 November Lyon was in the so-called *zone libre*, the part of France under the Vichy regime. But that façade ended when Hitler decided to extend the *zone occupée* to the rest of France, with the exception of a small area run by the Italians.

They called the new area *zone sud* but few people were fooled by that. In effect, they'd been occupied by the Germans before 10 November and now they were still occupied by them, only more so.

Just before noon that morning the atmosphere at Perrache railway station in Lyon's 2nd arrondissement suddenly became as cold as that outside as dozens of French gendarmes and a larger contingent of German soldiers – including a number of SS – descended on the station. Passengers milling around the main concourse were moved to the side and those waiting in queues to board their train were ushered through the ticket barriers and instructed to wait on crowded platforms. The few passengers who dared to question what was going on were told not to worry, no trains were going anywhere for a while anyway. They were used to life under the Germans usually being inconvenient, often oppressive.

They would have hoped this security clampdown was because of the Resistance and that more than compensated for any delay to their journey. They knew that the Resistance was more active in Lyon than in any other part of France and most took a good deal of pride in that. They also knew that the railways were a favoured target of the Resistance and the railway workers among its most active and effective members.

But those travellers who knew what to look out for noticed that the Germans weren't searching people or questioning them and nor were they looking in the waiting rooms, cafés and other parts of the station. Instead, they had formed a cordon of security around platform three. At ten past twelve a train that had left Gare de Lyon in Paris not long after nine-thirty that morning pulled into Perrache.

For a while the station was strangely still, the only sounds the shouting of the German officers, the barking of their dogs and the noisy escape of steam from the locomotive, signalling its relief at the end of the journey.

One person was watching the events unfolding below them with particular interest. Anna Rousseau had been waiting in the station café since eleven that morning and wasn't in the least surprised at the onrush of security. Unlike the other travellers, she was expecting it, so much so that she took advantage of the commotion as the concourse was cleared and slipped the lock on a door at the rear of the café. The door opened onto a narrow stairway, at the top of which was a dark corridor with a storeroom at the end. She pulled up a wooden box, stood on it, reached as high as she could and opened an air vent just enough to see what was happening below her.

Anna Rousseau watched as an excessive number of troops gathered round one of the first-class carriages. Moments later the carriage door opened and a short man – certainly no more than five foot six – appeared in the doorway. He paused for a few moments and looked up, conveniently long enough for Anna Rousseau to get a good look at him: a surprisingly young man who ran his hand through his dark hair, nodded as if satisfied that this was indeed his correct destination and then descended the steps, after which he was lost from view as a number of senior officers saluted, shook his hand and gathered around him.

By now Anna Rousseau had closed the air vent and stepped down from the wooden box. Her mission was accomplished: she'd been there simply to confirm what Mars – her Resistance group – was expecting.

The man they were expecting had duly arrived, along with his brutal reputation. There'd been a debate within Mars as to whether there should be an attempt to assassinate the man before he arrived at his new posting, or indeed, upon his arrival.

The debate had been quite intense, even heated, which Anna suspected was in a large part due to the considerable tensions that came with the life of a *resistant*.

Should we stop him before he can do us any harm?

But he'll be too well guarded – we'll be exposed. Let's wait until he's arrived.

Anna Rousseau had an ability to remain inconspicuous. She looked barely in her twenties – certainly younger than her twenty-five years. She was not so beautiful as to attract the undue attention of the Germans, but still pretty enough. She'd been the one to suggest using the vent in the corridor above the café to confirm Barbie's arrival. She'd also suggested that a good sniper with a good rifle may be able to get a clear shot and Marcel had even come to see the spot, but he said while it was a good idea – a commendable one, indeed – there was no chance of escape and there'd be too many travellers around who'd almost certainly be shot in reprisal.

–

Anna Rousseau left Perrache through the southern exit and headed down Cours Charlemagne. At the junction with Rue Ravat, she entered a boutique, though only after checking the deep blue scarf with a distinctive floral motif was on display in the window.

It was safe to enter.

It was the kind of shop she'd normally feel out of place in: expensive gloves and even more expensive silk scarves – all made in Lyon, of course. The shop was much favoured by German officers: according to the proprietor they tended to buy gloves for their wives and scarves for their mistresses.

The proprietor was Madame Madelaine, a tall, haughty woman who always had a disapproving look about her and gave the distinct impression that she too thought this was a shop Anna was out of place in. But Marcel assured Anna the shop was a perfect *bureau de poste* for Mars and Madame Madelaine kept detailed notes of the names of the German officers she served and – thanks to her fluent German and their tendency to confide in her – which units they served with.

'Can I help you?' Madame Madelaine barely looked up. She was pointedly using the formal *vous*. Anna should know her place.

'I see you have a pair of dark brown leather gloves in your window, next to the pale green scarf. May I ask if you have them in a small size?'

'I'm afraid not: we only have medium. I shall contact my supplier though. Good day.'

Madame Madelaine turned round as Anna left the shop. Even though no one else was there it was essential they both stuck to the agreed form of words. The proprietor would have understood that the enquiry about the brown gloves meant the man had arrived as expected at Perrache. Had she been asked about the black gloves with a fur trim that would have meant he hadn't arrived. An enquiry about whether she stocked white lace gloves would indicate there was a problem and Marcel should be contacted immediately.

Anna left the shop and headed back to work. She did wonder what Marcel would do next. Although he was a calm and stoic person she felt he could be too cautious, at other times too ready to take a risk, almost rash.

In truth, she knew little about him.

He was an enigma.

As were they all.

–

As Anna left Perrache station through its southern exit, the man whose arrival minutes earlier had caused such a fuss was being escorted through the northern exit.

Minutes later he strode into Hôtel Terminus, on Cours de Verdun. He paused long enough in the ornate entrance to admire the magnificent Art Nouveau décor and then announced he needed to get to work: straightaway. A man considerably taller than him and a good ten years older said that, with great respect, sir, we have laid on a very special lunch for you and would you not wish to refresh yourself after such a long journey – sir?

The man stopped and turned slowly to face him, an incredulous look on his face. 'After such a long journey? Where on earth do you think I've come from? I took the train from Paris. I travelled in comfort. It was hardly Napoleon's retreat from Moscow!'

Everyone laughed nervously, including the man who had made what transpired to be such an outrageous suggestion.

'And your name?'

'Otto Winter, sir, I am your aide-de-camp.'

'Are you indeed. You can have a cold lunch sent up to my office, Winter, if you're so worried I may starve. What you all need to understand –' he'd moved back to address the throng in the reception area, moving to the stairs so he appeared taller. 'What you all need to understand is that I'm here to do a job: thanks to the incompetence that appears to have been tolerated' – he spat that word out and looked around, as if searching for those responsible for this – 'the Resistance in this city appears to have been allowed to run the place and the city's full of Jews! Well let me tell you, that's all going to change!'

–

Waiting in an office on the fifth floor a woman in her fifties was telling the other women in the room, all younger than her, to get back to work. She said she really wasn't sure what all the fuss was about.

The younger secretaries did as she'd instructed: they knew better than to disobey her. Agnes Kléber had the title of office manager but she was more powerful than that. She was from Alsace, so technically French, but in practice more German than German. Her fluency in both languages and the fact there was little she didn't know gave her enormous power in the building. Even senior officers deferred to her and sought her advice.

She'd been as interested as the others as minutes earlier they'd all gathered at the window overlooking Cours de Verdun, curious to see what their new boss looked like.

'He's not even thirty, you know?' The others had heard that but nodded appreciatively at Fraulein Kléber, grateful she was taking them into her confidence.

'And he has quite the reputation, you know? He sorted out the Jews in Amsterdam and was then sent to Dijon.' All eyes were upon her and she seemed pleased to have such an attentive audience. 'And he so impressed Standartenführer Knochen in Paris that he himself arranged for him to be sent here. I understand –' she looked round, checking no one who shouldn't be was listening in '– that he will answer personally to Standartenführer Knochen!'

They were all suitably impressed.

Agnes Kléber was working out when would be the best time to introduce herself to Herr Barbie: she had every intention of making herself invaluable to the new head of the Lyon Gestapo.

The Mars Network met later that evening in the basement of a café on Rue des Capucins on the Croix-Rousse, the large hill at the north end of the Presqu'île peninsula.

The Croix-Rousse was the traditional heart of Lyon's silk-weaving industry: the area had expanded following Joseph Jacquard's invention of the silk loom. By the middle of the nineteenth century some thirty thousand *canuts* – the silk weavers – lived and worked in its cramped warren of streets and passageways. Buildings sprung up everywhere, their ceilings high to accommodate Jacquard's looms. The Croix-Rousse was steep and the area difficult to get around: the streets narrow and poorly lit, the buildings dark and the area frequently shrouded in fog. And although being the centre of the silk industry suggested glamour or even prestige, in fact the Croix-Rousse was anything but: the streets and alleys between the buildings were filthy, much of it was like a slum.

For these reasons, and the fact that it was built on a steep hill, it was a difficult area to get around. But over hundreds of years the silk workers had developed an intricate network of passageways and short-cuts, doors opening directly from the street into a corridor running between buildings, down steps into an alley, across a street into another doorway, and so on. They were called the *traboules*, a labyrinth known only to locals, traditionally a convenient way for the silk workers to move around the area and down to the rivers – and now offering perfect cover for the Resistance.

Anna Rousseau thought about this as she slipped into the *traboule* on Passage Thiaffait. Marcel himself had mentioned it to her one day. The Croix-Rousse was an area she was unfamiliar with, she told him, when he gave her instructions to take a package there. He explained how the *traboules* could have been designed and built by the Resistance.

'It offers us protection; it means we can move around the area unseen.'

'But what about the police – and the Germans?'

'They don't understand the *traboules*: only locals do. Most of the police are from outside Lyon, they have no knowledge of how the different *traboules* connect with each other. When you enter a *traboule* it's often unclear as to which way to go: the passageway could lead to a small courtyard and there may be four or five turnings from it. You need to know the area to know which one to take, and so on.'

He'd arranged for a retired *canut* called Luc to be her guide and soon she became familiar with the *traboules*.

'One thing you must realise,' Luc told her as they climbed a set of stairs leading into a cobbled alley, 'in the Croix-Rousse there are no concierges as in Paris. Here people rely on themselves: we don't need busy-bodies watching us.'

Once inside the *traboule* on Passage Thiaffait Anna paused. She was as certain as she could be that no one had followed her as she'd slipped in through the street door, but now she needed to be sure she was still alone. Attached to the wall just inside the entrance were some thirty letter boxes and there were a similar number on the wall opposite. The boxes were identical: made from dark, varnished wood, with a small door and lock on the front and a slot at the top for envelopes. The boxes were for the apartments and workshops throughout this complex of buildings: some had a name or an apartment number on them, others were blank. One or two had a first name chalked on the front and on one was the word '*chien*' and a drawing of a dog next to it.

Anna went to a box in the middle row, on the end furthest from the door. It had the name 'Blanc' on the front. She slipped her hand into the slot at the top and pulled out a sheet of paper. To all intents and purposes, it looked like a shopping list, but in the bottom right-hand corner was the letters 'RdC'. At the top of the sheet were a dozen tiny tears on the paper. She added one more and replaced the sheet in the letter box.

It was one of the dozens of ghost letter boxes in the *traboules* the Resistance used as a method of communication. She now knew she needed to go to the café on Rue des Capucins and she knew from the little rips on the sheet that a dozen others at least would be there.

–

They sat in a circle, fifteen of them, ensuring an oppressive atmosphere in the low-ceilinged basement. It was the first time Anna Rousseau had been to such an important meeting of the circuit: usually she just attended meetings with no more than two others present. She was in the outer circle of the room, her back against the rough, damp wall. Marcel was in the centre, of course, but to her surprise, so was Madame Madelaine: rather than being someone who passed on messages she appeared to be far more important.

Maurice was also in the centre circle, with Michel next to him. But what was interesting was how the three leaders deferred to Madame Madelaine. As the meeting went on, Anna realised that the stern woman who ran the glove and scarf boutique and who barely glanced at her was actually the leader of the Mars Network.

'There is no question that we are now faced with a most serious problem.' Her tone was less formal than when she spoke in her shop. Her voice was quiet and the people in the outer circle leaned forward to catch what she was saying.

'When he was in Amsterdam, Barbie had a reputation for brutal efficiency. When he was in Dijon… well, we know what he was like there. The man is brutal and very, very clever: the word one most commonly hears used to describe him is determined. And remember how young he is. He's been sent here to track down the Jews and break the Resistance. We are more fortunate in that we have a much lower profile and by and large we operate independently, but we must not become complacent. From now on, we simply cannot allow one single mistake.'

Chapter 5

Brandenburg, Germany
December 1942

The air raids in Hanover were to blame.

His predicament – and there was no getting away from the fact that Heinz-Wilhelm Schütze was in a serious predicament – was the fault of the British. He'd told this to the men in the long white coats who came in three times a day to give him food and medicines. He hoped that if he blamed the British then they'd realise he was on the right side, but they didn't seem interested. A tablet in the morning and one at lunchtime and they'd stand over him watching him swallow it and then in the evening his injection – *take down your trousers, face down on the bed* – and the next thing he'd know it was morning.

The first air raid which was to blame was in June 1941, not long after he'd completed all the new identities and he was beginning to feel less anxious, so much so that Dr Köhler noticed this on one of his regular check-ups and said if this improvement continued then he'd be able to reduce the medication to just one tablet every three days.

Dr Köhler wrote to Klara in Berlin as he did every month and said her brother was making excellent progress and gave no cause for concern.

A week later there was an air raid in the middle of the night and the following afternoon he was at the café on Baring Strasse when he overheard someone say that Artillerie Strasse had been badly hit. After his lunch he strolled over to Artillerie Strasse and was shocked to see that the block where Dr Köhler's surgery was had been levelled to the ground. He knew that Dr Köhler lived in an apartment above the surgery.

He hung around the area for a while, helping to move rubble, which was something expected of passers-by and it dawned on him that for the first time since he was eight or nine, he no longer had a doctor. He was no longer subject to their prying and restrictions. Even though Dr Sperling had been kind and Dr Köhler pleasant enough, they still required him to take medication, which in his opinion was quite unnecessary.

He had, over time, removed a number of sheets of headed notepaper from the surgery on Artillerie Strasse and forging the doctor's signature and official stamp was no problem at all for someone who'd become so skilled at forging far more complicated documents.

He rarely saw his sister Klara these days, maybe once every two or three months. But she seemed pleased that according to Dr Köhler he was doing well and was still taking his medication and as a result his allowance continued.

He had to say, not taking the medication appeared to have no detrimental effect, which rather reinforced his point that he'd never needed it in the first place. He felt more clear-headed, though he didn't sleep as well and stopping the medication appeared to coincide with the reappearance of some of the men who first began to watch him in Berlin. He even noticed people following him in the street, though he was always able to lose them.

Once a week he'd visit one of the four cities he'd chosen for his new personas and use the day to test the identity and add to it, queuing for ration cards, learning more about the places he was meant to be from.

He spent the Christmas of 1941 in Berlin with his sister and brother-in-law. His nephew – who just a few years before he'd flown kites with in the Tiergarten – had joined the SS and spent the two days he was at home shouting about Jews. His brother-in-law Günther talked about being sent to the front line and his sister spent most of the festive season crying.

Heinz-Wilhelm of course, being no fool – on the contrary, actually – knew that recently he'd become somewhat excitable so a week before Christmas he resumed the tablets he had left from Dr Köhler. This meant that by the time he arrived in Berlin and for the duration of the stay he was perhaps the calmest person in that tense household in Charlottenburg.

But soon after he returned to Hanover matters began to deteriorate.

The British bombing of the city was nowhere near as bad as it was in Berlin, Hamburg or the big industrial centres in the Ruhr, but it was still disconcerting and as the woman who ran the café on Baring Strasse said, it wasn't so much the bombing that shredded her nerves, it was the anticipation of it.

He agreed with that. He never went down to air-raid shelters because that was his idea of an utter nightmare, being cooped up with all those strange people. During a raid he hid under his bed, a pillow over his head as he hummed any tune he could think of.

But matters got worse. He was banned from swimming in the Masch Park because apparently he was frightening people by swimming underneath them and holding onto their feet, even though he'd done that as a child at the *stadtbad* on Krumme Strasse in Berlin.

Then the woman who ran the café on Baring Strasse asked him to stop coming because he was upsetting the other customers and when he asked her what she meant she said that sitting at the table and weeping so loudly and not eating his meal was well... not pleasant. Heinz-Wilhelm told the woman she had no idea what it was like when nearly everyone in the city was against you and the next thing he knew she'd called the police and he was taken to the police station on Am Waterloo Platz.

They were fine there, actually. He'd calmed down and taken one of Dr Köhler's tablets and he explained how the bombing had got the better of his nerves and the policeman – another one who looked like he'd been brought out of retirement – said he knew the feeling, but this wasn't to happen again, and Heinz-Wilhelm said of course not.

He was well behaved for a week or two after that. In March there was an unpleasant incident which he realised was his fault when he shouted at a group of schoolchildren who he thought were laughing at him. He deeply regretted having hit one of the boys and he was lucky that an apology seemed to suffice. But there were further incidents over the spring: reporting his elderly neighbour for being a British spy only served to annoy the police on Am Waterloo Platz, as did his attempts to arrest a woman who pushed in front of him in the grocery store in Markt Platz.

The final straw as far as the authorities were concerned was all due to what he saw as a misunderstanding, though on reflection he could see how the police had a problem with it. He'd been in the bath on a Thursday morning in June when he was convinced he heard an air raid overhead. He jumped out of the bath and ran out of the apartment and into the street and he was halfway down it before he realised he was naked but he carried on running because at least he was alive and decided to jump into the Leine so he wouldn't be burnt alive and was standing on the bank of the river when a policeman pulled him to the ground.

He spent the night in a cell at Am Waterloo Platz and the following morning was brought before the duty officer and he expected to be released with a warning as usual but the duty officer said he'd ignored too many final warnings and now he was going to be dealt with elsewhere.

Heinz-Wilhelm was calm and collected: could he return to his apartment and collect one or two things? He'd be fine then, he thought. He'd take his new identities and disappear. Heinz-Wilhelm Schütze would be no more.

He'd become Friedrich Roth from Bremen for a while. He'd always liked Friedrich Roth: Friedrich from Bremen and his wife, Franziska – he must remember her papers too.

But the duty officer refused. He was going straight to another place, he said. He wouldn't need anything there. Not even his clothes.

'They'll look after you there,' he said, a grin on his face, and Heinz-Wilhelm noticed all the other policemen laughing as he was led away.

–

He was so near to Berlin, the city which despite all its faults was the place he still called home. Had he been offered the opportunity he'd have happily walked out of the hell he was in now and walked barefoot back to Berlin.

When he was a child, they'd visited Brandenburg from time to time. He seemed to remember there was an aunt or a friend of his grandmother's there. He couldn't remember exactly, and he would have asked his sister, except Klara had only been to visit him once in this accursed place and then she'd not stayed for long. His brother-in-law had been more often, but he'd forgotten to ask him. He was forgetting a lot these days.

But the point about Brandenburg was that he knew it well enough to know where he was. He was on Neuendorfer Strasse, not far from the Havel and in the building that was the old prison and was now called the State Welfare Institute and the place where people with psychiatric illnesses were kept, which was utterly ridiculous because he may be many things – different, excitable possibly, brilliant certainly – but not psychiatrically ill.

They'd brought him here from the police station in Hanover and he'd assumed it would be for a few days, maybe a couple of weeks as they sorted out his medication and while he wouldn't have gone as far as to say he wasn't bothered, he saw this as no more than a temporary setback. As soon as he could he'd be back in his apartment in Hanover where he'd retrieve his new identities and then disappear.

They'd never catch him again.

But that was a year and a half ago and it had been a complete nightmare since then.

He spent much of the first few weeks strapped to a narrow bed in a dark cell. He was given different injections, some of which knocked him out, others of which woke him up. Then around the end of the summer he started the first of the sessions with a psychiatrist. It all seemed to be a complete waste of time because their starting point was that he was mad and he had to spend all his time trying to persuade them he wasn't and he had to admit that all too often he lost his temper, which as far as they were concerned seemed to prove he was mad.

On one occasion he did attack the psychiatrist, although he didn't think he hurt him as much as they said. The chair he threw caused just a glancing blow but he had to admit it was a mistake because a few days after that he was sitting in front of a panel of three psychiatrists and they told him he had a psychiatric illness and the very fact that he argued so vehemently that he didn't was further proof of how ill he was.

After that he was sent to a ward on one of the top floors. It was a mixture between a prison and a hospital, with the difference being that most of his fellow inmates – there were around twenty of them – were mad, which meant that there was little opportunity for rest: some people spent the whole night screaming, others did that during the day.

At the start of 1942 a new inmate moved in and was allocated the bed next to Heinz-Wilhelm's. Karl was similar to him in some ways, also in his late thirties, from what would be called a respectable background and, like him, not mad. The two became close, though their opportunities to talk were limited. Because of the medication both were on they had just an hour or two each day when both were in between medication and therefore lucid enough to talk.

In March 1942 there'd been some kind of disturbance on the ward – an inmate tried to kill one of the men in white coats and very nearly succeeded. In the chaos they missed a whole round of medication and Heinz-Wilhelm and Karl had the whole afternoon to talk and he was shocked at what Karl told him.

'You notice how people disappear from the ward, Heinz-Wilhelm?'

'What do you mean?'

'What I mean is that some of our neighbours, they're here for a few weeks or a few months and then they leave and never come back. What do you think happens to them?'

'I assume they're moved to another ward, don't you? They're usually the ones who are most disturbed, not like you and I.'

Karl looked around and came and sat next to him on his bed, which wasn't allowed but the men in white coats were too distracted to notice. Karl edged closer to him, their shoulders touching, and he spoke quietly, his mouth close to Heinz-Wilhelm's ear.

'There are rumours that some people in hospitals like this one, that they're disposed of.'

Heinz-Wilhelm looked at him blankly and said he didn't understand what he was talking about.

'Before I was brought here, I was living near Hamburg—'

'I know, you've told me, Karl.'

'One morning after an air raid by the British, people in my area found leaflets that the British planes had dropped. It was the text of a sermon that the Bishop of Münster gave last summer criticising the euthanasia programme.'

'What is that?'

'It's what I'm trying to tell you, Heinz-Wilhelm. The state is killing people with serious illnesses, including psychological ones. And cripples too.'

'But you and I aren't like that.'

'Try telling the authorities that! They're killing people here in Brandenburg. They gas them. Have you noticed something: when they come to take someone out for the last time they never take their possessions with them, do they? They collect those a day or two later. And there's something else, Heinz-Wilhelm.'

'What's that?' Heinz-Wilhelm sounded less sceptical now, more worried. He'd noticed that too and had wondered about it.

'When they come to take someone for the last time, they never look directly at them, do they? The rest of the time they lord it over us, don't they? They shout in our faces. But when they come to take someone away, it's like they're... I don't know... embarrassed. Keep your eyes open, Heinz-Wilhelm.'

—

They came for Heinz-Wilhelm Schütze on a bleak Tuesday morning in December, three days before Christmas, and there seemed to be something of a rush on to tie up loose ends before the festive season.

His fate had been sealed the day before. The institute's psychiatrists had met for their regular Monday meeting and the main item on the agenda was to decide which patients were to be disposed of that week. Heinz-Wilhelm was number three on the list.

'Heinz-Wilhelm Schütze, age thirty-nine. Originally from Berlin, last resident in Hanover. He's been with us since last June.'

'And his diagnosis?'

The psychiatrist who had the file laughed and told his colleagues they could take their pick. 'Delusional behaviour. Obsessive habits. Manic at times and prone to shouting inappropriately and occasionally resorting to violence.'

'So as mad as all the others?' All three laughed.

'He is well-connected though. His brother-in-law Günther Förster is a colonel based at army HQ in the Bendlerblock in Berlin.'

'Really? Surely he could have pulled rank and saved Schütze, couldn't he?'

'He did pull rank, as it happens, but in the opposite direction, if you get my meaning.'

When they came for Heinz-Wilhelm Schütze they had to shake him by the shoulder to wake him up. They told him to get up and get dressed and put his shoes on and it was only then that he remembered what Karl had told him.

…they never look directly at them, do they?

Karl himself had been taken away a few weeks before and he'd never seen him again, and he'd noticed then that the men in white coats hadn't looked at him. Now there were two of them standing by his bed, one helping him up by the elbow, the other handing him his clothes.

Heinz-Wilhelm didn't move. He felt sick as an awful realisation began to dawn on him. Where, he demanded, was he going?

Neither of them looked at him. The man helping him up actually looked away while the one getting his clothes was staring at the floor.

And that was when Heinz-Wilhelm Schütze knew.

Chapter 6

Lyon, France
February 1943

René Dupont was resigned to the fact that he was destined to be one of life's deputies.

He'd overheard his mother-in-law, whose tongue was at least as waspish as that of his wife, describe him as such when she was talking with his wife and clearly didn't realise he was in the next room.

'And did your husband get that promotion, Jeanne?' Always 'your husband', never 'René'.

'I'm afraid not.'

'So, he remains a deputy bank manager?' He imagined her smiling as she said it, her yellow teeth glowing like a dragon's.

'It is still a position of some importance, Mother.' His wife sounded unconvinced.

'Come on, Jeanne, how many branches does Crédit Lyonnais have in the area and how many deputy managers are there? After all this time one would have thought...'

And René Dupont knew that was basically true. One would have thought... one would have thought he'd have risen above assistant manager at the furniture factory he'd joined after school and one would have thought that he wouldn't have remained there for ten years and then one would have thought he'd have done better at the large bakery, where he'd expected to become the manager but then saw someone promoted over him. And then he'd joined an accountancy firm and had begun to sit the exams, but he struggled and he began to think that the fact the firm was Jewish-owned, as had been the furniture factory, was possibly no coincidence.

He'd joined Crédit Lyonnais, which as far as he could tell was not Jewish-owned, and eventually became a deputy manager, though admittedly in a very small branch. And that's where he remained.

One of life's deputies.

–

In 1938 he'd joined the Parti Populaire Français, which had been set up two years earlier by Jacques Doriot. Its hard right wing and openly anti-Semitic policies appealed to him, though membership of it wasn't something he advertised. He was a low-key member, not very active, but he did attend monthly meetings for a while.

But then at the end of 1942 life changed and for the first time in many years René Dupont began to feel optimistic. He knew he was in the minority of those in Lyon who welcomed the German occupation. His view was that it brought order and much needed structure to society. In his opinion, the Jews, the socialists, the liberals and the communists had been allowed their own way for far too long and they'd only have themselves to blame if the Germans were going to come down hard on them.

And when the Vichy regime formed the Milice Française René Dupont was a natural recruit. The *milice* was a fascist paramilitary organisation and although René Dupont had never seen himself as a military person – it was difficult, with his asthma – he did feel he fitted in with the organisation in other ways.

The *milice* recruited heavily in Lyon, where the new head of the Gestapo, a man called Barbie, was especially keen on it. He liked the idea of local people using their local knowledge. Doing the Gestapo's dirty work, he heard someone describe it, unkindly.

And they seemed rather keen on René Dupont, so much so that he was allocated to the Franc-Garde, which was the full-time section of the *milice*. It was quite an honour, even if it did mean taking a pay cut after leaving the bank. It also meant spending a few nights a week in the *milice* barracks, which he found uncomfortable. But all that was offset by the prestige that came with the role. And the uniform.

He'd very much hoped he'd be made a *chef de centre*, commanding his very own unit. But it was pointed out that while he was a very efficient administrator and there was no question as to his loyalty, he lacked military experience. An elderly veteran of the Great War was put in charge. René Dupont would be his deputy, the *chef de centre adjoint*.

He'd remain one of life's deputies.

–

It didn't take long for Klaus Barbie to make his presence felt in Lyon: he was a careful man, who'd learnt that planning and preparation paid off in the long run.

As the head of Gestapo in the city he was clear his targets were the enemies of the Reich. But he knew that was a very wide brief and there was a danger he could spread his forces too thinly. He was of the view that some of his colleagues at the Cours de Verdun had far too casual an approach in this regard. When asked who were the enemies of the Reich, they'd respond by saying all the French and then talk at length about how no French person could be trusted and they should all be treated as threats to the Reich.

In his first few weeks, Barbie was happy enough for them to talk like this. They may have been unfocused and unclear, but at least it gave him a sense of the city and who to be worried about in it. He listened to what they said and sometimes had to bite his tongue, like on the occasion when one officer complained to him about the old woman who'd served him in a grocery shop and not only didn't smile at him but refused to return his greetings.

But by the start of 1943 he'd begun to be clear in his own mind as to what his priorities should be. The Gestapo had something like a dozen sections devoted to enemies of the Reich: the communists, liberals, the Resistance, Protestants, Catholics, Jews… there were plenty to choose from. But Barbie decided the Gestapo needed to concentrate on two groups: the Resistance and the Jews.

He'd needed to be disciplined about this: the Roman Catholic Church in Lyon in particular was a cause for concern. The archbishop of Lyon – who also had the title of primate of Gaul – was an especially annoying character. After the Armistice, Cardinal Pierre-Marie Gerlier had initially supported Marshal Pétain, but more recently he'd publicly condemned the deportation of Jews from France and it was no secret that he'd asked his churches and other Catholic bodies to shelter Jewish children.

Just before Christmas 1942 Barbie had visited the cardinal at the Cathédrale Saint-Jean-Baptiste. He'd actually invited the cardinal to lunch at the Hôtel Terminus but the reply had been that the cardinal felt that was inappropriate and Klaus Barbie decided not to argue and agreed to meet at the cathedral on the left bank of the Saône.

It was notable he'd not been invited to the archbishop's residence. Instead, they met in a narrow building on Place Saint-Jean, and 'lunch' turned out to be a generous description of the meal: a single plate containing a sparse salad, cold potatoes and a small slice of fish. The meal was cold in more ways than one, the atmosphere tense and the conversation limited.

The cardinal explained that he answered to a higher authority than the Gestapo and it was his job, let alone his moral duty, to speak out against injustice whenever he saw it. It was also his duty to save God's children, of whatever faith.

Klaus Barbie was uncharacteristically thrown. He started talking about the threats to society posed by the Jews and the Resistance, who were often one and the same, and then he was interrupted by the cardinal, who asked him if he wanted more water and a few moments later when he explained he was about to start Grace.

Barbie left the meeting furious, walking back to his office across Pont Tilsit. He'd turn his attention to the cardinal sooner or later, but he had to remember his priorities.

The Jews.

And then the Resistance.

The Rue Sainte-Catherine is a narrow street running west to east in Lyon's 1st arrondissement, more or less at the point where the Presqu'île joins the Croix-Rousse district to its north.

The street traditionally had a reputation for drinking and bad behaviour, but that was not the reason why a dozen Gestapo officers appeared there shortly after lunch on Tuesday 9 February. Led by Klaus Barbie, their destination was 12 Rue Sainte-Catherine, the offices of the city's five-thousand-strong Jewish community.

They'd chosen the day carefully. Tuesday was when members of the community could go to the offices on Rue Sainte-Catherine to receive food parcels and see a doctor free of charge.

The thirty people already on the premises were arrested. During the course of that fateful afternoon a further sixty people turned up at 12 Rue Sainte-Catherine. It would have been many more, but a couple of people managed to escape from the building by persuading the Gestapo they were there by chance and nothing to do with the Jewish community. They, in turn, managed to warn others.

By late afternoon eighty-four people were in custody and Klaus Barbie was pleased with his day's work. It was very much like being back in Amsterdam, where he'd overseen the arrest, imprisonment and then deportation of the Jews.

He'd taken the precaution of bringing the *milice* with him and a very helpful *chef de centre adjoint* called Dupont turned up with a couple of dozen men and they'd kept good order in the street.

If the truth be told, this Dupont was a little too eager to ingratiate himself with Klaus Barbie. Every time the Gestapo chief turned round this Dupont was there, wringing his hands, his head slightly bowed and asking a series of frankly inane questions.

At one point he asked to see Barbie in the corridor. *In private, sir – you understand.* He leaned close to him, his breath smelling of garlic as he explained how a young man in the street appeared to have spat at one of his men.

'I was wondering, sir, do you think we should shoot him?'

'Who?'

'The man who spat at my man?'

'Don't be ridiculous! If you do that then we'll have a riot on our hands and some of these Jews could escape. Have him arrested. Make sure you search him.'

Dupont backed off, somewhat shame-faced, and explained apologetically – wringing his hands in front of him – that actually the young man had got away and...

'In that case, you fool, you wouldn't have been able to shoot him anyway, would you?'

But all in all, it had been a good day. The operation to deport the Jews of Lyon to the east had begun.

Now he could turn his attention to the Resistance.

Chapter 7

On a Thursday afternoon in the first week of June Klaus Barbie was summonsed to Paris.

He took the last train out of Lyon and stayed overnight on Rue de Copernic, which was a short walk to 84 Avenue Foch and the headquarters of the SD: the Sicherheitsdienst was the counter-intelligence branch of the RHSA, the Reich Central Security Office, which had a number of branches, of which the Gestapo was one. The organisation was not without its tensions – who was responsible for what – but by and large they'd learnt to rub along together. It helped that they were on the same side.

Barbie went straight to the office of his boss, Standartenführer Helmut Knochen, who was in the process of buttoning up his greatcoat.

'Put your hat back on, Klaus, and keep your coat on. Our meeting is elsewhere.'

Knochen looked annoyed as they headed down to the street. It was only when they were in the car that Barbie felt able to ask where they were heading.

'Hôtel Lutetia.'

'Really, sir?'

'Yes, really.'

'Surely, they ought to be coming to us?'

Knochen said nothing as he stared out of the window. They crossed the Seine on the Pont des Invalides and it was only when they were on the Left Bank that he replied.

'The Abwehr called the meeting, Klaus. They have something important for us, apparently. I'm told they feel nervous when they come to us. They think we're going to arrest them!'

'And not without good cause, sir.'

Knochen half-laughed. 'I'm hearing good reports from Lyon, Klaus. You're finally dealing with the Jews, I understand. What about the Resistance?'

'Not as straightforward as the Jews, I'm afraid, sir.'

'As is the case throughout France, Klaus. We found plenty of them in the round-ups in the summer of 1941, but God knows how many more are in hiding. I'm pleased you're using the *milice* properly.'

'Thank you, sir – they're very useful. They're like prefects at school: natural bullies and anxious to help teacher.'

'That's what I want to see everywhere, Klaus: get them to do our dirty work for us. The French may have a reputation for being bothersome but fortunately a number of them are proving to be quite co-operative. And I hear you've moved your headquarters?'

'Yes, sir. I felt we needed to move away from Hôtel Terminus, it somehow felt too comfortable, as if the staff had become complacent there. We're across the river now, in the old army medical school on Avenue Berthelot. It's more convenient for Montluc prison.'

The Hôtel Lutetia on Boulevard Raspail was the headquarters of the Abwehr, German military intelligence. Under Admiral Canaris the Abwehr had a reputation for being efficient and effective, with an impressive network of agents throughout Europe. The quality of its intelligence was consistently good. But the Abwehr was distrusted by many, not least those in the RHSA. Canaris and many of his senior officers weren't even members of the Nazi Party. They saw themselves as professional intelligence officers rather than servants of the Party. There were countless rumours about the loyalty of the Abwehr. Barbie was not alone in being suspicious of them.

'And do we know what this meeting is about, sir?'

'The so-called French Resistance I believe, Klaus. The meeting's been called by an officer called Georg Lange. Not too senior, but I have to say, a very effective officer with an enviable network of agents. He's supposed to be running a top agent into England. I did try and get him to join us but Canaris made a fuss and then I discovered the man's not even a Party member.'

'Let's hope for his sake, sir, he's not going to waste our time.'

Standartenführer Knochen sighed and turned to face Barbie. 'If he's invited us to the Hôtel Lutetia then it won't be a waste of time.'

—

There was a dozen of them in a smart, oak-panelled room on one of the upper floors of the Art Nouveau building. The room smelled pleasantly of polish and the carpets were deep; it was like walking on an immaculate turf. The high windows ensured the room was bathed in light.

Those present were from the SD and the Gestapo, gathered in a semi-circle facing three chairs, two of which were occupied by senior Abwehr officers. The middle chair was empty and remained like that for a couple of awkward minutes, during which time there was much sighing and annoyed glancing at watches.

When the door opened, a short man hurried in. As he bustled past his visitors, they caught a whiff of cologne, which was met by a series of disapproving looks. When he sat down between his two colleagues, they got the impression of someone who was decidedly not one of them. He was wearing a finely cut suit, certainly not one made in the Reich. His age was hard to judge – possibly late thirties, maybe early forties. He was slim and his thick hair was swept back. Not a military man.

He smiled at his guests and adjusted his jacket, pulling up the sleeves just far enough to expose jewelled cuff links.

He smiled again. He had the attitude familiar in so many Abwehr officers: an arrogance, an unspoken contempt for the Gestapo, the SD and the SS in general. A sense they were the professional intelligence officers, above the messy business of politics.

When he spoke, he introduced himself as Georg Lange. He had a slight Hessian accent and spoke in a confident voice, explaining he'd be pleased to take questions after he'd spoken.

'I need to share important information that is of significant concern with regard to the Resistance operations here in France. And at this point may I say that we are talking about all of France here – the Occupied Zone, what was the Free Zone, the Italian Zone and the east of the country: Alsace, Lorraine and the northeast region.

'Up until last year our general assessment of the Resistance was that it was an annoyance: certainly something we could do without but as a threat to our occupation of France and our operations, it was insignificant. As you know there have been some cases of sabotage, but they have been very limited. There have been plenty of incidences of disobedience and civil unrest – underground newspapers, the distribution of inflammatory leaflets, graffiti and the like – but we have been able to contain them and—'

'Excuse me, Herr Lange.' It was a senior Gestapo officer from Paris called Wagner, short and overweight, his face florid and angry as he stood up. 'I fail to see why the Abwehr is so dismissive of the Resistance. If you've brought us here to tell us you've now discovered we ought to be paying more attention to them, well I can assure you that the Gestapo at least has been paying ample attention to them and will continue to do so!'

Georg Lange waited until the man had sat down before thanking him very much indeed for pointing that out but in fact if he would be so good as to hear him out then he would understand the importance of this meeting, though he would stress that the Abwehr had never been complacent about the Resistance.

'As a military intelligence body our assessment is that the Resistance should be recognised as a collection of disparate groups, varying in size, usually very amateurish and with little to unite them in terms of ideology. The different groups have different structures, different aims and very different politics, all characterised by a confused approach – are they political organisations or military ones, for example? They have been poorly resourced in terms of equipment, such as explosives and radios. Some of the groups are in dispute with each other: there are strong ideological differences, sometimes quite profound – monarchists and communists tend not to make good bedfellows. There were also splits between the groups in the south of France – which tend to be stronger – and those in the north, which had struggled under full German occupation. All of this, frankly, was working to our advantage.

'But that began to change last year. We received reports from our sources in London and in Marseilles that General de Gaulle had begun to take an interest in the Resistance. He decided he needed to bring the Resistance under his control; that it needed to be shaken up – unified, with a clear structure and proper objectives and strategies.

'Our intelligence from other sources appeared to corroborate this. The British Government in particular is of the view that the Resistance could be turned into a highly effective force that could be of invaluable help to the Allies if and when they open their second front and launch an invasion of—'

'That is defeatist talk, Lange: you sound like a collaborator!' It was Wagner again.

'In that case, Herr Wagner, why has the Führer ordered the building of defences on the northern coast of France, eh? Why are our Seventh and Fifteenth Armies permanently based in northern France – are you telling me the Führer is defeatist? Of course not! He is showing his usual impeccable judgement and being prepared. As are we.

'We understand a leading member of the Resistance going by the name of Mercier travelled to London in the autumn of 1941. We do not know the true identity of this Mercier but our understanding is that at one point he was based in Marseilles. In London he met with de Gaulle, who appointed him to be his emissary to the Resistance. He returned to France in January last year – 1942 – with instructions to turn the Resistance into a more unified body, concentrating on both military and political objectives. The groups would be expected to take orders from this Mercier, who in turn would be acting on instructions from de Gaulle. He would be de Gaulle's delegate, his papal nuncio.

'In return they would know they have the support of the Allies and be part of them, if you like. They would receive money – we understand he may have brought a substantial amount back with him – and the British would send weapons, explosives and radio equipment. Mercier has had a degree of success, though not without some difficulties: the groups have been reluctant to compromise their independence and start taking orders. But our intelligence suggests that the bigger groups such as Francs-Tireurs, Combat, Libération-Sud are now co-operating and together they've formed something called the United Resistance Movement.

'We had one excellent source, a communist who was in Francs-Tireurs: our code name for him was Tourist and since April he'd been providing us with excellent information. He told us that the emissary travelled to London in January and returned to France towards the end of March. When he did so it was to form the National Council of the Resistance. They're also forming something called the Secret Army.

'Last Monday, Tourist informed us that the National Council of the Resistance was meeting here in Paris three days later, on the Thursday – the twenty-seventh of May. He said he'd been asked to be one of the lookouts, watching the building where the meeting was taking place from across the road. All the leaders of the main Resistance groups would be there, including this Mercier. Tourist was due to be given the address of where they were meeting on the Wednesday morning, the day before the meeting. We'd arranged to meet him that afternoon. And then…'

Georg Lange paused, looked down at the plush carpet and then up at the audience and at Wagner in particular.

'And then, Herr Wagner, you arrested Tourist.'

All heads turned to face the Gestapo man, whose face turned even more red.

'Last Wednesday, you say?'

'Correct: The twenty-sixth of May.'

Wagner pulled a large handkerchief from his top pocket and wiped his forehead. 'Now you mention it, yes… was this Tourist's surname Blanchet?'

'Yes.'

'We did arrest him last Wednesday. He was spotted at Gare St Lazare talking to someone we'd been following and—'

'That was most probably the person giving him the address where the meeting was taking place!'

'Well, we weren't to know that, were we? Perhaps if you'd shared your secrets with us… The man we were after got away but we arrested this Blanchet character and brought him back to Avenue Foch. He was distinctly non-co-operative and I'm afraid he tried to attack one of my interrogators and I accept they may have gone too far in restraining him and—'

'And you killed him?'

'He died under questioning, Standartenführer Knochen, sir. It happens.' Wagner shrugged and everyone in the room nodded. They'd all been there. French prisoners could be so… difficult.

'In any case, Lange: if Tourist was an informant, then why on earth did the fool not think of mentioning it to us?'

'Possibly because he was frightened or too badly hurt? Who knows? Maybe you didn't give him the chance.' Georg Lange had raised his voice at this point but now composed himself. 'So as a consequence, a meeting of the National Council of the Resistance took place here in Paris last Thursday and there was nothing we could do about it.'

'As I said, you should have told us.'

'And what would you have done, brought Tourist back from the dead? But all is not lost.'

Georg Lange stood up and paced the front of the room. 'Tourist did give us more information the last time we saw him.

He said that Mercier – the emissary – is now using the code name Max or Rex at the moment, possibly both. And also, the plan is for the Council to meet once a month. May I ask, is Herr Barbie with us?'

Klaus Barbie half-raised his hand.

'The next meeting of the National Council of the Resistance is to be in Lyon. We also understand that your city is now to be the headquarters of the French Resistance.'

—

Caluire-et-Cuire is a pleasant suburb in the north of Lyon, situated on the Saône side of one of the hills on the north of the peninsula formed by the two rivers.

As suburbs go it's close enough to the centre of Lyon for it to still feel more urban than rural – very much like the city, with little hint of the expanse of countryside to the north of the city.

It's a pleasant walk up to Caluire-et-Cuire from Croix Rousse, perhaps not one best taken when it's too hot or after having eaten a good meal, though most Lyonnais these days would remark that as far as the latter was concerned, chance would be a fine thing. Rations were making life most unpleasant. There'd even been a letter in *Le Nouvelliste* suggesting that given the city's gastronomic status, the Lyonnais ought to be given extra rations.

The final stage on that walk is on Rue François Peissel, which leads into Place Castellane, and on that small square was to be found – behind a high wall – the home and surgery of Doctor Frédéric Dugoujon.

And on a warm Monday afternoon – 21 June – some patients in the waiting room for the afternoon surgery may have noticed it seemed busier than usual. Around two o'clock five men had entered – not all at the same time – and were shown to a room on the first floor rather than the ground floor waiting room. At three o'clock the maid answered the door again and showed the three men standing together outside into the waiting room, joining the six of the doctor's patients already sitting there.

The patients were most probably unaware of the consternation among the three men who'd just come in. They weren't to know the men should have been shown upstairs and nor were they to know that the meeting they were there for was forty-five minutes late in starting. And, of course, they were quite unaware it was a meeting of the National Council of the Resistance.

But what they did know was that shortly after three o'clock on that warm Monday afternoon in June, the front door of the house burst open and the premises were filled with armed Germans, some in uniform, others in the distinctive civilian dress of the Gestapo.

In the chaos, one of the eight Resistance leaders managed to escape, though he was shot and later captured. All eight and Doctor Dugoujon were taken to the Gestapo headquarters on Avenue Berthelot and then to the nearby prison of Fort Montluc.

Both at his headquarters and at the prison, Klaus Barbie wasted no time in interrogating his prisoners.

And there was one thing he needed to find out as a matter of urgency: which one of the prisoners was Max, the head of the Resistance in France, the emissary of General de Gaulle in London.

—

It was not until the middle of July – more than three weeks after the Gestapo raid on the doctor's surgery in Caluire-et-Cuire – that the Mars Resistance group felt it was safe enough to meet again. Until then the sheer panic and fear that gripped the *resistants* in Lyon and beyond ensured they suspended all their activities.

They met on the afternoon of Thursday 15 July. Midweek meetings usually took place in the evening because leaving work early could arouse suspicion, but since the raid the curfew had been enforced even more harshly. They normally met on the Croix-Rousse but Madame Madelaine decided this meeting would have to be held in her boutique on Rue Ravat.

In the past she'd never got on very well with the proprietor of the small café next door: she felt the woman was too coarse and she objected to the noise and the smell, which disturbed the refined air of her own premises.

However, earlier in the year Madame Faure had confided in her. She hated how the Germans came into her café and behaved so badly, how they put their boots on the tables, how her late husband would have been so appalled. She told Madame Madelaine that her elder son, Gilbert, had been sent to Germany to work in a factory where he was treated as a slave and... and then she took Madame Madelaine aside, into the small kitchen behind the counter, and turned on the tap and whispered, so she could only just be heard above the noise of the running water.

'You know my younger son – Jacques?' She leaned close to Madame Madelaine. 'Between you and me, he's in the countryside now... he's joined the *maquis*. I'm so worried, but so proud...'

Madame Madelaine had been sympathetic and assured Madame Faure her secret was safe with her; she could be trusted. But she did nothing with the information, waiting a few months to be sure it wasn't a trap she was being drawn into.

In June she decided that Madame Faure appeared to be trustworthy, but gave her a test. She told her a man who was on the run from the Germans would be staying in her apartment above the boutique the following night. Please could she let her know if she saw anything suspicious? But nothing happened: no one watched the premises, let alone tried to enter it.

Madame Madelaine could now confide in her.

'Sometimes I have friends... if you understand... they may wish to meet in the boutique... would it be possible if...'

And then they came up with a plan. The basements of the boutique and the café were linked. If Madame Madelaine held a meeting, then Madame Faure's basement could be a possible escape route and the café an entry point. And more than that: whenever there was a meeting Madame Madelaine would of course close her shop, but Madame Faure would keep a lookout. She was very practised at observing the comings and goings on Rue Ravat.

And on that Thursday in July there was a succession of visitors to Rue Ravat. Over a period of two hours, starting at lunchtime, some came to Madame Faure's café and when it was safe made their way through her basement to that of the boutique next door. Others came to Madame Madelaine's boutique and were shown straight to the basement.

The meeting began at three o'clock. There were fifteen people present, crammed into the basement, which had been used as a storeroom but had now been cleared out. On the wall was a brass bell, which Madame Faure would ring from the café if she saw anything suspicious.

There was a newcomer too, a medical colleague of Dr Dugoujon from Caluire-et-Cuire. Doctor Hubert was a friend of Maurice. He'd been sympathetic to the Mars group and the raid on his colleague's surgery had spurred him to join.

'I don't know how much you know about our group, Doctor? You should know our origins are in the Communist Party. When the war began there was the pact between the Soviet Union and Nazi Germany so the line from Moscow was that the communists should remain neutral. Some of us disagreed with that so we left the party and started Mars. We felt it was appropriate we should name our group after the red planet! We decided that not only should we remain independent of the main Resistance networks but that we would remain a secret organisation, even to them. Our philosophy is to be very disciplined, to recognise we are limited in what we can do now but nearer to the time when the Allies begin the liberation of France, then we can become of some use. In the meantime, our role will be confined to intelligence gathering and possibly carrying out important operations. We have a link to the British in Switzerland. That is very important. Perhaps, Doctor Hubert, you could bring us up to date with the terrible events of recent weeks?'

The doctor leaned forward and shook his head. 'It is a disaster, of course. One or two of those captured at the surgery were released because the Gestapo believed their stories that they were just there for the afternoon surgery. Dugoujon was released too: he told them he had no idea what was going on, and this man Barbie had actually seen Doctor Dugoujon treating a patient when they raided the premises. They gave him the benefit of the doubt.

'Frédéric says Barbie wanted to know just one thing: which of them was Max? They knew the leader of the Resistance movement was going to be there and they knew this was his codename. As a result of his interrogations and torture they discovered the man going under the name Jean Martel was in fact Max. I understand he'd previously gone under the name Mercier and was de Gaulle's emissary to the Resistance. His real name is Jean Moulin and before the war he was a prefect in Chartres. From what we can gather he was tortured dreadfully here in Lyon and then transferred to Paris where at some stage he fell into a coma. We don't know how much information he divulged, if anything. Last week he was being transferred by train to Germany. According to the Germans, he died en route. The death certificate given to his family says he died in the railway station at Metz.'

There was silence in the basement, the noise from the café upstairs only just audible. Everyone shook their head and Madame Madelaine said of course they'd heard the rumours, but to hear this confirmed was... too terrible, too terrible.

'This is a disaster for the Resistance, but we are in a privileged position in that no one knows about us.'

'What should we do now?'

'For now, we do nothing: when I consider it is safe, we will try to contact the British in Switzerland. They will know what to do. But first we wait: it's too dangerous to do otherwise. I don't know who we can trust in Lyon.'

'What do you mean, Madame Madelaine?' It was Michel.

'The Gestapo raid on Doctor Dugoujon's surgery in Caluire-et-Cuire: it was led by Klaus Barbie himself, wasn't it? And he knew he was looking for Max and that he was de Gaulle's personal emissary. They were betrayed.'

There was a stunned silence in the room and then everyone looked up at the bell as they heard a clattering of chairs and a door slam in the café upstairs. But the bell remained silent and then the laughter from upstairs resumed.

'There is a traitor in Lyon.'

Chapter 8

Harold Dickson encountered a ghost on Haymarket.

When he'd felt the hand on his shoulder and turned in the direction of the familiar voice, a feeling of overwhelming fear swept through his body. He thought he was about to faint before realising he wasn't dreaming and that jolted him as if he'd been hit by a car and at that moment, he knew his life had been darkened forever.

–

After he changed his name at the end of 1933, Harold Dickson had little difficulty in thinking of himself in his new identity. It had come surprisingly naturally to him. For the first couple of months he did occasionally hesitate if his old name was called out – but only for a second or two and certainly not so that anyone would notice.

It almost certainly helped that he'd started his new job and at the same time had moved to the very pleasant apartment in Highbury, funded to a substantial degree by the generosity of Nicholas. It was a new life, a new beginning in more ways than one. He'd flourished in his new job: his manager told him that he'd taken to it like a duck to water and he hinted that if he carried on like this he'd soon be in line for promotion.

But around this time his opinions began to change, he started to see the world differently. Looking back on this period in his life he recognised that this change was in a large part because he'd begun to take a more positive view of the world and how he fitted into it. He recognised that being resentful and negative – having a chip on his shoulder, as his father used to put it – coloured his views. Previously, he'd been too quick to look for people to blame for things, too ready to look for scapegoats and feel hard done by.

As he began to prosper in his new department, he saw that maybe life hadn't dealt him such an unfortunate hand after all. He'd just needed to find his right role, something he was suited for. And now he'd appeared to be doing that, he saw things differently.

For a start he recognised that his political views had been far too simplistic. Blaming the Jews and Communists for everything was too easy and probably quite flawed. There'd been a Jewish chap in his new department, a kindly and patient man called Bernard who was also from Manchester and who went out of his way to ensure Harold had all the help he needed, and even invited him round for lunch with his family one Bank Holiday weekend after Harold had let slip he had no plans. And there was Reg, minus one arm after the Great War, who looked after the post and carried messages around Whitehall and who everyone called Red Reg on account of his politics and even though Reg obviously wasn't a communist because he wouldn't be working where he was if that were the case, he was unquestionably on the left. He was more than happy to talk politics after work, happy to lend him books, but he avoided preaching. Reg was always pleasant, always happy to hear another point of view and invariably ended their chats, as he called them, by saying they should agree to disagree.

And he began to read more widely, including the books lent by Reg. He wouldn't go so far as to say that his views changed dramatically, but they were certainly altered. He became more balanced. More moderate. More tolerant of other points of view.

And then at the end of 1935 came his promotion and his first posting overseas. It was quite unexpected and only came about because the person who was due to take up the post had to defer because his wife became pregnant and then the man next in line was due to be promoted elsewhere. All of which meant that Harold Dickson found himself in the right place at the right time.

He was duly posted abroad at the end of 1935 and his view of the world continued to change. If his views had moderated somewhat during 1935 while he was still in England, once overseas it was as if he'd become a different person.

This was due to far more than his new-found status giving him more confidence. It was a perhaps inevitable consequence of what he saw on the Continent. Experiencing the reality of Nazism at first hand had a profound effect on him. He still saw countries in crisis and he still saw communism as a threat. But the biggest change was in his attitude to Jews. He didn't exactly become a philo-Semite like one or two of the people with whom he worked, but he certainly stopped being an anti-Semite. He realised they were much like other people, some quite friendly, others less so but all in an increasingly desperate situation through what he now realised was no fault of their own.

The one cloud on his horizon – and it was a considerable one – was Nicholas. He'd seen Nicholas just before he left for his posting at the end of 1935 and he'd been told to keep his head down and there'd be a time 'sooner or later' when they'd call on his services.

He lived in fear of being contacted by Nicholas, of some dreadful demand being made upon him. Many a time he toyed with the idea of owning up to what had happened, hoping it may be forgiven as an indiscretion and mitigated by the information he'd pass over in return. But he knew that was unlikely: given the job he now had it would be seen as too serious an offence, certainly a disciplinary one, if not criminal. It would be the end of his career at the very least.

He coped with the situation by reckoning the longer he went without hearing from Nicholas, the more likely it was that he'd forgotten about him – though he did realise there was a good deal of wishful thinking in that. Then in early 1938 – about a week before he was due to return to England for a fortnight's leave – he received a letter from Nicholas, at his place of work. Nicholas understood – Harold had no idea how he understood – that he was due to be in London soon and how about they meet on the evening of the first Tuesday in March in The Hope in Kenton Street in Bloomsbury, which he was sure he remembered.

–

Nicholas was thinner than before, his complexion more pallid. Every aspect of him was now thin and pinched: the lips, the smile, the way his eyes appeared not to be fully open, even the voice, which was as if he was nursing a sore throat. He'd found a corner of The Hope where they could talk privately and Nicholas did so in an urgent tone. Very soon, he assured Harold, he'd be called upon. Any time now.

'Are you ready to serve the cause?'

Harold Dickson had hoped to broach the possibility of him pulling out of whatever Nicholas had in mind for him. He'd rehearsed a short speech on how he'd previously been in a position to help but no longer felt able to do so – at least for the time being – but if there was a point in the future when he felt able to help once more then he'd certainly be in touch. And then he'd add that Nicholas was not to worry: all of their dealings would remain between them. He had no intention whatsoever of saying anything to anyone.

But he never got the chance. When he asked him whether he was ready to serve the cause Nicholas had gripped him tightly by the wrist and leaned forward so their faces were just inches apart and he could see the thin red lines in Nicholas's eyeballs and smell the whisky on his breath and feel the tiny flecks of warm saliva on his face as he spoke.

'You're not having doubts, are you?'

'Doubts about what?'

'Doubts about the cause and the commitments you made five years ago. If it wasn't for me you'd still be a clerk in the Ministry of Labour and living in an unpleasant bedsit. Whether you like it or not, you're one of us. You work for me. You do understand that, don't you?'

Nicholas was still gripping his wrist, his face too close and he nodded though Nicholas didn't look convinced and when he removed his hand from Harold's wrist it was to remove an envelope from an inside pocket. He said nothing as he removed three photographs and fanned them out in front of him.

'Do you remember John, who used to deliver messages to you on my behalf? These photographs show you with him: these two are especially clear, considering the distance they were taken from. John is actually Denis Arthur Andrews, currently serving time in one of His Majesty's prisons for offences of violence committed while acting as a bodyguard for Oswald Mosely. The authorities know he is an active fascist. The authorities would, I dare say, take a dim view of this evidence of you consorting with him. As they would of this...'

Nicholas slipped the photographs back into the envelope and removed a bank document, which he told him detailed a transfer of money to him back in 1933 which enabled him to rent a new apartment. 'The authorities will know that in 1933 this account was one operated by the British Union of Fascists. All of which means that should you ever entertain any doubts and prove to be less than co-operative you'd do well to consider what I've just shown you. I hope you understand?'

He thought about protesting that this was blackmail but knew that would be pointless because Nicholas would disappear into the night and soon his life would be ruined. So, he said of course he understood and there was really no need for all that and naturally he remained committed to the cause though it would be very helpful if Nicholas could explain what serving the cause actually entailed and Nicholas moved even closer to him, if that was possible, his tall body almost enveloping him.

'Where you're based at the moment is most useful to us. We will be requiring confidential information: names, files – that kind of information. We may require you to help people we send your way. There are people who'd require the correct papers. You are going to be very important to us.'

He found himself – against his better judgement – saying 'thank you'. It was his nerves again, making him respond so inappropriately.

'But not yet: bide your time for a while. You need to be patient.'

Dickson promised him he would be, relieved he wasn't being given any instructions that evening.

'When we last met, I may have intimated that a number of us were forming the view that Oswald Mosley was too moderate and reluctant to embrace the ideals of National Socialism. Since then, our position has been vindicated: Mosley has been tentative at best in forming meaningful ties with Germany. Last year a small group of us left the British Union of Fascists and formed the National Socialist League. We see our role as doing what we can to serve the Nazi leadership in Germany. That can take a number of forms, but it includes having a number of people sympathetic to us in positions of influence and importance. People such as you.'

Dickson only just stopped himself saying thank you again and had to grip the counter to stop himself falling off his chair as the realisation hit him that he was, to all intents and purposes, a Nazi spy.

–

That was March 1938. He returned to England later that year and fully expected Nicholas to find out he was in London, but there was no word from him and he allowed himself to hope he'd been forgotten.

He did read in *The Times* that the National Socialist League had disbanded in August 1939 with a number of its senior members interned under wartime regulations, but as far as he could tell, Nicholas was not one of them, though he was by no means convinced that Nicholas was his real name.

He continued to be nervous about being contacted again. Nicholas had a habit of appearing in a mercurial manner and he doubted he'd heard the last of him.

It was to be more than three years before he next heard of him. They received bundles of English newspapers at work every fortnight or so, somehow finding their way from Lisbon, to where they were flown on a regular basis. They were devoured by everyone and it meant reading newspapers in a random manner and sometimes many weeks after their publication. *The Times* was the main newspaper in the bundles but there'd be the *Daily Telegraph* too, and it was a copy of the latter that he was reading one Sunday afternoon in late September. The edition was from Friday 1 August, 1941.

POLICE APPEAL IN MURDER HUNT

Police in Sussex have appealed for the assistance of the public in their hunt for Jeffrey Morgan (pictured) who is wanted in connection with the death of his wife, Dorothy Ethel Morgan.

The body of fifty-nine-year-old Mrs Morgan was discovered on the morning of Tuesday 29 July by a tradesman visiting the couple's isolated cottage south of Edburton and two miles north of Shoreham-by-Sea.

The tradesman noticed an outhouse had been burnt down, with the embers still smoking. Upon further investigation he discovered the body of a female in the outhouse. The body was identified as that of Dorothy Ethel Morgan and at a subsequent post-mortem the cause of death was found to be a broken neck.

Inspector Matthew Carstairs of Sussex police said the last confirmed sighting of Jeffrey Morgan (63) was in Shoreham-by-Sea on Saturday 26 July. Police believe Mr Morgan has contacts in the London area.

He stared at the report and particularly the photograph of Jeffrey Morgan for a good while. The image was unquestionably that of the man he knew as Nicholas. The distinctive, pinched features, the thin smile, the eyes that appeared half-closed. It looked to him like a police photograph, well-lit and perhaps taken a few years previously – certainly around a time in the mid to late 1930s when Harold would have known him.

His first reaction was one of relief: surely a man on the run – wanted for murder no less – would have more important things to worry about than contacting him. Then he began to think: what if Nicholas – or Jeffrey Morgan as he appeared to be – was caught? What would he reveal under police questioning? Would he offer up his name and other information in a desperate attempt to evade the hangman's noose?

Two months later, in early December, all his prayers were answered. He no longer had to worry. The good news came in a copy of the *Daily Telegraph* dated Tuesday 9 September and which had taken the best part of three months to reach them.

SUSSEX MURDER HUNT CALLED OFF
AFTER BODY FIND

Police in Sussex have confirmed that a body found in the Devil's Dyke valley last Wednesday is that of Jeffrey Morgan (pictured), the Shoreham-by-Sea man wanted in connection with the murder of his wife on or around 29 July this year.

Inspector Matthew Carstairs of Sussex police said the body was found in deep undergrowth by walkers. The state of decomposition indicated the body had been there for some time. Mr Morgan (63) was identified through his clothing and papers, which were found on his body.

Sussex police have confirmed they are no longer looking for anyone in connection with the murder of Dorothy Ethel Morgan.

An inquest held in October concluded that Mrs
Morgan's death was the result of foul play.

His relief was immeasurable. He no longer felt like a man under
constant suspicion, nervous of every glance in his direction,
frightened whenever there was a knock on the door or the bell
rang or he received a summons to meet with one of his superiors.
It went without saying that he bitterly regretted the initial contact
with Nicholas and his foolishness in allowing it to continue. He
resolved to lead a decent and uncomplicated life from now on,
in so far as his job – which was not without its own considerable
tensions – allowed him.

At the start of August 1943, he returned to England for the
first time in a number of years. Personally, he was in no hurry
to return, but apparently it was required: an annual review – a
number of years' worth of annual reviews, actually – a medical
and home leave. The journey home was naturally not a straightforward one and somewhat fraught at times but once he was back,
he was glad he'd made the effort.

The weather was not as close as he remembered it could be
in August, London not as oppressive. The meetings all went
well: the annual review concluded his service continued to be
commendable and he was to move up one grade. The medical
included a session on his morale, as they delicately put it, and
that noted he was in good spirits and deemed him to be of 'an
optimistic and positive nature'.

He was to be in England for three weeks. The first week
was taken up with his work commitments and then he visited
Manchester for what turned out to be a fairly pointless weekend:
there was no one there he especially wanted to see and he felt no
nostalgia for his home town. He was shocked at the bomb damage
and walked around the area he used to live, but then returned to
London. He was staying at a bed and breakfast between Lavender

Hill and the northside of Clapham Common and spent much of his time walking round the city, enjoying the bustle and not being at work.

In his last week he took to walking along the north bank of the river and strolling into the centre of London, especially the West End. His employers had been generous with ration cards – as he was on what they described as 'service leave' he was entitled to extra rations. He was also flush with cash so was able to afford to eat in the few decent restaurants that were still open and took in as many shows as he could.

He especially enjoyed *The Lisbon Story* at the Hippodrome and *Sunny River* at the Piccadilly but the play he enjoyed most was *Flying Colours* at the Lyric, with Binnie Hale and Douglas Byng. So much so that two days before he was due to return, he booked to see it for the second time. It was a matinee performance and when he left the theatre on Shaftesbury Avenue it was still warm and sunny and he decided to head south to the small restaurant he'd found in Cockspur Street where in return for extra coupons and a generous tip they were able to serve something that tasted remarkably like steak.

He was on Haymarket when he recalled thinking how pleasant and agreeable life was and how good it was to have no care in the world other than his stomach problems, which the doctor at the medical had assured him were really nothing to worry about.

He was opposite His Majesty's Theatre when he felt a hand on his shoulder, as if in greeting, and when he turned round an older man – bearded and tall and thin – said, Harold, well fancy that, if it isn't you, who'd have thought we'd bump into each other like this and what a pleasant surprise and we can't let an opportunity like this pass, can we?

Dickson said no, they couldn't, and he felt he was sleep-walking as he allowed Jeffrey Morgan – the man he'd known as Nicholas and who he'd spent the past two years believing was dead – to steer him south, across Pall Mall and then the Mall and into St James's Park where they found an isolated bench in front of the lake. A family of ducks appeared expectantly in front of them.

'I presume you know that I'm officially dead?'

'I'd heard, I mean, I read... I...' In the distance two police officers were strolling towards them. Nicholas didn't even flinch.

'I can heartily recommend death: wipes the slate clean, all one's problems disappear. No more debts, no more obligations. Of course, it's not without complications, but compared with what went before – marvellous.'

He'd briefly removed his trilby and swept it in front of him as if to emphasise how marvellous everything really was.

'What happened?'

'Once the war began, I laid low for a few months but it soon became apparent that the authorities weren't on to me. I'd been clever with my identities, you know, far cleverer than many at the top of the British Union of Fascists or the National Socialist League. We moved down to the south coast.

'Dorothy was really quite unaware of my line of work and of my connections. We didn't discuss politics. I told her we were moving to the coast to be away from the bombing and I found this place in Sussex which fitted the bill perfectly. Quite isolated and with an outhouse where I could rig up my radio equipment. Once a week I'd travel to London, collect messages from various dead letter boxes and return to Sussex. Then I'd encode and transmit them. They were short messages, too short for the trans-missions to be tracked. All was fine until that evening at the end of July 1941 when Dorothy came into the outhouse, which she had very strict instructions not to do: I'd persuaded her I'd turned it into a darkroom and didn't want the photographs exposed to light. I'd actually rigged up a bell system from the outhouse to the cottage, which she was to ring in the event of an emergency or if anyone came along and of course I also locked the door. But on this particular occasion I hadn't locked the door properly and as far as I can work out, the bell didn't work. Dorothy caught me *in flagrante*, so to speak. Transmitting, all the radio equipment on view, my headphones on.

'If she'd have left straight away maybe I'd have… who knows, but what I do know is that she stood there staring at me and said what on earth was I up to and then she said – these were her very words – was I a spy? She turned to leave the outhouse and I rushed after her and grabbed her by the neck. I imagine if I were to end up in court, I'd say something about just wanting to stop her and it all being a terrible accident, but I knew what I was doing. I simply couldn't risk her knowing what I was up to. It took longer than I thought it would but then she stopped struggling. As I soon as I checked her I knew she was dead.

'I was very organised after that. I dismantled all the equipment, broke it up and buried it under the outhouse and then collected what I could carry – papers, money, a few clothes and before I left set fire to the outhouse. I thought I may have a few days lead on the police but as far as I gather some chap turned up at the cottage the following day and, suddenly, I'm Britain's most wanted man. I was hiding in London by then: a comrade had a safe place for me. But I realised I needed to do something about the police so a week or so later I drove down to Brighton, found a vagrant who was a similar height and build to me and I plied him with enough alcohol to render him senseless. I then drove him north of Brighton to the Devil's Dyke, suffocated him and dressed him in a set of my clothes and left my papers on him. I took a risk that it would be a while before the body was found, but I also counted on the passage of time and wildlife interfering with it enough for the police to assume it was me.

'Seems to have worked a treat. I keep my head down, I've altered my appearance, as you can see, and most importantly of all I've been very careful. But that has, of necessity, meant I've been less than productive for the cause. I'd always hoped you'd return, of course. At one stage I'd given up and lost track of you, but let's say I had one or two sources and one of them paid off and I heard you were back in London a few days ago. It was easier to find you than I feared it was going to be. Now we have renewed our acquaintance…' He paused at that point, pleased with his clever joke, amused to see the other man's shocked reaction. 'Now we have renewed our acquaintance I shall be able to be more productive. You look worried?'

'I'm not sure what my role is in this.'

'You recall when we first met you indicated your willingness to serve the cause?'

He paused and turned to face him on the bench, lifting his trilby just enough so his full face was on view. Harold Dickson knew he had an opportunity here to say there'd been a misunderstanding, that circumstances had changed but he also knew he'd never get away with it and apart from anything, he assumed Nicholas would still have the photographs and the bank document that proved he was a traitor. He shrugged his shoulders in the most non-committal manner he could.

'I did say there would be a time when I'd call upon your services. Now is that time.'

He said nothing as he watched the ducks paddle away, so fast it was as if they sensed something was up.

'What would that entail?'

Nicholas said he wanted to know everything about his job and indeed his life. And for the next hour they walked around the park and he told Nicholas what he did – far more than he intended, but he was nervous and the older man was skilled at wheedling information out of him. After an hour Nicholas said there was no question he'd be of enormous use, the intelligence he could – would – provide would be invaluable.

'We will meet tomorrow, by which time I will have a plan as to how you will pass on the intelligence to me. I suggest we meet in The Hope in Bloomsbury, for old times' sake. How does that sound to you?'

It sounded like a nightmare to him but he knew he had no alternative but to say it sounded fine.

All he could think of as he walked back to Clapham was the fateful day exactly ten years ago, in August 1933, when he had been in half a mind whether to go to the meeting at The Hope. He bitterly regretted not listening to his instincts, which told him not to go, but now it was too late.

And when he arrived at The Hope the following lunchtime, he couldn't help but think of the Dante's warning quoted at him that day by the annoying little man whose name he couldn't remember.

'Abandon hope, all ye who enter here!'

Chapter 9

'*You'll meet him very soon: but he's terribly senior. Outranks me!*'

It was the middle of September, some four weeks since Sophia and Jack had been sitting in the library of the British safe house just outside Berne where Basil Remington-Barber had informed them their next mission would be in France.

And from now on, he told them, someone else would be looking after them. Someone more senior than him.

At the beginning of September Sophia and Jack had moved into a flat in Berne overlooking the Aare on Badgasse, not far from the Kirchenfeldbrücke. Looming over the entrance of the building on Badgasse was the high wall of the Münsterplattform park.

It was the fifth place they'd seen and that in itself had caused something of a row with Basil Remington-Barber because he made it very clear to her that as the Service was paying the rent then they really ought to be grateful for whatever they were given. But Sophia was having none of it: one flat was too cold, another too damp, one had an unpleasant smell and the fourth was on the wrong side of the river as far as she was concerned. The flat on Badgasse was small but bright and cosy.

Basil did insist on referring to it as a 'love nest', which was a bit grating. They should wait in their 'love nest', he told them, until instructions came through regarding their next mission.

'And when will that be, Basil?'

The older man shrugged. He was none the wiser. 'When the new chap arrives in Berne, which could be any day now. I'm told he'll find you, you're not to worry.'

'And how will we know it's him?'

'He'll introduce himself as Mallory, I'm told.'

—

On a wet Wednesday afternoon Sophia and Jack returned to Badgasse. They'd been for a walk in the Münsterplattform when the weather suddenly turned, as it was prone to do in Berne: gloriously sunny one minute, storm-like the next – something to do with the Alps. Everything to do with the weather in Switzerland seemed to be to do with the Alps. By the time they reached their apartment building the rain felt as if it was horizontal and they barely looked up as a tall man wrapped in a long raincoat held the main door open for them. They giggled as they climbed the stairs: so wet it no longer mattered, and Sophia said she'd have a bath first and Jack had suggested perhaps they share one.

They were still laughing when they reached the door to their apartment, nervously excited at what lay ahead. Sophia leaned over to kiss Jack as he tried to place the key in the lock and he told her to try and contain herself for a minute at the most and she replied thirty seconds was as long as she was prepared to wait.

It was only when they were in the hallway of their flat that they became aware they'd been followed into it. As Jack turned to shut the door the tall man with the long raincoat who'd held the door open for them outside was inside their doorway. As Jack reached for the pistol he carried in his jacket the man removed his trilby hat, a shower of rain spraying from it as he did so.

'No need for that, Jack. It's me – Edward, Edward Campion! Sophia, how wonderful to see you: I trust you also remember me?'

The two of them stood quite motionless for a good minute as the shock registered. Neither of them had seen the man standing in front of them since before the war, four years previously.

The man they both knew as Edward Campion was the British spymaster who'd originally recruited them in Berlin, though 'recruited' hardly described the protracted and clandestine process adequately.

'I'm pleased to observe that you two are getting on so splendidly! Perhaps we could go into the lounge? Basil says your "love nest" is very cosy and is costing him a fortune.' He was speaking in German now.

They said little as they removed their coats and shoes and sat in the lounge: the Englishman on the single armchair, Sophia and Jack on the sofa. There was a little small talk: Edward Campion said how wonderful it was to have a view of the river and no thank you, he wouldn't like a drink at the moment.

'Awkward time of the afternoon, I find: a bit too late for tea but a shade too early for anything stronger.'

'Would it be naïve to ask what on earth you're doing here, Edward?'

He smiled at Jack and wondered whether now was the time to tell them that Edward Campion as such had ceased to exist after his last trip to Berlin in 1939. He'd been going by his real identity since then: Barney Allen, MI6 spymaster. But for the purpose of him being in Switzerland… it was a bit complicated.

'I was just passing by!'

They looked at him as if he was mad and he burst out laughing and said no, no – of course not. Far more important than that, he said, and perhaps they should now be serious because he had something very important to say.

'I'm Mallory, you see.'

–

It had been quite some meeting on the last day of August at the MI6 headquarters in St James's – head office as those who worked there were want to call it.

Piers Devereux had called the meeting with two of his senior officers, Tom Gilbey and Barney Allen, along with his boss, Roland Bentley, and Bentley had mentioned it to Sir Roly Pearson, the Downing Street intelligence man, earlier that morning and he said he'd very much like to be there too and of course he knew both Gilbey and Allen – he was at school with both of them!

'I'm concerned about Switzerland.'

There was silence as everyone in the room stared at Piers Devereux wondering if he was going to elaborate.

'Do you think they're going to join the war?'

'No, of course not, Roly! I'm concerned about our operation there – Berne Station.'

'I thought it was doing rather well? Ran the German woman and the American reporter in Berlin very impressively, didn't they? Got them out and back in again and then safely back, eh?'

'Yes, Roland, they did indeed. But they have an awful lot on their plate: vetting refugees from Germany who say they want to work for us, running clandestine operations, sorting escaped RAF aircrew, intelligence inside Switzerland itself – it's an enormous operation, as you know. And the Swiss are reluctant to let us increase our diplomatic cover there: they don't want to upset the Germans. Basil was on the verge of retiring when the war began and I think the pressure is beginning to tell on him, to be frank. He has a few officers there, of course, but it's not enough. Noel Moore is one of them and I saw him when he was back in London and he says Basil is struggling. Could do with some help.'

'We could get someone out there, I guess, just need to work on their cover: that's always tricky with the Swiss, isn't it?'

'It is indeed, sir. However, there's been an important develop-ment which means we need to reinforce Berne at a senior level.'

'How senior?'

'Above Head of Station level.'

'Really, Piers – why is that?' Roland Bentley was looking up now from the papers in front of him, which Piers Devereux suspected were probably to do with his next meeting – or the budget: he was always going on about his budget. Now his interest was piqued.

'Tom has something to share with us.'

Tom Gilbey had removed his jacket, the only person in the stuffy room to have done so, and had also rolled up his sleeves. As he began to speak he loosened his tie and Sir Roly huffed in disapproval. Letting down the old school.

'I have a contact in Geneva, chap I'd not heard from for over a year. He's French, from Lyon. Goes by the name of Benoît Roux and he was a university lecturer at the École Centrale in Lyon but fled to Switzerland when the Nazis occupied France. I think there's a Swiss wife, which helps matters.

'Roux was part of a small group in Lyon who'd left the French Communist Party in August 1939 in disgust at the Nazi-Soviet Pact and the French Communist Party's support for it. Early in 1940 Benoît Roux turned up at our embassy in Berne looking to co-operate and he met Basil. Seems they never hit it off: took an instant dislike to each other. Basil's take on it is that Roux was very demanding and wanted money but was very cagey about how it was going to be used. Benoît felt that Basil was dismissive of his offer to supply us with intelligence and distrusted him because he's a communist and insisted he should reveal the names of all his contacts.

'As far as Basil and Benoît were concerned, that was it, but later that year – this would be 1940 – I was put in touch with Roux via a contact of mine in London. We managed to meet once and got on well and since then he's been a reliable source of intelligence: not a lot of it but everything I've got from him has been good. I'd describe him as a useful source rather than a top agent, but good nonetheless.

'I heard from him last week. He was able to corroborate the dreadful reports we've been getting from France on the Gestapo raids on the Resistance in Lyon and the death of Jean Moulin, who was de Gaulle's man over there and meant to be sorting the Resistance out. As we know, it's all a terrible mess and a big setback for us: we've been relying on the French Resistance getting organised before the second front.'

'Winston is most concerned,' said Roly Pearson. 'Someone clearly informed the Gestapo about the meeting of the Resistance leaders in Lyon where Moulin was arrested. There's no doubt they were betrayed and de Gaulle is trying to blame us as usual and is demanding Winston sorts it out. There is no evidence whatsoever we're to blame, of course, but they're looking for a scapegoat. Does this Roux have any idea who it was?'

'Not as such, Roly, I don't think so at any rate – but the group of former communists he has links with in Lyon have formed themselves into a Resistance group. He tells us that this group is quite independent of all the other Resistance networks, operates separately from them, no one knows about them, apparently. As a result, they've remained intact – they've survived the Gestapo's purge on the Resistance. And he's offering us the chance to work with them. They have excellent contacts in Lyon. If we can send them weapons, explosives, money and whatever else they need, then we can be part of their intelligence operation. They're even suggesting we send in agents to work with them.'

'With communists? Winston won't be awfully keen on that!'

'They're former communists, Roly, and not all of them are communists. Anyway, the communists are now our allies, are they not?'

Sir Roly huffed once more. 'And does this group have a name, Tom?'

'Mars, apparently.'

'Like the chocolate bar?'

'Named after the planet, I suspect,' said Roland Bentley. 'The red planet.'

Piers Devereux coughed to attract the attention of the others. 'My feeling is that this is such an important opening that we should send our best agents to Lyon. It's an opportunity for us to help get the French Resistance back on track and if we succeed in that, then the prospects for the second front are significantly improved. I propose sending Sophia and Jack to Lyon to work with the group.'

'When did they get back from their last operation in Germany?'

'Beginning of July, sir: two months ago. I think this operation is so important we ought to run it from Berne or Geneva with someone very senior – so senior we can run it discretely from Basil's outfit.'

A long silence in the room as they waited to see who would ask the question hanging over it.

'And um… any thoughts as to who that may be?'

'Someone,' said Piers Devereux, 'who has the clout here to get Mars what they need and ensure that the intelligence we get from them goes to the right places: someone who can ensure the Resistance is properly organised and that its aims are focused on what the Allies need. Someone senior, as I say. And someone who knows Sophia and Jack, who they trust.'

Barney Allen shuffled uncomfortably as what Piers Devereux was saying began to sink in.

'Who recruited them, Piers?'

'It was me actually Roland: I think we all know that.' Having avoided looking at him before, all eyes were now on Barney.

'Fancy taking it on, Barney? More fun than sitting behind a desk in London, eh?'

'It rather sounds to me, sir, as if the decision may have been made.' Barney frowned, as if he was thinking about it. Sir Roly Pearson stretched over and put his hand on Barney Allen's arm.

'Can't stress how vital this is, Barney: it's our opportunity to get the Resistance back on track and effectively to have our own network at the heart of it. But it will require skilful handling. You're just the man for it. Winston will be thrilled: I promise you it will not go unnoticed.'

When Barney Allen looked up, still in shock, he saw that everyone else in the room was looking at him and nodding and then Roland Pearson stood up and leaned over the table to shake him warmly by the hand – two hands clasping his – and say, 'Well done… well done indeed, knew you wouldn't say no.'

The London intelligence community could move painfully slowly. It tended to be a world where caution prevailed and notwithstanding the nature of the work they were engaged in, risks were approached with a good deal of suspicion.

It was, Barney Allen realised, a consequence of the intelligence bodies having grown out of the civil service and a very British tendency to avoid mistakes. But the world of intelligence could also move at astonishing speed.

And this is what happened after the meeting at MI6 where it was decided he'd be sent to Switzerland. The meeting had been on a Tuesday. As soon as it had finished, Piers Devereux took Barney into his office.

'I had taken the precaution of making one or two arrangements, Barney.' He patted a not insubstantial folder in front of him. 'We're sorting out your trip, but the plan is for you to leave this country on Friday the tenth of September. Between now and then you'll be fully briefed.'

Barney Allen said this all sounded rather... sudden and Piers Devereux said yes of course, but there was no point in hanging around and, as it was, he'd ideally have liked him to be out there a week or so earlier, but there we are and...

'You were saying, Piers?'

'And you'd better tell your wife: keep details to the absolute minimum, no locations, nothing like that. She knows Tom, I understand?'

'Yes, of course. We were in the same year at school.'

'Tell her Tom will be her contact but she may not hear very much: she's to treat no news as good news.'

–

Margaret Allen had taken the news very badly. Barney had travelled home to Oxfordshire that night and as he wasn't expected until the weekend, she'd known straight away that something was up.

He'd decided to tell her in the garden and did so in front of the rose bushes to which she tended with such care. She'd fixed her gaze on the flowers as he spoke and when he finished said nothing as she continued dead-heading.

'And that's it, Barney?'

'It is, I'm afraid, Margaret dear. That's as much as I can tell you.'

'That you're going to be away for work for quite a while and if there's any news Tom Gilbey will be in touch. Really, Barney, you can't say any more? I mean, will you even be in this country?'

He told her that was as much as he could say and then she started to cry and asked if he was in trouble and he said of course not, in fact, on the contrary and she asked what on earth he meant by that and he said he couldn't really say but he was sure he'd be fine and she walked over to the yellow roses, which she'd cultivated to bloom so late in the year.

He remained at home in Oxfordshire that Wednesday, sorting out his affairs and paperwork as Piers Devereux had advised him to do, and wrote letters to his wife and children in the event of anything happening to him. He left home after a largely silent lunch on the Thursday, driving to an MI6 safe house just south of Newbury.

He spent the next week in the company of Piers Devereux and a succession of other MI6 officers and trainers.

There'd been some small arms practice and radio work – codes and the like – but the most important part of the week as far as he was concerned was spent with an elderly man he'd seen around head office from time to time, a man people spoke of with awe as having spent the whole of the Great War behind enemy lines.

He appeared to be well into his seventies, walked with a limp and told Barney Allen he could call him Oliver. Oliver explained that he should avoid the mistake of regarding Switzerland as a neutral country. It was, technically, of course, but as soon as he arrived there it was best to regard it as enemy territory.

'That way you'll be alert and careful from the outset. I know you were in Berlin, but that was before the war. Now you need to adopt the mindset of a spy rather than a spymaster. In my book, spies need to operate with a degree of paranoia: you need to be suspicious of everyone. If you do this then you'll cut down the errors you're bound to make. Only involve people you absolutely have to. Resist the temptation to share information with people who don't need to know it. It's pretty lonely out there, sometimes quite frightening. You'll be very grateful to have people there who are friendly, like colleagues, and without realising it you can find yourself telling them information you shouldn't be sharing.

'And have your own secrets: if you get a new contact, think twice and then again about who else should know about them. You're not working for Berne Station, remember. You're working for Piers in London. From what I gather Basil's not running the tightest ship.'

He received detailed briefings on his new identity: Arthur Mallory, from Canada. He was given a closely typed twenty-page document with Arthur Mallory's biography. An important aspect of this was that Arthur Mallory had moved around Canada: it would be hard to tie him down. He'd been born in Winnipeg, moved to Calgary and then Edmonton before going to college in Toronto where he'd married before getting divorced and then moving to Vancouver and most recently, he'd been back in Toronto.

Always be vague about dates, volunteer as little in the way of facts as possible.

He could refer to having made a good deal of money in engineering before selling the company and so being able to afford his passion for watches: Swiss watches in particular. Hence his presence in Switzerland.

'How do I explain being a Canadian who happens to turn up in Switzerland while there's a war on? Canada's at war with Germany too.'

'You were in France when the war started and then moved to Spain. You have no desire to be involved in the war and little interest in it: you are a wealthy man, more interested in watches than in your country. In Switzerland discretion is a national trait: people ask very few questions. As long as you are involved in buying and selling watches you will be seen as having a satisfactory reason for being there.'

And then a man called Richard turned up and spent a day tutoring Barney on watches. He gave him a well-thumbed guide to Swiss watches and pointed out that serious collectors tended to specialise. He suggested an interest in the luxury brands manufactured in the Canton of Geneva. And then Piers joined them and said there'd be enough money in a Swiss account for him to purchase watches.

'All seems excessive, if you ask me, Barney, but I have to admit, it's an excellent cover. Be as careful as you can be with the watches because when this is all over, we'll need to sell the bloody things. Otherwise the Service will go bust!'

Early on the Friday morning he was driven to Whitchurch airport, just outside Bristol. He was on the noon BOAC flight to Lisbon, which left on time. The flight on the DC-3 took four hours, flying at low altitude so the Germans would recognise it as a civilian flight.

At Portela airport in Lisbon he was met by a driver who took him straight to the British Embassy on Rua de São Domingos. There he met the head of station, Sandy Morgan, who told him he'd spend the night there and be driven to Madrid from where he would take a train to Barcelona and a flight from there on the Monday morning to Locarno.

'In Switzerland.'

'Yes, I know that. Thank you, Sandy.'

'Just that it sounds Italian! Wouldn't send you into enemy territory though, would I? Basil will have someone waiting for you there and then you're all set!'

Chapter 10

Lyon
July, August, September 1943

René Dupont would never have gone so far as to say he was enjoying life, that would be overstating matters. His life continued to be a web of worries and concerns – about money, his health and about the lack of respect he was shown and the way his family regarded him, not least his wife, Jeanne.

But that aside, his life had unquestionably taken a turn for the better.

By the end of July, he'd been an officer in the *milice* for some nine months. Of course, he was no fool. He was not so naïve as to imagine that everyone in the city liked the idea of the French having their own militia to work with the Germans. He knew that some people even thought of them as collaborators, which was a ridiculous and actually quite insulting attitude. What did they want: for the Germans to run France without the involvement of the French? Surely it was better to have French militia and police who could work with the Germans and, at the same time, for the people of France?

As he saw it, working with the Germans was helping to ensure law and order prevailed in Lyon and also that the communists, the Jews, the socialists and the liberals – the lot of them – were put in their place. At the same time, it enabled the French to have a say in their own affairs.

René Dupont was quite certain his was the right course of action. The problem was that so many of those he came into contact with outside of work didn't seem to agree. The tension at home was considerable: Jeanne seemed happy enough with the extra rations he was entitled to but an undeniable *frisson* had emerged between them.

He wasn't pretending that the marriage had been without its difficulties before. He was aware that he'd not been as successful in his career as she and her family would have liked. He put this down to their different backgrounds, his own being very low middle class, hers more prosperous.

But over the years they'd managed well enough, he supposed: arguments tended to be resolved or forgotten about and they still made love once a week. He couldn't fault her cooking or the way she kept the house, the children were well brought up, even if they were somewhat distant from him. They were certainly more her side of the family.

But since joining the *milice* all this changed. The atmosphere at home was so awkward that he began to spend more nights at the barracks, returning home on Friday for the weekend unless he was on duty. Coming home was not the pleasure it ought to have been: for a start there were his neighbours, who he'd always got along with well enough but now none of them would even return his greeting and the man across the road – who he'd always suspected of being a socialist – had even taken to turning his back on him.

René Dupont tried to remain calm about this. He made a careful note of all the neighbours, along with the people at the local shops and the café where it was made clear he was no longer welcome. When the time was right, they'd be dealt with.

Then they'd soon be knocking at his door.

They'd soon want to be his friend again.

Then it would be too late.

At home the atmosphere deteriorated considerably. The children more or less ignored him and Jeanne seemed even more remote. He couldn't remember the last time they'd made love other than that it had been such a tense business that it had all ended most unsatisfactorily. He'd even thought about mentioning it to the *milice* doctor, but couldn't quite bring himself to discuss such an intimate matter with another man.

And then there was his wife's family.

He knew full well they looked down on him and he didn't think it was his imagination that they treated him as a figure of fun. More than once he sensed they were laughing at him behind his back and since he'd joined the *milice* this seemed to be a regular occurrence.

His wife's younger sister, Henriette, was married to a man who Dupont particularly resented. Marcel appeared to be everything René wasn't: charming, good-looking and very successful. He was still in his mid-thirties and in his teens had been a successful athlete, even competing in the national trials in Paris, something which cropped up in conversation with an annoying regularity.

Marcel had trained as a mechanic to work in his father's garage in Brotteaux in Lyon's 6th arrondissement. He was still in his twenties when he took over the business, transforming it from a solid little business to a highly successful one. They had a Citroën concession and Marcel had made the wise decision to concentrate on the best-selling Traction Avant. He also ensured they had the local Michelin dealership. When the war started, he compensated for the drop in sales of cars and the restrictions on driving by building up the repair side of the business.

René Dupont found Marcel so irritating he generally tried to avoid conversation with him, but towards the end of July, not long after the Gestapo raid on the Resistance leaders, he found himself sitting opposite his brother-in-law at a family lunch for his wife's birthday. Dupont grudgingly asked Marcel how business was.

'Satisfactory, thank you, René: we sell very few cars, as you know, but people still wish to drive when they can and my mechanics have become very skilled at defying the laws of engineering!'

He paused as the others round the table laughed at his wit and topped up René's wine glass with far more than he'd intended to drink.

'We could of course increase our business if I took on work for the occupying authorities, but so far… I've managed to avoid that. We get our hands dirty enough as it is!'

More laughter around the table, René unsure whether to join in.

'They could order you to service their vehicles, you know, Marcel.'

'I know that, René: tell me, with your elevated position in the *milice* are you going to use your considerable influence and get that Klaus Barbie to order me to service his vehicles?'

'He's a busy man, Marcel: he has far more important things to do than worry about cars.' René laughed at his own joke but no one else joined in.

'I hear you work very closely with him, eh, René?'

Dupont shrugged, hoping the conversation would peter out before it became too uncomfortable.

'I was told you were at Caluire-et-Cuire?'

'I work all over the city, Marcel.'

'For the *milice*.'

'For France.'

And this time the others around the table did laugh at what he'd said, but it all felt very… bitter.

'I hear,' said his wife's uncle, 'that you took part in the raid at Doctor Dugoujon's house Caluire-et-Cuire. The one where the *resistants* were captured. Is that true?'

Jeanne turned to their children and suggested they go out to play and perhaps their cousins would care to join them. He waited until they'd left the room.

'I'm unable to discuss my work, you should understand that. But please be assured that what I do – my sole motivation, I can promise you – is for the maintenance of law and order in our city. The military situation in France is beyond our control as citizens, but surely, we have an obligation as citizens to ensure that there is no trouble and no civil disorder. The people who cause trouble, the *resistants* as you call them, they're just trouble-makers, left-wing agitators – you should know that!'

There was an appalled silence around the table. A few people shook their heads and he heard some tutting and then his mother-in-law said she was far from being a socialist, heaven forbid, what about de Gaulle? Wasn't he calling for people to support the Resistance and, surely, he was no socialist?

'Let me ask you a question,' said Dupont. He smiled at Marcel, hoping to reduce the tension. 'Surely you agree that it is preferable that French people like my colleagues in the *milice* and the police are working with the Germans?'

'Why?' Marcel was looking at him with disdain.

'Well, surely, you'd rather be arrested by a French person than by a German, wouldn't you?'

Marcel's look of disdain hardened. 'I think,' he said, as if giving the matter serious consideration, 'that on balance I'd rather not be arrested by any of you!'

-

Since the Mars network had met at the basement on Rue Ravat in the middle of July they had gone into hibernation, as Madame Madelaine put it.

'We do nothing,' she'd told them then. They were trying to contact the British through their contact in Switzerland. That could take some time. 'And in any case,' she'd said, 'there is a traitor in Lyon.'

One month later, in the middle of August, she'd met with her three closest comrades: Maurice, Marcel and Michel.

'We've heard from Benoît Roux in Geneva,' she said. 'I don't know what he's been up to – he can be elusive. He's sent a message to England: he's told them he wants to meet with someone important. We'll have to wait and see what happens.'

'Surely it would be quicker for him to go to Berne?'

'He refuses to. He doesn't like them.'

They all sighed. Benoît Roux was not the easiest of characters and there was some resentment at how he'd left Lyon and was trying to call the shots from Switzerland. Refusing to go to Berne because of what seemed to be a personality clash with the head of British Intelligence there just seemed like an indulgence.

But Madame Madelaine said they had no alternative but to go along with him. 'He may be exasperating at times but there's no question that we can trust him totally: he's one of us. If we are to maintain our tight security then we cannot risk any other way of approaching the British. We must be patient.'

That patience paid off, though not until later in September.

Madame Madelaine called another meeting in the basement of her boutique, again just her and her closest confidantes. They met late on a Monday afternoon, the basement now beginning to feel chilly and slightly damp.

'We've not had a problem for many years. I hope it remains that way. But I have news: I heard from Roux in Geneva this morning.'

'It's good news, I hope?'

'He has heard back from the British: it appears that his insistence on meeting a top person has paid off. He is meeting someone tomorrow, in Geneva.'

'Do we know who it is?'

Madame Madelaine shrugged. 'I don't know their name. But they are very important, apparently.'

—

As August had turned into September life continued to look up for René Dupont. He was now based full time at the Gestapo headquarters in the former Ecole de Santé Militaire building on Avenue Berthelot.

Klaus Barbie had recruited around thirty Frenchmen to work for the Gestapo: some had been members of the *milice* and others members of the Parti Populaire Français, which meant that Dupont was an obvious recruit. The section he belonged to was the Mouvement National Anti-terroriste, the National Anti-Terrorist Movement. It was run by Francis André, who Dupont had known before the war in the Parti Populaire Français.

Dupont had little doubt that he was now part of Klaus Barbie's inner circle. The German had a reputation for trusting few people, but René was pleased to say that he was one of them. He'd mentioned this to his wife one evening during one of the long silences that accompanied their meal times. He'd hoped, perhaps misguidedly, to impress her but as soon as he'd mentioned it, he realised it had been a mistake to do so.

'So the head of the Gestapo in Lyon trusts you, does he, René? Is that something to be proud of or ashamed of?'

He said she shouldn't be so cynical.

'And how do you know he trusts you?'

Because Barbie had said so himself, he replied. Only earlier that week in fact. His section had carried out a series of raids on Resistance contacts and they'd arrested all the people on their lists and furthermore he'd started a programme of going into the secondary schools in the city to question children about the activities of their parents and Barbie had been impressed with his initiative.

He didn't mention all this detail to Jeanne but he did hope she'd be impressed with the fact that Klaus Barbie trusted him. She shrugged her shoulders as if she didn't care and when he said she ought to be pleased with the extra rations she said nothing as she picked up the plates and headed to the kitchen, though he was sure that as she did so he heard her say that she'd rather starve.

He did notice he was no longer invited to any events with his wife's family, which suited him fine. But towards the end of September, he did see his brother-in-law, the charming and faultless Marcel.

Except Marcel didn't see him.

Perhaps Marcel wasn't nearly as smart as everyone seemed to think he was.

It was a Monday afternoon and Dupont was returning from a meeting in a Gestapo staff car. As they drove up Cours Charlemagne the road was blocked and Dupont suggested they turn right and then left. They turned into Rue Ravat, which was when he saw his brother-in-law.

There was no question it was him: the athletic build, the confident walk. He told the driver to slow down and watched as Marcel paused by a shop selling scarves and gloves and glanced at the window before entering.

That was odd, he thought. Rue Ravat was a strange place for Marcel to be on a Monday afternoon. Indeed, it was a strange place for him to be at any time and in a ladies shop too. It was a long way from his garage in Brotteaux.

He told the driver to carry on and wrote in his notebook, glancing at his wristwatch to check he'd made a note of the correct time.

This was something he really must look into.

Chapter 11

'We've only just moved in here, Barney, and now you want us to move again?'

Barney nodded and said perhaps they ought to get used to calling him Arthur, though the more he thought about it the less he felt like an Arthur. 'My mother had an uncle called Arthur. A bank manager – in Southampton.' He shook his head and fell silent and Sophia and Jack looked at each other, unsure what was more of a problem: being a bank manager or in Southampton. 'We're going to Geneva. I'll tell you more when we get there.'

'And Basil – he's all right about all this?'

'Basil is… Basil is Basil, isn't he? On the one hand he's a bit put out and one can hardly blame him: you're both first-class agents and who wouldn't want to run agents like you? On the other hand, he's got so much on his plate this is a probably a relief.'

They all fell silent as the sun dropped low over the Aare and filled the lounge with a soft light. Barney looked at the pair in front of him with a good deal of pride. He'd been sent to Berlin in 1936 as a new MI6 officer on a mission to recruit his own spy ring. He'd met Sophia von Naundorf during the Berlin Olympics of that year, through her husband, Karl-Heinrich, a senior SS officer.

His instincts told him she was a potential British agent but each time he'd approached her over the following years she was clearly sympathetic and hadn't said no, but nor had she said yes. She'd intimated that there may be a time and he said when that time comes, here's the address of an Annemarie in Interlaken, in Switzerland. If and when she sent a letter, then he'd know she was willing to start.

And on the same trip to Berlin that August 1936 he'd met a young American reporter, Jack Miller. Miller was there to cover the Olympics but was looking to remain in Germany, so fascinated was he by the country. Barney arranged for him to get freelance work from British newspapers and allowed him to develop the perfect cover. It wasn't until the following year, on a visit to England, that Jack realised he'd been recruited as a British spy.

And then in October 1940 a letter arrived at Annemarie's address in Interlaken from her old penfriend, Sophia in Berlin.

She was ready.

Since then, she and Jack had become two of MI6's finest agents in Nazi-occupied Europe. And somewhere along the line they'd become a couple. Barney felt like a matchmaker. He was looking at them with pride when he realised Sophia was talking to him.

'I beg your pardon, Sophia?'

'You seemed miles away, Barney.'

'The journey here rather took it out of me.'

'I was saying: did Basil mention Siegfried to you – Siegfried Schroth?'

'He didn't, no. Name rings a bell though.'

'It ought to, Barney,' said Jack. 'When you came to see me in Berlin at the end of 1938 you suggested I look him up when I was next in Düsseldorf.'

'Beginning to ring a bell – an actor, wasn't he?'

'Correct, with the Stadt-Theater.'

'I remember now: MI5 had spotted him when they were touring England earlier that year: overheard criticising the Nazis. MI5 tipped us off and Tom Gilbey met up with him. Wasn't too keen, felt he could be prone to indiscretion.'

'You asked me to look him up when I was next in Düsseldorf, which I did. I liked him, he was good company and clearly no Nazi but I agreed with your colleague's view: seemed a bit too keen on gossip.'

Jack Miller went on to explain how he'd been desperate when they were in Düsseldorf on their last mission. With Sophia in prison and about to be handed over to the Gestapo, he had to do something and so he approached Siegfried Schroth. The actor had risen to the occasion and thanks to him they managed to escape from Düsseldorf.

'And you brought Siegfried back with you? I recall hearing that.'

'He was quite magnificent, Barney.' Sophia smiled sweetly. 'He was totally convincing as a police officer and as a Rhine boatman. He played a part, as if he was on stage – as an actor he's a natural secret agent. But Basil's not keen on him. He's put him up in a hotel somewhere while he says he's checking him out and won't let us have any contact with him.'

'Sophia's quite right, Barney. He's magnificent. If you're going to send us somewhere, we want Siegfried along too.'

'Another member of the Wolf Pack then? It sounds like I'd better meet him!'

–

By the end of September Sophia and Jack had moved to Geneva. Barney had found an apartment block on Rue François-Bonivard, overlooking Place de Mont Blanc, away from the Old Town and where they'd lived before. He'd chosen the apartment carefully. It was on the top floor of a block, with Lac Léman just visible over the rooftops on the other side of the square. The top floor had three one-bedroom apartments and Barney had been able to rent them all. The war, said the landlord, had been bad for business. He'd been hoping for more refugees – wealthy ones.

The third apartment was for Siegfried Schroth. The actor had been the subject of an argument between Barney and Basil, with the latter insisting he was yet to be convinced that Siegfried could be trusted. He was still checking him out.

'How, Basil?'

'How what?'

'How are you checking him out, as you say? As far as I can see you've put him in a hotel. If you were that concerned about him, you'd be watching him in a safe house, surely?'

Basil muttered something about there being a limit on the number of safe houses he had access to.

'Sophia and Jack speak very highly of him. They say they owe their lives to him.'

'Sophia and Jack don't have the same type of responsibilities as I have, Barney. You ought to know that.'

'I would say that the judgement of two agents who've operated so successfully inside Germany for years is impeccable, wouldn't you?'

Basil shrugged, evidently finding the conversation uncomfortable.

'Look, Basil, if Siegfried weren't to be trusted then, surely, he'd have informed on Sophia and Jack when they were in Düsseldorf, or as they were about to cross the Rhine back into Switzerland?'

'Maybe the idea was for him to come here, Barney, and find out what he could about our operation – and become involved in other missions. It could be a sophisticated trap by the Germans.'

'I doubt they'd have let Sophia and Jack get away like that.'

Basil said he could see Barney's point and maybe he was being too cautious and if Barney was happy to take the risk, then as far as he was concerned Siegfried was all his, though he still wasn't sure how much he trusted him.

'You'll take him to Geneva then?'

Barney nodded.

'And then into France?'

Barney didn't respond.

'And what news of this operation?'

'I'm about to find out, Basil: I'm meeting someone tomorrow.

–

When the Quai des Bergues branch of Credit Suisse opened at nine o'clock precisely on the morning of Tuesday 28 September a handsome man in his late forties was the first to enter the bank, not exactly pushing past the other two customers who'd also been waiting outside, but certainly making sure he was in before them.

He told the receptionist that he wished to see Madame Ladnier. When asked if he had an appointment he said not as such, but they'd been in touch and he'd been assured he was to ask for her.

'And your name, sir?'

'Roux: Benoît Roux.'

Madame Ladnier was a model of calmness when she appeared soon after. Perhaps Monsieur Roux would care to join her downstairs?

She remained calm and business-like inside the basement office. He noticed she'd checked the two rooms either side of the one they entered were unoccupied and then asked to see his identity card.

'I am your point of contact, Monsieur Roux, you realise that.'

'Of course. I received a message to come and see you.'

'Indeed. A gentleman has arrived in Geneva who wants to meet with you.' She paused and glanced at a piece of paper she was holding. 'At twelve noon today, you are to go to Brasserie Genevois on Rue de Chantepoulet. You are to ask if a Mr Mallory has arrived. If not, then you are to leave. At six o'clock you should go to the Centrale on Rue de la Croix-d'Or and ask the same question – but I don't think the fall back will be necessary.'

Benoît Roux duly presented himself at Brasserie Genevois on Rue de Chantepoulet at twelve noon. The restaurant was quiet and three waiters approached him as he entered.

Monsieur Mallory? This way, please.

The upstairs dining room was empty apart from a man sitting in the far corner who stood up and gestured Benoît Roux over. They quietly introduced themselves to each other and Barney Allen said they ought to order now because they didn't want to be bothered by the waiters while they were talking. They waited until the food was served. Both had ordered veal escalope with potato salad and Barney suggested the Frenchman order the wine, which inevitably was an expensive Bordeaux.

Barney Allen explained he was a colleague – indeed a friend – of Tom Gilbey and he wanted to say at the outset how very sorry he was that his previous experiences with British Intelligence in Berne had been so unsatisfactory, but he wanted to assure Benoît that he was now very much a priority for British Intelligence, that he was most valued by them, so much so that he himself had come from England to work directly with him.

Benoît Roux was nonchalant, as if he'd barely been listening. He ate more veal and drank his second glass of wine before asking the waiter for some more bread.

'And you are who, if I may ask?'

'I'm the man you're to trust, Benoît. I'm a senior officer in London. We wish to work closely with you and your colleagues in Lyon. I have people I work with who will be able to work with you...' He waved his fork; aware he wasn't sounding clear. The Frenchman was being so non-committal that Barney worried he didn't trust him.

'We would wish to send people to Lyon. We want to be able to access what intelligence your group there has. We would be able to arrange for your group to be supplied with what you need: money, weapons, explosives, radios – whatever you need.'

'Whatever we need?'

Barney Allen nodded. He wondered whether he'd promised too much. He was concerned he'd also said too much and the Frenchman had said nothing in return. He wondered quite how well he was handling this but at that moment the Frenchman placed his cutlery on his plate to indicate he'd finished his meal and drank some more wine before pushing his chair back a little from the table and looking up at him, now smiling and looking relaxed for the first time.

'We will certainly need money. That should be paid to me in cash and I will arrange everything else: the exchange rate of the Swiss franc is very good against the occupation currency in

France. As for weapons and the other things you mention… that is to be decided. I am hoping that very soon a representative of Mars will be visiting Geneva. We will meet and see how to best co-operate. You say that you have people you wish to send to Lyon to work with us?'

'Indeed, I—'

'I will need to meet them first: if I find them… acceptable then I will arrange for them to meet with our group here.'

—

Siegfried Schroth arrived in Geneva with Sophia von Naundorf and Jack Miller. Barney Allen was quickly charmed by the German actor. The evening they arrived they sat in the lounge of Barney's apartment on Rue François-Bonivard and talked into the early hours of the morning.

Siegfried talked of how committed he was to defeating the Nazis, how Barney and indeed everyone else in England probably underestimated how much unease there was in Germany with the regime and then there was something of an argument as Sophia said there was overwhelming support for the Nazis, though she agreed with Siegfried that much of this support was born out of fear.

'And you're happy to work with us, Siegfried?'

'Of course.'

Barney looked at the three of them, who in turn were watching him intently.

'There is a Resistance group in Lyon with whom we plan to work. This mission will depend entirely on their co-operation. I have met with a representative of their group who's based here, in Geneva. Any day now a member of that group will arrive from France and they will wish to meet us.'

—

They arrived in Geneva on the last day of September, two days after Benoît Roux had met with the nervous Englishman who'd insisted on talking about such serious matters while they were actually eating.

Despite that, what he'd had to say was important, far more important than he'd allowed himself to let on. As soon as he'd left the restaurant, he'd sent a message to Lyon.

Essential you come to Geneva.

Maurice arrived in Geneva accompanied by Anna Rousseau. They'd travelled separately from Lyon, meeting up in a farmhouse near the village of Échallon, where they'd waited until nightfall. She was surprised quite how nervous Maurice was, given he was one of the leaders of the group. He paced up and down the barn they were waiting in, constantly looking at his watch, checking his pistol and wondering out loud whether they should abort the mission. At ten o'clock they became aware they were not alone in the barn: a man had appeared in it without them hearing a sound. He gave the correct code phrase and they responded likewise and he said they ought to get a move on: the border was not too far and there were no reports of German patrols, but nevertheless...

They crossed the border north of the village of Péron, crossing the Rhône and finding themselves in a forest and suddenly alone, their guide nowhere to be seen but moments later Benoît appeared in front of them and said they were to hurry: they were now in Switzerland but it would be a problem if the Swiss border guards found them.

The following morning Benoît took Maurice and Anna to a workshop owned by a friend of his close to Cornavin railway station. In a room above the workshop, they were joined by the Englishman, accompanied by two men and a woman.

And for the next two hours they talked, the seven of them sitting in a circle, leaning in close to hear each other against the noise of the station and the workshop. There'd been a good deal of suspicion at first, Anna and Maurice uneasy at the presence of two Germans, and the meeting wasn't helped by the fact that Barney was having to translate between French and German.

But after a time, the atmosphere gradually changed. Barney gave what he had to admit was a rather moving account of the bravery of his colleagues – pointing to Sophia, Jack and Siegfried – and although of course his friends from France would understand he couldn't possibly go into any details he could assure them that the courage they'd shown had been of incalculable benefit to the Allied cause. He added that this was only matched, of course, by the bravery and the resourcefulness of the French Resistance and that brought him to the purpose of this meeting – how they could work together, how the British would like to help the Resistance to be more effective.

'And you propose to do that by sending two Germans and an Englishman to help us?'

Jack said actually he was American, but that wasn't the point. 'Sophia and Siegfried being German is surely an advantage in a country occupied by the Germans?'

'I think that is a good point,' said Benoît.

'If I may say, I think it will work. We need to check when we're back in Lyon, but I think we have an ideal opening for Sophia.' The two women smiled at each other. 'You don't speak French?'

Sophia shook her head.

'That isn't a problem, this opportunity I have in mind is for a German. You will find out more. You will need to sort out identity for the two men though, but I think in maybe a week or so we will be able to tell you more.'

They stopped speaking as the room shook, a train was pulling into Cornavin. They all smiled at each other and then Maurice spoke, explaining how vital it was they received help.

'You have no idea of how terrible the situation is in France. The occupation is dreadful and in Lyon particularly so, especially after the raid in Caluire-et-Cuire on the twenty-first of June and the murder of Jean Moulin.

'We need all the help we can get.'

Chapter 12

Switzerland
October 1943

The watch expert called Richard had recommended Arthur Mallory show an interest in top-quality watches manufactured in the Geneva area. He'd also recommended that Mr Mallory visit the Ecole d'horlogerie in Geneva.

'It's been around for over a century: it's where all the watch-makers are trained but is also a very important place in the Swiss watch industry. They have a library and hold talks in the evening. I suggest going along there: it's an ideal place to meet people and establish your alibi.'

The Ecole d'horlogerie was on Rue des Terreaux-du-Temple by St Gervais, a short walk from the apartment on Rue François-Bonivard. He visited it on his second day in Geneva and returned the following day to register for a series of talks in October and met the assistant director of the school who asked him what his particular interests were and Barney said the premier brands made in the Geneva area.

'Chopard, Patek Philippe and Rolex of course: ones certified with the Geneva Seal.' That was a validation which carried some weight if and when he sought to re-sell the watches in the United States or Canada.

'Of course, sir. And you are interested in buying?'

Barney said he was, but only of course if the prices were reasonable and the man said naturally, that was always the case, especially with more discerning buyers. He introduced himself

– Emile Jeanneret – and said he hoped Monsieur Mallory didn't mind if he asked but what kind of budget did he have in mind and when Barney told him he noticed the man blink in surprise and smile unctuously before suggesting perhaps Monsieur Mallory would care to join him in his office for a coffee?

Emile Jeanneret waited as their coffee was brought in and then gestured Barney should move his chair closer. 'Although this institution is not involved with the purchase and sale of watches, I myself do take an interest in this area, if you understand me. The market has been volatile in recent years. From 1937 onwards, maybe even before that, we saw a large number of watches coming onto this market as a result of refugees leaving Germany in particular. Jews, you understand…'

Barney nodded.

'As a result of the higher number of watches for sale, the price dropped. However, since 1941 the market is back to where it was before, and prices are higher. I have an associate in Zürich and he informs me that next week there is a private auction of watches including a dozen Patek Philippe and a few Chopard too. The auction is by invitation only but if you were interested then I'd be happy to arrange an introduction.'

–

Basil Remington-Barber had been most difficult about it. Barney had telephoned him to say he was planning to visit Zürich and Basil had said that his understanding was that Barney would be based in Geneva and he regarded Zürich as his territory and this could make matters even more awkward in a city where it was difficult enough as it was for the Service to operate.

'I don't want to appear difficult, Basil, but I need to go to Zürich: it is important that my cover is as credible as possible. If I'm supposed to be collecting watches then this is an ideal opportunity for me to show it.'

Basil had grunted down the phone line.

'I understand you have a chap in Zurich?'

'I hope you don't think you're going to—'

'I need a contact there, Basil. Just in case.'

'Just in case what, Barney?'

'If you'd be so good as to give me his details. And there's one more thing: I'm taking Sophia with me. She'll be acting as my assistant and will be able to translate. Arthur Mallory doesn't speak German.'

They stayed at the Carlton-Elite on Bahnhof Strasse, Sophia in a small room on a lower floor, Barney in a larger one on an upper floor.

The evening they arrived, Barney went on his own to meet Basil's man in Zürich. He was in a small apartment above a hardware shop on Basteiplatz. According to Basil, Rolf Eder was an Austrian social democrat who'd fled his own country after the Anschluss and was a committed anti-Nazi. He wasn't a front-rank agent, Basil had explained, but more of a fixer than anything else. Totally trustworthy though, he assured him.

Rolf turned out to be friendly and helpful. He was happy to help in any way he could he explained. 'Zürich is full of German agents. The Nazis have their money here in the city and their business is very welcome and, more than anything else, the Swiss don't want any trouble: they certainly don't want to offend the Germans.'

They spent a while drinking the remains of a bottle of whisky and Rolf explained the situation in Austria and the difficulties getting anyone out of there and the problems of working in a neutral country that wasn't nearly as neutral as it pretended to be and then... would Mr Mallory mind if he raised an awkward matter?

'Of course not, Rolf.'

'Mr Remington-Barber is very busy, I understand that. However, there is a matter I have raised with him and despite mentioning it a few times now he hasn't dealt with it yet. He says it's on his list. I wouldn't want him to think I was going behind his back, of course, but...'

'I understand, Rolf, but you shouldn't worry: I know full well Basil has a lot on his plate. If you tell me about it then I can tell Basil.'

The young Austrian nodded.

'Basil doesn't trust the British consulate in Zürich: a few of the staff are Swiss German. Occasionally they have visitors, usually people from Germany, who offer to help the British and the instructions at the consulate are that all such approaches should be referred to him in Berne. Basil looks at all these approaches and the ones he regards as less of a priority he asks me to vet, to meet with them and see what they have to offer: I ought to add that the consulate know nothing about me.

'Three months ago – that would be late May, I think it was – I met with one such person. Her name is Johanna Brüderlin – originally from Berlin but married to a Swiss and has lived here in Zürich for some time, certainly since the early 1930s.

'Frau Brüderlin's message was that she wished to pass on to the British authorities information about the treatment of sick people in Germany and Basil didn't think this sounded like a priority so asked me to meet with her. When we met, she was very distressed. She had a brother called Heinz-Wilhelm Schütze. In December 1942 – so some six months before she and I met – her brother had died at a psychiatric hospital in Brandenburg.

'Frau Brüderlin says her brother had a mental illness, although she describes it as not serious: she says it was more that he found it difficult to fit in with society rather than that he was mad. Because she is in Switzerland the responsibility for him fell to their sister, Klara Förster, and her husband, Günther, who is a colonel in the army. I got the very clear impression that Johanna Brüderlin is not close to her sister and doesn't share the politics of her and her husband. She says that her sister sold their parents' house and her brother rented an apartment in Berlin, but he was so frightened by the bombing that he expressed a desire to move away from the city.

'It appears that Klara and Günther Förster encouraged this: Frau Brüderlin says they found Heinz-Wilhelm an embarrassment and were pleased to see him away from Berlin. They helped find him an apartment in Hanover and he moved there in 1940 and Frau Brüderlin believes he began to deteriorate after that. He was living on his own and she believes he stopped taking medication.

'As far as she can gather there was an unfortunate incident in June 1942 when Heinz-Wilhelm had some kind of breakdown and was taken to a psychiatric hospital in Brandenburg and according to Johanna Brüderlin it's one of those places where the Reich disposes of undesirables, as they see them. You've heard of that? We're receiving many reports – physically and mentally ill people are simply killed.'

Rolf stopped and shook his head, clearly appalled, and Barney Allen shook his head too and said there had been rumours. Rolf nodded and remained silent.

'And is that it, Rolf, is that what she wanted to tell us?'

'Johanna Brüderlin was just told that her brother had died and his cremation had already taken place. She wasn't able to travel to Germany until April, nearly four months after his death. She says that her sister and brother-in-law were very cold about it and were more bothered by the fact that they were still paying rent on his flat in Hanover and they wanted it cleared out so Frau Brüderlin decided to go there and sort everything.

'She says that her brother was very clever, very interested in history and details like railway timetables. He was also very good at art: she says his ability to do complicated drawings was extraordinary. He could copy a picture with remarkable accuracy. When she went to his apartment, she discovered he'd turned one room into a studio and he'd evidently devoted a lot of his time to working on diagrams and drawings. She made the point that he'd have made a fine draughtsman, if only people had concentrated on his abilities rather than his problems.

'It took her a few days to sort everything out. According to her there was box after box of his papers – cuttings from newspapers, notebooks, diagrams she couldn't understand. Then in one box – it was under another box – she found an envelope at the bottom, wrapped in tape. And when she opened it up there was the *kennkarten* and other paperwork for seven people.

'Frau Brüderlin says they are quite extraordinary. She believes they are fake because she found some notes about the identities he'd created or stolen in various notebooks, but she says as far as she's concerned, it's impossible to tell. Each of the five men and two women had a life, as she says, and that life was in that envelope.'

'And where is all that now?'

'She brought it all back to Zürich. She disposed of almost all of his paperwork and everything else, but managed to smuggle these out with her: she had some framed photographs of her brother's and she hid them in the frames.'

'And Basil wasn't interested in this?'

'I wasn't able to give him all the detail about the identity documents: I wanted to do it properly, give him the background – the proper context.'

'And where are all these documents, Rolf?'

'Frau Brüderlin has them: she showed one of the *kennkarten* to me and it looked authentic, but of course I'm no expert. I did, of course, express an interest in them – they'd be invaluable to us, wouldn't they? I even offered money, but she said she wants various assurances and wanted to see someone important from Britain, that's how she put it. I think she meant she wants to deal with someone who's British rather than Austrian!'

'And you say she's in Zürich, Rolf?'

'Correct.'

'Tomorrow morning, I am attending this private watch auction. Can you arrange for me to meet her later in the afternoon?'

–

Johanna Brüderlin was a nervous woman in her late forties, eyeing them suspiciously in Rolf's apartment on Basteiplatz and clearly unsure of whether she was doing the right thing.

Rolf had introduced her to Mr Mallory, who he explained was a very important man from England. What clearly helped was that Sophia was also there. She was introduced as Mr Mallory's assistant and translator. Once Sophia began to speak, Frau Brüderlin began to relax. The two women smiled at each other and Frau Brüderlin asked Sophia if she was from Berlin and Sophia said many years ago and Frau Brüderlin nodded and said she thought she recognised the accent and Sophia laughed and said she thought she'd managed to lose it – *nowadays people say I sound Swiss!*

And then Frau Brüderlin told her story, much the same as Rolf had recounted it, but it took much longer and was accompanied by a good deal of emotion. On reflection, the family had never made much effort to understand Heinz-Wilhelm, she said – to help him.

'It was all about doing what we could to minimise the embarrassment. My parents felt comfortable if he was in the house, but when he wasn't they felt awkward. My sister and her husband were the same.'

'You say there are seven identity documents?'

Frau Brüderlin nodded. She explained how her brother had created wives for two of the men. 'I don't know why he did that, it was always hard to work out Heinz-Wilhelm's mind. Maybe he felt that having proof of their being married gave the identities added credibility, who knows? But it does mean that I possess seven excellent German identities. I did wonder whether at some point they'd be of any use to me – but the more I thought about it the more I realised I have no intention of returning to Germany while this ghastly war is going on. So...' She turned to face Barney Allen. 'They are yours if you want them. I don't want to know what you plan to do with them, not that I imagine you'd ever tell me.'

Barney Allen thanked Frau Brüderlin very much, stopping quickly when he realised he'd spoken to her in German. Sophia explained he spoke a few words and said how sorry she was at the dreadful circumstances of her brother's death and then Barney asked her to ask what she would like in return. Money, perhaps?

Frau Brüderlin waved away the suggestion, as if insulted by it. 'I just want to feel that by handing them over to you I'm in some small way getting justice for Heinz-Wilhelm.'

Barney Allen had thanked Frau Brüderlin profusely and promised he'd do what she asked. Rolf returned with her to collect all the documents.

Barney and Sophia walked back to the hotel, a pleasant early evening now in Zürich, a gentle breeze from the Zürichsee.

'I take it you're not going to tell Basil about these identities, are you?'

Barney said of course not and they both laughed. He remembered what the man called Oliver had told him during his briefing.

…have your own secrets: if you get a new contact, think twice and then again about who you need to tell about them…

He had his own secrets now.

And he was feeling altogether more confident about what lay ahead.

Chapter 13

Lyon and Geneva
November 1943

They were always distrusting of anyone who approached them: it was a lesson drilled into every member of the group by Madame Madelaine. Even if it was a person that a member of Mars already knew and trusted, she was nevertheless insistent they should be treated with the utmost caution and wariness.

You never know... it could be a trap... look what has happened to the other groups... we have a traitor in Lyon, don't forget! It's why we've survived intact.

Madame Madelaine had taken this approach with Madame Faure who owned the café next door to her boutique on Rue Ravat. It was she who'd approached her, but she still waited months before recruiting her to work for their Resistance group.

But the person who approached them in the autumn of 1943 was a different case altogether. She was someone they needed to be especially wary off. Someone who they had every reason to be suspicious of, but also someone who could be of enormous help. Someone they would never normally have dreamt of recruiting.

Someone who could be the best possible source of intelligence.

–

'So what do you think? You shouldn't look so shocked – I think it's a great idea.'

They were in Barney Allen's apartment on Rue François-Bonivard in Geneva, five of them: Barney and Benoît Roux on one side of the dining table, Sophia, Jack and Siegfried Schroth facing them. In between them was an empty bottle of wine and one that was half empty, or half full, depending on who was in what mood. Despite the wine there was a formal air in the small room, an undeniable tension.

No one had replied to Barney's question for a while and then Jack said that – with the very greatest of respect – it was easy for someone who didn't operate in enemy territory to think of it as a great idea but people like us – he'd nodded towards both Sophia and Siegfried at this point – who have operated clandestinely, we have to be far more circumspect.

Jack leaned back and looked pleased with himself. He'd started to learn that Englishmen like Barney and Basil – and Noel too – responded best to understatement and apparent good manners. Losing your temper could be quite counter-productive. He'd begun to understand that the phrase 'with the greatest of respect' could really be quite lethal.

'And Sophia – Siegfried – what do you both think?'

Sophia said it would be helpful if Benoît himself could go through it, but this time in more detail.

Siegfried nodded in agreement and he would be the translator: it had turned out he was fluent in French, so much so that he'd even acted in France in the early part of his career. Benoît pulled his chair closer to the table and took one of the cigarettes offered to him. He waited until Jack had poured them each another glass of wine.

'A few weeks ago, Maurice – one of the leaders of our group in Lyon – was approached by a woman.'

He paused briefly, as if to allow the others to wonder about the nature of this approach.

'Maurice is a carpenter and a woman had asked him to come to her apartment on Rue Servient, close to Part-Dieu station. The door frame at the entrance to her apartment was warped and she needed it to be fixed. Maurice spent most of the day working on it and needed to return the following day and she gave him a key and said she'd return at lunchtime to check on everything.

'When she did arrive, she was rather flustered: she said she'd been delayed at work and the trams weren't working properly and so she'd had to walk and when Maurice asked her where she'd walked from, she replied from Avenue Berthelot. It seems she said it without thinking and appeared to have regretted saying it: Avenue Berthelot is where the Gestapo has its headquarters, in the old military hospital. Of course, Avenue Berthelot is a very long avenue – it runs from the Rhône to past the Guillotière cemetery and she could be working at any one of dozens of places, but somehow everyone in Lyon understands these days that when you talk about Avenue Berthelot you're talking about the Gestapo. If she worked somewhere else, she'd have soon enough said so.

'According to Maurice what happened next was quite extraordinary. The woman broke down. She started sobbing and then apologised and said she didn't know what had come over her and everything was getting too much for her and so he suggested they go into her lounge and she poured a pastis and he had one too and the way he described it, the woman unburdened herself to him. Perhaps if I can have another glass of wine?'

Benoît drank half of it and lit another cigarette before continuing. 'The woman's name is Agnes Kléber: she told Maurice she works as an office manager for the Gestapo. She said she's from Colmar in the Alsace and as with so many people in that area she'd thought of herself as more German than French – she spoke both languages.

'At the time of the invasion she was working for the police in Colmar as a clerk and she was asked to apply for a posting in the Free Zone: French nationals from the Alsace found it easier to get security clearance. She found herself working for the Gestapo in Lyon.

'It wasn't a problem for her at first: she told Maurice she believed in law and order and despised what the French had done in Alsace and she was opposed to communists and socialists and, in any case, for her it was a job and one she turned out to be very efficient at. But apparently Klaus Barbie trusted her and she became more involved in their work, more familiar with what the

Gestapo was up to. However, Agnes Kléber is a devout Catholic and the archbishop in Lyon is very opposed to the Nazis: the Church's disapproval of them is very evident in the sermons. This resulted in a moral conflict for her and that had come to a head when she had to type up a report about a family where the parents had been caught distributing anti-occupation leaflets: the father was executed, the mother was sent to a concentration camp in Germany and the two young children were sent to an orphanage. She had to organise the documentation to give the children new identities and this was the final straw for her. That is why she broke down in front of Maurice.'

'But how did this woman know she could confide in him?' Sophia was leaning forward, looking directly at the Frenchman.

'And more to the point, did it not occur to Maurice this could be a trap?'

'Of course, it did, Jack, of course. But he said nothing, he just said he was sorry to hear what she had to say and suggested she find her comfort in the Church and left it at that. He told the other leaders of Mars and they decided to wait, to see what happened. They had Agnes Kléber followed from Rue Servient to Avenue Berthelot and it was clear she did indeed work there, and Maurice was extra careful to ensure he wasn't being watched. They only had to wait one week. Maurice was contacted by Mademoiselle Kléber to say she had a problem with another door. Please could he come round.

'When he did so she had information for him. She gave the name of a school in Les Brotteaux where she said there was a teacher suspected by the Gestapo of being a courier for a Resist-ance group. She gave Maurice the name of the teacher and told him the woman's apartment was to be raided the following day and so was her locker in the school: they suspected she was using that to keep Resistance material. Maurice asked why was she telling him that and she said she believed he may be involved in the Resistance and...'

'Hang on, hang on – she works for the Gestapo and suspects Maurice of being a *resistant*?'

'Let me finish, Jack. According to her she'd come across a list from 1938 of members of a Communist Party branch in the city. There were only a dozen names on it and she was meant to check it – to see if the names and addresses matched the current records – and then pass it on for investigation. She kept it. I think it coincided with her beginning to have doubts about the morality of her job.'

'It took her that long to realise there may be a problem working for the Gestapo?'

'I agree, but people are different, aren't they? Maurice went to see Madame Madelaine and despite normally being so cautious, she decided they had to act. Anna was sent to see the school teacher that evening. It turned out she was indeed a courier for one of the Combat group cells in the city. She was able to remove all incriminating evidence from her apartment and the school. Sure enough the Gestapo did turn up the following day, but found nothing.'

'So, Agnes Kléber is to be trusted?'

'Yes.'

'And this information she has – that Barney was telling us about?'

Benoît briefly closed his eyes, as if trying to ensure he remembered exactly what he'd been told. 'According to Mademoiselle Kléber, Klaus Barbie increasingly distrusts the French administrative staff and has requested some Germans to come and work for him. She says that they'd just been told that a woman called Luise Brunner was being sent to Lyon from Berlin. This woman had been based at the Gestapo headquarters on Prinz-Albrecht-Strasse. She has all her details and passed them on to Maurice.'

There was a long silence in the room. Both bottles of wine were now empty, as was the cigarette packet on the table. No one moved, no one said a word, but Jack and Sophia exchanged worried glances and Siegfried looked confused, unsure what was going on. Barney Allen was the next to speak, consulting a pocket diary as he did so.

'Today is the seventh of November. From what we're told, Luise Brunner is due to finish work at Prinz-Albrecht-Strasse on this coming Wednesday, which is the tenth. The following day she travels to Lyon. According to the information Mademoiselle Kléber has, Luise Brunner arrives in Lyon on the Friday – the twelfth of November – and starts work at Avenue Berthelot on the Monday, the fifteenth. She's been allocated a small apartment on Avenue de Saxe, just north of Place Jean Macé. Is that correct, Benoît?'

The Frenchman said it was: no more than ten minutes' walk from the Gestapo offices on Avenue Berthelot.

'We know she's travelling by train,' said Barney, 'because she is due to arrive at Part-Dieu at twenty past one on the Friday afternoon – Mademoiselle Kléber has been told to meet her at the station with a car from Gestapo headquarters and take her to the apartment and give her all her paperwork.'

'If she is travelling by train and leaves Berlin on the Thursday,' said Benoît, 'and arrives in Lyon at twenty past one on the Friday then we can work out her route. It is most likely she'll take the early morning train from Berlin to Frankfurt and then change to catch a train to Strasbourg. There is a train which departs Strasbourg at five to nine on the Friday morning and arrives at Part-Dieu station in Lyon at twenty past one.'

'Which means she'll stay overnight in Strasbourg,' said Barney.

'Where we have very good contacts,' said Benoît. 'The Germans use two hotels in Strasbourg for visiting officials: the more important ones stay at the Maison Rouge on Rue des Francs-Bourgeois, close to the canal. More minor officials stay at a *pension* on Rue de la Course, which is a short walk from the station. That is where we think Luise Brunner will stay on the Thursday night. But we have a contact in the *pension*: we will be able to confirm it twenty-four hours before.'

Barney and Benoît both looked at Sophia who sat calmly and nodded her head in anticipation of what they were about to say. Jack reached out for her hand and held it tightly.

'The plan is, Luise Brunner will arrive in Strasbourg at around seven o'clock next Thursday evening on the train from Frankfurt. She will depart at five to nine the following morning on the Lyon train.' Barney paused. 'But the Luise Brunner who arrives on the Thursday will be very different from the Luise Brunner who leaves the following day.'

Chapter 14

Strasbourg and Lyon
November 1943

They knew they had to move very fast: the operation was so finely choreographed there was no room for even the slightest mistake.

Four of them had travelled to Strasbourg from Lyon. Madame Madelaine and Anna – posing as a demanding mother and her dutiful daughter – were scheduled to arrive at Strasbourg station just twenty minutes before Luise Brunner arrived from Frankfurt. Maurice and Michel arrived in the city separately on the Thursday, meeting up at a café close to Notre Dame cathedral at a quarter to two that afternoon. Shortly before two o'clock a young couple entered the café and moved to the back, totally engrossed in each other, their bodies pulled close and their faces touching. They didn't look at anyone else as they approached a door at the rear. Michel was the closest to them and watched as the boy pushed the girl against the door to steal a kiss while the girl slipped her hands behind her to surreptitiously unlock the door.

Michel waited until the couple had moved to a table before he slipped through the unlocked door. Minutes later Maurice followed him. They climbed down a steep set of steps into a cold basement. Moments later they were joined by the couple. They were their contacts from a Resistance group in Strasbourg.

'You don't think you may have been drawing a bit too much attention to yourselves, behaving like that?'

The couple looked at Michel and laughed and the boy said romance was alive and well in Strasbourg even if it wasn't in Lyon, and then he introduced himself as Hugo and the girl said they could call her Marie and they better get a move on.

'We have a plan,' said Hugo. 'If there are no German patrols, it can work.'

'Isn't the centre of Strasbourg full of German patrols? It's a big gamble to take, planning on there not being any.'

'What you've asked for our help with is a big gamble,' said Marie. 'But Strasbourg is quite well behaved these days: in any case, we'll have plenty of lookouts.'

They spent the next hour going through the plan, consulting a map attached to the wall and they all agreed it could work. Marie suggested they rest for any hour.

'And when does the other woman arrive?'

'She's already here. She's waiting upstairs.'

—

Sophia von Naundorf had arrived in Strasbourg on the Wednesday night. She'd crossed the border just west of Basel into France on the Tuesday night and hid in a farmhouse until daylight, when a farmer's van took her to Mulhouse, where she was handed over to another courier, who accompanied her on a bus to Colmar from where they caught the train to Strasbourg.

Since her arrival she'd been in a small apartment above the café close to the cathedral, resting as much as she could and going over and over in her mind the instructions from Barney and Benoît. It had all happened so fast: the gathering in Barney Allen's apartment on Rue François-Bonivard in Geneva on the Sunday night, travelling to Basel on the Monday, another safe house, more briefings, a hurried goodbye with Jack on the Tuesday evening and then across the border.

She had no idea what their relationship would be like without the constant frisson of danger. She understood that you can forgive someone an awful lot when you know the time you're spending with them is quite possibly limited. She'd once wondered out loud whether they could ever be a normal couple or whether their love existed only because of the clandestine nature of their lives. Jack had looked at her in that innocent way of his and smiled and said she was being far too serious and to come back to bed. Nonetheless, when they'd said goodbye on the Tuesday, she had noticed a catch in his voice and the hint of a tear in his eye.

Jack had told her he thought the plan Barney and Benoît had come up with was a clever one. It was audacious, of course, and it needed an experienced agent like her to have a chance of being carried off, and in any case, she wouldn't be alone. There was the Mars Resistance group in Lyon and when he'd suggested to Barney that maybe he and Siegfried could join her there, Barney had thought it was a good idea.

'He thought Siegfried being there was a good idea, Jack, not you. You don't speak French.' Jack had said not to worry, something would be sorted out.

Around five o'clock on the Thursday afternoon she was taken down to the basement of the café where she was introduced to two men from Lyon, Maurice and Michel. Michel spoke a little German but the young man called Hugo spoke it well and they went through the plan carefully.

When they'd finished Hugo said they should all wait in the basement. Timing was of the essence and it wouldn't do if they were too early.

At six o'clock Maurice and Marie left, saying they'd see them soon. Sophia remained in the basement with Michel and Hugo, alone with her thoughts and the knowledge that even if all went according to plan, it would still be dreadful.

–

The train from Frankfurt arrived in Strasbourg at ten to seven that Thursday evening. Luise Brunner was tired after her early start and very excited, of course: this posting to France was one she'd been hoping would come about for some months now. The past year had been awful. She'd been due to marry her darling

Kurt in March but the previous summer the 6th Army had been posted to Stalingrad and although at first his letters home had been optimistic and full of cheer, by the autumn their tone had changed.

'When' he came home became 'if' and 1942 turned into 1943 and what little news there was from the Eastern Front was utterly depressing and by the time the authorities admitted early in February that Stalingrad had been lost, she'd not heard from Kurt for weeks.

Berlin hummed to the sound of rumours: there were hundreds of thousands of casualties and hundreds of thousands of prisoners, all kept in sub-zero temperatures, hundreds dying each day. Everyone seemed to know someone who had a relative or a neighbour or a friend who'd been at Stalingrad – and none of them had returned. By the start of March, it was evident she was unlikely to ever see Kurt again.

She'd spent Easter with her mother's sister, a clever woman, the headmistress of a school in Brunswick, who'd lost her own fiancé in the Great War. Her aunt told her that she had to snap out of it: the only way she'd survive was by putting this behind her and thinking of her future. Her advice was to keep herself very busy. In her case she'd devoted her life to her career and had progressed from being an assistant in a school to where she was now: a headmistress.

And that was when Luise decided to apply for a transfer. She knew there were openings at Gestapo bureaux around Europe and she hoped for Paris but then Lyon had come up and she'd heard they were very keen on her and the man in charge there, Klaus Barbie, was known to be very ambitious and ran the kind of efficient operation she'd revel in.

It all sounded rather fun: she'd have her own apartment, generous rations, more responsibility and the opportunity to learn French. Although she was still mourning Kurt, there was a large garrison in Lyon and plenty of young officers…

Of course, there were those who said the war was going badly, but she had no cause to doubt that victory was assured.

If we'd listened to the pessimists in 1939, where would we be now?

She'd had her trunk sent ahead and it would be waiting in the apartment and now she just had to think about the next stage of the journey: it was, she'd been assured, a short walk from the station in Strasbourg to the small hotel on Rue de la Course, where she'd be able to change and there'd be a supper for her. Then a train to Lyon the next morning, just over four hours, which wasn't too bad, and she'd be met there by a very nice-sounding lady called Agnes Kléber, whose German was excellent and who assured her she'd be looking after her.

She paused at the exit of the station: she'd been told to find the Place de la Gare and head to its south-west corner. At that moment a charming lady paused and asked if she needed help. The woman spoke decent German – with a French accent, of course – and was accompanied by her daughter, and they both seemed very friendly and willing to help, so unlike what she'd been told about the French, that they were unfriendly and even resentful of the Germans.

But this woman said of course she knew Rue de la Course and in fact she and her daughter were heading in that direction and she should accompany them, and they crossed the Place de la Gare and she knew they were going in the right direction because after the Place de la Gare they crossed the Rue Déserte, which she'd also been told to look out for.

Just then they came to a small alley and the woman asked which hotel she was staying at and Luise told her and the woman said she knew a short cut, if they went down this alley then they'd be able to enter through the rear and she followed them down the alley – followed the mother that is, the daughter was behind her – and she began to become a bit unsure because the alley turned, so they seemed to be moving in the wrong direction, but the woman continued to chat in a friendly manner – how beautiful Berlin was, how she adored Munich, how France was moving in the right direction these days. Ahead of them was a van with the word *boulangerie* on the side, which Luise knew was something to do with bread, and then the back door of the van opened and before she had a chance to react, she was grabbed from behind and shoved into the van.

Sophia was in the van, along with, Marie, Maurice and Michel. Hugo was waiting in the driver's seat.

At one stage Sophia had thought about asking whether it was really necessary to go this far, but she realised there was no alternative. Another woman had helped push Luise into the van and crouched behind her. Michel forced a cloth against the woman's face: she struggled violently at first and then lost consciousness, at which point Marie held the woman's head while Maurice grabbed her jaw with one hand and her face with the other and twisted both swiftly with an enormous amount of force and Sophia was shocked at how loud was the sound of the woman's neck snapping. It seemed to echo around the sides of the van. For a few moments there was silence in the van.

When they turned her on her back Sophia stared into the face of her alter ego as if trying to glean something about her from the now lifeless body. Her eyes were still wide open and in utter fear, her make-up smudged and her mouth open, her teeth marked with bright lipstick.

'Help me,' said Marie, who'd already begun to undress the woman. Sophia helped to remove her clothes. They'd been insistent: everything must be removed, every single item of clothing. Everything that Luise Brunner came into the van with would leave it on Sophia von Naundorf.

Maurice and Michel helped too, which surprised Sophia, but she knew every second counted. Now Luise Brunner lay on the floor of the van completely naked. Only then did the two men turn round as Marie helped Sophia to dress in Luise's clothes. She handed her the handbag and they quickly checked its content: all her identity papers, money, the rail ticket to Lyon, the make-up. She took out a brush to tidy her hair and a compact so she could sort her make-up.

'Put these on.'

It was the woman's spectacles. They made Sophia squint but the frames were quite distinctive and made her look more like Luise Brunner's photograph on her *kennkarte*. Marie handed her an engagement ring and the woman's watch.

'Are you ready?'

Sophia said she was, did she look all right and Marie said she looked fine, maybe adjust her hair later, and then Hugo called from the front to get a move on and Michel knocked twice on the side of the van and when there was a response of three knocks, they opened the door and Sophia hurried out.

Except she was no longer Sophia von Naundorf.

She was now Luise Brunner, a native Berliner, twenty-nine years of age which was four years younger than Sophia but it didn't show. She was an employee of the Gestapo, excited by her positing to Lyon and still grieving her darling Kurt but managing to put it all behind her.

There was an older woman waiting in the alley. She handed Luise's suitcase to Sophia and said she should follow them. When they passed the *pension*, she was to carry on in.

'Tomorrow, you will see us on the train to Lyon, but you are not to acknowledge us, you understand?'

Sophia nodded. She realised her heart was still beating fast and she was breathing heavily. She knew she needed to calm down.

'If you think you are in trouble when you're on the train then remove your gloves.'

She thanked them, and they stood aside as the van with *boulangerie* on the side reversed past them. She knew they'd be on their way to dispose of the body.

'The woman who'll meet you in Lyon—'

'Mademoiselle Kléber?'

'Correct. You are to trust her, but say nothing to her about your involvement with us and she will do likewise. It is to be assumed. You understand?'

Sophia said she did. Now they were walking to the end of the alley, about to turn into Rue de la Course, and the older woman paused and smiled briefly, gripping her wrist as she did so.

'Don't worry: we will be with you in Lyon. We've been told you're the best.'

And then the women moved briskly ahead of her and soon they were past the *pension*, which she walked into. A tall woman with a severe haircut asked in German if she had a reservation and she replied that she did and then the woman said that in that case perhaps she'd be so good as to give her name and she said of course.

'I'm sorry, it's been a long day: I left Berlin at dawn and I still feel as if I'm on a train!'

She laughed and the woman allowed herself a tight smile.

'Of course: and your name?'

'My name is Brunner, Luise Brunner. Fraulein Luise Brunner.'

–

It was a strange feeling, to feel less oppressed in a foreign country than in the one you'd been born in and spent your whole life in and whose language was the only one you spoke.

France was not nearly as relaxed as Switzerland, of course. It was an occupied country and there was an unquestionable tension about. And it was not easy having to cope with the unfriendliness of local people. Everyone seemed aware she was German and this was certainly the case on the train, where the ticket inspectors and gendarmes deferred to her and the German security officers treated her with great respect.

Was she comfortable?

There's no need to open your case, Fraulein, thank you.

We wish you a pleasant journey.

At one point a young girl – maybe five or six – wandered up to her seat and said something in French and Sophia – Luise – indicated she was German and the mother hurried over and pulled the child away, all the while avoiding looking at her.

126

They headed south through Colmar and Mulhouse, west towards Besançon and Dijon and then south through Mâcon, where there was a half-hour delay and the ticket inspector walked through the carriage making an announcement in French and it was only when the train moved on that she noticed they passed mounds of tangled metal and twisted rail tracks and she assumed it was bomb damage and she took that as a sign that if the Allies could hit a target this far south then maybe the war really was coming to an end.

There was a shorter delay just north of Lyon and the train finally pulled into Part-Dieu station just after two o'clock. Even before the train stopped a young German officer appeared by her seat. He would help her with her case and she was to come with him he said, and for a brief moment she wondered if there was a problem, and if there was what on earth would she do in a country where she didn't speak the language, but the officer was very friendly and spoke with a Berlin accent. She asked where he was from and he said Schönefeld, and she said she had many happy memories of Schönefeld.

By now they were on the platform and a woman in her fifties stepped forward and introduced herself as Agnes Kléber. 'Welcome to Lyon, Fraulein Brunner. How was your journey?'

They'd begun to walk towards the exit. Her case had been handed to what she took to be their driver, who was walking in front of them. She replied that it had been a long journey but a pleasant enough one.

'Uneventful, I hope?'

You are to trust her, but say nothing to her about your involvement with us...

'Very uneventful indeed.'

'Very good, our car is here. It is a short journey to Avenue de Saxe but it is better to arrive in some style, eh?'

Sophia nodded and when they were in the back of the car the woman asked how she found Strasbourg.

'Rather pretty: more German in appearance, I must say, Fraulein Kléber.'

'You must call me Agnes. But all went well in Strasbourg?'

She hesitated before replying but the woman smiled, and Sophia did too and said it all went well, and the *pension* was most comfortable.

—

The apartment on Avenue de Saxe was smaller than Sophia had expected but it seemed clean and well equipped, though these were the least of her concerns. What mattered was, as Jack had reminded her, to check out how secure it was.

Remember what Basil always tells us: make sure it's not bugged, see if there is more than one exit, check who your neighbours are…

Agnes Kléber showed her round the apartment. They were alone in it, but she was very correct and said nothing unexpected.

'This is the bathroom; the kitchen is small but quite modern and through this door…'

She opened a narrow door at the back of the kitchen.

'This leads to the fire escape. Some people use it to take their rubbish down. At the bottom of these stairs are the rear doors to the building.'

She closed the door and indicated Sophia should join her at the sink. She turned the taps on and said this is the hot water one, though there was only hot water in the evening. She leaned towards her.

'Although the Gestapo does not normally listen in on German staff, it is best to act as if they do. Do you follow me?'

She was speaking softly. Sophia nodded.

'I've shown you the rear exit. Maybe check it out soon. It is important you are familiar with it. It opens onto an alleyway which runs parallel to the street. If you go to the end, you can get back onto Avenue de Saxe.

'I will show you the way to where you'll be working: you are to walk south through Place Jean Macé and then turn left on Avenue Berthelot. Everything is on this map. I've marked here the food shops that are less hostile to German customers.'

'Only two of them?'

Agnes Kléber nodded. 'There are ten apartments in this building: two on each floor. Half of the occupants are Germans working for the authorities and the French residents have all been vetted. Your trunk is in the bedroom. Unpack and settle in. Take a look around the area by all means, but my advice would be not to speak unless it is really necessary: Germans are not popular in Lyon. Do you have any questions?'

Sophia felt reassured that the woman had been so thorough. The questions she'd been thinking about on the journey to Lyon had by and large been answered. She felt calmer and more relaxed than she'd expect to in the circumstances: posing as a Gestapo employee in occupied France was about as dangerous an assignment as she could imagine, and she assumed that her calmness was down to experience. She'd learned that an agent's best chance of survival depended on keeping a clear head and not allowing themselves to be distracted by fear and panic. Her mind must have wandered because the woman tapped her on the arm.

'I asked, do you have any questions?'

'I assume someone will contact me soon?'

'Wait: be patient.'

Chapter 15

Lyon and Geneva
November 1943

'Do come through, please, Fraulein Brunner: there's really no
need to stand in the doorway like that – I won't bite your head
off, you know!'

Sophia von Naundorf was shaken by that because she knew full
well that Klaus Barbie was prone to serious violence. He'd been
running the Gestapo in the city for a year now and was already
known as the Beast of Lyon. She smiled and nodded in what she
hoped came across as a grateful but not too servile a manner.

She'd found playing the part of Luise Brunner to be harder
than she imagined. Although she came from a humble background in Berlin, since marrying Karl-Heinrich in 1932 she'd
been the wife of first a lawyer and then a senior SS officer. She
now realised that this position gave her a certain standing and
seniority and with it a degree of confidence and assurance that
she'd not fully appreciated, and which she'd perhaps taken for
granted. Over these past few days, she'd had to adjust to being
in what would best be described as a less important position in
society. Someone who'd know her place.

She was a secretary working for the Gestapo – not an unim-
portant role – and being German in France unquestionably gave
her a certain status. But she was a secretary and she had to act
as if she knew her place. She had to be less charming, more
anonymous.

Klaus Barbie gestured for her to come closer and as she
approached his enormous desk, he pointed to a chair in front

of it. Behind him was an oak-panelled wall, attached to it a large street map of Lyon. The window to his right overlooked the courtyard of the Gestapo headquarters, Avenue Berthelot just visible through its cloistered entrance. Agnes Kléber had told her that when they'd moved into this building Barbie instructed that none of his officers should sit too close to the windows. His own had been reinforced, she said. It was the secretaries and French staff who sat near the windows. They'd be the ones to take the force of any explosions.

'How is the mood in Prinz-Albrecht-Strasse, Fraulein Brunner?'

'I would describe it as serious, sir, determined. Everyone is very clear as to the importance of our work.'

'Of course: it is some time now since I've been there, but I always found it to be a place where there was a clear sense of mission.'

'Indeed, sir.'

'And you've been with us how long now, Fraulein Brunner?'

'I arrived in Lyon last Friday, sir, and started work here on Monday, the fifteenth of March. So, four days.'

'And are you settling in, Fraulein Brunner?'

'Yes, thank you, sir: obviously there is much to get used to but I am beginning to find my way around and Fraulein Kléber has been most helpful, I must say.'

'She's French, you know.'

'I do realise that, sir, though her German is excellent.'

'She's from Alsace.' Barbie waved his hand, which could have been taken as meaning to be dismissive of Alsace, or pointing in its general direction.

Or both.

'So, I understand, sir.' Her stomach tightened as it suddenly occurred to her that she'd forgotten to greet him with 'Heil Hitler' when she'd entered the room. He hadn't seemed to notice.

'Which in itself is not a problem as she is very efficient and *appears* to be someone who is to be trusted, but...'

He paused and took a cigarette from the packet on his desk and lit it using an improbably large lighter, which he needed to hold with two hands. 'How can I say this... what I mean is that the German authorities in Lyon – indeed, in France in general – have to employ a large number of French citizens. And by this I don't mean people in jobs like the police and town hall – civil servants. I mean French citizens who we employ to work directly for us. Without them, I have to say that our ability to keep control of this country would be quite limited. The French call it collaboration, you know: I prefer to call it co-operation.' He smiled, evidently pleased with the clever distinction he'd just drawn.

She nodded.

'The extent to which citizens of countries we have occupied are prepared to collaborate with us never fails to amaze me, Fraulein Brunner. I saw ample evidence of it when I was based in Amsterdam and notwithstanding what one hears about the French so-called Resistance, the French make very good collaborators, I have to tell you. Of course, if I was speaking in public and not within the privacy of this room, I'd say that right-minded citizens of France and the other countries in Europe realise that the Reich is helping to liberate their countries from the tyranny of socialism and liberalism and the evils of world Jewry and the bankers and...'

Barbie paused, perhaps aware he was now raising his voice. He finished his cigarette and stubbed it out before running his hand across his forehead.

'All of which is true, of course, and I do appreciate that one ought not to be ungrateful for the people who so willingly work for us. But having said that, I doubt very much that in the unlikely event of Germany ever being occupied there'd be many German citizens willing to co-operate. What do you think, Fraulein Brunner?'

She was surprised he'd bothered to ask her opinion, so surprised that she replied she wasn't too sure and maybe the communists and others like them and the Jews, of course, maybe they'd collaborate – she quickly corrected that to co-operate

– and then thought she'd gone too far in expressing an opinion, but Barbie nodded and said that was true, there were always the enemies of the Reich, though thankfully their numbers were decreasing by the day.

'Do you know, Fraulein Brunner – we have already disposed of more than one hundred thousand Jews who lived in Germany, and last year the Reich eliminated two million seven hundred thousand Jews!'

He clapped his hands in amazement and smiled and Sophia joined in, smiling and wondering if she was meant to say anything.

'All of which, Fraulein Brunner, is a long way of me getting round to the purpose of our meeting. I felt we were relying too much on the French people who work for us. I wanted to bring in more Germans to work here at Gestapo headquarters. I raised this with Berlin and am delighted you've joined us. I feel I can only fully trust fellow Germans. Perhaps you could tell me something about yourself?'

Sophia coughed gently and allowed herself another smile and paused for a moment or two, recalling the advice Siegfried had given her in Geneva when she'd been told she was to become Luise Brunner.

You're an actor playing a role… the most important thing to remember is that when you are on the stage the audience will be pre-disposed to believing you are the character you're playing: they have no reason to disbelieve you. But I always feel it is important not to be too expressive, if you understand what I mean. Actors call it hamming it up, or over-acting. Hold something back, without being mysterious, allow yourself to be somewhat enigmatic. And most importantly, don't think of yourself as playing a role: think of yourself as really being that character. And learn your lines!

'Well, there's nothing that's terribly interesting, I'm afraid, sir. I am twenty-nine years of age and was born in Berlin.'

'Whereabouts?'

'In Prenzlauer Berg, sir, where my parents lived.'

'Do they still live there?'

'I'm afraid not, sir: my father was killed at Verdun in 1916. My mother died five years ago. I was an only child.'

'Do continue.'

'I did a variety of jobs, sir, including working for a bank and for a law firm. In 1938 I began working as a clerk in the Gestapo office attached to the police station in Wedding and in 1940 I was promoted to a full secretary and transferred to Prinz-Albrecht-Strasse. I've worked in a number of departments there, including records and finance.'

Barbie nodded and looked slightly bored. She'd been ready to recount her story and had been advised to keep it simple. She wanted to sound as boring as possible.

'And you live where in Berlin, Fraulein Brunner?'

'In Wilmersdorf, sir, on Duisburger Strasse – between Brandenburgische Strasse and Konstanzer Strasse. Do you know it?'

Barbie shook his head. She'd been told that he'd never been based in Berlin and wouldn't know the city. But it sounded as if he was going through the motions rather than trying to catch her out. But maybe that was where any danger lay: if she made even a small error or so much as hesitated, he'd almost certainly spot it.

'I hope you don't mind me asking, Fraulein Brunner, but I see you're wearing an engagement ring…'

Luise Brunner had packed dozens of letters she'd received from her fiancé, Kurt, along with her diary and Sophia had read every word. The letters and diary were clearly not intended for anyone else's eyes and reading them had felt quite intrusive. She lowered her head and adjusted the engagement ring. It was still quite loose on her finger: Agnes Kléber had said she'd need to get it adjusted.

'My fiancé, Kurt, was with the Sixth Army at Stalingrad, sir. The last letter I received from him was sent at the end of December last year. I've heard nothing since. He's listed as missing and I—'

'You must not lose hope, Fraulein Brunner!'

'I do understand that, sir, and as people never fail to tell me, no news is good news, but not knowing is… very hard. The only comfort I have is that if he has been killed then he made his sacrifice in the name of the Reich and the Fuhrer, sir!'

Barbie nodded approvingly and appeared to glance down at a file on his desk. 'You have my sympathies Fraulein Brunner, but as you know, we all make sacrifices for the Reich. But I can see from your photograph here that the strain has taken its toll on you: you do seem to have aged. It is understandable.'

'The photograph would have been taken some years ago, sir.'

'Indeed.'

Klaus Barbie closed the file and didn't seem unduly concerned. Wearing Luise Brunner's spectacles helped considerably and, on the day after she'd arrived in Lyon, Agnes Kléber had taken her to a hairdresser who had styled her hair in the same way that Luise Brunner wore it on her *kennkarte* photograph. She was wearing Luise Brunner's clothes, which were slightly larger than she'd normally wear. It made it look as if she was underweight.

She was surprised to feel a wave of emotion sweep over her and realised she was now becoming Luise Brunner, rather than playing the part of her. She felt tears forming in her eyes and although her instinct was that a Gestapo secretary should not be given to such an overt display of emotion, in this case it did no harm. Klaus Barbie coughed in a slightly embarrassed manner and then came over and pulled a chair to be next to her and said she must be strong and then patted her on the knee, two or three times, and by the third time it was considerably higher than the knee and he allowed his hand to linger there for a while, causing her skirt to ride up and squeezing her thigh as he told her that if she ever needed a shoulder to cry on then she knew where he was.

She thanked him very much and said she really must get back to work. Klaus Barbie said of course, of course… and as he did so he stepped back, as if very slightly embarrassed at his behaviour.

'You are based in our finance department at the moment, I understand?'

'Yes, sir.'

'And it is very busy?'

'Extremely busy, sir. I understand you issued a directive that it should only be staffed by German nationals and as a result the unit is short-staffed.'

'I realise that. Is there anyone in Prinz-Albrecht-Strasse you think would wish to be transferred here? I did ask but they said it was hard enough releasing you.'

She paused in the doorway. 'I'll make some enquiries, sir.'

—

'Do you think you can pull it off, Siegfried?'

Siegfried Schroth looked at Barney Allen with something close to disdain. 'An actor never turns down a leading part, Mr Allen! I feel I have been resting for too long. It is as if this part has been written for me.'

'Well, I'm not sure I'd go so far, would you, Jack?'

Jack said nothing, leaning back until his chair was at a dangerous angle, still looking at the *kennkarten* spread out in front of them. There were four of them in the apartment on Rue François-Bonivard, still digesting the news Benoît Roux had received from a courier from Geneva.

'Go through it once more, Benoît.'

The Frenchman sighed, unsure of why he needed to repeat himself. 'Agnes Kléber met with Madame Madelaine to tell her that Klaus Barbie himself had asked Sophia if she knew of a German to work in the finance department at Avenue Berthelot. Apparently, they are desperate, and it seems Barbie no longer wants French staff working there.'

'Why?'

'He doesn't trust them to do anything other than dirty work, Jack, but Sophia thinks the finance department is connected to informers – local Lyonnais who sell information to the Nazis. If she's correct, that's very important for us.'

'If there is a traitor in Lyon,' said Barney '– someone betraying the Resistance – then that may be the place to find their identity.'

'Exactly.'

'So, Sophia thinks she can recommend Siegfried and he turns up in Lyon and starts work for the Gestapo and now we have two people working in their headquarters? All sounds a bit too easy to me.'

'Just because something is easy, as you put it, Jack, doesn't mean there is no merit in it.'

'Sophia is just a secretary and has only been there a couple of weeks, yet somehow the head of the Gestapo in Lyon thinks to consult her about recruiting staff from Germany?'

'One can be cynical, of course, Jack, but by the sounds of it, Barbie is desperate for more German staff. One imagines he's asking all the Germans there if they know of anyone. What do you think. Siegfried?'

The German actor put on his spectacles and looked again at the identity papers on the table in front of him – the papers created by Heinz-Wilhelm Schütze. 'This one would make most sense – if only because the person is closest to me in age.'

It was the *kennkarte* for Erhard Schröder, a forty-five-year-old clerk from Bremen.

'He's six years younger than me, but the photograph is not a problem and nor is the fact that he's from Bremen – I can do the accent easily enough. But his back story – what would we have for that? I doubt I can suddenly turn up and say I'm a clerk from Bremen?'

–

'You say you know him personally, Fraulein Brunner?'

Walter Möller was the head of the finance department, always stressed and appearing put-upon, someone who appeared far older than he was, which Sophia thought was no surprise: at least once a day Klaus Barbie would stand in the open doorway of his office and shout at him, usually about something that he'd expected to be completed the previous day. No sooner had Barbie left than Möller would hurry out to the toilets and when he eventually returned – white-faced – he'd pace around the office, his hands shaking so hard that he had trouble guiding his next cigarette towards his mouth.

He was an old-fashioned accountant. He wasn't used to being rushed and certainly not used to being shouted out. On the first day he met her he told Luise Brunner that the biggest mistake he'd ever made was admitting to speaking French: he ought to have kept quiet and remained in Germany.

So, when Luise Brunner – the very helpful young woman sent from Berlin – had told him that Klaus Barbie himself had asked her if she knew of anyone who may be suitable to work there, he was surprised. He was even more surprised she was now telling him she thought she had found someone.

'I have only met him once or twice, Herr Möller – he was a friend of my cousin in Bremen who I met when visiting family there. But I do know he is a man of the most outstanding probity and integrity. He is a senior finance clerk and also, as I understand, a member of the Nazi Party. His wife died earlier in the year and I believe he'd welcome the opportunity to get away from Bremen.'

'Who wouldn't!'

'And there's something else, Herr Möller.'

'Go on.'

'He speaks French very well. Just think how helpful that would be?'

For the first time, she saw Herr Möller relax. He smiled broadly and leaned back in his chair and when he raised a cigarette to his lips, she noticed for once his hand wasn't shaking. As his chair swivelled round, she caught a glimpse of the safe behind him – the door of the cupboard which housed it was open and so too was the safe.

The safe was where she knew she'd find details of the Gestapo's informants.

And the name of the traitor.

'Did you hear what I just said, Fraulein?'

'I beg your pardon, Herr Möller, sir.'

'I said, the correct protocol would be for the recommendation to employ this Erhard Schröder to come from me. I'll be frank: Herr Barbie is very demanding of me and for me to be able to recommend such an ideal candidate would do much to help restore my standing in his eyes. It will also ensure he can start work that much sooner.'

On the last day of November, which happened to be a Tuesday, Erhard Schröder arrived at Part-Dieu station on the right bank of the river Rhône after a lengthy journey from Bremen.

The final leg of the journey had been from Strasbourg, which was in fact where Siegfried Schroth officially became Erhard Schröder. Siegfried had arrived in Strasbourg the previous day after being smuggled into France over the Alps.

He was met at Part-Dieu by Luise Brunner, as one would expect an old family friend to do. She'd been given leave to meet him by a delighted Herr Möller, still basking in Klaus Barbie's gratitude at his having found someone so well qualified. And a Party member too!

The recruitment had gone very smoothly. If Walter Möller was totally honest he'd admit it had been rather rushed through, but then needs must and he had taken the precaution of involving Barbie's aide-de-camp, Otto Winter, and he saw no problem. The man would only be a clerk, after all.

And he was a Party member.

Luise Brunner and Erhard Schröder greeted each other formally at Part-Dieu and barely spoke as the Gestapo car took them to Avenue de Saxe, where Agnes Kléber had arranged for him to have one of the vacant apartments.

They were able to talk properly later that afternoon, walking through the 7th arrondissement towards the river and then along the banks of the Rhône on Quai Claud Bernard. Sophia was amazed at how Siegfried appeared to have become Erhard Schröder in almost every respect: from the way he spoke with a north German accent, to his slightly hesitant and even mumbling speech, the way he walked – as if weary and perhaps with a bad knee – to his whole demeanour. He was asking her about the nature of the work he'd be expected to undertake.

'I don't think it is especially complicated, Siegfried.'

'Erhard!'

'I'm sorry. I think it is more a matter of being organised and diligent. Most of the work in that department is to do with gathering records of payments made by the Gestapo and entering them into ledgers, reconciling them and then passing them through to Walter Möller to be signed off. Nearly all of the entries are in a code and most of them seem to be payments to people.'

'What does the code look like?'

'A letter followed by a series of numbers. There doesn't seem to be any pattern. The codes could be for an individual or for each payment, I'm not sure. You'll be working more closely with the codes, if you get my meaning. As far as I can tell Herr Möller has a ledger he keeps in his safe which lists names against the codes. When he gets it out he usually closes his office door: I spotted it on his desk once when the door was opened briefly.'

'Is he a Nazi?'

'Who?'

'This Möller.'

'I'm not sure: he may well be a Party member but he doesn't seem interested in that kind of thing, Erhard. He's an accountant and very overworked. If you can help him then who knows, he may begin to trust you more. He doesn't seem like the kind of man who'd ever trust a woman anyway.'

'And you'll be working with me?'

'I think I'm being moved again. The Gestapo has five different sections, Erhard, and between them there are more than twenty different subsections. Obviously, that's more organised in Berlin, but even here they try and divide the work according to these sections. Agnes Kléber has arranged for me to be moved to Section 4A, which deals with the Resistance. Hopefully I'll pick up useful intelligence there. But where you are, that's critical. The Resistance has to know who its hidden enemies are, those it cannot see.'

They walked along to Pont de Midi and watched the river for a while as it flowed quickly through the city as if in a hurry to get away from it. They turned into Avenue Berthelot to work back that way, enabling Erhard to see where he'd be working.

They were stopped by a police patrol just as they turned into the Avenue, the French gendarmes saluting them and apologising once they saw their papers identifying them as Germans.

'This is what it's like being a member of the master race, eh?'

Sophia shrugged. 'It does feel like that. Being German here means that we are seen as being superior and privileged.'

'Not by the French though.'

'We are by some of them, but not many.'

'And the rest of them?'

'They hate us, absolutely despise us. You can see it in their eyes and in every sinew of their bodies. You can even see it in the way they hold themselves. If you're in a shop or a café and they realise you're German – and believe me, Erhard, they know – then there's something about the way they react. They take half a step away from you as if you're infected with some terrible disease. And at the same time, I'm not sure how to put it, but their bodies seem to tense up, as if they are about to attack you.

'I've seen old ladies look at me as if they'd happily knife me and then the mothers who move their children away from me. Every time this happens, I want to weep, but I know we deserve it. And more than that, Erhard, it's the reason we cannot fail in our mission.'

Chapter 16

Berne
November 1943

From Noel Moore's workplace at the British Embassy to where he lived on Marzilistrasse was a comfortable twenty-minute walk: up Thunstrasse, crossing the Aare on Dalmazibrücke and then the short walk in Marzili, just south of the Altstadt and although not exactly quaint, a pleasant enough area to live.

Most of the embassy staff lived on the other side of the river, some closer to Thunstrasse, others in one of the pleasant suburbs to the south-east of the city with their dramatic views of the Bernese Alps on a good day.

It suited Noel Moore to live away from other people: he liked to have a separation between where he lived and where he worked. The apartment on Marzilistrasse could be described as quite isolated, even slightly bleak. It was at the end of a block, with scrubland to one side and at the rear a factory from which there was a near-constant hum of machinery. The stretch of the Aare that ran parallel to Marzilistrasse was particularly windy, meaning that Noel Moore's apartment had the noise of the factory from behind and the wind from its front.

But it suited Noel Moore fine: when he found the apartment on his third week in Berne, he knew it was ideal. The building had three apartments, his being on the top floor, and it had its own entrance, reached via an external staircase, which led to a small porch.

By the time he climbed the external staircase just after six o'clock on a bitterly cold Wednesday evening in the third week of November, Noel Moore was exhausted. It had been a difficult day. It had begun at seven that morning when he had to debrief an escaped RAF navigator who'd arrived at the embassy the previous day. That had taken up most of the morning, and then Basil Remington-Barber said he wanted to see him in his office.

Urgently.

It turned out not to be urgent but instead something he'd become increasingly used to over recent months: a shoulder for Basil to cry on.

Had he, Remington-Barber asked, discussed him when he was back in London in August?

'Discussed you with who, Basil?'

'You know, Noel, with the powers that be. Head office.'

'Well of course your name came up as in "how is Basil" and that kind of thing but nothing more than that really. It would have been most odd had they not asked after you, don't you think? That would have been reason to be concerned, I'd have thought.'

'And when they asked you how I am, how did you respond?'

'I cannot remember exactly, Basil, to be frank. I imagine I said something along the lines of how busy you are and indeed how we all are and how Switzerland is now centre stage and we're not really adequately staffed. Nothing that you and I haven't discussed many times. You look bothered, Basil?'

'Of course I'm bloody bothered, Noel! What do you think? Barney Allen pitching up in Switzerland and acting like he owns the place and taking over my best two agents and he doesn't even have the grace to be where I can see him in Berne, instead he's building his own little empire in Geneva and next thing I know I'll be told I'm past it and once this damned war's over I'll end up somewhere dreadful in the Home Counties without the knighthood I'd been given to understand I'd get and… Christ…'

His voice tailed off and he stared out of the window and Noel Moore noticed that somehow Basil had not just aged in recent months but had certainly started drinking more. He'd never been exactly abstemious, but he could hold his drink, there was no question of that. But now he invariably turned up at work looking hungover and seemed to start drinking well before lunchtime. Noel noticed the familiar redness to his complexion.

'I mean… Barney Allen… decent chap and a good family, the right school, well-connected of course… I understand all that, Noel – but you could hardly accuse him of having any experience of espionage, could you? He's never operated in hostile territory, has he? Never been on a clandestine mission, never had his life in danger – has he? He won't know what it's like to stand in the ruins of a building in the damp and cold for hours on end in the hope that an agent may turn up, unsure that if they do, they won't turn on you. He won't know what it's like to have a gun pulled on you or to go on the run and know your chances of making it are—'

'He did—'

'Please don't tell me he fought in the Great War, Noel. Everyone fought in the Great War: even my brother-in-law fought in it, for heaven's sake! Barney probably spent most of it copying maps three miles behind the front line in a comfortable manor house with a decent cellar.'

'While I see your point, Basil, I think it is fair to point out that Barney was operating covertly in Berlin when I first met him in 1936 and—'

'Exactly Noel – 1936. We weren't at war with Germany then, were we?'

'Nonetheless, Basil, he did recruit Sophia and Jack, so the fact that he's running them now would seem to be reasonable enough.'

Noel Moore wondered if he'd perhaps gone too far. There was no question that Basil's nose had been put out of joint by the arrival of Barney Allen and it was also true that when he'd been back in London in the summer he'd been asked about Basil and he had said that the workload was all a bit too much and what with his age, Basil was rather struggling. And he could see how Basil was concerned with Barney running an operation from Geneva that was so secret even he didn't know about it.

And it was certainly an operation Noel would like to know about too.

He managed to placate Basil, but it took long enough. He told him how London was in awe of the work he did, not just the quantity of it but also the quality, and although he wasn't privy to anything, he was sure the reward at the end of the war when Basil finally was able to retire would be something that Basil felt was appropriate.

But it had taken long enough to get to this point. It was now well into the afternoon and Noel had a report to write up on the RAF navigator and then he had to look at the paperwork on a woman who claimed she'd escaped from Munich and wished to work for the British and who he was due to interview tomorrow.

By half past five he was so tired he decided to head home and not for the first time would bend the rules – well, break them, if the truth be told – and take home the report on this German woman. He'd have a bath, then some supper and read the file then before having an early night.

He climbed the external staircase carefully: it could be quite precarious in the icy wind. He was a bit annoyed that the porch door was open: it needed fixing and sometimes it was enough effort to get the bloody thing to close. He really must have a word with the landlord about it. He'd mention the mould in the bathroom while he was at it. And the light in the hall cupboard.

It was only when he'd removed his shoes and put on his slippers and was standing in the small hallway that he realised something wasn't quite right. He paused and stood very still but couldn't hear a sound, at least not at first. He looked round and noticed that the door to his bedroom was open and he usually closed it and then he noticed some marks on the wooden floor, which he was sure hadn't been there in the morning, and as his hearing tuned in to the silence of the apartment, he thought he heard a faint sound from within the lounge, which sounded like someone breathing.

Which was, of course, ridiculous.

So ridiculous that he decided he really was exhausted and needed to pull himself together if he wasn't to end up becoming paranoid like Basil. And with that he strode into the lounge and turned on the light and blinked in utter shock.

Sitting on the sofa, facing the door, wearing his coat and trilby but otherwise looking quite at home was the man he'd first met as Nicholas ten years previously and who he now knew as Jeffrey Morgan.

'Good evening, Harold. Perhaps you'd care to put the kettle on?'

–

He didn't even bother to ask Jeffrey Morgan – though he still thought of him as Nicholas – how he'd found him. He knew he'd just shrug and smile in that knowingly superior way of his and not for the first time he'd feel like a fool for asking a question that would be batted away in a contemptuous manner. Instead, he waited until he'd recovered something of his composure, which took a while, and then sat down at the table, facing Nicholas on the sofa.

His visitor asked him how he was, and he didn't reply, determined this time not to come across as compliant and obedient.

'You always looked so shocked to see me.'

'Last time it was because I thought you were dead.'

'True: but last time was just four months ago, and I did say I'd be in touch, did I not?'

The last time they'd met had been in August, back in London, at the Hope public house. Nicholas had told him that he'd be asked to start working for them 'sooner or later' and he'd asked then how he'd know when and Nicholas had told him not to worry about that.

And here, in the small apartment on Marzilistrasse in Berne, it appeared that the 'sooner or later' that had haunted him for ten years, that had hung over him like an executioner's axe, that had caused him sleepless nights and never-ending stomach problems and a constant state of anxiety… that 'sooner or later' was now.

The time he had so dreaded had come.

'How did you—'

'How did I find you? Easy enough, I do know where you work after all.'

'I was going to ask how you got here – to Switzerland. I thought you were a wanted man?'

Nicholas shrugged in that dismissive manner of his, the one he used when he had no intention of answering a question and was surprised Noel Moore had the temerity to ask it.

'It wasn't easy, I'll leave it at that. But being here is very... refreshing. Hearing German spoken so ubiquitously is a true pleasure. But...' He clapped his hands then rubbed them together before removing his hat and coat. 'We have work to do, eh? Heaven knows, we've waited long enough! And I must say, well done, you... your metamorphosis from Harold Noel Dickson to Noel Moore has been a joy to behold. How long is it now?'

'As you know, I changed my name at the end of November 1933, before starting my new job at the Foreign Office in January 1934. I'm amazed no one suspected—'

'I told you – I arranged for the letter from the solicitor handling your change of name on our behalf to the Foreign Office to be removed from the files. For a brief time in 1935 we had someone with access to Registry and she was able to fillet a few files for us. Without that letter and a form subsequently completed about your change of name, no one would be any the wiser that Noel Moore had in fact been Harold Noel Dickson. That was important, of course, when you moved to Berlin to work in the Passport Control Office and became involved in espionage work.'

Nicholas leaned back in the sofa and suggested it was time for Harold to put the kettle on. When he returned with a tray of tea he'd removed his jacket too, ready now to start work.

'Of course, it was never the intention that we would wait quite so long before we turned you into an active agent. But then the war did throw up a number of insurmountable obstacles and, of course, my own difficulties and the need to disappear and then you being in Switzerland... but –' he clapped his hands so loudly that Noel Moore jumped '– here we are!'

Noel Moore coughed nervously and started to sip his tea until he realised his hand was shaking too much. 'Can I just point out that my role at the embassy is not what you... what I'm trying to say is that you may have a somewhat exaggerated view of what I do. I'm little more than a clerk, really.'

Nicholas looked at him long and hard, during which time his demeanour darkened and even though he didn't say a word, Noel Moore felt frightened.

'That is not my understanding.'

'It's not that I don't want to help but—'

'You give every impression of not wanting to help.'

'What I am trying to say is not that I don't want to help but that I fear I may not be in a position to help... much.'

'So, this has all been a waste of time, then?'

'I beg your pardon?'

'The past ten years... our meetings during that time, the *considerable* help we gave you, the promises you made... our expectations... the subterfuge we arranged and you so happily colluded with... what I believed was an agreement that we had – that has all been a waste of time, has it?'

Noel Moore shrugged. He'd been staring at the floor but when he looked up, he noticed Nicholas was putting on his jacket and standing up.

'Maybe you're right, Harold Noel Dickson. Maybe you are little more than a clerk, though that would be contrary to what we understand. In that case, you've clearly misled us. Maybe it's best if I cut my losses and disappear once more.'

He was putting on his overcoat now and adjusting his scarf. Noel Moore wondered if he was about to be let off the hook.

'I hope there's no hard feelings.'

Nicholas stopped and turned towards him, stepping so close that their faces were no more than six inches apart. His eyes were veiny and red and his face pinched and aged but there was an undoubted venom when he spoke.

'No hard feelings? Really... no hard feelings? Let me assure you, Harold Noel Dickson, that I have enough hard feelings to occupy every moment of what remains of your life. Maybe I cannot force you to work for us as you've promised…' He was gripping Noel Moore's arm now, very tightly, and as Moore tried to step back his grip tightened even further as the other man pulled him closer.

'You're my last hope, Harold Noel Dickson. If you don't come up with the goods then I'm finished. But I promise you one thing: if I go down, you're coming with me.'

He pushed Noel back, so roughly that he stumbled against the chair and had to steady himself against the table. Nicholas looked as if he was about to attack him.

'Don't forget, I have everything: the details of your membership of the British Union of Fascists, your original birth certificate, the letter informing the Foreign Office of your change of name and the form that was filled in subsequent to it and I even have photographs, photographs of you meeting with me in 1933 and 1934. They'll know who I am. You'll be finished, Harold Noel Dickson: they'll have all the evidence they need to convict you of High Treason. And just in case you're wondering, by the time they get all this, I'll have disappeared once more. You know how good I am at that.'

He stepped back, breathing heavily through his nose, his chest heaving and his face bright red. Noel Moore sat down and was relieved when the other man did likewise.

'I fear that there may have been a misunderstanding. I didn't say I wasn't prepared to pass on information. I just didn't want you to think I was more important than I am.'

Nicholas looked at him as if he didn't believe a word he'd said.

'I want something big: not some minor morsel of intelligence, something that amounts to little more than gossip or something the Germans will already know or is out of date. Don't try and pull a fast one like that on me, understand? I'll spot it a mile off. Give me something consequential that our German friends will truly value. Then I'll be satisfied, and I'll be across the border and in Germany before you know it and our relationship will have run its course. Understand?'

He nodded.

'Do you have something in mind? I've waited ten years, Harold Noel Dickson, and I'm not prepared to wait any longer.'

Noel Moore's shoulders slumped. He knew the game was up. Nicholas had outmanoeuvred him, and he knew unless he co-operated, he was doomed.

'I do have something in mind actually, yes.'

'Good... I knew you would. And it's something big, I hope, nothing trivial?'

'You don't need to worry. This will be very big.'

Chapter 17

Geneva and Lyon
December 1943

'And then there were three…'

'I beg your pardon, Jack?'

'It's a children's rhyme, Barney: ten kids go out to play and one by one they disappear or die and each time that happens the rhyme goes "and then there were seven" or "then there were six", and so on.'

'And how does it end?'

He hesitated before answering. 'And then there were none.'

That had the effect of drawing a silence over the room in Barney's apartment in Geneva, three of them alone with the thought of none surviving, a sense of doom. It drew out the fear they all had but rarely admitted to themselves, let alone discussed with anyone else.

'And you say that's a poem for children, is it, Jack?'

'It's the fault of you British, Barney – all your kid's rhymes seem to be so dark. Isn't "Ring a Ring a Roses" to do with the great plague?'

The discussion was interrupted by Benoît Roux coughing, anxious to bring them back to what they were meant to be talking about.

'Perhaps we don't have time to talk about children's poetry?'

'Perhaps not, Benoît, but I was making the point that a month ago there were five of us here and then Sophia goes to France and we were down to four and then Siegfried is sent to join Sophia in Lyon – which is why I said now we are three.'

The Frenchman shrugged in a manner which made it clear he had little time for such distractions. There was an evident tension between him and Jack, the two had very different personalities. Jack had told Barney Allen he didn't think Benoît trusted anyone who wasn't French. Barney said he got on with him fine, but he had to admit he was a very serious type.

'I crossed the border last night and met with Maurice in a farmhouse near Motz,' said Benoît.

'Did he say how Sophia is?'

Benoît glanced up at Jack, annoyed at the interruption. 'He said the operation is going very well, so I assume she is well. She and Siegfried are settling in and seem to be established at Avenue Berthelot. He said Madame Madelaine is very pleased with them and she meets regularly with Agnes Kléber and she is optimistic that soon they will get a breakthrough and discover who is betraying the Resistance, but…'

Benoît paused and took a sip of his coffee. 'Madame Madelaine is a proud woman: she has always been determined that the Mars group would be independent and be able to operate inside Lyon without any help, if you understand me. Clearly this does not mean the two Germans, that is different. But she does recognise that they need help, especially with communications between Lyon and us in Geneva and with London too. Her view is that relying on couriers or me crossing the border is too risky.

'The message Madame Madelaine sent through Maurice is that Mars needs a person in the city to communicate with us and vice versa. I think the phrase Maurice used was a "radio-man".'

He looked up and at Barney who nodded, and Jack got the impression that Barney had been aware of what the Frenchman was going to say because he responded so promptly.

'Which all makes a good deal of sense, do you not think, Jack? Mars is stretched enough as it is in Lyon and if we are to make the most of the splendid work Sophia and Siegfried are doing then we do need a radio-man in Lyon, eh?'

He was looking at Jack, waiting for some kind of response and Jack hesitated because he suspected that as far as Barney was concerned, he and this radio-man may well be the same person.

'I've not operated a radio before,' he replied.

'You'll be trained. Basil has a chap in Berne that looks after this type of thing. He says you can pick up the basics in a week or two. And then we'll get you across to Lyon.'

'Carrying a radio transmitter?'

'No, that will arrive separately. London will look after all that.'

'It sounds as if this has all been planned for some while?'

'One has to make plans all the time.'

'The problem as I see it is, Jack.' Benoît gestured towards the American.

'I've operated inside Nazi Germany, Benoît, in case you didn't know.' Jack stared hard at the Frenchman, resisting the temptation to point out that was something Benoît had not done.

'I understand that, Jack, and I don't doubt your ability and your... courage, certainly. But you're an American. You will stand out in Lyon for sure if you're neither French or German.'

'For Christ's sake, don't you—'

'Please!' Barney raised his voice. 'Can we please not squabble like this? Of course we know that Jack is American, but I ought to point out that we have sent over dozens of radio operators into France. Once there they tend not to wander around, their job is to stay in hiding – with their radio sets. Jack will not be going to Lyon to hang around the bars and cafés. And we'll make sure he has a reasonable identity. It's being worked on.'

'When will I go?'

'Basil's chap reckons you ought to be proficient after ten days, which may be pushing it, but you're a bright chap. He arrives tomorrow. Then you'll travel to Lyon.'

Jack nodded and looked at Barney and Benoît, gesturing at the pair of them.

'And then there were two.'

Luise Brunner was moved to Section 4A of the Gestapo in early December. This was the section which dealt with what the Gestapo described as 'enemies of the state'. She thought they could just as well say they meant most of the population of Lyon. And France.

In her new section the Gestapo officers would write their reports in long-hand before passing them over to Luise or one of the other two German secretaries to type up. This version would then go to a senior officer who'd make notes and corrections before returning it to a secretary to re-type. It was a laborious process and one she was pleased to see added an unnecessary amount of time to any investigation. After her first week in the department, she was able to differentiate between reports that had serious consequences for the Resistance and those which didn't. She tried to delay typing the former, never by more than a day, but she knew that even half a day's delay could impede an investigation.

And it wasn't as if the Gestapo officers helped: they all insisted *their* reports were the most pressing and the most urgent, the ones which *had* to be typed up first and this meant that Sophia could never be accused of choosing which report to delay.

What did surprise her was the extent to which the Gestapo relied on what she would describe as low-level informers. That seemed to account for a high proportion of their work. She was amazed at the sheer pettiness of the information the Gestapo was acting on and which she could also see was clogging up the system. She even mentioned to Agnes that if Mars wanted to impede the Gestapo, they should ensure that they were deluged with reports from neighbours, work colleagues, acquaintances and even family members passing on what amounted to tittle-tattle with little to corroborate it.

I am a PATRIOT and I asked my daughter's teacher why there was no picture of Marshal PETAIN in her classroom and she said nothing but now my daughter is receiving LOW MARKS and I am sure the teacher is a MEMBER of the Resistance...

My neighbour two doors down... she makes disrespectful gestures BEHIND THE BACKS of German officers... and when you question her please ask her to return the money she owes me...

You should know that there's a man called Etienne who works in our storeroom who I think writes 'RESISTEZ!' on the inside of boxes before they're sent out! I am sure I heard him talking about BOMBS...

I hope you realise this is in CONFIDENCE but my sister's father-in-law often disappears for days on end — and he fought in the Great War...

You will understand that I am a loyal family man, but I heard my nephew — he's FIFTEEN and should know better — and his friends talking about something they heard on a BBC broadcast...

The reports had a pattern to them: the sour smell of the settling of scores; a distinct lack of evidence; the random use of capital letters.

She had wondered why so much time and attention was devoted to these informants but on her third day in that section Barbie himself had come in to address the officers and from the back of the room she overheard him say that no piece of information should be regarded as too small, no informant too petty. All should be investigated; you never know when a seemingly inconsequential piece of information may tally with other information we have and turn out to be the last piece in the jigsaw.

After a while Sophia began to make some sense of the process. When the first, typed version was returned by the senior officer it would have his initials under those of the original investigating officer and alongside it either one, two or three asterisks. At first, she thought these related to the rank of the officer, but she soon realised it was the senior officer's assessment of the importance of a report, grading it to show how seriously the informant should be taken.

And the informants accorded three asterisks — fewer than a tenth of all reports — were clearly the ones she began to take interest in. They would be the ones investigated first and paid most attention to.

And these informants – the ones with three asterisks – would next appear on a *pro forma*, with 'Verified Source Report' printed at the top. Her job then was to copy the contents of different sections within the report onto separate index cards and file them accordingly.

Sophia began to realise some of these 'verified' sources were from the original reports of the informants, others were from established sources. By the time they became a 'verified source' these key informants had a code name: Source Antoine, Source Armand, Source Félix, Source Eugénie, Source Renée among dozens of others.

And Luise Brunner began to notice that a small number of the sources – Source Armand, Source Félix, Source Eugénie – cropped up more frequently. And at the top of those reports, on the *pro formas*, would often be written a figure and Sophia wondered if these correlated to the payments they were receiving, and which were being processed in the finance department.

Could Source Félix, for example, with the figures '1200' circled at the top of their *pro forma* be the same as M7499 in the ledger, with the figure 1,200F against it?

She discussed it one evening with Siegfried in his apartment below hers on Avenue de Saxe. He agreed there could be something in it. He'd make a note of the larger sums and see if they equated to the figures written on the 'Verified Source Report' *pro formas*.

And two days later he caught up with her as they both walked back to Avenue de Saxe after work. 'J128.' He was slightly breathless as he spoke, struggling to keep up.

'What about it?'

'Does it mean anything to you?'

She shook her head.

'Today I had to process the payment of two thousand francs to J128. It's the largest sum I've seen to date.'

Sophia let out a low whistle. 'That's one hundred Reichsmarks! I certainly don't recall seeing a Verified Source Report with two thousand on it.'

'And there's something else – maybe you can slow down a bit? I'm not as young as you. Alongside that entry on the ledger were the initials "NB" in the "special approvals column". You know who that is?'

'Tell me.'

'I reckon it must be Barbie: his proper name is Nikolaus and that's how he signs official documents. When I got the ledger back from Möller I looked for who else had a "NB" against their payments. J128 was the only one. Apart from that two thousand francs payment they'd had four other large payments since that ledger began in September: two more of two thousand francs; one of two thousand five hundred, and one of three thousand.'

'I need to see if I can find which source is J128.'

'And then we need to find out who they are.'

'Of course. You do realise the significance of this, don't you?'

Siegfried nodded, saying nothing as they allowed an elderly couple to stroll past them. 'J128 is the traitor.'

–

Johannes van Leeuwen arrived in Lyon on the 22 December. His *kennkarte* revealed that he was an engineer, from the Flemish city of Turnhout in Belgium. He was also in possession of a letter authorising his journey to Lyon on account of his expertise in repairing railway machinery.

Barney Allen was decent enough to admit to Jack Miller that while it was a good enough identity, it was a long way from being perfect.

'There's the small matter of my not speaking Dutch.'

'I understand that, Jack, but London took the view that we couldn't risk giving you either a French or a German identity because you'd be bound to be caught out by native speakers. Being Belgian you can be expected to have some knowledge of French, but at the same time a very good excuse for not being fluent in it and certainly for speaking it with an accent. It was the best we could rustle up in a short matter of time. I'm sorry. But the purpose of the identity is just to get you into Lyon. Mars will sort you out then.'

'And what if I bump into a Dutch speaker?'

'Well, I'd say you'd have been awfully unlucky.'

–

A man called Lawrence who looked after Basil Remington-Barber's communications with London had arrived in Geneva to begin Jack's intensive radio training. Lawrence was tall, with a Birmingham accent and a pipe that seemed to be permanently wedged in the corner of his mouth. He told Jack the transmitter he was being trained on would be identical to the one he'd be using in Lyon.

'It's a Type Three Mark Two B Two, if you're interested in that type of thing... we started using it a few months ago and it's regarded as an excellent piece of kit... the tubes in the transmitter provide thirty watts of power and the receiver has a four-tube heterodyne set... probably a bit too much detail, but suffice it to say that as far as radio receivers and transmitters go, this is about as good as you'll get...'

Jack said that was very interesting though a bit above his head, if he was honest, and Lawrence – who seemed like he could talk about the technical capabilities of the Type Three Mark Two B Two all day – looked slightly disappointed but then said what he was about to say was important.

'The Germans are bloody good at radio-detecting, if you'll excuse my language. They can triangulate a transmission to within ten miles and then they use vans with special detectors which can pick up a radio – not just when it's transmitting, but when it's receiving too. This machine is quicker and a bit harder to detect... but only a bit. Always transmit in code: only use clear in an absolute emergency, like when they're trying to break down the door. And there's something else…'

Lawrence reached under the table and pulled out a suitcase. 'It's more compact – it will fit in a suitcase like this. Your radio will be flown into France and will be waiting for you wherever you're going to – I've not been told where, quite rightly, I don't need to know. It's versatile enough to be able to move around. And that's important: don't make the mistake of transmitting from the same place too often. If you do, the Germans will catch you in no time!'

Chapter 18

Lyon
December 1943

By Sunday the twentieth, Lawrence agreed that Jack was ready. Or as he put it in his flat Birmingham accent, 'Ready enough, I suppose'. It sounded a bit grudging.

He travelled to the border with Benoît, where a guide took over, escorting him into France and the village of Bellegarde-sur-Valserine. From there another escort, this time to Ceignes and then an uncomfortable journey under a pile of vegetables in the back of a lorry to Ambérieu where he spent the night in the house of an elderly woman, who stayed up all night praying.

In the morning a man arrived at the house. He introduced himself as Michel, a member of Mars. He would be Jack's escort into Lyon.

They travelled into Lyon by train, the two met sitting apart but within sight of each other. There was only one security check on the journey into Lyon Part-Dieu: it came as the train approached Montluel on the outskirts of Lyon, the city already emerging on either side of the track. A French gendarme wanted to know why Monsieur van Leeuwen – he made a meal of pronouncing the name – was on this train and could he show any other papers? The overweight and bored-looking German soldier waiting behind him was in the early stages of becoming interested. At that point another passenger came over and said excuse me in a more polite manner than the gendarme was used to these days and proceeded to push between the gendarme and the other passenger, reached for his case on the luggage rack, directly above the Belgian and then to his horror it burst open and all of its contents spilled out. It was almost entirely shoes – he explained he was a shoe salesman… *here is my card* – and the gendarme had to help pick them up, along with some of the other passengers.

At that point the German soldier said in bad French that enough was enough and told the gendarme they should move on. When Johannes van Leeuwen sat down a minute or so later after helping pick up the shoes he nodded at Michel, his companion and the man who'd apparently been so clumsy with his luggage. And as he did so the elderly man sitting opposite him, so close that their knees touched, smiled and tapped his nose.

Jack realised the old man knew.

He wondered if he was the only one.

There was a broad grin on the man's face, pleased to have played a tiny part in something he wasn't sure of, but he reached into his pocket and took out a packet of cigarettes and pressed them into Jack's hand and patted it.

Jack felt more relaxed than he ought to have done, an enemy agent venturing into hostile territory. He attributed that in part to the fact that he was an experienced agent now, with years of clandestine operations under his belt. He knew it was good not to be too nervous but at the same time, he worried there was a danger in being too complacent.

But he realised there was another reason he felt so relaxed. He would soon be reunited with the love of his life. He didn't know what the circumstances would be or how long they'd be able to spend together and more than anything else, how it would all end, but he did know that given the choice he'd rather spend one more day with Sophia than a lifetime apart from her.

He lit one of the old man's cigarettes as they pulled into Part-Dieu, unaware of how prophetic that may be.

–

He followed Michel out of Part-Dieu and onto a tram which took them as far as Rue Duquesne and he then spotted the woman in the dark green raincoat with a blue beret and, as instructed by Michel, walked behind her across the Rhône on the Pont St Clair.

Michel had told him he'd be led into the Croix-Rousse and he was struck how different it was to the right bank of the Rhône. Here it was narrow, cobbled streets, high buildings, filth everywhere and the walls seemed to lean into the streets, their surfaces blacked and uneven.

On Place Bellevue the woman disappeared into a *boulangerie* and that was his cue to walk on to the church, Église St Bernard, where an older woman with the large umbrella was waiting as he'd been told she would be, carefully studying the church noticeboard and not glancing even once in his direction, and Jack was impressed, he couldn't work out how she'd even seen him. He followed her across Place Colbert and from there into Rue Lemot and at that point the woman's pace slowed slightly and she glanced round, peering behind him and when she was satisfied they were alone in the narrow street nodded and carried on walking. Moments later she opened a door and indicated he should follow her, quickly.

They were in a dark passageway, their footsteps echoing loudly around them. The woman walked into a courtyard surrounded by buildings on all sides and with a pile of refuse in the middle. She continued walking to one corner where she headed into another passageway and then down a set of dark steps and into what to all intents and purposes was a tunnel, which soon opened on to an alley, a building to their left and a high wall to their right. And then across a bridge leading to an open-air set of quite steep steps and he followed her down, and at the bottom she pointed to another alley and she waited until he was in it before moving away.

Halfway down the alley a door opened and a man hurried him in, anxiously looking up and down as he did so. The man closed the door, locked it and then indicated they should stand where they were – in the dark, musty entrance, in complete silence apart from Jack's heavy breathing. They waited for three or four minutes and then the man gestured for Jack to follow him, down into a cellar, along a narrow passageway and into a room that was surprisingly warm and bright.

He introduced himself as Maurice. Jack should make himself at home, he must be tired. There was a camp bed against one wall, a small table with two chairs opposite it and Jack smiled and said thank you and apologised for his French and Maurice said it was no problem, it was fine and he should wait in here, he'd be brought some food and there was a room next door where he could wash and use the toilet and soon someone would be along to see him.

Jack found it hard to rest because he was convinced that the person who'd soon be along to see him was Sophia and the excitement – that wasn't the right word, it was far more than that – meant that he'd sit on the camp bed for a minute or two and then get up to pace the room.

When he heard footsteps approaching, he knew instinctively it wasn't Sophia. It turned out to be the older woman he'd followed from Église St Bernard. She introduced herself as Madame Madelaine and asked if he was comfortable and if he needed anything and Jack thought about asking for a towel but decided not to: he was a secret agent, in a foreign city on a clandestine mission and asking for a towel didn't feel quite right.

Madame Madelaine explained that the radio had arrived in France – the British had flown it in the previous night and she expected it to be in Lyon soon.

'It's a Christmas present to us from the British: they have sent us weapons too.'

Jack laughed and wondered whether he should ask about Sophia. He wasn't sure if he was even meant to ask about her. He had no idea how senior this woman was – he had the impression she was quite important, but he worried he'd only just arrived and asking so soon about her may seem wrong.

'When the radio arrives, you can start transmitting and receiving. You will be based in the Croix-Rousse, it is the hardest place for the Germans to track us down, the place is an enigma for them. We will move you around the area: we are told you should never use the radio in one place more than once.'

Jack said that was true.

'In the meantime, I have to tell you that tomorrow you will have a visitor. We will bring you a change of clothing – and you'll need a towel.'

–

Sophia arrived at Jack's hideout in the Croix-Rousse on the Wednesday, the 22 December. It was a good time to get away early from Avenue Berthelot. More than half of the German staff had been granted home leave for Christmas and Section 4A was quiet. Agnes Kléber told her she could have the Wednesday afternoon off.

Tell people you're shopping for Christmas!

She left the office at the start of her lunch break. It had been a productive morning. Now that the office was so quiet, she was able to look through the files on other desks. She was convinced she was close to finding the identity of the traitor.

She'd already narrowed down J128 to one of four probable sources.

From Avenue Berthelot she took a tram to the Presqu'île and got off at Perrache station. She was sure she'd not been followed but her concern was more that she'd bump into someone from work and have to explain why she was there. From the station she headed north towards Place Bellecour and allowed herself half an hour in the shops, shocked at how poorly stocked they were, shocked too at how miserable everything was. Even in Germany there was a bit more cheer at this time of year. It was as if in France they couldn't be bothered.

She knew she was being impatient but the thought of being so near to Jack hurried her along. She took a tram north to

Rue Terme and from there the funicular up to Boulevard de la Croix-Rousse, her excitement building as the funicular climbed the steep hill. She did at least remember to check she'd not been followed when they reached the top. She crossed an almost deserted Place de la Croix-Rousse and entered the café in the north-east corner. The barman watched her carefully as she came in: suspicious at first and then as if he was delighted to see her, showing every sign that he'd been expecting her. It was all a bit too obvious, not nearly subtle enough.

Nonetheless she asked him if she could use the toilet and he said she'd find it at the back and she thanked him and said it was not nearly as cold as she was expecting and he said that was true, though he thought it would be over Christmas and smiled as he said it and his whole manner was a bit too knowing and had it not been for the thought of seeing Jack, she'd have aborted it there and then and told Agnes to tell Madame Madelaine exactly what she thought.

When she returned from the toilet a boy was waiting by the bar and he nodded and Sophia followed him. He moved fast, through the *traboules* and then into an alley and the boy disappeared, as if into thin air and at that moment a door opened and she entered.

Her recollections of what followed were expressed more through the emotions she experienced rather than a precise sequence of events: the tightening of her chest as she climbed down into the cellar, the quickening of her heartbeat, the sobs as she first saw Jack silhouetted in the doorway of the room, the way he held her as if never going to let her go and the fact that they didn't exchange a word for a long time and then constantly reassured each other they were fine and repeatedly asked how are you.

They had no idea of how long they'd been left on their own for but there was a knock at the door and when Madame Madelaine came in, she said she was concerned: it was already getting dark outside and she thought it would be dangerous for Luise to be out and about in the Croix-Rousse when it was dark.

Either we can try and get you out now or you stay overnight – and hope no one spots you weren't at your apartment.

–

Sophia left the building on the Croix-Rousse at seven o'clock the next morning with the promise that they'd be able to spend the Christmas weekend together. She wouldn't have missed the time she'd just spent with Jack for anything, but now she was worried. She was too exposed. If she was stopped, she'd have no excuse for being on the other side of the river, let alone on the Croix-Rousse.

She took the funicular down from Boulevard de la Croix-Rousse to Rue Terme and a tram from there to Cours du Midi and once outside Perrache wondered whether to walk to Avenue Berthelot from there – it wasn't too far – or take the tram.

And then she had an idea. She'd take the tram but get off it at the junction with Avenue de Saxe, past the Gestapo building. Then she'd walk back, as if coming from the direction of her apartment, as normal. It was, as Basil would say, a good example of how she'd come to think instinctively like a secret agent.

The tram was crossing Pont du Midi when she noticed him and more to the point, he noticed her. He looked surprised and smiled when he saw her and moved from his seat across the aisle to one next to her and wished her a good morning, doffing his trilby as he did so and she responded and asked how he was and he replied all the better for seeing her and laughed and she joined in.

'I had no idea you lived on the Presqu'île, Fraulein Brunner!'

Franz Boehm was one of the Gestapo officers in Section 4A, an overweight Bavarian with bad breath who'd barely spoken to her before. His reports were the worst ones to type up: his handwriting was tiny and barely legible and his grammar was shocking.

She shrugged by way of an answer and said it was a fine, crisp morning.

'I thought you lived on the Avenue de Saxe?'

She stood up, slightly too early for their stop but it enabled her to avoid replying.

Whether she'd got away with it was another matter.

–

It was eight o'clock when she settled into her desk. Her heart was still beating fast, from the excitement of seeing Jack and the encounter she'd had with Boehm on the tram. She tried to think of an alibi in case he questioned her again.

Her priority that day was to conclusively match J128 with a named source. She was sure she'd have come up with something by the end of the day. The desk next to her belonged to Maria, who'd returned to Münster for Christmas. She had a feeling J128's file would be on her desk.

She spent the morning working through the reports. She typed up three from the previous day and checked the rest on her desk. None of them were Verified Source Reports so she casually leaned over and placed them on Maria's desk and picked up the stack of files she'd replaced them with.

Just before lunchtime she found it – a Verified Source Report from Source Armand with the number '2200' written across the top.

If that equated to 2200 francs, as Siegfried suspected, then Source Armand was almost certainly the same person as J128, the source who according to the entries in the ledger had already received so much money.

Which meant Source Armand was the person most likely to be the traitor.

She glanced through the report. It wasn't a straightforward one: the information in it was vague, replete with references such as 'as disclosed in person to officer'… 'will confirm location of new safe house in person'… 'followed up with telephone call 17 December'.

But she realised that the very fact that this report was so sparse marked it out from the other verified sources. The more she read, the more she was convinced Source Armand was the traitor. She decided to work through her lunch break to take advantage of the office being empty. She'd be able to make copious notes on anything she could find on Source Armand.

She bent down to collect some carbon paper from a drawer when she became aware of someone standing over her. When she looked up it was Franz Boehm, grinning.

'You are such a diligent worker, Fraulein Brunner – working through your lunch break: the Fuhrer will be proud of you!'

He was leaning on her desk, his breath rancid and warm, and he looked down and angled his head so he could see the report she was working on.

She said she was keen to get as much finished as possible because she understood they would be finishing at noon on Christmas Eve and she was anxious to—

'Anxious to what, Fraulein Brunner? Anxious to get back to spend Christmas at your apartment on Avenue de Saxe or anxious to spend Christmas with your mystery lover on the Presqu'île?'

She felt every part of her body freeze.

'I checked, you know, Fraulein Brunner – or may I call you Luise?'

'Whatever you wish, Herr Boehm.'

'Franz, please... call me Franz, I insist. You see I was puzzled when I saw you on the tram this morning coming from the Presqu'île when I thought you lived on Avenue de Saxe. But you know, I'm tired, I work hard and I thought I could be mistaken, no? So, I checked this morning – always a Gestapo officer, eh? And where does Fraulein Brunner, our pretty new secretary from Berlin with the lovely legs live? And I think you know the answer: Avenue de Saxe!'

He'd reared back when he said that, underlining the drama of his revelation. His grin was even wider now. Some of his teeth were missing and his lips were moist as he ran his tongue over them.

'And then I thought, why would Fraulein Brunner with the pretty face and the lovely legs be on the Presqu'île at such an early hour of the morning and I applied all my skills as an investigating officer to work out what you were up to over there and do you know what my conclusion was?'

She was unable to reply but smiled as sweetly as she could manage.

'A man – you have a man over there. But who could it be? Maybe you wish to tell me, Luise Brunner?'

'Really, Herr Boehm…'

'Franz.'

'Franz, I know you may find this hard to believe but the explanation is far less interesting. You see… would you care to sit down?'

He eagerly pulled up a chair, pulling it in close to her, his feet touching hers.

'I lost my fiancé, Kurt, at Stalingrad: he was with the Sixth Army. My grief is sometimes so overwhelming that I wake early and go for a long walk, as was the case this morning. I found myself on the other side of the river when I realised it was time to come to work.'

'When was this, Luise?'

'Just before eight o'clock.'

'No! I mean when did you lose you fiancé?'

'I've not heard from him since the start of the year and I—'

'Well then –' he slapped her thigh, hard enough for her to flinch '– surely by now… that was what, nearly a year ago! I'm sure you're interested in one of those young SS officers, boys in their twenties, all that energy, eh? Quite understandable, Luise. But don't worry…' He was patting her thigh now, his hand moving under her skirt and although she moved back, he didn't let go. 'I tell you what, Luise: what you need to get over your fiancé isn't one of these young bucks, but the wisdom and comfort that an older man can give you. What do you think?'

She said maybe that was the case but actually she found she took comfort from dedicating herself to the Reich through hard work and it was an honour to be able to work here, especially with officers as talented and devoted as him and—

'So, tomorrow night, Luise – Christmas Eve – you will join me for dinner! There is a wonderful little restaurant on Place Garnot, near where I live. They are most hospitable to Germans. You will be my guest!'

—

Franz Boehm's 'wonderful little restaurant' turned out to be not so little and certainly not so wonderful. It was noisy and steamy and full of German officers and a few local women. The best that could be said about the food was that there was plenty of it, but it had none of the refinement which she'd been told typified Lyonnais cuisine.

Sophia's experienced sharply contrasting emotions the afternoon before, the Thursday. At first, it was sheer relief that Boehm clearly had no idea about Jack or that she'd come from the Croix-Rousse. She'd been rather pleased with her story about being so grief-stricken about Kurt that she'd gone for a walk. He seemed to believe it and she felt it was another example of her thinking intuitively like an agent. She assumed he'd check out the story about the fiancé missing at Stalingrad – he was a Gestapo man after all – and would discover it was true.

But this relief was soon overcome by a gnawing dread at having to have dinner with Franz Boehm. She had no doubt he had more in mind than just dinner, the way he'd groped her in the office made that clear. She had been hoping to go to the Croix-Rousse after work on the Friday and spend the Saturday – Christmas Day – with Jack and return to Avenue de Saxe on the Sunday afternoon. Madame Madelaine had even agreed that Siegfried could join them on the Saturday.

But on the Thursday afternoon she'd told Agnes Kléber about her dinner with Boehm and her encounter with him on the Thursday morning and that night Agnes turned up at Sophia's apartment with a message from Madame Madelaine.

This is too dangerous now… you are to return to Avenue de Saxe after your dinner and remain there over the weekend… there will be no more visits to the Croix-Rousse in the foreseeable future…

And that meant there was another emotion Sophia had to cope with: being in the same city as Jack but now unable to see him. Over the past few years, since becoming a British agent, she'd learnt to live with the fear and the omnipresent danger of living a clandestine life. But now the loneliness and despair were becoming too much.

There were times when she felt overwhelmed.

Franz Boehm had been civil enough at first in the restaurant on Christmas Eve as he insisted on recounting his life story. He was from Halle in Saxony – she could tell that by the accent – had fought in the Great War (though she got the impression he'd not done much fighting) and then had been unemployed for much of the 1920s, joining the Nazi Party in 1926, which was his route into the Gestapo.

As the meal moved from the hors d'oeuvre to the main course Boehm became increasingly drunk and maudlin, talking about how he missed his family, how he missed his dog – more so than his family it seemed – and how he missed Germany. And as the main course was cleared away – *you have left so much of your meal, Luise!* – he became more indiscreet: how Klaus Barbie was such a demanding boss to work for and how he sometimes wondered if he was up to it and then he talked about the course of the war, leaning over towards Sophia so that his head was so close to hers that he had to move the candlestick. As he did so she felt something touching her knee and she edged back then realised it was his hand, clutching the knee tightly at first to stop her and then, as he grinned at her with his yellow teeth and moist lips, his hand moved up to her thighs, stroking them much as she imagined he'd stroke his dog – an owner expecting obedience rather than any expression of tenderness.

Did she realise that the war was not going so well, he asked? That there had been some… setbacks… that events in the east were especially… he turned round to check no one overheard him and then sobered up enough to realise that perhaps he'd gone too far and waved his hand, as if to dismiss what he'd just said.

'But you should understand that is how a war goes, Luise: there are setbacks and disappointments, but there is no question we will triumph! We may lose battles but we will surely win the war!'

'Of course, Franz. I'm sure the Fuhrer will—'

'We have to be especially careful in this city, you know: you realise that the French Resistance see this as their most important city in France? I fear there are Resistance members everywhere, though none in this room of course!'

He leaned back, laughing heartily and finished his glass of beer and then called the waiter over for more wine. By the time it arrived he'd craftily moved his chair so he was even closer to her. This time his hand strayed under her skirt and as she tried to move her chair back he'd placed a foot there to stop it. His hands were clammy and warm and she worried about what was going to happen.

She had no idea this was about to be the least of her worries.

'You mustn't worry though, Luise – are you sure you won't have another drink, it is Christmas, after all? You will be safe: look on me as your personal protector. Between you and me –' he leaned closer again, beckoning her to do likewise '– Herr Barbie is looking to strengthen our operation here in Lyon. He is bringing a very senior SS officer over from Berlin. In fact, he's currently based at Prinz-Albrecht-Strasse. Maybe you know him?'

She smiled sweetly and said there were hundreds if not thousands of people who worked at Prinz-Albrecht-Strasse and she knew very few personally, especially SS officers and—

'His name is Brigadeführer Konrad Busch – does that ring a bell? Are you all right, Luise, you look unwell?'

Chapter 19

'Take a moment, Sophia, you need to calm down. And do try to be quieter: we can't risk waking any of our neighbours, can we?'

They were in the tiny lounge of Siegfried's apartment on Avenue de Saxe, which was one floor below her apartment and she'd knocked on his door at one o'clock on Christmas morning.

He was shocked at the state she was in: normally so composed and immaculate, now her face was white and her eyes filled with terror. She shook uncontrollably as he led her into the lounge and towards the sofa. She spoke incoherently, something about having to leave Lyon.

Straight away!

That was when he told her to calm down and to be quieter. He leant over to pick up the bottle of schnapps, which had been his sole companion that Christmas Eve, and poured a glass for her. Sophia sipped at it at first and then finished it in one go and held the glass out for a refill. Siegfried never failed to be amazed at the restorative powers of schnapps. When he was on stage there was always a bottle waiting in the wings in case an actor needed it. It could, he believed, cure stage fright.

'That bastard, Boehm… he tried it on with me of course but thankfully he got so drunk that by the end of the evening he could barely stand. When it came time to leave, he insisted I should go back to his place with him, but fortunately a couple of Luftwaffe officers saw what was going on and arranged for him to be taken home. They kindly had their car bring me back here.'

She paused and sipped at the schnapps and Siegfried said he could quite see how unpleasant that was and more than once he'd rescued a young actress in similar circumstances but at least she was back here and by the sounds of it, Boehm would have such a dreadful hangover that he wouldn't remember a thing.

'That's not why I'm so worried, Siegfried. Boehm told me at dinner that Barbie is bringing a senior SS officer over from Berlin in the new year to work with him and wondered if I'd heard of him. It couldn't be worse, Siegfried.'

She fell silent and shook her head and held out her glass for him to refill, which surprised him because she wasn't much of a drinker.

'The senior SS officer who's coming to work here in Lyon is Konrad Busch – Brigadeführer Konrad Busch. I've known him for something like ten years: he joined the SS at the same time as my late husband, Karl-Heinrich, and they were great friends. We often socialised with him and his wife. I couldn't stand either of them. When I escaped from Berlin in March, I went to see Busch to get the papers to enable me to travel to Switzerland: I appealed to his greed – I told him I was travelling to Zürich to access Karl-Heinrich's safety deposit box which was full of money and jewellery and other valuables he'd stolen from Jews. I promised Busch he'd get five thousand Reichsmarks if he helped me. So, when he arrives here, he's bound to see me and of course will know I'm Sophia von Naundorf and not Luise Brunner: he'll know straight away what I'm up to. The game's up, Siegfried: we're going to have to get out of Lyon before he gets here. I don't know what to… and what about Jack, he—'

'Calm down, Sophia: we need to think of something. You say Boehm said this man is coming to Lyon in the new year?'

'That's what he said. It could be any time in January, I guess, but we must assume it will be early in the month.'

'Which gives us a week – we have to get to Jack so he can let Barney know what's going on as soon as possible.'

They were back at work at Avenue Berthelot on Monday 27 December, as if Christmas hadn't taken place that year. Section 4A was back to being busy and Sophia was relieved that Franz Boehm left her alone all day, nodding nervously if their eyes caught.

As she was beginning to get ready to leave, he gingerly approached her desk. He wanted to wish her a very happy Christmas, he said, and she thanked him and wished him one too and he asked if he might have a word and she said of course, convinced he was going to say something about Konrad Busch or ask her out again, but instead he said he wanted to apologise for Christmas Eve.

'I'm afraid I had too much to drink. You know how it is, being away from home and the time of year, which causes one to reflect… I know I drank more than I ought to have done and it wasn't until late the following morning when I finally woke up that I realised I must have abandoned you in the restaurant and I want to apologise for that. I hope you got home all right.'

'I did, thank you, Franz, you really mustn't worry.'

'I'm afraid I recall so little of the night… I do hope I wasn't indiscreet in any way; I have no memory of what we talked about.'

'Mainly about your dog – but nothing to be concerned about, you don't need to worry. And I enjoyed our dinner very much, thank you.'

Franz Boehm kept a polite distance from Luise Brunner and more than anything else she was relieved he appeared to have no memory of having mentioned the imminent arrival of Konrad Busch.

That evening she met with Jack and he promised to make an urgent transmission to Geneva. And on the Wednesday, came a breakthrough in identifying Agent Armand. Sophia and Siegfried had agreed that discovering the real identity of the traitor was like filling in a jigsaw. Realising it was J128 was one piece, linking J128 with Agent Armand was another, but significant gaps in the jigsaw remained.

That Wednesday afternoon Sophia noticed that Franz Boehm was in the side meeting room of Section 4A where he appeared to be involved in a heated argument with one of the French Gestapo officers, a nervous-looking man called René Dupont. She'd come across Dupont on a few occasions, one of a group of around thirty French fascists who worked for the Gestapo. He spoke some German and seemed to have an inflated view of his own importance, trying to hold himself in a military manner and hand out orders.

At the same time, there was an awkwardness about him, as if he knew this strange life he was leading was an aberration. She noticed how he'd stride into a room or down a corridor full of swagger, only to turn round and glance nervously over his shoulder.

But he didn't seem to be displaying too many signs of nerves with Franz Boehm. She heard raised voices but she couldn't make out what they were saying. There was a line of filing cabinets alongside the outer wall of the meeting room and she moved over there, busying herself with some filing.

I don't care, Boehm, I'm not telling you... why? Because I don't have to tell you: he's my agent and I report directly to Herr Barbie on ALL matters relating to him... Source...

At that moment two other officers walked by, talking loudly enough for what Dupont said next to be obscured.

Whose side are you on, Dupont, eh? I need to talk to him... from what I gather he'd be the best placed person to help me...

Well talk to Herr Barbie then, how about that?

Franz Boehm stormed out of the meeting room at that point, his face red with fury as he marched over to his desk. He was followed out by René Dupont, smoothing his jacket and straightening his tie as he did so.

She waited until towards the end of the day, choosing her moment to take some typed copy to put in the in-tray of a senior officer whose cubicle was close to Boehm's desk.

'How are you, Franz: you look like you've had a bad day?'

This was all Franz Boehm needed to hear. Yes, as it had happened, he'd had a very bad day. If Luise would do him the honour of joining him for a drink after work, then he'd even tell her all about it. She replied that it would be a pleasure: after all, Franz, a problem shared is a problem solved, is it not?

–

They ended up at a bar on the corner of Quai Claude Bernard and Rue Parmentier, close to the Rhône. There was a room above the bar where they found a table in the corner with no one else close by and by the time Boehm had finished his first beer and his schnapps chaser, he was ready to unburden himself.

'What I am going to share with you is in complete confidence, Luise, you do understand that?'

'Of course, Franz. It goes without saying that—'

'Of course it does, Luise, I know if anyone's loyalty to the Reich is beyond question it is yours. Where do I start? Between you and I, my position here has become rather difficult: Herr Barbie is a very demanding boss and I think his opinion of me as a Gestapo officer is that I may not be quite up to it. I think if I'm being totally frank, I'm seen as someone who is diligent enough, but a bit of a plodder – that was the very word he used to describe me in my annual review, would you believe? Barbie seems to want officers who are very good at gaining original intelligence and the like. Me, I think there's a place for both: the bright boys who find all the new intelligence and then the so-called plodders like me who actually do something about it. Will you have more schnapps... no?

'There was even talk I could be transferred, possibly to Poland, heaven help me. But a few weeks ago, I had a lucky break. I won't go into too much detail because I know you'll be bored by it but let me just say that through a mixture of perseverance and what I acknowledge is luck I discovered a communist cell was operating in La Mulatière. Have you heard of it?'

'I don't think so, no.'

'It's an area on the left bank of the Saone, more or less opposite La Confluence, which is the point where the river splits – the bottom of the peninsula, if that helps.'

She assured him it did, and she wasn't bored by his story at all.

'But tracking down the actual names of the members of this communist cell is proving to be very hard and without those the intelligence is of very limited use. I know some of their nicknames and where one or two of them work, but beyond that... it's tricky. They are a political group rather than part of the Resistance, but dangerous nevertheless, and if I could break them up and capture members, well – that would be a big feather in my cap, eh? May stop me being transferred to Poland, God help me.

'Now, that bastard Dupont... he's found himself running an agent who Barbie regards as our best source on the Resistance in the whole of Lyon.'

Franz Boehm paused and looked round to check they were still alone. He leaned closer to her.

'This source is a leading communist. I believe Dupont came to be running him because this source made an approach to the Gestapo but insisted on dealing with a fellow Frenchman for some reason, maybe it makes him feel less of a traitor. I'm told this source doesn't regard himself as a sympathiser with the Germans: his motivation is that helping us in the way he does helps his own cause – communism.'

'I'm not sure I understand that, Franz.'

'Communists are highly disciplined, Luise: they only care about one thing – communism. They have no loyalty to anyone else. Look at how the Soviet Union entered into a pact with us at the start of the war! For them, the ends justify the means. And at the moment, they are involved in a big battle for the control of the French Resistance. As far as we can gather, de Gaulle has managed to gain control of the Resistance. And the communists hate that. And they're doing what they can to undermine it, to the extent that...'

He turned round once more and then lowered his voice: he was speaking barely above a whisper. 'Do stop me if you find this boring, by the way. This was before you came to Lyon, but in June Dupont's communist informer told him that all the Resistance leaders in France would be meeting at a doctor's surgery in Caluire, in the north of the city. His information was correct: Barbie raided the place. He knew the man running the Resistance in France on behalf of de Gaulle was code named Max and he was one of those arrested.'

'What happened to him?'

Boehm drew his hand across his throat and smiled. 'He ended up at Fort Montluc where he was tortured and they discovered his real identity – Jean Moulin. As I understand it, Dupont's informer may have been there too – so he is an important man. All I wanted was for Dupont to give me access to him so I could ask him about this communist cell in La Mulatière, but Dupont is like a child who won't let go of his ball. He refuses to let me have anything to do with him.'

'Do you know his agent's name?'

Boehm shook his head vigorously. 'If only! All I know is that he works in a laboratory in La Mulatière and lives in that area too.'

–

'Are you sure about it?'

They were crammed in the basement of a café on Rue des Capucins on the Croix-Rousse: Jack, Sophia, Siegfried along with Madame Madelaine and half a dozen members of Mars. It felt a bit too crowded for Sophia's liking and she'd said as much, but Madame Madelaine waved away her concerns. We've survived for nearly four years, she said. We know what we're doing.

But now they were listening to Siegfried – they knew him as Erhard Schröder – describe how he thought he'd identified Source Armand.

'I'm as certain as I can be that André Martin was the informer, the man who'd betrayed the Resistance meeting in Caluire in June. I believe he is the man referred to as J128 in the ledger and is also Source Armand, the source being paid so much money.

I'm not sure what else you want short of Klaus Barbie signing a document confirming his identity.'

Sophia looked at the Mars members. 'Do you know of André Martin?'

'I've heard the name,' said Michel. 'He's associated with the FTP.'

'What is that?'

'Francs-tireurs et partisans – it's the main communist Resistance group. Martin is the most common surname in France, so I've always assumed it's a *nom de guerre*.'

'I knew most of the leading communists here in Lyon before the war and I don't recall an André Martin,' said Madame Madelaine, 'but I imagine he'd have changed his name at least twice and may well be from another part of France. Remind me of how you've linked André Martin with Source Armand?'

Siegfried pulled his overcoat tightly round him: the basement was cold and damp and the vapour of their breath was visible whenever someone spoke. 'I was in Walter Möller's office yesterday morning trying to sort out some mess he'd got himself into. His secretary came in and said Barbie wanted to see him urgently and it was as if she'd shouted "fire" because he rushed out of the office. I noticed his safe was open and I could see the blue ledger: the normal ledgers we work from are dark red and quite thick but I've noticed that Möller often copies details from these ledgers into a thinner, blue one. I've always assumed this one contains the most sensitive information. I reckoned I'd have no more than ten minutes so I risked it: I removed the ledger from the safe and checked it. Alongside two dates – one in November, one in December – were the sums of two thousand francs and alongside them, the name of André Martin. At the front of the ledger Möller had written the name of an optician's laboratory against the name André Martin.'

'Which I checked out,' said Marcel, 'and it's a workshop in La Mulatière, which makes lenses and spectacles for opticians. André Martin works there and lives in an apartment in the next street.'

There was muttering in the basement before Madame Madelaine clapped her hands. 'We must waste no time. We will eliminate him as soon as possible.'

'Do you want me to clear it with Geneva?'

'There's no need, Jack. Geneva will want to check with London and by the time they have a meeting to decide and reply... no... it will all take too much time. We have to act quickly. We must disperse now: we will leave in pairs at five-minute intervals.'

Madame Madelaine indicated to Sophia and Jack that they should wait until the others had left.

'Jack has heard back from Geneva about that German officer,' said Madame Madelaine.

'You mean Busch? What did they say, Jack?'

'They said it's all in hand.'

Chapter 20

Berne and Berlin
January 1944

'What I don't understand, Konrad, is why you have to leave so soon for Lyon?'

'It's not so soon, Hannelore my dear. I leave on Monday: that's nearly three weeks after I was informed of the posting. I work for the SS, you realise, not a bank!'

'And you don't know when you'll be back?'

'I have no idea, Hannelore: I'm very lucky I'm not being sent back to the east.'

'But your leg, Konrad?'

'My leg is fine, unlike this beef – it's not as good as usual. You need to have a word with Else, she's normally such a good cook. Are you all right, Hannelore? You've gone terribly pale… Hannelore? Oh my God!'

—

There was nothing quaint or appealing about Schützenmatt-strasse, a bleak road a few metres from the west bank of the river Aare, just north of Berne's historic Old Town.

It was here, in a room at the rear of a damp and derelict office building, that three men met on a Saturday morning, the first day of 1944. Harald Mettler was the last to arrive: he was in his late thirties but looked younger. He also looked edgy that morning as he walked down Schützenmattstrasse, twice past the office building, eyeing it suspiciously. On the second pass he spotted the black bicycle with a red saddle propped up on the side wall and knew it was safe to enter.

Mettler was there at the instruction of the man who'd originally recruited him in 1936 as a British agent. Mettler was then a clerk at the Federal Political Department, the Swiss foreign ministry. And at the behest of Basil Remington-Barber he'd applied for a posting in Berlin. This had come up in 1938 and since then he'd been a senior clerk in the consular department of the Swiss Embassy on Corneliusstrasse. He had also been one of Basil Remington-Barber's most important agents in Berlin – and since Jack Miller had left the city at the end of 1941 and Sophia von Naundorf in March 1943, one of the only ones.

Normally Harald Mettler reported to Noel Moore. Messages would be passed between them through a news kiosk on Budapester Strasse, but one of Mettler's roles played a big part in his effectiveness as an agent. He was a courier between the Swiss Embassy in Berlin and the ministry in Berne. Every two or three weeks he'd make the trip. It was the perfect way to carry British intelligence and receive his instructions.

But this meeting was most unusual. For a start, he'd not been summoned by Noel Moore through the news kiosk on Budapester Strasse. He'd returned to Berne on New Year's Eve and after delivering the diplomatic bag to the Ministry had gone to his apartment on Zähringerstrasse, near the university, for the weekend. He was too tired to do anything on the Friday night: he'd planned to have a quiet weekend, possibly meeting a friend for lunch on the Sunday and then on the Monday back to the Federal Political Department to collect the return diplomatic bag and the long journey to Berlin.

But he'd been woken early on the Saturday morning with a telephone call. It was Basil Remington-Barber who asked him how he was and without waiting for a reply told him to be at their usual meeting place at ten o'clock. It was most odd, the first time the British had not followed their normal protocol.

And now he was there, his hat and overcoat doing little to keep out the cold, looking at the other Englishman who was with Basil, a man who'd only been introduced as his colleague and at least spoke decent German.

'Where's Noel?'

'Noel is out of town, Harald, which is why I contacted you and I apologise for not doing so in the normal manner, but this is a matter of some urgency. Perhaps if my colleague were to explain everything?'

Basil gestured to Barney Allen who stood up and walked over to shake Harald's hand, removing his gloves before doing so. The three men pulled up their chairs so they were closer together in the middle of the dank room.

'We have a most important mission for you to undertake in Berlin, Harald.'

'Everything I'm asked to do in Berlin is most important, Noel tells me.'

'This is the most important yet, Harald, so much so that Basil assures me your services will not be called upon for quite a while after you've completed this mission. That is correct, Basil?'

Basil said it was: they'd need him to keep his head down for a while.

Barney Allen said if Harald was ready, he'd explain everything. It took getting on for two hours to talk through the mission. Harald rather liked the other Englishman: he was obviously more senior than Noel, the other Englishman who usually gave him his instructions. And he was certainly better informed and more to the point than Basil, who tended to ramble.

But the Englishman whose name he was never given was clear and direct and seemed very respectful of Harald's role and nor did he take the seriousness of the mission for granted.

Yes, he knew how dangerous it was and yes, he knew it was asking an awful lot and if he wanted to be pulled out of Berlin after that and sent to Britain then that could be arranged.

Basil looked a bit unsettled at this point and said that was the first he'd heard of it and perhaps one thing at a time and Barney said fair enough and they went through the plan they'd just concocted one more time and by the time they'd finished even Basil had to agree it was a clever plan.

'The lives of some of our agents and others in another country depend upon it, Harald.'

–

Harald Mettler returned to Berlin the following day: Basil Remington-Barber had met him before he left and handed the small package to him and told him to be very careful with it. Barney Allen returned to Geneva at the same time, unsure whether the Swiss Embassy clerk was up to the mission he'd been given.

It would require extraordinary bravery and careful execution.

And he knew that if it failed, they'd have to abort the mission in Lyon and get Sophia, Jack and Siegfried out before it was too late.

At least Sophia had provided all the information they needed.

–

Konrad Busch lives with his wife, Hannelore, and their five children in a large villa on Beyme Strasse in Schmargendorf in the south-west of Berlin, it's in the Wilmersdorf district. Their house is in the section of the road between Hubertusbader Strasse and Jagow Strasse.

I know an excessive amount about their domestic lives because whenever we met socially, it was all Hannelore Busch talked about: the perfect and organised life she'd created for Konrad, their perfect children, their perfect meals...

Their life is one of strict routine: Karl-Heinrich told me that Konrad had complained about this to him on more than one occasion, but it was something he never dared question with his wife. Part of this routine is that every Friday night the children go to bed early and Hannelore and Konrad sit down to a dinner of roast beef, the best possible cut.

They have the meat delivered on the Friday morning from what Hannelore Busch always insists is the best butcher in Berlin, Vorgesetzter Metzgerei on Hohenzollerndamm.

Harald Mettler moved fast once back in Berlin. On the Tuesday he volunteered to work the early shift that week at the embassy, which meant he finished work in the middle of the afternoon. On the Wednesday he took a series of trams from the centre into Schmargendorf, eventually getting off on Forckenbeck Strasse and taking a circuitous route to check out the Busch home on Beyme Strasse.

The following day – the Thursday – he made the same trip, this time leaving the tram further down Forckenbeck Strasse and walking from there through a series of side streets to Hohen-zollerndamm, where he went in to Vorgesetzter Metzgerei, apparently the best butchers in Berlin.

It was certainly the most expensive one he'd ever been in, so busy that thankfully no one paid much attention to him as he bought the cut of beef he'd been told to purchase. It was eye-wateringly expensive and he used up a whole month's meat-ration coupons in the process. The assistant did ask him if he was new to the area and who it was for, but he made out he was in a hurry. His hat was pulled low over his face and he wore a pair of heavy spectacles. He hoped the disguise worked.

Back at his apartment on Luther Strasse Harald Mettler was grateful that he no longer shared it with anyone else. It could sometimes be quite lonely, but now it enabled him to get on with the job in hand.

He unwrapped the beef and avoided the considerable tempta-tion to cut some off for his dinner. He removed the watery paste from the bottle that was in the package that Basil had given him at the airport on Monday morning. And then he set to work inserting it into the joint of beef, using a sharp knife to create cuts deep in the joint, applying some of the paste in there and then repeating it elsewhere. It took him longer than he expected and he kept stopping to wash his hands, terrified some of the poison may remain.

When he finished, he wrapped the joint up carefully and covered it in ice he'd bought on the way home.

–

At seven-thirty on the Friday morning Harald Mettler walked to a coin box on Budapester Strasse and telephoned Vorgesetzter Metzgerei. He'd checked the previous day and this was the time they opened.

As far as I know, the meat is usually delivered later in the morning, just before lunchtime. I was there once when it was delivered, and she insisted on showing it to me, so I'd appreciate how good it was.

'Good morning: this is Hauptsturmführer Karl Muller from Brigadeführer Konrad Busch's office in Prinz-Albrecht-Strasse. The Brigadeführer has asked me to call because unfortunately Frau Busch has had to leave Berlin on a private matter and they will no longer be requiring their normal delivery today. I beg your pardon? Monday? Yes, please make the normal delivery on Monday, of course. Heil Hitler!'

His next call was to the embassy: he was dreadfully sick, he feared he must have eaten something. He was so sorry he wouldn't be in today.

On his way back to the apartment he stopped at a clothes shop and bought some overalls, an apron and a cloth cap with a wide brim. It was as close to a butcher's boy's outfit as he could manage.

She always has her hair done on a Friday morning, at around ten-thirty at a salon on Hubertusbader Strasse.

At ten-thirty Harald Mettler arrived in Schmargendorf. He was dressed in a suit and was carrying a small holdall. In a cubicle in the public toilets on Elster Platz he changed from his suit into the overalls, apron and cloth cap, putting the others back in the bag. He removed the beef from the case too, making sure the Vorgesetzter Metzgerei packaging was in place.

The toilets were as deserted when he left the cubicle as when he entered it. It was a nervous five-minute walk from there to the

Busch's house on Beyme Strasse. No one seemed to pay him any attention. It was something he'd noticed about people in Berlin, they avoided looking too obviously at others.

In the Busch's driveway he hid the holdall behind a large shrub and went to the back entrance. The woman who answered the door said he was late and was he new and Harald grunted that he was and she said that must be why and thank you very much.

Minutes later he was back in the cubicle in the toilets on Elster Platz and ten minutes later was on a tram back to the centre.

He was exhausted and only now did the enormity of what he'd done and the danger he'd been in – and was still in – hit home. He found himself shaking uncontrollably. When he closed the door of his apartment he burst into tears and then staggered into the bathroom where he was violently sick. He knew he had to dispose of the overalls and the apron and the cap and the suitcase too, but that would have to wait.

For now, he wasn't leaving the apartment.

–

Konrad Busch stared at his wife in utter shock.

Hannelore Busch had indeed turned pale, as white as the expensive table cloth they were eating on. She was sitting very still, her hands gripping the edge of the table, her eyes glazed over as if she wasn't there. Then her body arched up and she vomited blood all over the table, so violently that some of it sprayed him and when he tried to leap up to get out of the way he realised his legs weren't working.

It was as if he was strapped to the chair.

When he called out for help, no sound came from his mouth.

Now he felt bitterly cold and could feel his body trembling. In front of him Hannelore continued to vomit blood before collapsing onto the table.

He started coughing violently and noticed he was bringing up blood and for the next few, agonising minutes, the final ones of his life, he thought something wasn't quite right and his last conscious thought was that he hoped it was nothing to do with the beef.

Chapter 21

Geneva and Berne
January 1944

Barney Allen was in a particularly good mood on the afternoon of Thursday 13 January. He'd lunched at a very good brasserie he'd discovered on Rue du Prieure where they served a superb veal pan-fried in butter and excellent rosti. He'd had a very agreeable Swiss pinot noir and realised that any reservations he'd had about Swiss wine were misplaced: he even begun to toy with the idea of importing it after the war. He'd always fancied the idea of being a wine merchant. He found it hard to think of a job that would be less stressful and more satisfying.

After lunch he permitted himself the indulgence of a long walk on the Quai du Mont-Blanc and although he knew he really ought to get back to work he nonetheless stopped at a café overlooking Lac Léman where he drank strong coffee and a small Armagnac and allowed himself to reflect on the past few days.

He had to admit things had gone really rather well and even though he'd been brought up to eschew being too full of oneself, he did think he'd handled a series of tricky matters in a very sure manner.

London had said as much. Piers Devereaux had most been effusive in his praise.

The operation in Lyon was going splendidly and getting his three agents in there and beginning to produce first-class intelligence was something to be proud of. The news just after Christmas that the SS officer who Sophia knew so well was being transferred to Lyon had been a serious concern, but he'd handled the matter expertly. Sophia had played her part too, as she always did. She'd provided excellent background information on Busch and then he'd travelled to Berne to seek Basil's assistance.

Basil had been in something of a flap. He did have a very good chap in Berlin, he said, in fact he'd recruited him a number of years ago, but these days he was handled by Noel and Noel was out of town, tied up in Luzern where he was trying to sort out two escaped RAF pilots.

But he'd insisted that Basil contact this agent – his name was Harald Mettler – and as luck would have it, he turned up in Berne on New Year's Eve and the next day they'd met with him.

Barney was very impressed with Mettler. They'd got on well. He didn't shirk at the mission he was asked to undertake, as perilous as it was. He was, Barney thought, terribly practical – the type of chap he liked.

In fairness to Basil, he had managed to get his hands on the poison on the Sunday through a Jewish refugee in Basel, a professor of chemistry from Frankfurt who'd not asked too many questions but clearly knew what it was all about and seemed to relish the task.

And he'd persuaded Basil to move his radio-man from Berne to Geneva. A bit of gentle persuasion from London helped, it had to be said. He'd moved Lawrence into Siegfried's apartment, next door to his on Rue François-Bonivard, and it certainly made communications with Jack in Lyon considerably easier.

And then the news this morning: Harald had left the Swiss Embassy on the Tuesday afternoon and travelled across Berlin to Schmargendorf, which Barney felt was rather taking a risk but then they had prevailed upon him to find out what had happened to Konrad Busch and his wife.

The message had come in code in a letter Harald sent ostensibly to his tailor in the diplomatic bag on the Wednesday.

Area around the Busch house on Beyme Strasse cordoned off: police guard at front of house. Did not approach. Vorgesetzter Metzgerei on

Hohenzollerndamm closed: police guard outside. Asked in bakery on Hubertusbader Strasse why Beyme Strasse closed and woman said a couple had died tragically there on Friday and the police were treating it as suspicious and it was tragic as they had five children. Made donation to collection box.

Barney did worry about Harald wandering around Schmargendorf asking too many questions, but the most important thing was that Konrad Busch wouldn't be going to Lyon.

Or anywhere else, for that matter, other than an overcrowded military cemetery.

Lawrence had already sent the good news through to Lyon.

–

But Barney Allen's very good mood did not last very long. No sooner did he reach the top floor of the apartment building on Rue François-Bonivard than Lawrence appeared in the hallway between the three apartments.

'We have a visitor,' he announced.

The visitor was Noel Moore and Barney was struck immediately by the man's odd demeanour. He'd always regarded Noel as a very solid, reliable type – never someone who, to use Basil's description, was going to open the batting but a solid middle-order type. And one of his characteristics that had always struck Barney was how he was calm and clear about matters.

But he wasn't that afternoon in Geneva.

'I need to talk with you,' he announced, and Barney took him into his flat and told Lawrence he was fine, no need to join them.

There was no small talk, so much so that Noel hadn't yet removed his coat when he began. 'I'm very concerned about matters, Barney; an operation is being conducted behind my back, which is really not on. It must be obvious to you by now that Basil is struggling: he's no longer got the grip on matters that he once had. It's not surprising – I told them that in London in August. He's getting on and the workload here is considerable. That is one of the main reasons why you're out here, after all.

However, it's wrong I'm being kept in the dark. I know you have something going on in France with the three agents, but I don't know what or where. I also suspect something has been going on with Mettler in Berlin, but I'm told nothing – other than to be informed by Basil on Monday that Mettler is off limits for the foreseeable future. It's not on, Barney, it really isn't, it—'

'Hang on, Noel, hang on…' Barney was struck not just by what Noel was saying but also the way he was saying it: he spoke quickly, almost gabbling, his voice was loud and he appeared nervous. Barney poured them both a large Scotch, but Noel waved his away.

'It is essential I know what is going on.'

'But you know as well as I do, Noel, that is not the way these matters work, is it? Our protocol is that only those directly involved in an operation know the details of it, otherwise our security is compromised. It's not that you're not trusted.'

'But what if something happens to Basil?'

'Then you would be told.'

'Or to you?'

'Then I imagine Basil will brief you. But I doubt anything is going to happen to either of us. But why are you so concerned, Noel? You've enough on your plate, surely? You've come all the way from Berne to ask me about an operation when you know I cannot discuss it with you.'

Noel Moore said nothing, sitting slumped on the sofa staring at the carpet and when he did look up, he appeared frightened – that was the only word Barney could think of to describe his appearance – and said maybe he would have that Scotch after all and then he said was there anything – anything at all – which Barney could tell him about the operation, even where it was taking place and who was involved and what was it about?

'But why are you so desperate to know, Noel?'

'I am not desperate!'

'You sound it.'

'Maybe because I feel I'm not trusted. Look, I know Sophia, Jack and Siegfried are involved and I know they're in France and—'

'That is as much as you need to know, Noel. In fact, it's probably a good deal more than you need to know.'

–

Noel Moore left Geneva soon after, his questions unanswered and his mood just as bad as when he'd arrived. Barney waited until he'd left and then went next door to ask Lawrence how he'd found Noel and he said he didn't appear to be his usual self.

But Barney continued to be bothered about the visit: it was the man's nervousness, his persistence with questions he must have known he had no right to ask, the way in which he tried to interrogate him, the almost desperate and even fearful way he came across.

He went out for another walk along the Quai du Mont-Blanc to try and clear his mind but by the time he returned he was still uneasy.

Something wasn't right.

He thought of going to Berne to have a chat with Basil about it, but then Noel would most likely hear of it. When he returned to Rue François-Bonivard he told Lawrence he needed to send an urgent message to Piers Devereaux in London.

–

They met as arranged in the Bernisches Historisches Museum on Helvetia Platz, a place Noel Moore often visited at weekends, when he found it a relaxing and interesting diversion from his everyday life.

Now there was nothing relaxing about the museum.

It was the Saturday morning, two days after what Noel recognised was his unsatisfactory encounter with Barney in Geneva: 'botched' was the word he thought described it best. The plan was to meet in the section on the upper floor where they'd find each other among the fifteenth- and sixteenth-century armour and if that was busy then they'd move to the Ecclesiastic Room on the same floor where there was a collection of stained glass, which Noel always felt could do with a good wipe.

Noel entered the armoury at ten past eleven, as per Nicholas's instructions. He found him staring at a suit of armour for horse and rider and with a brief movement of his head gestured he should follow him. The Ecclesiastical Room was deserted and the two men walked separately past the stained glass until they came to a large, fraying tapestry with no one else within sight.

'You have something to tell me, I sincerely hope, Harold Noel Dickson?'

'There's a major operation underway in France. It's so important that a senior officer from London has been sent over to run it. His name is Barnaby Allen and he's based in an apartment on Rue François-Bonivard, in Geneva. Much to Basil's annoyance, Basil's radio-man has been sent there to work with him.'

Nicholas nodded in a manner to indicate this was interesting, but he clearly wanted to know more.

'So, as you'll gather, it is a major operation.'

'So you said. And where is it?'

'France.'

'You said that too: but France is twice the size of Great Britain. It would be rather helpful to know where in France.'

Noel Moore took a step away from Nicholas and said he wasn't sure, and Nicholas said what in Christ's name did he mean, he wasn't sure?

'I mean, I don't know where in France, but I do know that Barney Allen has sent in three British agents who'd previously worked in Germany. Two of them are German.'

'I don't suppose you have their names, Harold Noel Dickson?'

'As it happens, I do: there's a German woman called Sophia von Naundorf from Berlin. If your contacts in Germany check her out, I think you'll find she's a fugitive, married to a senior

SS officer and fled the Reich last March. The other agent is an American called Jack Miller who worked there as a journalist in Berlin until Pearl Harbour. And the third one is a German actor called Siegfried Schroth. Von Naundorf and Miller met him in Düsseldorf last July when he helped them escape. They brought him back with them.'

Nicholas nodded. This was a bit better, though only a bit.

'Wherever they are in France they'll be using different identities.'

'Oh, will they really?' Nicholas glared at Noel Moore, his voice hissing with fury. 'Do you take me for a complete idiot? I realise that: what I want to know is whether you have any idea of the identities they're using?'

'I'm afraid not, though I am doing my best to find out. But I do have this for you.'

Noel Moore stepped back and walked behind a cabinet displaying ecclesiastical robes. From where they stood, they had a good view of the room, while remaining partially obscured. Noel removed an envelope from inside his jacket and passed it to Nicholas.

'It's a photograph of Siegfried Schroth. I don't have access to ones of either the American or the German woman, though I imagine it will be possible to find pictures of them in Germany? I have this photograph of Schroth because I had to check him out when they brought him back from Germany with them.'

Nicholas opened the envelope and looked at Siegfried's photo, studying it for a while. He thanked Noel and apologised if he'd been a bit short, but he was sure he understood, and Noel said yes, of course he did, and it all does rather get to us, doesn't it?

Nicholas said they'd meet the same time and same place next week and hopefully Noel will have more then, and Noel said of course, although he was surprised that Nicholas was arranging to meet at the same time and in the same place.

That was against all the rules as far as he was concerned. Maybe the other side had different rules.

But he didn't get a chance to say anything as Nicholas was already on his way. He wondered if he should have told him more – about Harald Mettler for instance – but he thought he'd need to keep something up his sleeve.

Nicholas smiled as he left the museum. This was certainly something for him to go on: it was by no means perfect and the Germans would have plenty of questions, but they would have the photograph of this actor from Düsseldorf and he didn't think it would be beyond them to get photos of the other two.

And if his German contacts agreed this was a big enough piece of intelligence then, as they'd promised him, he could be across the border into the Reich within a matter of weeks – possibly by the end of the month. He'd be going to the place he'd only been to once before – seven years ago – but which he'd long regarded as home.

Chapter 22

Lyon
February 1944

André Martin proved to be most elusive, which as far as members of Mars were concerned only helped to prove he was indeed Source Armand, the German's most importance agent inside the French Resistance.

The traitor.

They identified the optician's workshop in La Mulatière easily enough and when they noticed it was advertising for someone to work in their accounts department Madame Madelaine decided Anna Rousseau should apply.

Anna Rousseau started there on Monday 7 February and by the Thursday she'd found André Martin's file, but as far as she could tell there was no sign of him at the workshop. She waited until the following week when she was working on the payroll: she was sitting opposite an elderly man called Pierre who was in charge of the payroll and who'd told her to ask him any questions, he was there to help.

She spent most of the morning asking about various members of staff – where does so and so work… this Gilbert, which department is he in… this one here, can't read the name, where are they? He'd smile sweetly at her and patiently do his best to help and when she asked about André Martin, Pierre said he wasn't sure about him, he used to work full time but was now only around occasionally and when Anna asked what he did he said he was a very skilled technician.

'And so, there is no payment due to him?'

'Not if he's not been working, no: we're not a charity, you know!'

Anna laughed and Pierre said she reminded him of his grand-daughter and Anna said she'd check his file to check the payments for him were up to date.

'The file is more or less empty: it doesn't even have his home address. Do you know where that would be?'

Pierre said he was impressed at how thorough she was and of course the files should be more up to date and if she'd give him a few minutes he'd see what he could find.

Minutes later he came back with another folder: André Martin had lived just round the corner from the workshop but early in January he'd moved; here's the new address.

'He lives on Rue Saint-Jean, behind the Palais de Justice. Date of birth: 4 March 1902. Here, you take this and make sure it goes into his file.'

'I will do: I think I may have seen this André Martin in the reception the other day. He's quite short and fat, isn't he?'

'That would have been someone else, my dear: André Martin is very tall and very thin, walks with a noticeable stoop – but don't we all these days!'

That evening they met to decide what to do with André Martin. Sophia and Siegfried were strongly of the view that he needed to be interrogated: they had to find out what he knew, who his contacts were, who he'd betrayed – everything. Madame Madelaine said that was all well and good and, of course, in an ideal world that is what they'd do but it wasn't as easy as that.

'We'd have to be sure we can capture him without anyone being aware of it and then get him to somewhere safe where we can hold him and be sure of keeping him for as long as it takes to get the information out of him. It's too much of a risk. We have to be clear as to what our priority is, and I have no doubt it is to eliminate André Martin, to stop him providing any more information to the Nazis.'

And then she said the discussion was over and everyone was to listen very carefully. 'Marcel, you will lead a team to identify André Martin: exactly where he lives, what he looks like – we already know some of this from Anna – and what his routine is. Once we have this information Maurice will lead a team to kill Martin. Today is Wednesday the sixteenth, is it not? The assassination must take place early next week, we cannot lose any more time. Michel, your team will be responsible for making sure the area is safe and helping Maurice and his team to get away. Luise and Erhard, you carry on as normal.'

But the following day – the Thursday – was very far from normal at Avenue Berthelot. It was only through a stroke of extraordinary good fortune that it didn't turn out to be a complete disaster, though it wasn't very far short of it.

The stroke of extraordinary good fortune didn't start out like one. Luise Brunner was at her desk in Section 4A when Agnes Kléber came into the office. The clerk on duty in the transmission office was off sick, she announced. She needed someone to cover for him. No one volunteered: the transmission office was in the basement of the building, the noise deafening due to the machinery and the smell awful thanks to an outlet from the sewer system nearby. But when Agnes came over to her desk and said, please, it would only be for one day, Luise agreed.

The job of the clerk in the transmission office was to monitor the incoming communications. These came in through the noisy machines: the telegrams, the telex and the Belino, which was a wirephoto service, capable of transmitting photographs over a telephone line. The clerk had to check all transmissions when they came in and then place them in appropriate trays, the contents of which were then collected by a messenger every half hour and taken to the different offices around the building. If there was a transmission that was marked as urgent then the clerk would telephone the duty office and a messenger would be sent down to collect it immediately.

It was often a struggle to stay alert in the basement office, it was too easy to be distracted by the noise and the smell. For the first two hours Sophia pulled each transmission from its machine, checked who it was for and whether it was urgent and then placed it in the correct tray and was beginning to wonder if anyone would relieve her for a lunch break when Siegfried Schroth appeared in front of her.

He appeared very gradually, as his head and shoulders slowly inched their way out of the Belino machine. She knew it was Siegfried she was staring at, even before the transmission ended, with the words 'Schroth, Siegfried' under the photograph. And no sooner had that come through than the telex clattered into life and what emerged through that shocked her to her core.

MOST URGENT
FROM: Standartenführer Helmut Knochen
REICH CENTRAL SECURITY OFFICE 84
Avenue Foch, PARIS
SUBJECT: ENEMIES OF THE REICH:
WANTED FOR ESPIONAGE
TO: ALL LOCAL GESTAPO OFFICES,
FRANCE

FOR HEAD OF GESTAPO OFFICE ONLY

Acting on information received from source reporting to Gestapo Counter-Espionage Section lV4/D5 Berlin, we inform you of the following URGENT information:

Reliable source reports THREE BRITISH AGENTS CURRENTLY operating within France on an important British espionage operation. Operation believed to be connected with the Resistance. Exact location within France unknown.

Siegfried Schroth (Düsseldorf) – SEE PHOTO-GRAPH

Sophia von Naundorf (Berlin) – NO PHOTO-GRAPH at present

Jack Miller (US or British subject) – NO PHOTO-GRAPH at present

ALL THREE LIKELY TO BE USING AN ALIAS!

'Did you hear me?'

'Pardon?'

'I said, is this all there is?'

It was the messenger, checking the trays to see what documents he had to deliver. She was so shocked at the transmissions she'd just seen and was clutching in her hands that she'd not noticed him coming in.

'Yes, thank you.'

'Shall I take those?'

'Take what?'

'The ones you're holding.'

'No, no – I need to sort them first, but they don't seem urgent.'

As he left she was thankful that the photograph was concealed by the telex. At least the messenger wouldn't have seen she was holding a photograph.

But as consolations went, that was a pretty small one.

She knew she couldn't risk keeping the documents. Trying to smuggle them out of the building would be too dangerous. She waited until someone came down to allow her to take her lunch break and then went into the toilet in the basement: there she tore the photograph and the telex into tiny shreds and dropped them into the sewer.

Then she went to Agnes Kléber's office. Fortunately, all the other staff were on their lunch break.

'You shouldn't come up here, Luise.'

'I know, but it's urgent. We have a very serious problem.'

Rue Saint-Jean runs through the heart of Vieux Lyon, the oldest part of the city, on the left bank of the Saône, and home to the city's cathedral and the Palais de Justice. Like most streets in the area, it is narrow, with the sense of walking through a ravine as a result of the high buildings on each side, the cobbled surface tapering to a narrow drainage gully, which made progress difficult.

Marcel found André Martin on the Friday, the day after the Mars group had met. He wasn't difficult to find: he lived under that name – which surprised Marcel – in a bedsit on the top floor of a building facing the rear of the Palais de Justice. The ground floor was occupied by a large, dusty shop selling silk. When Marcel entered, he got the impression from the owner that business was so bad he only survived by letting out the rooms above the shop.

'I may be interested in renting one: are there any vacant at the moment?'

The owner eagerly showed him round: two bedsits per floor, four floors, two vacant – one on the second floor, one on the fifth. Marcel said the one at the top was exactly what he was looking for. The owner told him without much conviction that it was likely to go soon so if he wanted it he'd need to pay a deposit and a month's rent now and Marcel said that was no problem and handed over the money.

He moved in on the Saturday. That afternoon they waited until André Martin was seen leaving the building and then he took Maurice and three of his team in through the rear entrance.

Marcel's work was done.

From the window in the bedsit Maurice could see into the narrow alley at the rear of the building. At nine o'clock that night he opened the window and a man stepped out from the shadow of a doorway opposite. It was one of Michel's men: as agreed, he walked to the end of the alley, disappeared from view for no more than a minute and then returned. He'd removed his cap, the agreed signal that all was clear.

Maurice knew he had to move now. There were three others in the bedsit with him: Alain remained by the window in case the lookout raised the danger signal. Maurice knocked on the door of André Martin's bedsit. When he opened it, Maurice apologised for disturbing him and explained he'd just moved in opposite and introduced himself and André Martin happily gave his name and Maurice said he realised he had no matches and would it be possible to borrow some, and André Martin said no problem, I have a spare packet.

Emile followed Maurice into the bedsit while Georges took up position on the small landing between the two bedsits.

Maurice was surprised how – he wasn't quite sure of the right word, he explained the next day to Madame Madelaine – how docile he was? Compliant, maybe – unsuspecting? Madame Madelaine had asked him what he meant, and Maurice said if you're living the clandestine life that we do then we all know how every waking moment and most of your sleeping ones your senses are on alert, as if you're expecting something at any moment, but this Martin character he seemed so innocent: maybe unsuspecting was indeed the right word.

André Martin had looked mildly surprised when Emile had appeared in his bedsit and slightly more surprised when both men followed him into the main room and he only began to react when Emile grabbed him from behind and Maurice produced his knife and by then of course it was far too late. The fact that he was so tall made it difficult for Emile to hold him and this meant that rather than cutting his throat and having it all quickly over and done, Maurice first had to stab him in the stomach, which was not only messy – very messy, actually – but also meant André cried out and although much of the sound was muffled by Emile's hand over his mouth, it was still something they could have done without.

It did have the desired effect though of Martin doubling up and then Maurice was able to stab him in his back – three times, once in the neck and twice through the ribs and when he was finished, he and Emile dragged the body over to the bed and managed to get it under the covers and although André Martin didn't exactly look peaceful and at rest, it somehow felt better than someone finding him on the floor covered in his blood.

They sent the message to Michel's lookouts that the deed had been done.

They'd agreed it would be too risky for them to leave the building during curfew, so they waited until early on the Monday morning: Emile and Alain left first, Georges and Maurice a few minutes later.

Both pairs made the same journey: out of the rear of the building, into Rue Saint-Jean and then through an innocuous-appearing doorway at number fifty-four which took them into La Longue Traboule, the longest in Vieux Lyon. They hurried through the *traboule*, through four buildings, down a spiral stair-case, across five courtyards before emerging in Rue de Boeuf.

Opposite the exit stood a man and a woman, two of Michel's lookouts. Both had their coats over their arms.

It was safe to continue.

–

There was no sense at all that matters had been sorted or that they could feel any sense of satisfaction or even achievement.

Sophia felt that the killing of André Martin had been a wasted opportunity. Surely, she asked, he could have been questioned – even for a few minutes before they killed him.

'You mean torture him, do you?' asked Maurice.

'Well, ask him a few questions at least – if he thought his life was at stake, he may have revealed something, like his contacts – that kind of thing.'

Maurice shook his head and told her that information gained through torture is rarely reliable and, in any case, it's a noisy business. 'Any noise could have led to us all being caught.'

Madame Madelaine said there was nothing more to discuss: what mattered was that Source Armand was dead. They should continue their operation and see what further intelligence they could gather at Avenue Berthelot.

And that was when Sophia and Agnes told her about the telex and photograph that had been sent by Gestapo headquarters. The news was received in complete silence, although it was notable that the breathing in the room became heavier and the atmosphere more charged.

Marcel, Maurice and Michel looked in shock at Madame Madelaine who remained impassive. Even in the gloom of the basement, Jack and Siegfried looked pale.

'That was when, did you say – last Thursday?'

'Yes, madame, and it's Monday today so five days ago. I destroyed the photograph.'

'So you said, but that doesn't mean we can relax.'

'I realise that, Madame Madelaine,' said Agnes. 'The way Gestapo HQ operates is to re-send alerts like this every two days for perhaps a week. Fortunately, the clerk was also sick on the Friday, so I placed Luise there. And today too. I understand he may return tomorrow, but I can move him elsewhere and do my best to keep Luise there. There was another transmission today.'

'Yes, of the photograph and the telex,' said Sophia. 'What concerns me are two things: firstly, that sooner or later one of these documents may find their way into the system – maybe overnight or at a weekend or someone speaking to someone in Paris on the phone. And secondly, the telex makes it clear that they have no photographs of either Jack or I "at present". But they're bound to find them sooner or later. With the records they'll have in Berlin… it's only a matter of time, though I do know that when the section I work in here requests a photograph from the files in Germany it can take two or three weeks – and we could be lucky: some records have been destroyed in the bombing.'

Madame Madelaine said she needed a moment or two to think and the others watched her in respectful silence.

'There was a reference in the telex to another part of the Gestapo?'

'The counter-espionage section. They have a fearsome reputation.'

'We must continue to watch the transmissions for at least another week. And—'

'Shouldn't we pull Luise and Erhard out? What if the photographs come through when Luise isn't on duty? They'll be sitting ducks!'

Madame Madelaine nodded at Agnes and said that was true, but her instinct was that the two of them suddenly disappearing would be a guaranteed way of putting them under suspicion and where would they go?

'There's a limit to how long we could hide the two of you. And remember, the Germans would have your photographs: they'd know exactly who they're looking for. It would put the whole group at risk. But we'll need to see what your Englishman in Geneva thinks. Jack, you will do that tomorrow.'

–

That was the Monday night. Sophia and Siegfried discussed it later at Avenue de Saxe and they agreed that they were damned if they did and damned if they didn't. They would just have to be on the alert for their photographs coming through.

They walked separately to work the following morning and entered Avenue Berthelot five minutes apart.

Neither of them could imagine how much worse matters were going to get.

And how quickly.

Chapter 23

London, Geneva and Berne
February 1944

They came for Stephen Summers shortly after half past seven on a chilly Wednesday morning, the 2 February.

Marjorie Summers was making breakfast and even though he'd told his wife he was running late and really needed to be leaving for work, Stephen Summers had been ordered to ensure all three of their children were up and dressed.

When the doorbell of their pleasant suburban home in south London rang, he assumed it was the postman and didn't listen as his oldest son opened the door. He was in the doorway of the kitchen when his son appeared in the hallway.

'Some policemen are here to see you, Daddy.' The boy looked excited.

Behind him were two men in plain clothes and behind them the hall gradually filled with policemen in uniform. Stephen Summers blinked in shock as one of the two men in civilian clothes announced he was under arrest under Section 1 of the Treason Act. He would be handcuffed and the house searched, he was told.

He was driven to Canon Row police station in Westminster, a journey which was long enough for him to gather his thoughts.

Despite assuring Marjorie before he was taken away that he had no idea whatsoever what this was all about and he was sure it was an unfortunate misunderstanding, he knew full well what it was all about.

And it was no misunderstanding.

He'd been expecting an outcome like this since foolishly becoming involved with that chap Nicholas and his far-right lot some ten years previously. It had started with a single act of utter madness on his part: an indiscretion with a young man no more than sixteen years of age in a public lavatory, the boy had run off and emerged a minute or so later with his friend and this friend turned out to be Nicholas and Nicholas said they could either let justice take its unpleasant course through the police and the courts, or Mr Summers could co-operate.

'Co-operate' turned out to mean doing all of the legal dirty work for Nicholas and his lot. He'd been blackmailed and there was nothing he could do about it. A few months later he worked out he'd been set up by Nicholas. The boy had encouraged him and then he realised where he'd seen Nicholas before, at a meeting of a patriotic discussion group, as it liked to call itself.

Nicholas had had his eyes on him.

Fortunately, Nicholas was smart enough not to get Stephen Summers to do anything illegal, as such. Certainly, some of his requests required him to operate in what may be termed the grey area of the law, but most of it was family law, conveyance, certifications for banks.

And as time moved on and he began to feel increasingly trapped in his work for Nicholas, he made a decision. When he was caught – he knew he'd be extremely lucky if that never happened – then he'd co-operate from the outset.

He'd tell them everything.

And he'd give them everything.

–

He was strip searched at Canon Row, which was quite the most humiliating experience of his life, not least because it was witnessed by half a dozen police officers. He was then given some shabby clothes to wear, the trousers too big and with no belt.

He was led into a room in the basement, dark around its sides, the table in the centre brightly lit. And there he was interviewed by two men, with a third sitting against the wall, barely visible in the dark.

Stephen Summers assured them he didn't need a solicitor.

He'd represent himself.

One of the officers – he had a Scottish accent and introduced himself as a Superintendent something or other – laid out the charge: that on or about the 28 December last year he had conspired with Jeffrey Morgan and others to illegally and fraudulently obtain papers for the aforementioned Jeffrey Morgan, knowing him to be a fugitive from justice and…

It became something of a blur after this. They mentioned the National Socialist League and it being a proscribed organisation and his membership and involvement in it and at that point he knew the game was up.

He waited until Superintendent something or other had finished and then said he was guilty as charged and had been anticipating this, so much so that if they cared to visit his office in Clerkenwell, which he had no doubt they intended to do, then in a safe concealed in the basement – he'd give them the combination code – they'd find half a dozen folders with all the paperwork they needed to catch a good number of associates of Mr Morgan and there was also a letter in the safe addressed 'to whom it may concern', setting out in some detail his activities over the years.

Stephen Summers leaned back and while he didn't exactly smile, he was pleased with how he'd handled matters. He knew he'd be sentenced to a few years in prison, which would be most unpleasant, and he'd lose his job and most probably his family, but he was sure he'd done enough to escape the hangman's noose.

–

Piers Devereux was surprised to hear back from Maguire so soon. Just the previous week he'd asked their security man to check out

Noel Moore. 'He's on the Foreign Office books but is one of our chaps in Berne... works with Basil. Barney's just wondering if there's anything about him...'

Maguire had asked what he meant by 'anything about him' and Devereux said he wasn't sure, but Barney had good instincts and was a bit unsettled by him and it wouldn't do any harm to check. A week later Maguire said Noel Moore was fine, nothing questionable on his file, joined the consular section of the Foreign Office in January 1934, posted to Berlin the following year, worked for Foley... glowing reports, et cetera, et cetera...

But a week after that, Maguire turned up in his office just as he was about to leave on a Thursday evening. He said it was urgent.

'It's about Noel Moore, sir, the man you asked me to check out a couple of weeks ago.'

'You said he was fine.'

'He was then but...' Maguire looked a bit uncomfortable and asked if he could sit down and Piers Devereux said of course.

'I dealt with our person in the Personnel Department of the Foreign Office, very reliable lady called Joan Drew. Joan rang me half an hour ago to say that MI5 had been in touch with her to say that yesterday morning they and Special Branch arrested a solicitor called Stephen Summers who was suspected of being involved with the banned far-right group the National Socialist League and of helping that fugitive, Jeffrey Morgan.

'No sooner had this Summers arrived at Canon Row than he confessed to everything. According to MI5, they only had scant evidence against him, but he told them to go to his safe in his office. There they found extensive files that detailed what he'd been up to over the years on behalf of first the British Union of Fascists and the National Socialist League.

'In effect, he'd been acting as a solicitor on their behalf. MI5 contacted Joan because within the files was proof that in November 1933 – just prior to Noel Moore starting work there – Summers had organised his change of name. When he began work there in January 1934, no one was aware that he'd previously been known as Harold Noel Dickson. Had they known that and looked into him, they'd have discovered that Harold Noel Dickson had connections with the British Union of Fascists, which would have meant Moore would most certainly not have obtained clearance to be posted in a job as sensitive as the Passport Control Office in Berlin and subsequently as an intelligence officer.'

'But wasn't that letter on his file in the Foreign Office Personnel Department?'

'It should have been, but it had been removed along with all the paperwork relating to his change of name. Joan says they don't know when, but it would have been well before the prospect of his transfer to Berlin came up.'

'So what do we make of all this, Maguire?'

'I would say it raises very strong concerns about Noel Moore – or Harold Noel Dickson. It seems that Mr Allen's instincts may well have been correct. We need to handle this very carefully. I'd suggest not telling Berne at the moment, but perhaps Mr Allen could investigate further?'

–

Barney Allen was to break every rule in the book.

This was despite Piers Devereux being very clear when he got in touch late that Thursday night.

Serious security concerns now about Noel Moore... otherwise known as Harold Noel Dickson... links with far-right in early/mid 1930s... Proceed with caution... Await further advice but cease contact with Moore until advised accordingly. Basil to remain unaware for time being...

Barney Allen was furious when he heard there were 'serious security concerns about Noel Moore', which was Piers' way of saying he was most likely a traitor and now he was seething, eager to confront him. The fact that his instincts had been vindicated was of little consolation: there was a good chance that his agents in Lyon could be betrayed and that was unimaginable.

He was aware Devereux had said to await further advice and have no contact with Noel Moore, but his view was that Piers hadn't said anywhere this was an instruction and on top of this, Piers was in London, and while he was if not exactly behind enemy lines, then certainly an awful lot closer to them than Piers was.

He decided it was in order for him to use his discretion and judgement. He had, after all, been vindicated where Moore was concerned. He'd suspected something wasn't quite right about him. His instincts had told him as much and now he felt justified in continuing to rely on those same instincts.

It was only when he was on the train to Berne that it occurred to him he may be being a bit too impetuous: perhaps he should at least have told Lawrence where he was going. Or Benoît. But his instinct told him to go and sort Noel Moore out.

–

Barney Allen toyed with the idea of getting in touch with Moore and asking him to pop down to Geneva – perhaps luring him there by saying that on reflection he felt he did owe him a more thorough briefing on the French operation.

But he decided that as Moore had been so edgy when he'd been to see him before that this may just alert him that something was up.

And then he recalled some advice he'd been given in the Great War when a brigadier who'd been at school with his uncle told him about the importance of always being in control of a military action.

Always make sure the battle takes place at a time and place of your choosing: never let the enemy take the initiative. And never underestimate the strategic value of a surprise attack.

The following day he made sure his Webley Mark lV service revolver was cleaned, oiled and in good working order. He went for a long walk through the Old Town, calming himself down and doing his best to ensure that the plan he was formulating in his mind was logical and clear.

He travelled to Berne on the Saturday and stayed at the St Gotthard hotel on Bubenberg-Platz, a more anonymous location than the Altstadt with its grander hotels and busier streets.

Barney Allen found Marzilistrasse on the map and scouted it out on the Sunday. The plan he'd come up with was based on the fact that to get to work Noel Moore would have to walk down Marzilistrasse to cross the river on Dalmazibrücke. He found a spot on Marzilistrasse close to the bridge. He'd wait in an alley until Moore walked past, slip in behind him and with the help of his Webley force him to walk down the alley he'd been hiding in until they reached an empty warehouse.

He'd already found a door on the side of the warehouse that he'd managed to force the lock of and in a small room he had a chair waiting along with lengths of rope to tie up Moore. There he'd interrogate him and find out everything he'd been up to.

He wasn't too sure what he'd do after that, but he knew what was most important was finding out what Moore had told the Germans.

It was a reasonable plan: he'd need to be decisive and also be careful about the revolver – the Swiss weren't used to seeing them waved around on the street – but he was sure as long as Moore knew he had it he'd co-operate.

And above all, he'd chosen the battleground and it would be a surprise attack.

–

Except it wasn't.

At midnight on the Saturday Noel Moore was woken by knocking at his door, which at first he thought was the porch door playing up again, but it continued and when he went to check he saw a figure through the frosted door.

Nicholas shouted through the wind.

Open the bloody door!

It was a brief and urgent conversation, conducted with both men standing in the tight hallway, Noel in his dressing gown and slippers, Nicholas in his overcoat and still wearing his trilby.

'I don't have much time so listen.' He was breathing heavily, sweat glistening on his face despite the cold. 'I got a message this afternoon: they heard from London. Stephen Summers was arrested last week. He was the solicitor who sorted out your change of name back in 1933. Apparently he's confessed to everything and given MI5 evidence of everything he was involved in, including your name change. They'll be on to you.'

'Christ – what do I do?'

'The first thing you need to do is pull yourself together. The one thing in your favour is that we can assume they don't know you know. The question is who they've told over here: Remington-Barber or that Barney Allen in Geneva. I'm told Allen left the city yesterday. My guess is that he's come here to deal with you, Noel – for heaven's sake, man, take a grip! Listen to me: this is what we'll do.'

—

Noel Moore left for work at seven fifteen on the Monday morning. He'd been up all night and with his nerves frayed was having trouble remembering his instructions. Nicholas had told him he was convinced this Barney Allen would approach him somewhere between his home and the British Embassy.

'That's my hunch, but he doesn't know which building you live in, otherwise he'd have come here by now: my guess is he'll find you either just before the bridge or when you're on it.'

'And if… when… he comes up to me…?'

'I've told you: do as he asks, don't make a fuss. Leave it to me.'

Nicholas had told him not to look around, but just to act as normal as possible, which was all very well but as it was his legs were like jelly and he was having trouble remembering a route he took every day, let alone managing to act normally. But it was quiet on Marzilistrasse at that time and none of the few people around looked like Barney Allen and he thought about what would happen if he got to the embassy on Thunstrasse and if Basil knew something and suspected him and if he did what would happen to him and...

'You'll do as I say, Noel, understand?'

Barney Allen had appeared half a step behind him and there was something sticking in his side, into his ribs, and when he looked down to see what it was Allen pulled open his coat so he could see it was a revolver. He then told him they'd be crossing the road and going down that alley and if Harold Noel Dickson had any clever thoughts about running off or something like that then he should know that he'd used a revolver like this before and would have no hesitation in doing so again.

Noel Moore said he understood and crossed the road as instructed and then into the alley, which was narrow, the surface wet and uneven, and he'd managed to look around as they crossed the road and he couldn't see any sign of Nicholas and was beginning to think the whole business was a trap when he became aware of a crumpling noise behind him and when he looked round Barney Allen was in a heap on the floor, his body writhing slowly and Nicholas standing over him, pulling the long blade of a knife from the fallen man's body.

'Don't just stand there: help me get him into this doorway!'

He was heavy to move and clearly still alive. He moaned, softly at first, and then the moans became louder and Noel saw Nicholas look around before plunging the knife once more into his victim, this time into the neck, just below the jaw and for a few seconds Barney's eyes shot open, staring directly at Noel. He looked sad as much as anything else and when he opened his mouth and moved his lips, no words came, just a trickle of frothy blood and Noel stood there in complete shock.

'Move out of the way, you don't need his blood all over you. You need to get a move on now. Go to work and act as normally as you can. Don't look so bloody petrified: everything will be fine now.'

Noel said thank you, thank you very much, and he hoped he didn't mind him asking, but what was going to happen to him because surely London would be on to him and was it really safe to go to the embassy?'

'Go in today: I'll come to your place tonight. In the meantime, I'll make arrangements to get us over the border.'

Chapter 24

All Luise Brunner could do was stagger into the lady's cloakroom and sit in a cubicle for a few minutes in an attempt to regain her composure. The longer she sat there the worse she felt as she breathed heavily, trying to swallow against the tightness in her throat and dabbing the sweat from her brow.

She realised she'd been away from the office for too long, which could be seen as suspicious and things were bad enough without that so she left the cubicle and washed her face in cold water and drank some water, even though it had an unpleasant, metallic taste. She was brushing her hair when someone came alongside her, a woman she recognised from another department whose name she didn't recall, and the woman asked if she was all right and she replied she was fine, thank you very much, and the woman said that was good because she didn't look too well.

'You know what it's like, the time of the month... today's the first day.'

The woman said the first day was always the worst for her too and she swore by these mints, fumbling in her handbag and pressed a packet into Sophia's hand.

And then Luise Brunner steeled herself.

She'd have to return to the office and act normally, despite what she witnessed just a few minutes before being her worse nightmare.

It was ten o'clock on the Tuesday morning and the Croix-Rousse was unusually quiet.

The area could be like that from time to time: normally it was noisy and bustling, full of people moving round, the dark, narrow streets busy with pedestrians and the very occasional vehicle.

But at other times it was as if the area had decided to pause, like an elderly person stopping on a walk, ostensibly to admire the scenery, but really to catch their breath.

These quiet periods in the Croix-Rousse had a tendency to start very suddenly, as if the residents of the area had been alerted by an unheard signal. Some said these were a more recent phenomena, one which they attributed to the German occupation. Certainly, news of a German raid or the sudden setting up of a new police checkpoint would spread through the area with the speed of the wind whipping in from one of the rivers.

The quiet that descended over the Croix-Rousse that Tuesday morning began about ten minutes after Jack Miller left the building that had been his refuge for the past four nights, which was longer than he normally remained in one place. He'd been staying in an attic in the building on Rue Pizay in the south of the Croix-Rousse, more or less where it blended into the rest of the Presqu'île.

Emile had come to collect him just before ten and gave him a quick briefing: they'd enter a *traboule* at the end of the road, emerge into Rue de l'Arbre by which time they'd be well into the 2nd arrondissement, then pick up the *traboule* again as it worked its way south, through Rue Mulet and Rue Neuve before coming out behind the Église Saint-Nizier with its odd mix of Gothic and Renaissance, though ecclesiastical architecture was not at the forefront of Jack Miller's mind that morning.

In truth, Jack wasn't totally confident with Emile: he trusted him, but wasn't sure how careful he was. Emile spoke passable English and this was the main reason why he was more often than not Jack's guide around the area. It meant his briefings were clear, but once on the move he always appeared to be in a hurry and unsure how close he should be to Jack, sometimes alongside him as if they were companions, other times too far ahead.

The previous night – after their meeting – he'd hoped to have a few minutes at least alone with Sophia, but it wasn't to be. She'd been hurried away with Siegfried, and Gilbert had escorted him back to Rue Pizay and had then taken the radio set. It would be waiting for him tomorrow, he said. Ready for his transmission to Geneva.

On Rue Neuve Emile told him to wait in a doorway at the end of a passageway while he checked ahead. Jack knew this was not quite right: the journeys through the *traboules* were always conducted if not at speed, then certainly without stopping, which drew attention. Standing on his own in a doorway didn't feel comfortable.

And then there was the question of his identity: for his journey to Lyon, he'd been Paul Mertens, a Flemish engineer from Turnhout in Belgium. He'd been assured that once in Lyon the Resistance would sort him out with a new, better identity, but that hadn't happened. Madame Madelaine had studied his Belgian *kennkarte* carefully and said she doubted they could do much better, given they couldn't risk giving him a French identity.

'Your French is just not good enough: if you were stopped by a gendarme you'd be found out. Making you Flemish with some knowledge of French was actually rather clever.'

Jack did have another *kennkarte* with him, that of Johann Neumann, a thirty-six-year-old teacher from Bielefeld. Barney had given it to him before he left and said he was only to use it in an emergency. He knew his German was far better than his French and he thought he could use it if he was stopped by a French policeman, but then he'd need a backstory to explain what a German school teacher of military age was doing wandering around Lyon.

That was his plan: the Belgian identity if stopped by a German, the German one if stopped by a French officer.

And if that wasn't enough to worry about, there was the constant concern about the radio transmissions. Lawrence had explained how the main German radio-detecting station in Paris was bound to pick up any unauthorised transmission and be able to triangulate where it was coming from to an accuracy of around ten miles. That was fair enough, ten miles covered the whole of Lyon and the German radio receiver vans would be searching for a needle in a haystack. But that was no reason for complacency: even though they never transmitted from the same location, the Germans were skilled at narrowing down the source of transmissions and were especially good at pinpointing radio sets receiving messages, which was when they were at their most vulnerable.

It was ten minutes before Emile returned and he looked tense. There was a change of plan, he announced: German soldiers were all around Église Saint-Nizier and it would be too risky to come out there. They'd continue into another *traboule* to Rue de la Poulaillerie and then they'd just be one road away from Rue Dubois where the radio set was hidden. This shocked Jack: it was an absolute rule that he wasn't to know the location of the radio set until they got there. The information was too valuable for him to have if he was caught.

But he didn't say anything, hurrying after Emile until they came to the exit on Rue de la Poulaillerie from where they'd walk the short distance on Rue de l'Hôtel de Ville until they reached their destination.

Which was when disaster struck.

It may not have happened had Emile not hurried ahead of him as he crossed the road, causing Jack to quicken his own pace and as he did so, bump into someone who was crossing his path, sending the man sprawling across the pavement, which would not have been so bad if the man hadn't been a gendarme. He hauled himself up and told Jack to come here.

Jack spotted Emile hurrying off.

He was all on his own.

The gendarme brushed himself down and looked angry, doing his best to ignore the smirks of passers-by.

Identity papers.

He reached into the pocket where he kept his German papers. Johann Neumann, a thirty-six-year-old teacher from Bielefeld, smiled and said he was very sorry and the gendarme raised his eyebrows and gave the impression that the last thing he needed was to get involved with a German citizen, even one who'd just knocked him over. He looked as if he was about to send Jack on his way when two German officers appeared by them.

What is the problem?

The officer spoke in French and the gendarme replied that there was no problem of course, sir, he was just checking papers and...

He handed the *kennkarte* to the German.

Where are you from, why are you here, where are you going, do you have any other papers...

Jack did his best. He'd been told his German was more fluent when he imitated a Berlin accent and he obviously did this well enough because the other officer asked him if he was from Berlin and Jack said yes, he was from Wilmersdorf, and the officer said he knew it well, whereabouts? and Jack said Sächsische Strasse, which he knew well enough because he'd lived there, but this wasn't going well because he was speaking far too much and knew they'd suspect something sooner or later.

And what are you doing in Lyon?

He had a story of sorts – how he'd visited Lyon before the war and it was where he'd proposed to his late wife and it held a very special place in his heart and as he had a few days off he felt he'd visit and...

'You're a teacher, yes?'

'I am: in Bielefeld.'

'So how come you have a few days off: the schools are not on holiday in the Reich at the moment?'

He shrugged and said of course, but he'd volunteered to serve the Reich and was soon to join the army and he had a week off and...

Both officers looked unconvinced and that was when the taller one, the one who knew Wilmersdorf, said there was something about him that didn't add up so perhaps it would be best if they took him somewhere where they could sort it all out, because they had better things to do and if he followed them, they had their car around the corner.

'Where is it you're taking me?'

'Avenue Berthelot.'

Luise was still working in the Transmission Office on the Tuesday. It was so noisy and oppressive in the basement that she was allowed a short break every couple of hours. Agnes agreed it would be too risky for her to be replaced by someone else, so she'd hurry up to the courtyard, walk around it for five minutes to get some fresh air.

Her first break that morning was around a quarter to eleven: no sooner had she entered the courtyard than she decided it was too cold to hang around but at that moment a grey army staff car swept into the courtyard turning at speed to stop just past the main entrance.

She watched as an officer got out and opened the rear door and a man climbed out and although Sophia was perhaps fifty metres away and the man had his back to her there was something very familiar about him. She moved closer to the car and as the man followed the officer down the steps he turned to his right and for a couple of seconds she saw his face.

It was Jack, his fair hair blowing in the wind, the features and the smile which she knew so well and which she loved so much and for a fleeting, foolish moment she thought of shouting his name and running over and saying it was fine and he was with her but then Jack was gone, the officer grabbing him roughly by the elbow and pushing him down the steps and it was all Sophia could do to get herself to the cloakroom without collapsing.

Jack had no time to gather his thoughts. He'd somehow imagined he'd be put in a cell and there at least he'd be able to come up with a story that would at least buy him time because this was the one thing that had been impressed upon him throughout his training.

One of the trainers in England had been disarmingly frank: *once you've been caught, you'll be extraordinarily lucky if you get away with it. The most you can hope for is to hold out for long enough to give your comrades sufficient time to escape or cover up their tracks.*

Twenty-four hours was generally regarded as the minimum time a captured agent should try to hold out for and he'd been instructed on how to do that, with a long story with just enough plausible detail for them to at least have to check it out.

But as soon as he was handed over to the Gestapo he was searched and was being asked to explain why he had two *kennkarten*: one for a Belgian citizen named Paul Mertens and another for a German teacher called Johann Neumann.

Jack Miller shrugged and said it was a long story and the Gestapo officer, who looked as if he couldn't believe his luck, said he had all day and if he'd like to follow him, he could begin this long story.

He knew he never stood a chance. He had no idea of the time, other than that it must have been around eleven when he entered Avenue Berthelot. He explained that he was in fact Johann Neumann, the teacher from Bielefeld, and as for the Belgian *kennkarte*, well he had no idea about it because he'd bought this coat in a flea-market only the other day and it must have been left in it and, yes, he had told the other officer that he was from Berlin because that was where he was born, but he'd lived in Bielefeld for many years and…

At that point the Gestapo officer burst out laughing and asked if that really was the best he could do, and Jack could see his point, it was pretty poor. At this rate it would take them minutes rather than hours to break his story.

For the next hour he explained at inordinate length how he was a teacher in Bielefeld, how he'd volunteered for the Wehrmacht and was enjoying a few days before reporting for training, how his dear wife had died of pneumonia the year before and they'd visited Lyon before the war and the city had such happy memories for him.

The Gestapo officer was carefully taking notes and when he paused to ask him more questions, he looked at Jack in an incredulous manner. Jack managed to switch to the one aspect of Bielefeld he did know something about. In his previous life as a sports reporter, he'd covered Arminia Bielefeld so he talked about what a good football team they were, how much he enjoyed visiting the Alm with Hans and Klaus and half a dozen other very good friends and...

At that point the officer said that was enough: it was all clearly nonsense, he said, but it would need to be checked and then they'd want to know who he really was and what he was up to. 'And there's something else you may wish to think about,' the officer said as he prepared to leave. 'I don't believe you're German. You may wish to tell the truth before we get it out of you.'

—

The telex had come through at three o'clock that afternoon. It had been a quiet afternoon in the Transmissions Office and when the machine clattered into life she jumped.

FROM: Knochen, Paris
TO: Barbie, Lyon
DATE: Tuesday, 22 February
STATUS: URGENT
DELIVERY: IMMEDIATE

At your suggestion, I met with your Source Armand in Paris today and made it very clear to him how disappointed we are with his recent reports: I was quite explicit – that we are interested in the quality of intelligence rather than the quantity of it. We have plenty of the latter. We rely on him for the former. He seems to be under the impression that the information he provided last June on Caluire is enough to ensure his long-term liberty. I assured him this is in fact dependent on future intelligence, not intelligence now getting on for a year old, as excellent as it was. He returns to Lyon tomorrow: You are to now take personal control of him. I no longer want him run by that Frenchman.

–

It was six o'clock before Sophia was replaced by the night clerk.

She went straight to Agnes Kléber's office. Fortunately, she was on her own. She kept it brief.

'I thought you'd come down at some stage today?'

'It's been too busy up here. What is it? You look worried.'

'Jack's been arrested. He was brought here at around eleven o'clock this morning by a Wehrmacht officer. I've no idea what's happened to him and I—'

'Try and calm yourself my dear: no one must see you in this state. But I can quite understand why you're so worried. I'll try to find out what—'

'And that's not all.' Sophia moved closer to Agnes. She was trembling. 'A telex came through at three o'clock, from Knochen in Paris for Barbie. It's dreadful news: Source Armand is still alive, Knochen met with him this morning.'

'Good Lord—'

'Two days after we were supposed to have killed him!'

Chapter 25

Berne
February 1944

It was unquestionably the worst day of Basil Remington-Barber's professional life, though the day had begun in much the same way most days did at the British Embassy.

He'd arrived at Thunstrasse later than intended, still feeling slightly the worse for wear and wondering if he could manage an abstemious day or two. His secretary followed him into his office with a long to-do list and as he listened to her, he began to doubt how abstemious he'd be after all.

Much of it was what he'd expect: the overnight telegrams; reports from his officers; meetings in the embassy; a cancelled lunch with the chap from the American Embassy and a message from Lawrence in Geneva to call him urgently.

He groaned: he was forever telling his staff he didn't like the overuse of the word 'urgent'. He assumed, he told them, that any matter they needed to discuss with him was important. But there was a distinction between that and urgent. Urgent was to be used for matters of life and death.

He said he'd call Lawrence in due course and perhaps if he could have a coffee, and his secretary pointed out one was already waiting for him on his desk and he said thank you very much and please could you ask Noel to pop up and see me.

'He isn't in yet, sir.'

'Isn't in? He's always in before me. Tell him I want to see him as soon as he gets in.'

Go to work and act as normally as you can.

It had been all well and good for Nicholas to tell him that, but he was in no fit state to go to work. He'd remained staring at Barney's lifeless and bloody body for longer than he should have done after he'd helped Nicholas haul it into the doorway of an empty building in the alley off Marzilistrasse.

Eventually Nicholas had pushed him out of the door and he headed to work, across the river on Dalmazibrücke and then towards Thunstrasse. But by the time he reached Helvetia Platz he knew he was in no fit state to go into the embassy for a while. He stopped at a small café he sometimes visited on a Saturday where as a treat he'd have some of their wonderful *Zuger Kirschtorte* – a rich, layered cake flavoured with cherry brandy. He'd hoped it would fortify him but instead each mouthful made him feel sick.

They also served a very strong Italian-style coffee, two cups of which did help him. He walked around the area for a bit, trying to calm himself down, concentrating on his breathing, and when he looked at his watch it was ten o'clock and he knew if he didn't get a move on, even Basil in his current state would suspect something.

Once he arrived at the embassy, he was told to go and see Basil who asked him why he was late but didn't bother to wait for an answer.

'Lawrence has been on to me: says it's urgent. Do me a favour will you, Noel? Ring him up and see what he wants; I imagine it's something terribly tedious.'

But when he called Lawrence, something wasn't right: he told him he had no intention of discussing anything on an open line and, in any case, he didn't want to speak with him but with Basil.

Only Basil.

Noel thought about it: this wasn't like Lawrence to be so curt. He could be dour and understated, but not so unfriendly.

It didn't feel right, but then nothing did today.

Basil Remington-Barber took the call just after two o'clock that afternoon. He'd been contacted by Captain Gerber from the central police station in Bern, a man he trusted.

'I don't know if you've heard anything,' he said, insisting as always on speaking in English, which wasn't nearly as good as Basil's German, 'but a body has been found, in an alley off Marzil-istrasse, close to the Dalmazibrücke. It looks like a case of murder: the victim had been stabbed. Several times.'

Basil said he was terribly sorry to hear that and he imagined that Captain Gerber and his colleagues would be kept busy on this and was about to ask what this had to do with him when the policeman said the body was that of a Canadian subject.

'How do you know this?'

'We found his papers on him.'

'Well, I'd have thought this would be a matter for the Canadian Legation. They're perfectly capable of handling this kind of thing. I'm not sure why you're telling me about it?'

Captain Gerber coughed and sounded hesitant when he eventually replied. 'Because… as you know, I am responsible for political matters, and as part of my job I have to be aware of foreign nationals in Switzerland who are working in your field. I believe the man found with Canadian papers this morning may be an associate of yours.'

It had taken a moment or two for Basil to draw the connection and when he did, he felt a sense of profound disbelief.

'I would have thought that if there were a British connection, Captain, this would be a matter for our consular section.'

'His name is Arthur Mallory, Basil. Does that name mean anything to you?'

Basil asked if it would be all right if he called the captain back and, in the meantime, would he mind sitting on this and not raising the matter with anyone else? Gerber said he'd try to do so, but this was a murder. We don't get too many of them in Berne, he said. He could hold it for an hour, two at the most.

When he replaced the receiver Basil felt so cold, he began to tremble violently and felt his throat tighten.

Barney Allen was dead.

Murdered.

How on earth would he explain that to London.

—

By three o'clock Captain Gerber was back on the phone. He really couldn't sit on this very much longer. If this man was in fact connected with the British Embassy in some way he needed to be told. Only then could he intervene and ensure the investigation was handled with a degree of discretion.

Basil replied it would be best all round if this was indeed handled with an enormous amount of discretion. The less publicity the better and in the meantime if all the man's possessions and most especially any documents that were on him could be passed over to him, he'd be terribly grateful.

He then asked his secretary to come through.

'Are you all right, sir? You look rather shaken.'

He asked her to arrange a meeting with the ambassador as soon as possible. 'Ideally now, please: tell his office it's urgent.'

'Talking of urgent, sir, Lawrence has been on again from Geneva: he wishes you to know that he too must speak with you urgently.'

'Tell him I'll call later.'

'He really is most insistent, sir. He asks that you call him on the secure line.'

—

Noel Moore left the embassy at four-thirty that Monday afternoon.

He'd arrived in a bad enough state and the phone conversation with Lawrence, brief as it was, had shaken him even further. And now there was a rumour of a body being found off Marzilistrasse and it may be that of a foreign national.

Somehow, he'd imagined – hoped – the body would remain concealed for a while, at least until he was out of Berne. He'd assumed Nicholas would sort that.

He'd briefly toyed with the idea of going to see Basil and coming up with some story about Nicholas and implicating him in everything, but he knew it was a hopeless idea. Nicholas was too smart for that.

He was damned if he did and certainly damned if he didn't.

He took a long route back to his apartment, avoiding Dalmazibrücke and entering Marzilistrasse from the end furthest away from the alley where Barney Allen had been killed.

I'll come to your place tonight.

He was terrified at the prospect of going to Germany, but even more terrified at the prospect of staying. For the next hour he shuffled round his apartment, picking which items to go in a small suitcase.

At seven-thirty there was a knock at the door and Nicholas was standing in the porch.

'How long before you're ready?'

'I'm ready now, just need my coat and hat on and—'

'What is that case for?'

'To take with me.'

'Only bring what you can carry on your person. Get a move on.'

There was a car waiting for them in a narrow turning off Marzilistrasse. Noel sat in the back, Nicholas in the front next to the driver, a thickset man who spoke in a sharp Bavarian accent.

They were stopped a few times as they headed north, but the papers that the driver showed ensured a smooth passage. They eventually stopped in Rheinfelden, just yards from the border crossing.

They waited in the car until a Swiss police officer came over. The driver passed him a thick envelope, which the man opened, and then he said that seemed to be in order. He said they should follow him on foot.

Two minutes later they'd crossed the border. A German officer told them a car was waiting for them by the road.

'Welcome to the Reich!'

—

The ambassador had taken the news of Barney Allen's death very badly. He was convinced it would reflect badly upon him and above all there'd be all the paperwork and he hoped London didn't have clever ideas about repatriating the body because that was out of the question and Basil told him not to worry because he'd sort everything, though if he could have some assistance from the consular section, it would be appreciated.

There was more to do, phone calls with Captain Gerber, a visit to the morgue, Barney's possessions being discreetly handed over, back to the embassy, a meeting with the consul-general who was actually terribly helpful, and then Basil's secretary – who'd remained at work despite the fact it was now well past eight o'clock – said he really must telephone Lawrence on the secure line.

'I do hope I'm not being out of order, Mr Remington-Barber, sir, but I'm concerned about Mr Allen: I handled a communication between him and Mr Devereux in London on Thursday night in which Mr Devereux very clearly stated that there were security concerns about Noel Moore, this was in response to concerns Mr Allen had raised with Mr Devereux.

'He was told to have no contact with Mr Moore under any circumstances, but he left Geneva on Saturday and I've not heard from him since and I'm worried he may have contacted Mr Moore after all.'

Basil Remington–Barber did think of going to Moore's apartment himself with a couple of security officers from the embassy but decided to ask Captain Gerber.

It was a quarter to nine when he heard back from him.

Noel Moore's apartment was empty. It appeared he'd left it in a hurry, with an open suitcase in the hall. A neighbour said he'd heard him leave less than an hour ago.

Chapter 26

Lyon
February 1944

They met in the cellar below a furniture shop on Place d'Helvétie on the Thursday evening, two days after Jack's arrest and the shocking discovery that Source Armand was alive after all.

Place d'Helvétie was at the very northern end of Avenue de Saxe, easy enough for Sophia and Siegfried to reach by tram after work. It was on the right bank of the Rhône, close to Pont St Clair, which led into the Croix-Rousse. Madame Madelaine had been given the news the previous evening and insisted they needed to be even more cautious for this one, so those attending arrived one by one over a period of two hours.

There were ten of them altogether: Madame Madelaine was joined by Marcel, Maurice, Michel, Agnes and Anna while Emile and Gilbert acted as lookouts. Sophia had been the second person to enter the cellar, Siegfried the last.

When she began to speak, Madame Madelaine's voice was hoarse, in the manner of someone who was exhausted and for whom even speaking was an effort.

'There's a saying – that bad news comes in threes.'

She left it at that for a few moments, leaving Sophia and Siegfried to wonder what the third piece of bad news could possibly be.

'Even before Jack was arrested, the communications with Geneva have been difficult for at least two weeks. Jack felt that the person he was communicating with in Geneva was not as forthcoming as he'd been before. He got the impression Barney wasn't directly involved.'

'Jack didn't mention anything to me?' Sophia looked uneasy.

'And nor should he have done,' said Madame Madelaine. 'I'm told a good radio-man has an innate sense of the person and the mood at the other end, even when communication is in Morse code. He felt it wasn't as it had been when he first starting transmitting.'

'And he was using the safety words?'

'Yes, of course – the agreed safety words from him at the beginning and end of transmission and likewise from Lyon. But this brings me to the third piece of bad news. When Agnes told me the news on Tuesday night, I decided to send Anna to the border. Anna, please...'

'I travelled yesterday morning to the farmhouse near the village of Échallon and luckily found the guide who was able to get a message to Benoît. He came to the farmhouse last night. I'm afraid that Barney Allen was killed in Berne just over two weeks ago, around the seventh of February. Benoît is running matters from Geneva as best he can with the help of the radio operator. He says he knows very little about what happened to Barney because the British in Berne won't tell him, but he thinks it is something to do with a traitor who's now escaped to Germany.'

Sophia and Siegfried both gasped in shock.

'Do we know who this traitor is?' asked Siegfried.

Anna shook her head. 'Benoît thinks it could be someone British, but he isn't sure. I explained the developments here to him as Madame Madelaine instructed me and he said we should continue with our operation at Avenue Berthelot. The priority remains finding Source Armand. If we discover who he is then we should send a messenger to the border with the news.'

'There we are then,' said Madame Madelaine, her voice still hoarse but now sounding more matter-of-fact. 'I told you it was more bad news. But for the time being, you remain at Avenue Berthelot. I cannot understand how we managed to identify the wrong person as Source Armand, but this is no time for a dispute over it. Our priority now is to find him and—'

'Our priority now surely is to rescue Jack,' said Sophia, her voice angry.

'Of course.'

They didn't lay a finger on Jack Miller until much later that Tuesday evening. Up until then the questioning had been nothing like he'd expected – and feared: it was long and very repetitive but he got the impression they were merely warming up.

He felt nervous, of course, and frightened too, but most of all he was angry with the British. Whereas on his previous clandestine mission into Germany he'd been well prepared with a solid identity and a good back story, now he felt that it was all rather second rate, a bodged job, as the English would call it. He'd always thought of British Intelligence as being like a Rolls-Royce car: unequalled and highly reliable. Now it felt like his father's car when they were young and never sure it would complete the journey. They'd managed to send him in with a Belgian *kennkarte* when he obviously wasn't Belgian, and the Johann Neumann back story wasn't good enough. In fact, there wasn't one. What he told them he'd had to make up himself.

They'd given him some boiled potatoes and carrots on a dirty metal plate and a mug of thin soup with a slice of stale bread and as soon as he'd finished that another officer came into the room and questioned him for a while, mainly going over questions he'd already been asked in the morning and then there was a knock at the door and a nervous-looking young Wehrmacht corporal entered and said he'd been sent for, and the officer introduced him to Jack Miller and said this is Jurgen and I'm told he's from Bielefeld – 'Is that correct, Jurgen?' – and Jurgen said, yes, that was correct.

'Jurgen and you can now reminisce about your home town!'

And Jack knew the game really was up now, though he did make something of an effort. Young Jurgen asked him a series of questions – the names of parks… and cinemas, where different shops were, which road came off this road and then where did that road lead to and which school did he teach at and where did he live?

After ten minutes Jurgen turned to the officer and shook his head and said wherever this man was from it certainly wasn't Bielefeld and, in any case, he didn't even have the right accent, and the officer thanked Jurgen and said he could go now and he then told Jack to stand up and he waited until the guard had handcuffed his hands behind his back before he was pushed roughly against the wall.

The first punch winded him badly and as doubled over he felt a heavy blow to his head which must have knocked him out briefly because when he came round, he was on the floor and that was when the officer kicked him in the face and he felt his nose crumple and a tooth break. He was hauled back to his feet and shackled to the wall and the officer told him he'd be given a bit longer to think about matters and decide when he was going to tell them the truth, because he should remember this: what had just happened to him was nothing compared to what would happen to him when he went to Fort Montluc.

–

Sophia had found working in the same building where Jack was being held prisoner to be almost unbearable. She remained in the Transmissions Office for the rest of that week and she was now glad at being on her own in the dark, noisy basement where the only visitor apart from Agnes was the messenger and, in the gloom, he couldn't see her tears or sense her distress.

Agnes promised she'd do her best to try and find out what was happening to Jack, but they both knew she needed to be careful. The best chance of finding out would be through the Prisoner

Transfer Forms, which were sent to her office to be processed every morning.

There was nothing on them on the Wednesday morning, which meant Jack was still in the dungeons at Avenue Berthelot, but on the Thursday morning his name – Johann Neumann followed by a question mark – was shown as being one of three prisoners transferred to Fort Montluc on the Wednesday evening.

She told Luise Brunner on the Thursday afternoon, not long before the meeting on Place d'Helvétie. She took the news surprisingly calmly, falling silent and nodding her head as if she was expecting it and then asking Agnes to help her persuade Madame Madelaine that they must make freeing Jack from Fort Montluc an absolute priority.

The only good news that week was that by the time Luise finished work on the Friday evening there'd been no further communications about them from Paris since the Wednesday morning. Agnes said this all made sense: it didn't mean they'd been forgotten about, but the immediate danger was over.

On the Saturday morning Sophia and Siegfried met in his tiny apartment on Avenue de Saxe. They both agreed it was up to them to devise a plan to free Jack from Fort Montluc.

'For Madame Madelaine, the priority is to discover the identity of Source Armand,' said Sophia. 'I understand that: she blames us for the death of André Martin. Jack is less of a priority for her: we know that Emile saw him arrested and that within minutes the radio was moved and the safe houses Jack was aware of were closed down. He knows very little if anything about the real identities of the Mars network, so they're not in immediate danger.'

'Whereas we are.'

'Exactly, Siegfried: we need to rescue Jack before it's too late. He could break down under torture or even be killed and Agnes said some of the prisoners are sent to concentration camps, hundreds of miles from here.'

They talked for hours, but no idea they came up with amounted to anything approaching a plan. It seemed hopeless.

Fort Montluc was a fortress, its high walls impenetrable and well-guarded.

Then Siegfried said, hang on… maybe he did have an idea after all and insisted Sophia listen carefully and when he'd finished, she sat silently, trying hard to think of a reason to dismiss it out of hand, which she clearly couldn't.

'It may work,' she said eventually.

'Of course, if you can think of something better then I—'

'No, no – I admit it's a clever idea, Siegfried.'

They discussed the plan with Madame Madelaine on the Sunday. Her reaction was similar to that of Sophia: she tried to find flaws in it but had to admit it was a good one.

'Your role in this, Luise, what you're being asked to do – you realise how dangerous that is, don't you?'

'Of course.'

'If we pull this off, you'll both have to disappear. You'll need to go into hiding with Jack until we can smuggle you across the border, which means we no longer have the two of you inside Avenue Berthelot to find out who Source Armand is. So, what I ask is this: please wait one more week – you'll need that long anyway to prepare the rescue, won't you? One more week to try and find who Source Armand is and then I'll ensure my network does all it can to make the rescue succeed.'

'But a week… Jack could be killed in that time, or sent to a camp?'

'I have news on Jack,' she said quietly. 'I was about to tell you. Gilbert's brother, Gilles, sometimes does work for us so is trusted, absolutely. There is a seventeen-year-old boy who lives on his road who was arrested for throwing manure at a German soldier – foolish boy, he was lucky not to be shot. They kept him in Montluc for a month, roughed him up and then realised he was nothing more than a hooligan, as they saw it. He was released yesterday, a bit shaken, but regards himself as a hero. Gilles saw him last night and the boy remembered that a foreign prisoner was brought in a couple of days ago from Berthelot. He said someone in his cell talked about the prisoner being an Englishman. They said he was a spy flown in by Mr Churchill. He said he'd heard Barbie himself was supervising his interrogation.'

Chapter 27

Lyon
February and March 1944

Fort Montluc was in Lyon's 3rd arrondissement, just off Cours Gambetta on the right bank of the Rhône. It had begun its long existence as part of the fortifications of Lyon before becoming a military prison. Its 122 four-metre square cells were spread across two wings and the Vichy authorities probably assumed they were being ruthless by forcing up to three prisoners into each cell. But when the Gestapo took over the prison in February 1943, they clearly saw that as an indulgence. By early 1944 there were as many as 850 prisoners – women and men – crammed into Fort Montluc.

Jack Miller had been taken to Fort Montluc from Avenue Berthelot late on what he assumed was the Wednesday afternoon, the day after his arrest. By then he was beginning to get confused and unwell: his mouth hurt from where he'd been kicked and his nose was painful and throbbing. He was hungry and above all thirsty but at the same time quite nauseous.

This wasn't the first time he'd been a prisoner of the Gestapo. He'd been arrested by them in Dortmund the previous April and although he remembered the all-consuming fear and the utter terror – feelings which had never fully left him and which often returned in his sleep – somehow now it felt worse. At least then he felt he had a better cover story. And he was soon rescued from the prison by one of his former agents, a doctor in the Dortmund prison infirmary.

But now his predicament appeared hopeless from the outset. The chances of him being rescued were remote and in any case, he had mixed feelings about any rescue attempt because it was bound to involve Sophia in some way and the thought of her being put in even more danger made him feel worse. The hope of somehow surviving this and the life together they'd promised each other was the one thing that kept him going. Her liberty being jeopardised even more was too terrible to think about.

He hardly slept on the Tuesday night in his dungeon in Avenue Berthelot and when he did drop off, he was soon woken by a guard who'd come in to check him. The following morning, he was taken back to the interrogation room. It was the same Gestapo officer from the previous day, the one who'd beaten him up so badly.

'Have you had time to reflect on your situation?'

Jack winced as he held the mug of lukewarm tea to his lips. His mouth felt as if it was full of shards of glass. He shook his head.

'Allow me to be clearer. You say you are Johann Neumann from Bielefeld. We know you are not. We don't believe you're German. Or French, or Belgian for that matter. So, my question is this: are you going to tell us who you are and what you are doing in Lyon?'

Jack repeated that he was Johann Neumann from Bielefeld and… and his voice trailed off and he asked him to repeat the question but the Gestapo man shook his head and called him an idiot and said he didn't know if he'd heard of Herr Barbie who was in charge of the Gestapo in Lyon, but now he was going to have the pleasure of meeting him and he'd soon bitterly regret being so difficult.

Barbie had turned up much later that morning – a guard had explained to Jack that he was delayed, sounding almost apologetic, in case the prisoner may be inconvenienced by the delay.

When Barbie did arrive, he was younger and shorter than Jack had imagined, business-like, as if he were a doctor in a hurry because he had a long list of patients to deal with. He removed his jacket, which he handed to an assistant, and rolled up his sleeves and then asked Jack who he really was because his story so far was total nonsense.

Jack repeated his story. Barbie sighed impatiently.

'Look: we know you're neither German nor French, which makes us convinced you are a British agent. Assuming that is indeed the case, let me say this: people in your predicament believe that if they confess, they will be horribly tortured and then dragged into a courtyard and shot against a wall.'

He stopped and leant back in his chair and studied the prisoner in front of him carefully. Jack did his best to remain impassive, but actually Barbie had described his feelings quite well and he felt himself shaking. The nausea swept all over him and he felt it rise into his mouth.

'I'm correct, eh? But let me disabuse you of this. The sooner you co-operate and the more you tell us, the less likely we are to treat you in the manner I've just described. You'll be surprised at how many British agents are being held in prison camps in the Reich: I'm not saying they lead a life of luxury, but they're alive. All you need to do is co-operate: I appreciate that what you would see as betraying your comrades may be an anathema to you, but it is your opportunity to remain alive.'

Jack realised he'd been biting his tongue so hard that blood was dripping from his mouth and when he spotted Barbie looking confused, he let his head drop and he drooled and began muttering before slumping in his chair and he didn't react when the German slapped him hard across the face. They brought a medic in who said the prisoner was fine and the next thing he knew a bucket of cold water was thrown over him and he was shackled to the wall once more and at that stage he decided to talk.

Most of it was gibberish, a stream of nonsense peppered with bouts of violent coughing and hyper-ventilating but there were enough facts to keep Barbie interested: addresses where he'd been hiding because he knew Mars would have abandoned them by now and he recounted a long story about a man called Claude who he met in the middle of the Pont de la Guillotière every Monday, Wednesday and Friday at eleven thirty-five precisely in the morning and, yes, of course he could describe him – which he did, at length. In his training he'd been told that in such circumstances you should have in mind someone you knew well so Jack's description of 'Claude' was in fact of his former maths teacher, an overweight, unpleasant man with a penchant for sadistic violence against his pupils.

This lasted for what must have been an hour, interspersed with beatings, but he could tell Barbie's interest had been stirred. And then he decided to tell them about the radio because he thought that by now the network were bound to have got rid of it.

It was a Type Three Mark Two B Two he said. And from somewhere in his memory, he remembered the tedious stuff Lawrence had told him about the tubes whatever they were having thirty watts of power and the heterodyne set, though how he'd managed to recall that he had no idea, but at least now Barbie looked almost impressed and said very well, they were getting somewhere, but it was late now and we've a lot more work to do.

'By which I mean, work on you!' Barbie laughed and said that would happen at a place where they were better equipped for that.

'Tonight, you'll be taken to Fort Montluc.'

–

It was on the Sunday – the 27 February – that Madame Madelaine had agreed to support the attempt to rescue Jack from Fort Montluc, on the condition that Sophia and Siegfried spent the following week trying to find out the true identity of Source Armand.

The rescue, they agreed, would be attempted the following Sunday, 5 March. They had one week to plan it. Madame

Madelaine said Siegfried's plan was a good one and she'd contact a chemist she knew and try to obtain what they were after.

Luise Brunner left it until the Monday afternoon before approaching Franz Boehm. *How are you, Franz, you look like you could do with a few days off?*

Boehm replied that he was tired and then corrected himself and said not that it was a problem, of course, it was all in the service of the Reich and Luise said of course, but certainly he looked like he could do with a break, and he said he had actually applied for home leave but he didn't rate his chances of getting back to Saxony too highly and Luise said how unfortunate that was and how he must miss his family and Boehm said yes, and his dog, of course.

'Maybe if you were to take me to dinner, Franz?'

'Really, Luise?'

'I regret that our dinner on Christmas Eve ended in the way it did: I feel responsible in some way, I should have perhaps dissuaded you from drinking so much, but then I felt it was Christmas Eve, that you work so hard and you must miss your family. Perhaps we could start afresh?'

Franz Boehm looked like a child who'd discovered a hidden stash of sweets, his eyes wide open and a broad smile creasing his ample face.

It would be a pleasure, he said, a pleasure and an honour and he'd be delighted and Fraulein Brunner would of course be his guest. 'Perhaps this coming Friday, Luise?'

She said of course, but she'd prefer Saturday night, she was so tired on a Friday and… she paused and leaned forward, close to Boehm, looking round to ensure no one was listening. 'Perhaps if it were on Saturday night, I'd be able to stay at your apartment?'

They had talked about this and Madame Madelaine worried it may sound too forward, not the way a proper young lady from Berlin would behave, but Luise said she doubted Boehm would argue about it and in any case, being from Berlin made such behaviour more likely.

So, she did her best to look suitably coy while Boehm managed to look at once shocked and thrilled. He was no longer a boy who'd discovered a stash of sweets, he'd now discovered a whole, hidden sweetshop.

–

Franz Boehm had booked a table at Café Neuf on Place Bellecour. He couldn't have been more attentive to Fraulein Brunner while at the same time clearly nervous and struggling to contain his excitement. She was worried at how little he drank during the meal, which was not the plan, but he was clearly mindful of his excesses on Christmas Eve.

At ten o'clock they left the restaurant and walked across Place Bellecour towards Rue du Plat where Boehm lived. She linked her arm through his and walked close to him and told him what a fine man he was, a true son of the Reich, and above all a gentleman and a very attractive one at that and Boehm could barely contain himself, making quiet animal-like whimpering sounds. He did mention something about wanting Fraulein Brunner – Luise – not to feel uncomfortable and if she wished to return to her own apartment, he'd quite— but she cut him short and said she was very comfortable.

She was most looking forward to spending more time with him.

To getting to know him better.

Once inside his apartment Sophia produced the bottle of Asbach Uralt from her bag. A token of appreciation, she told him, and one she'd been saving for a special occasion and he said it was quite unnecessary, her very presence in his apartment was appreciation enough, and why don't you come and sit next to me on the sofa here, patting the space next to him.

'Perhaps if we could have a drink first, Franz? It would make me more relaxed.'

Boehm opened the bottle of German brandy, his hands shaking.

The chemist had assured them he'd mixed enough chloral hydrate in the brandy to send a man to sleep for around twelve hours after he'd drunk three reasonable measures.

There'd been a discussion about how Sophia could avoid drinking it and incapacitating herself while at the same time encouraging Boehm to drink more. The solution was a large sponge concealed in her handbag.

She was pleased to see he'd poured himself a large measure and her a smaller one and when they said 'prost!' he downed his in one go, while she gave the impression of sipping daintily at hers. When he refilled his glass, she managed to empty the contents of hers into the sponge in the handbag.

As he finished his second glass, he spotted hers was empty and refilled it, though only after she ran her hand along his thigh and suggested he refill his glass too. She drank a couple of sips for appearance's sake and felt that shoot to her head immediately and by now Boehm was on his fourth and beginning to turn red faced and glassy-eyed.

'We'll have one more each, Franz, and then you will take me to the bedroom?' She leaned forward and kissed him on the lips and allowed her hand to move up his thigh.

Franz Boehm lasted until halfway through the fifth glass, at which point he suddenly yawned, closed his eyes and slumped back on the sofa, snoring heavily. She tried to pour the remains of the fifth glass into his mouth, though most of it dribbled out.

She moved quickly after that: removing his wallet, his Gestapo identification badge and other papers from his jacket pocket and his Mauser pistol from its holster hanging on the coat rail along with his handcuffs. She remembered to empty the remains of the brandy in the sink.

Madame Madelaine had been quite insistent about what she did next. *I know it's not going to be pleasant, but it will make him assume that something happened between the two of you. It will confuse him and may buy us time, which we'll need if he wakes early.* She steeled herself as she walked over to the sofa and then set about undressing

Boehm, loosening his tie and unbuttoning his shirt, removing his shoes and then pulling his trousers down to his ankles. And then the underpants, harder to dislodge but they too ended up by the ankles.

It wasn't a pleasant sight.

Madame Madelaine was right. When the poor man woke up, he'd wonder what on earth had happened.

By which time, she hoped, it would be far too late.

–

At a quarter past seven on the morning of Sunday 5 March a gleaming black Citroën Traction Avant pulled up in front of Fort Montluc as the sun rose above the city. A man in the distinctive civilian attire that marked him out as a Gestapo officer climbed out of the front passenger seat and approached the sentry on duty at reception.

He showed him his metal Gestapo identity badge and his Gestapo identity card and held out his *kennkarte* but the sentry said that really wasn't necessary, sir, and please do come in, sir, and would your driver like to come in, and the Gestapo officer said no, he'd remain with the car.

The Gestapo officer was escorted to the duty office where the handover between the night team and the day team was in progress. The time had been carefully chosen, of course. They hoped no one would be in a hurry to take responsibility at that time: the senior officer from the night shift was technically in charge until seven-thirty but he would just want to get to bed. The officer taking over for the day would be looking for a quiet start to the day.

Siegfried spoke with a Saxony accent, given that he was playing the part of a man from Halle. He asked who was in charge and the two officers looked wearily at each other and eventually one said he supposed he was, and Siegfried presented his papers and showed his Gestapo identification.

Franz Boehm.

Section 4A

Geheime Staatspolizei

Avenue Berthelot, Lyon

And then he produced the paperwork, which Sophia had so carefully prepared: a series of forms requesting that Prisoner Neumann – question mark – be released into his custody for further questioning at Avenue Berthelot.

'On a Sunday morning?'

'What's the problem: were you planning to take him to church instead?'

'It's most unusual for you to request a prisoner at this time on a Sunday morning.'

'It's most unusual for you to question a request from Herr Barbie!' Siegfried stepped back and allowed a half smile. He was enjoying being back on the stage. One thing he'd discovered early in his acting career was how much an actor fed off the audience. If the audience clearly believed you were who you were pretending to be then it made an actor more confident and convincing in their role.

'I beg your pardon?'

'I am surprised you've not looked at the documents more carefully: if you look here – no, this one, you fool – you will see it is signed and stamped by Herr Barbie. He is requesting Prisoner Neumann be released into my custody.'

The officer had gone red in the face and seemed unsure what to do.

'Of course,' said Siegfried, 'if you care to contact Herr Barbie and question whether—'

'No… no! There's absolutely no need for that,' and then he barked out instructions for Prisoner Neumann to be brought to this office and Siegfried said it would be altogether more convenient if the prisoner was brought to his car waiting at the front because that would be quicker and they wouldn't want to keep Herr Barbie waiting any longer, would they?

–

When Jack Miller was brought out, Siegfried was struck by the American's own acting abilities: not a hint of recognition of Siegfried, a distinct nervousness and he flinched when Siegfried pushed him into the back of the Citroën, which Marcel in his guise as a Gestapo driver had parked alongside the main door to the prison.

It was only when the car screeched away that Siegfried realised Jack may not be acting. He'd put his hand on his knee and assured him he was safe now, but Jack flinched again and looked at him uncomprehendingly. His nose was a mess, his left eye was swollen and his face bruised and puffy, with his upper lip badly split and an obvious gap in his mouth. He edged away from Siegfried and when he said he wasn't to worry, he was being taken to Sophia and she was safe, his right eye opened wide for a moment and then a trickle of tears fell from it.

Marcel had headed west on Cours Gambetta but instead of turning south towards Avenue Berthelot he waited until he was certain they weren't being followed and turned north onto Rue Boileau. This took him into Brotteaux in the 6th arrondissement.

He pulled into an alley to check once more they'd not been followed and edged through the narrow network of lanes that led off it until he came to the back of his garage business. His mechanics were already waiting. The large doors had opened and closed and within minutes the Traction Avant had a new number plate and was on a platform, minus its wheels.

Michel and Gilbert were waiting there to escort Jack and Siegfried to the safe house. They went through to the front of the garage and into a delivery van. It was a short journey from there to Boulevard du Nord, one of the smartest roads in Lyon, parallel to Parc de la Tête d'Or.

The van drove straight into the basement of an elegant white Art Nouveau building, five storeys high. By the time they arrived there, Jack was barely conscious.

–

Sophia waited anxiously in the luxurious apartment on the top floor of the building on Boulevard du Nord. She'd not slept at all since waking early on the Sunday morning, more than twenty-four hours before. The fear she'd experienced in that time was now being replaced by excitement at seeing Jack again. She gasped out loud when she spotted the van driving into the basement.

Any minute now.

The Saturday night with Boehm had gone to plan. It was eleven o'clock when she left Boehm's apartment on Rue du Plat. She'd walked quickly from there to Place des Célestins and in a narrow alley off it – barely wide enough for two people to pass – she'd found the steps leading down to a cellar and as she was about to knock on the door it opened and she was pulled in.

Agnes Kléber was there too and Sophia handed over everything she'd taken from Boehm and was told to wait. Early in the morning she'd be taken to the safe house. She'd sat quietly for the next seven hours on a narrow bench in the dank cellar, talking with Agnes in the dark, the only other sounds that of a dripping pipe and the scuttling of rats.

During the week, she'd managed to put together the papers necessary to secure Jack's release. Before she'd left on the Friday evening, she'd even managed to gain access to the Personnel Department where she removed the photographs of her and Siegfried they held on file.

And on top of all that, she'd had the breakthrough she thought eluded them.

She was certain that this time she had discovered the link that would lead them to Source Armand.

–

Franz Boehm was woken at nine-thirty on the Sunday morning in the most embarrassing circumstances imaginable. They'd been hammering at his door, but he was in such a deep sleep he'd not heard a thing.

Eventually, his colleagues broke the door down to found Boehm stirring on his sofa, confused and naked. When he saw them he leapt off the sofa, only to go sprawling on the floor as he tripped over his trousers.

Half an hour later he was in an interrogation room in Avenue Berthelot, on the other side of the table from which he normally found himself. He was doing his best to answer the questions being fired at him while at the same time struggling to clear his mind. He had the most dreadful hangover, the worst he'd ever had. And it was just beginning to occur to him what may have happened.

'Of course, I didn't give my identity badge and cards to anyone: do you think I'm a fool?'

'Yes, actually, Boehm, we do think you're a fool. You were seen last night at Café Neuf on Place Bellecour dining with Luise Brunner and observed leaving the restaurant with her heading in the direction of your apartment.'

'So what? She works for the Gestapo! I'm not one of those mixing with French women!'

'What happened when you got back to your apartment?'

'I can't remember. Why don't you ask her?'

It was only at that point that Franz Boehm realised that Klaus Barbie was in the room. He'd been standing behind him, but came in front of him. He spoke quietly, but it was clear he was furious.

'The reason we cannot ask her, Boehm, is that she is not at her apartment on Avenue de Saxe. We have no idea where she is. Also missing is Erhard Schröder, who Fraulein Brunner recommended for a post in our Finance Department. However, a man matching Schröder's description presented himself at Fort Montluc some three hours ago. He said he was Franz Boehm and he had all your papers along with documents requiring them to release into his custody the prisoner calling himself Johann Neumann, but who we believe to be a British agent.'

He jabbed Boehm hard in the chest and then grabbed his chin to force him to look up.

'The Red Army is now west of Kiev, Boehm – and I'm trying to decide whether you should be enlisted in the Wehrmacht and sent to stop them, or be put on trial in Berlin, or whether I should deal with you here and now!'

Barbie stepped back and glared at Boehm with a look of derision. The awfulness of his situation began to sink in: this was a death sentence, with no prospect of a coup de grace. The now former Gestapo officer began to whimper and then sob uncontrollably.

Chapter 28

It wasn't until the doctor turned up at the apartment on Boulevard du Nord early on the Sunday afternoon that they appreciated the gravity of the situation. Until then they'd assumed that while Jack was clearly battered, bruised and exhausted, with plenty of rest and the right medicine he'd be fine in a few days.

But when Doctor Hubert emerged from the bedroom after examining Jack, he looked worried. 'This man is very poorly. He is running a high fever and his blood pressure is very low: I suspect he may have some internal bleeding. You said he was a prisoner at Fort Montluc?'

'Yes.'

'He's got bruises all over his back and sides: this may be the cause of internal bleeding. I suspect his liver or kidneys have been damaged. It is possible that this bleeding may stop, we can only hope. As for the fever, we need to start him on medication now and get him on a drip: the next twenty-four hours will be critical. If there is no improvement by Tuesday then we will have to think about getting him into a hospital, though I do know how risky that is.'

Sophia was in shock, she said she couldn't believe that Jack's life was in the balance and sat on the sofa with her head in her hands, sobbing and saying she couldn't cope with the thought of losing Jack...

Siegfried told her to snap out of it. 'He needs you now. You go in there and sit with him. Hold his hand and reassure him. Wipe his face and talk gently to him. You will be the most important medicine for him.'

Doctor Hubert remained in the flat overnight, checking on Jack constantly. But there was no improvement. He spent most of the time asleep, but it was no restful sleep as he tossed and turned, sweat pouring from him, and occasionally crying out.

The doctor left in the morning and returned later that day with more medication. He spoke good German and was able to address Sophia directly. 'He should be in hospital: he may well need a blood transfusion, though moving him would be dangerous and it could also make him worse. But if there's no improvement by the morning, we'll have no choice. Otherwise...'

He shook his head.

'Otherwise, what, Doctor?'

'Otherwise he'll die.'

–

It was the previous Tuesday – the 22 – when Sophia had seen the telex arrive from Knochen in Paris informing Barbie that he'd met with Source Armand that day and he now wanted Barbie to take personal control of Source Armand.

René Dupont was off the case.

The following week was the one before the rescue attempt at Fort Montluc. As well as planning the rescue, Sophia and Siegfried were also under pressure from Mars to find out what they could about Source Armand while they still had the chance.

Sophia frantically scoured as many Verified Source Reports as she could, but found no reference to Source Armand. She concluded that since he'd come under the direct control of Barbie, the security around him had been tightened up. The contents of one of the Verified Source Reports she came across shocked her, although it was nothing to do with Source Armand. It seemed urgent and would need to be dealt with. She made a mental note and resolved to raise it with Agnes Kléber.

The breakthrough came early on the Wednesday evening, around six-thirty when there was a lull in Section 4A: the secretaries and the officers on duty during the day had mostly left and those on the night shift weren't due to arrive until closer to seven. Luise Brunner didn't want to remain in the office too late and draw undue attention to herself.

It was then that René Dupont came in, looking as if he was carrying the weight of the world on his shoulders, sighing and shaking his head as he put his bag on his desk and removed his raincoat. She remembered Knochen's telex: *I no longer want him run by that Frenchman.* That could explain his mood.

Dupont's German was quite reasonable so she asked him how he was and he pulled a face and shrugged his shoulders as if to indicate things were not so good and she said she hoped the night shift wouldn't be too difficult and he muttered something about it probably being the usual, adolescents writing *Resistez!* on walls to impress girls, and she asked him if he'd like a coffee and he seemed very grateful.

His desk was close to hers, easily within earshot in a quiet office and it was then the thought occurred to her. She was surprised she'd not thought of it before. She lifted the telephone, discreetly keeping a finger on the button to suppress the dialling tone in case Dupont heard it.

'Hello – is that Registry? I hoped I'd catch you before you left… of course… this is Luise Brunner from Section 4A: we had a request on Monday to send you any files relating to a Source… hang on, just let me check… here we are: Source Armand. Is that correct?'

Out of the corner of her eye she caught Dupont staring at her and leaning forward to catch every word. She nodded, as if listening to someone on the other end of the line.

'I know, I do realise that: we sent the files through, of course, but I'm just checking if you have them all now? I went through our outstanding files today and couldn't find any more but if you want me to keep looking… no, absolutely – I understand. Thank you. I wish you a pleasant evening. Heil Hitler!'

René Dupont didn't so much as take the bait as snatch at it. No sooner had she replaced the receiver than he appeared at her desk, thanking her so much for the coffee and she said it was a pleasure.

'I hope you will excuse me, Fraulein Brunner, but I couldn't help overhearing your telephone conversation with Registry and am I correct in thinking you were referring to Source Armand?'

'That is correct.' She was tidying her desk, preparing to leave.

Dupont nodded, shifting awkwardly from foot to foot, a forlorn expression on his face. 'Source Armand was originally my agent. And now...' He snapped his fingers like a magician making a handkerchief disappear. 'And now, he's been taken away from me. Into Registry so it would seem!'

Sophia smiled and said she really didn't know about such matters and she just did what she was told.

'Of course. Do you happen to know what has become of the Source Armand files? I only ask because if I happen to come across any in my possession then I can ensure they are sent to the correct place?'

'As I understand it, Registry are collating them and they are then being sent to Herr Barbie's office. Maybe if you were to—'

'No, no, no... no need, I was just wondering. To be honest, Fraulein Brunner, it's one less informer for me to worry about. I'm busy enough as it is, though I can't help feeling a bit resentful that an informer I recruited – perhaps the most important one in Lyon, if not in the whole of France – is no longer mine and, of course, I receive no credit.'

'That is the way of the world, Monsieur Dupont: one rarely gets credit for what one does.' She smiled sweetly, which seemed to encourage him. He pulled up a chair next to her desk and sat down.

'I hope you don't think I'm speaking out of turn, Fraulein Brunner, and I know these are not matters for you, but... these are difficult times for a patriotic Frenchman such as myself. Our motives are all too often misunderstood. We are called collaborators and even traitors would you believe, yet it is people such as myself who are upholding true French values: what could be more patriotic than defending France from the Jews and the socialists and the communists, I ask you?'

'I can certainly see your point.'

'When it comes to loyalty, they're the worse of the lot, I can tell you from personal experience.'

'Who is that, Monsieur Dupont?'

The door opened and someone entered, heading for the other side of the room. Dupont looked uneasy. 'The communists, Fraulein Brunner. They only have loyalty to the Soviet Union. Yet no one pillories them as they do the likes of us. They call them defenders of France, the great *resistants*, all of that nonsense. He's one of them, you know?'

'Who is one of them?'

'Source Armand, the man we've just been talking about. We were at school together: right up until we left at the age of fifteen – we even shared the same desk in our last year would, you believe? That's why he approached me: because he saw in me a kind of loyalty too – to a different cause, at the opposite end of the political spectrum, but at least I have my own determined point of view and I think he respected that. Neither of us just follows the crowd. Maybe he used me, maybe it was because he knew me and preferred to deal with a Frenchman so it wouldn't feel like he was collaborating... I don't know but... but what I do know is he chose *me* to pass on information to.'

He stopped speaking suddenly, as if realising he'd already said too much. Sophia said she could quite understand his position and it was so unfair that people like him who were acting in France's best interests should be criticised.

'Are you still in contact with this Source Armand?'

'I've been told not to. You know something, Fraulein Brunner: the information I passed on was the best the Gestapo had ever received. Herr Barbie himself admitted that. But I understand Source Armand's motives better than the Gestapo because I'm a Frenchman.'

Someone else had entered the office now. Dupont stood up and moved the chair back. He leant over Sophia's desk, his face inches from hers. 'In the so-called Resistance, they hate the other groups almost as much as they hate the Nazis. As far as some of them are concerned – especially the communists – the end justifies the means. I was smart enough to exploit that.' René Dupont stood up straight, his arms folded and a knowing smile on his face.

'Who is this man, then, this Source Armand? He sounds a complicated character!'

René Dupont shook his head as he backed away. Another of the French Gestapo officers had come to sit in his desk close to them.

–

Sometime on the Wednesday morning Jack Miller opened his eyes – or as much as his swollen left eye would allow him – and looked around the bedroom in the apartment on Boulevard du Nord.

When he saw Sophia, he smiled and held his hand towards her and she grasped it and leant over to kiss him on the forehead. Siegfried passed a glass of water, which he sipped, and then he allowed himself to be helped up into a sitting position.

Doctor Hubert took Jack's blood pressure and temperature. For the first time since Sunday, he didn't look so worried. The previous evening he'd arrived at the apartment after visiting Hôtel-Dieu hospital.

'I managed to get hold of Prontosil,' he said, tapping his briefcase. 'It's a sulphonamide: it's by no means certain if it will work but I'll give him the maximum dose. It's the best antibiotic available to us. I'm not sure we have any alternative.'

It had the desired effect.

By the Thursday Jack was still weak and feverish, but was well enough for just the three of them to remain in the apartment with a member of Mars coming in once a day. Gilbert had been to check on them on the Sunday morning. In the evening Sophia and Siegfried were sitting in the lounge when the door of the apartment opened and Madame Madelaine entered.

They knew immediately something was not right.

–

This would be Agnes Kléber's great triumph.

No longer would she be the reliable and accommodating person, steady and boring, someone who once the war was over would be easily disregarded and forgotten about.

She could see as well as anyone else the way the war was going – perhaps better than them, to be honest – and if she were lucky, she'd be regarded as just one of the many thousands who'd assisted the Resistance and she'd end up back in Alsace, or here in Lyon, or wherever – but she'd still be the spinster who people viewed with a mixture of pity and disinterest.

But once the war was over, she wanted to be seen as a hero of the Resistance, without the faintest trace of a question mark over her motives for working at Avenue Berthelot.

And this was her opportunity.

On the Thursday, Luise Brunner had recounted what René Dupont had told her the previous evening: that he'd been at school with Source Armand, they'd left school at the age of fifteen and had shared a desk in their final year at school. They agreed that nothing would be done about that until after the rescue attempt on the Sunday.

Agnes Kléber said to leave it to her and Luise Brunner said obviously you'll pass all this on to Madame Madelaine and she said of course, naturally. It was then that Luise Brunner had remembered something and handed her a piece of paper in her own writing.

Izieu.

'I found this place referred to in a Verified Source Report: I think you need to have a look at it, something from an informer. It looks urgent to me. Maybe Mars will know who to warn.'

She nodded and promised to find the report and slipped the piece of paper inside a notebook on her desk. She'd check it out in the morning, she said.

But she never did.

She had a more pressing matter on her mind and she had no intention of sharing the glory that would come from that with anyone else because she knew if she did so her role in exposing the great traitor of Lyon would soon be forgotten. She alone would find out their identity and she would present Source Armand's head on a silver platter to the Mars Network.

She waited until the Monday, the day after Jack's rescue from Fort Montluc. In the Personnel Department at Avenue Berthelot, she found Dupont's file and on it the name of the school he'd been at and the year he'd graduated.

She telephoned the school and was told that all records from before 1935 were stored in the basement of the Hôtel de Ville, the headquarters of the council in Lyon. She had to wait until the Wednesday to find a pretext for visiting the Hôtel de Ville on Place des Terreaux. There was a small Gestapo liaison office based there and she timed her visit for the start of their lunchbreak. She been sent to collect some housing details, she told them, from the records department.

'I'm happy to go and look myself, if that helps you?'

It took her an hour to find the correct records. The document listing those leaving the school in 1918 was divided into four classes. The class with René Dupont's name had twenty-six pupils, listed in alphabetical order. She studied it carefully, trying to see if there could be any clue as to which of the other twenty-five names was that of Source Armand.

But she did notice written in pencil alongside each name – in brackets and preceded by *b/* – was a number. There were thirteen numbers. Against Dupont's name was *(b/8)*.

It must be his desk.

The other pupil with *(b/8)* against his name was called Georges Moreau.

Agnes Kléber had found Source Armand.

She found Georges Moreau's family address in the same school records. She was able to check it with the most up-to-date directory for Lyon: his mother still lived at the same address in Montchat. The following day she found a file for Georges Moreau in the Registry in Avenue Berthelot. It contained a single sheet of paper, with two typed lines: one saying he was believed to have been a member of the Communist Party youth wing in 1919. The second line said he had been observed handing out leaflets for the Communist Party candidate in the legislative election of 1924.

Written underneath in pen was 'Refer RD: 4/11/1942', which proved he was handled by René Dupont. And she suspected that they had no idea that Georges Moreau was his original name. Had they done so, that file would have been removed.

Georges Moreau would have a different name now. Only Dupont would know he was now Source Armand.

And now she knew too.

–

Georges Moreau knew his past would catch up with him one day. He didn't labour under any illusions about the depth of his treachery and nor did he attempt to diminish it in his own mind by seeking to justify it. It was something he'd had to do, and all his attention and energy now needed to be devoted to ensuring he remained above suspicion. It was not as if there was a shortage of people who'd want their revenge on him. It could be people within his own organisation or those seen as their allies in the Resistance, but who were still political opponents. And then the Germans: he knew sooner or later they'd turn on him.

But Georges Moreau also knew how hard it would be to find him. He'd been careful in concealing his identity. He'd not used the name Georges Moreau since 1929 when he'd changed his name and then disappeared underground for three years. When he emerged, he used another identity until 1936 and then changed that one two years later to the name by which he was known now.

Georges Moreau had been – to all intents and purposes – dead for the best part of fifteen years.

But Georges Moreau did emerge once in a while, like a creature in the depths of a dark forest emerging for a brief period only to disappear again. Now he only emerged to visit his mother in Montchat in the east of the city. For many years his mother understood that if anyone ever enquired after him, she was to deny all knowledge.

She knew what to say.

Georges? I've not seen him for years. I'm told he's been sent to work in Germany. If you see him tell him to write to me!

But in recent months he'd begun to worry: he'd noticed how forgetful she was becoming, how she could be so vacant at times. He doubted he'd be able to risk visiting her for much longer. He cut his visits to once every five or six weeks, unannounced, slipping in through the back door and staying no more than half an hour.

When he turned up on the morning of Saturday 11 March his mother looked more confused than usual. 'Every Sunday, Georges, you arrive at nine and take me to church and then we come back here and we sit down to lunch with your father! So why have you come today rather than tomorrow?'

He sat in silence as he pondered the situation: his mother had imagined everything. 'Now you won't see the woman!'

'What woman, Mother?'

'The woman who came yesterday. She was asking for you. She said she knew you from schooldays and mentioned a few other boys I remembered from your class and she wanted to say hello, though to be honest, Georges, she looked older than you, but then the years do that to women. And I—'

'Did you get her name?'

'No, but don't worry: I told her you're here on Sunday morning to take me to church and I invited her for lunch!'

–

It was only as she walked down the path to the house that Sunday morning that it occurred to Agnes Kléber that perhaps she wasn't as well prepared as she ought to have been. She'd been concentrating on finding out Source Armand's identity and then tracking down Georges Moreau and had been so pleased with herself at doing this she'd not really thought of a plan of what to do now.

She had thought about telling the Mars Network what she was doing, perhaps leaving a note to say she'd identified Source Armand and giving his mother's address in Montchat, but then there was the chance that somehow she'd lose control of the situation and others would take the credit.

This was going to be her triumph. She decided the best course of action would be to confront Georges Moreau. She had a pistol, after all.

–

Georges Moreau had spelt it out very clearly to his mother. The woman who she'd invited for lunch was not coming. Instead, he told his mother, she was to go round to her cousin's and remain there for a few hours.

Moreau waited alone in the house that morning, concealed behind a curtain upstairs as he watched the street. At a quarter to one he spotted the woman, walking nervously down the street, hesitating outside the house before heading for the front door. She remained there for five minutes, knocking and then peering through the front window and at once stage calling out, 'Madame Moreau!'

When she left the way she'd come, Georges Moreau hurried downstairs. He left the house through the back door and ran down the alley at the rear, which ran parallel to their road. When he followed a turning of the alley he emerged onto the road, at a reasonable distance behind the woman. She headed east and turned into Boulevard de la Part-Dieu and he knew he'd have his chance when they passed the railway sidings, deserted on a Sunday.

It had occurred to him that there could be an innocent explanation to all this, that maybe it was someone from his past who did indeed want to catch up, but he doubted it. He couldn't recognise the woman who'd come down the path and who he was now following. And in any case, it was a risk he couldn't take. Georges Moreau disappeared fifteen years ago and he intended for it remain that way.

His chance came sooner than he thought: ahead of them was a gap in a fence leading to the back of a marshalling yard and the woman's pace had slowed so he hurried up. As soon as he reached her, he bundled her behind the fence and pushed her out of sight of the road. She looked confused and terrified and fumbled with her handbag, which he pulled away from her. He was about to ask her who she was when she started to scream. He punched her so hard she went sprawling in the rubble. By the time he'd jumped on top of her his knife was already out. He slashed at her throat, so hard she was almost decapitated.

He heard a shout from the road and ran off, not risking turning around, dropping the woman's handbag. He just managed to get across the tracks before a goods train passed, meaning his escape was assured. Minutes later he was sitting in a pew in the shadows at the back of Église de Dominicains, recovering his breath and gathering his thoughts.

It had been too close a call.

Georges Moreau would now disappear forever.

There would be no more Source Armand.

He would never see his mother again.

No one would ever find him.

Chapter 29

Madame Madelaine was far from her usual unflappable self when she arrived at the apartment on Boulevard du Nord that Sunday evening. Siegfried asked her if something was the matter and she ignored his question, asking instead whether Jack was awake. Sophia explained he'd been given something to help him sleep and Madame Madelaine said that was probably for the best and they must listen to her carefully.

'There has been a catastrophe.'

She glared at them as if inviting guesses as to the nature of this catastrophe.

'Agnes Kléber has been killed.' She held out her hands to emphasise the gravity of the situation.

'Agnes… are you sure?'

'Of course I am sure! Do you really think I'd risk my life coming here if I wasn't sure? We have a very reliable contact at Part-Dieu police station who got in touch with me this afternoon to say the body of a woman was discovered in some wasteland near the railway marshalling yard off Boulevard de la Part-Dieu. It would appear a passer-by heard a commotion behind a fence and saw a man attacking a woman. The man ran away, across the tracks, and managed to escape. When the police arrived, they discovered the woman's throat had been cut. The man dropped her handbag when he fled and when they opened it, they not only discovered who she was and where she worked but they also found the Webley revolver we'd given her. It will link her to the Resistance, it was one of the ones we got from the British. I mean…'

She shook her head in astonishment. 'It was for her protection, not to walk around the streets of Lyon with. What on earth was the woman thinking? She always gave the impression that she knew best. At first the police thought it was a case of robbery, but of course as it involves an employee of the Gestapo it's out of their hands now. I have no idea what she was doing there and who the man was but it's a disaster – and a tragedy, of course. And now we have no one in Avenue Berthelot!'

'She told you about Source Armand?'

'What do you mean?'

'The French Gestapo man – Dupont – gave me a lead on who he was: that he'd been at school with him.'

'When did you find this out?'

'The first of March, just before we rescued Jack, so – ten days ago? I told Agnes the next day. She said she was going to tell you about it.'

'And you didn't think to mention it since then?'

'I assumed she'd told you – it didn't occur to me she wouldn't have done so. And there were other things on my mind. I imagined you were working on finding out who he was.'

Madame Madelaine looked furious. She stood up and paced the room and when she sat down, she told Sophia to tell her the whole story from the beginning, to leave nothing out. Once Sophia had finished, they all agreed that Agnes had most probably decided this was something she could investigate herself.

'We will have to be even more careful, but at least we now know what you know, if you follow me: that Source Armand was in the same class as Dupont and shared a desk with him. The records will be at the Hôtel de Ville. We will look for him there.'

'It does rather sound,' said Siegfried, 'as if Agnes got to him first.'

They arrested René Dupont when he arrived for work at Avenue Berthelot that Wednesday morning, 15 March. As he'd entered the building with a *milice* colleague they'd joked about it being the Ides of March and how they'd need to be careful that day and Dupont had opened his coat to reveal his new Walther PPK he'd been issued with the week before, the so-called police pistol.

It was only then that they noticed Otto Winter standing in the reception area, flanked by two SS officers. Winter said Dupont should hand over his weapon and follow him.

He was taken down to the dungeon area where he was told to remove his clothes and place everything on a table and when he asked if that included his Gestapo badge he was told, 'Especially the Gestapo badge.'

He spent the next hour in a damp cell, the discomfort of his rough prison uniform the least of his worries. At first, he was too shocked to think anything and then he realised tears were running down his face and he was terrified they'd see him like that because they'd see that as evidence of his guilt, though he couldn't think of anything he could possibly be guilty of, unless patriotism was now a crime.

He was brought into an interrogation room and made to stand handcuffed in front of Otto Winter. Barbie's aide looked him up and down and asked him if he knew why he was there and he shook his head and felt tears welling in his eyes again.

'Over three weeks ago, Dupont, you were instructed by Herr Barbie to cease all contact with Source Armand and told that from then on, he would be handled exclusively by him. You recall?'

Dupont nodded. He felt himself swaying.

'Source Armand has disappeared. We were in contact with him last Friday. Since Monday morning there has been no trace of him. Nothing.'

René Dupont said he was very sorry to hear this but since he'd been told to hand Source Armand over to Herr Barbie he had, naturally, ceased all contact with him. He had no idea where he could possibly be.

'As you know, we are also investigating the disappearance of Fraulein Luise Brunner. Did you know her, Dupont?'

'By name and by sight only, sir: she was in the same office.'

'So, you never spoke with her?'

'Possibly good morning or goodbye, but nothing more than that. I can—'

'Don't treat me as a fool, Dupont – and stand still while you're at it. We have two witnesses – both Gestapo officers – who say that on the evening of Thursday 2 March you were seen deep in conversation with Fraulein Brunner in the Section 4A office. Do you recall that?'

'Not as such, I may have been wishing her a good evening, but nothing of any consequence I can assure you, I—'

'You appear to have taken a long time to say good evening, eh?'

'I was merely being civil, sir.'

'Fraulein Brunner is an enemy agent and an associate of Erhard Schröder, who was involved in helping the prisoner escape from Fort Montluc. We are also investigating possible links between Fraulein Brunner and Agnes Kléber, whose body was found on Sunday. In her handbag we discovered a British-issue revolver, of the same type they've been supplying to the Resistance. It has emerged that Brunner and Kléber spent a good deal more time in each other's company than one would have expected.'

He paused and glared at Dupont who had no idea what to say: he was concentrating as hard as he could manage on remaining standing still.

'It would appear that there was an enemy cell operating in this building and now with Source Armand disappearing – the same day as the killing of Kléber – we suspect there may be a link.'

'Herr Winter, sir, I hope you don't think I—'

'Don't think you what, Dupont? That you're connected with all this? Well, unless you can give us a very satisfactory explanation, we most certainly do!'

On the same day that René Dupont discovered he was suspected of being an enemy agent, Anna Rousseau turned up at the apartment on Boulevard du Nord.

They'd not seen her for a while and in fact Sophia and Siegfried hadn't seen anyone from the Mars Network since Madame Madelaine's visit on the Sunday evening when she'd told them about Agnes Kléber.

She had a bag of food with her and once that had been sorted, they all sat in the lounge, including Jack who was now able to sit in the armchair.

'I have bad news, I'm afraid.'

She seemed paler and thinner than when they'd last seen her. 'The information you gave Madame Madelaine – about Dupont telling you that he was in the same class as Dupont and shared a desk with him? You passed this on to Agnes Kléber, I understand: our contacts in the Hôtel de Ville searched for the records. However…'

She sighed and raised her eyebrows.

'In the file for that school a number of items had been removed – the four class lists for 1918, the year that Dupont left and also the directory of the pupil's home addresses. We have no way of finding out who Source Armand could be. Either it was removed by the Gestapo or more possibly by—'

'Agnes Kléber?'

'Exactly: Madame Madelaine is convinced she was no traitor but believes she wanted to make the discovery of his identity herself.'

'It would make sense,' said Sophia. 'If she discovered his identity, she may then have confronted Source Armand and he killed her.'

'That is the most likely explanation,' said Anna.

'But we shall never know,' said Siegfried.

René Dupont regarded his discovery of an apparent link between the shop on Rue Ravat and the Resistance as his insurance policy.

He'd obtained this policy just over six months before, on a Monday afternoon when he was a passenger in a German Gestapo staff car and they'd driven down Rue Ravat where he spotted his brother-in-law Marcel pausing outside a ladies' boutique selling scarves and gloves and then entering it.

It was most unusual: Marcel's garage business was in Brotteaux, on the other side of the Rhône. It made no sense for him to be visiting such a shop on the Presqu'île, let alone anywhere else in the city. He'd decided this was something he must look into, but it was another month before he was able to do so.

He visited the shop at the end of October but left it none the wiser. The proprietor was a taciturn woman who eyed him suspiciously and when she asked him what he wanted he realised he'd not really thought of a reason why he was there so muttered something about his wife's birthday and before he knew it, he'd bought her a ridiculously expensive pair of deerskin gloves.

Although there was nothing to make him suspicious about the shop, he remained unsure as to why his brother-in-law had visited it. He toyed with the idea of asking him, but Marcel was too smart to be caught out like that. The following week he returned to Rue Ravat: this time he had his story ready – his wife was delighted with the gloves, he'd say, and he was so pleased his brother-in-law had recommended the shop to him. And then he'd mention his brother-in-law and show the two of them together in a family photograph.

But the boutique was closed. He decided to visit the café next door, which on a wet Wednesday afternoon was deserted. The proprietor – a Madame Faure – was pleased to see him, so much so that she brought him an extra cake and ended up sitting down near to him, only too pleased to talk.

Her husband had died a few years ago, she told him. Running this business on her own was so unpredictable: sometimes it was too busy and she'd be exhausted, other times too quiet and she'd worry about money.

'Do you have any help?'

'My oldest son has been sent to Germany to work; you understand? My youngest, Jacques – he's not in Lyon.'

'Does he ever visit?'

At that point he noticed Madame Faure clam up, as if she'd said too much and he thought that was odd because all she'd said was that Jacques wasn't in Lyon.

He did ask her about the shop next door, the boutique – who is it owned by – and she was similarly reticent. Her behaviour was odd: she gave the appearance of being a woman who thrived on gossip and loved to talk and was now having to make an effort to say as little as possible.

But René Dupont's time with the Gestapo had not been wasted. He'd learnt how they operated. He understood the need to be unscrupulous and intuitive and to recognise that if you suspect something then there's probably a very good reason for it and therefore to follow your instincts.

When he returned to Avenue Berthelot, he checked the files. There was nothing on Madame Faure or her eldest son Gilbert. But there was a file on Jacques Faure: a suspected *resistant*, with links to the Combat Resistance group, last heard of in Lyon February 1942: an unconfirmed report from November 1943 he may be involved with the *maquis* in Limousin.

He returned to the café on Rue Ravat in the first week of November, waiting until the boutique was closed and the café was quiet. Madame Faure clearly remembered him, and he asked if there was somewhere they could talk in private?

'Maybe when I close, in a couple of hours?'

'It's about Jacques.'

She reacted more calmly than he'd expected and said very well, wait until those customers leave and I'll close up.

Half an hour later they were in a small room at the back of the café, sitting amongst the boxes and supplies. Dupont had just showed Madame Faure his Gestapo badge but told her not to worry, she wasn't in any kind of trouble.

She looked terrified. 'I can promise you Jacques is a good boy who is easily led. I beg of you to—'

He raised a hand for her to stop. 'I told you, Madame Faure, there is nothing for you to worry about. Everything I am going to say is between you and me. Jacques is not in trouble – yet. I can tell you he is in Limousin and is involved in the Maquis. You maybe suspected that, eh? Don't worry, we know he is no more than a messenger and if you do me a small favour, I promise to ensure he remains safe.'

He wanted her to become one of his informants, he told her. If she were to overhear anything in the café or in the neighbourhood or see anything that may be of interest to him then she was to tell him and he'd ensure no one suspected her. And in return, Jacques would remain safe.

She nodded slowly, realising she had no alternative and then he asked her about the shop next door, the boutique.

'Madame Madelaine's?'

'I've wondered if perhaps anything goes on there? I've noticed people going in…'

'She has meetings, in the basement,' Madame Faure said. 'I know nothing about them, I'm not involved. She just asks me if I'd ring the bell behind the counter if I ever see anything when they're meeting. I don't know who it is who meets there, but it is very… I'm not sure of the right word, clandestine? But you must understand: it is nothing to do with me!'

Dupont said of course, he understood, and could he show Madame Faure this photograph: do you recognise this man?

It was a family photograph, taken that summer. He'd covered over all the faces apart from Marcel's. Madame Faure held it close to her face and angled it against the light. Yes, she said, she did recognise him: she didn't know his name but he was always at these meetings.

'How often do they meet there?'

273

'Hard to say: it used to be more often. Now maybe every fortnight, perhaps three weeks? She tells me an hour or so beforehand so I can be on the lookout.'

And they then came to an agreement.

René Dupont gave Madame Faure his telephone number at Avenue Berthelot. When she heard a meeting was imminent, she was to telephone this number and say it was his optician and his new spectacles were ready.

And in return, Jacques would be protected.

Between the middle of November and the end of February he picked up three calls from her in time for him to go to Rue Ravat, there were another two which he missed as he got the message too late. He was careful though, still observing the boutique from a distance, spotting where the lookouts were, seeing how many people entered, making sure his hated brother-in-law was there too.

But he did nothing about it.

Not yet. The time would come.

This was his insurance policy, after all.

–

They were concerned about the three of them remaining in the apartment on Boulevard du Nord.

The idea had been to move all three of them, but Dr Hubert made it clear that Jack was too ill to be moved. But Siegfried did leave the apartment, taken east by Emile towards the Swiss border, which they hoped to smuggle him across.

This meant that for days at a time Sophia and Jack were on their own in the apartment and for much of that time, Jack was asleep. Sophia filled these empty hours pacing up and down and thinking and one day found her mind wandering, thinking about Agnes Kléber and why she'd not told Mars about what Dupont had told her about Source Armand and why had she been killed, was it linked to Source Armand: had she discovered him and had he killed her? It was hard to think there was no connection.

And that was when she remembered.

It was the same Thursday evening that she'd told Agnes what Dupont had told her. She'd been preoccupied with the plans for Jack's rescue from Fort Montluc, but she'd also told Agnes about a Verified Source Report she'd read that afternoon, one that struck her as urgent, the dirty work of an informer.

About children.

In an orphanage.

And for the life of her she couldn't remember the name of the place she'd written on a slip of paper.

But Dr Hubert was due to visit the following day.

She'd mention it to him.

–

René Dupont had been arrested on the Wednesday 15 March. He waited until the following day before he explained to Otto Winter that he was being asked to own up to something he'd not done and that wasn't fair, and Otto Winter said they only had Dupont's word that he had nothing to do with Source Armand's disappearance.

'But you have no evidence that I was involved.'

Winter shrugged. That was not his problem.

'How about if I were to give you some information I've been pulling together for a while?'

'What information, Dupont?'

'Information I believe could expose a Resistance cell: if my informant is correct, you could catch them red-handed!'

Otto Winter looked interested, interested enough to bring in Barbie who told Dupont to go through it in detail. When he finished, he nodded in approval. He was obviously interested.

'So let me get this clear: your source telephones your direct number upstairs about an hour before the meeting and says it's your optician and your new spectacles are ready?'

Dupont nodded.

'How often do they meet there?'

'It's uncertain, but I've not had a call for a couple of weeks, so it could be any time.'

'And you didn't think to tell us before?'

'I wanted to be sure: I was gathering the intelligence.'

They agreed to give it another week. Someone would remain by Dupont's telephone in case his optician rang, which Barbie and Winter thought most unlikely.

Which explained why they were so surprised when on the following Wednesday – the 22 March – the woman monitoring Dupont's phone called Otto Winter and said there'd been a call for Monsieur Dupont.

His new spectacles were ready.

Chapter 30

Lyon
March 1944

Madame Madelaine knew they were meeting too often at Rue Ravat. They ought to have used other venues, but most of those were in the Croix-Rousse and she was never comfortable there. Although the *traboules* made moving around the area easier, there was something about it that made her uneasy. It wasn't a place she was familiar with and she felt that its weak spot was when the members of the group moved in and out of the area.

So, against her better judgement, the basement under her shop became the regular meeting place. After all, she had confidence in the warning system she'd established with Madame Faure. The café owner had a good view of the street and she could discreetly press the buzzer they'd installed behind her counter to ring the bell in the basement.

The meeting she convened on the afternoon of Wednesday 22 March comprised herself, her three lieutenants, Marcel, Michel and Maurice, along with Dr Hubert and Anna Rousseau: all five were told of the venue that morning. The main item on their agenda was for the doctor to update them on the American and the German woman and also to discuss what would happen with Siegfried, who was currently hiding on a farm near Annecy.

She was also planning to broach a difficult subject with them – a proposal that with the prospect of the Allies landing any time now in northern and southern Europe, the group should cease all their activities until then.

They should hold their fire.

Madame Madelaine arranged for Georges and Gilbert to be on lookout duty at either end of the street. And an hour before the meeting she visited Madame Faure to tell her to keep an eye out too. If Madame Madelaine had the time to stop to think about it she'd have observed that Madame Faure had been in one of her dismissive moods: she could be like that, your best friend one day, barely stopping to say hello the next. But Madame Madelaine was too busy to think about it, other than to assume her neighbour was worried about her sons.

–

Madame Faure took up position behind the counter at one o'clock: twenty minutes later she spotted the two lookouts, both men she'd recognised, and soon after that the other attendees began to arrive. She was sad to see one of them was the pleasant doctor who Madame Madelaine had arranged for her to see when she had her stomach problem, but there was nothing she could do about it. It was such an unfortunate situation.

The first inkling she had of the Germans' arrival was at ten past two when she spotted the lookout on the corner of Rue Delandine remove his cap. She pretended not to notice, reaching under the counter to get something and when she stood up, she saw a series of Gestapo cars pulling up outside the boutique and her own café.

She froze in fear when the first of the Germans burst into her café and then in her panic, pressed the buzzer. No one could accuse her of doing nothing now.

And it was all a blur after that. Tables being turned over, glasses smashing, the sound of shouting and then screaming from the basement following by two, maybe three gunshots and more screaming. She became aware of someone coming behind the counter and pushing her aside and then lifting the cloth she'd placed over the buzzer and shouting as someone else grabbed her arms and pinned them behind her and before she could say a word, she was being bundled into a car.

–

Gilbert was in a dreadful state. He'd been the lookout on the other side of Rue Ravat and it had been Georges, on the corner of Rue Delandine, who'd spotted the Germans first and he'd been the one to raise the alarm. Gilbert had backed into a doorway and fortunately an old man had opened it and pulled him in before slamming it shut.

Gilbert had a clear view of everything after that. Georges was shot dead. From the boutique, Marcel and Dr Hubert had been marched out and thrown into the back of cars, and the same had happened to the woman who ran the café next door.

As that happened, he spotted Anna Rousseau, arriving for the meeting, evidently late. As she spotted what was going on she walked on by, not pausing, nor hurrying her step.

A short while later three bodies were carried out and dumped on the pavement: Madame Madelaine, Michel and Maurice.

Four of the Mars network were dead: two arrested. It was almost more than he could take. He remained in the old man's apartment for the rest of the afternoon, only daring to leave it just after five o'clock.

From there he made his way to the Croix-Rousse. There was a safe house – more of a safe room than anything else – to be used in case of such an event. The idea was that any surviving members of the group would gather there in the immediate aftermath, but then cease to use it within twelve hours of any comrades being captured.

Gilbert approached the room in a large silk workshop reached through a *traboule* off Rue Pouteau. Anna was there along with Emile, who she'd managed to alert. Gilbert told them what he'd seen: four dead, two arrested, along with the café owner. They sat in stunned silence in the dank room, its curtains tightly drawn and the only light coming from a small candle, which seemed to emit more smoke than light. Gilbert found himself weeping, while Emile struggled to stop his hands shaking as he tried to roll a cigarette.

Anna was the most composed of the three of them as she assumed control. They must leave this room now, she said. They couldn't rely on either the doctor or Marcel holding out for more than twelve hours. She told Emile he was to return to Annecy to ensure the German man was safe and try and get him over the border as a matter of urgency.

'And you go with him, Emile: you must escape to Switzerland, join Benoît there. Gilbert, you are to go underground here in Lyon: inform anyone else associated with Mars they are to do likewise, you understand? Tell Alain tonight and the others as soon as you can. I will remain in Lyon too to keep an eye on Jack and Sophia.'

The other two nodded, it made sense.

'The war continues, but for us, our battle is over. As a group, we no longer exist. We go to ground and when the time is right, we emerge and fight again. But for now...'

She paused and looked down and even in the gloom of the room the glint of tears in her eyes was clear.

'But for now, we say farewell.'

Chapter 31

In the neat Ain countryside, some fifty miles east of Lyon and a similar distance from the Swiss border, lies the pretty village of Izieu. On the outskirts of the village is the hamlet of Lélinaz and there, on the banks of the Rhône and surrounded by farms and green fields and on the edge of a forest, is a large house, the Villa Anne-Marie. With its own fishing ponds, an orchard and a large garden it is a perfect bucolic setting.

But in the first week of April, this pastoral idyll was about to be shattered by the most unimaginable horror, releasing an unseen terror which would settle on the area for many years to come.

Since May 1943 the Villa Anne-Marie had also been a place of refuge for Jewish children hiding from the Nazis. There were forty-four children in the home, most of them orphans, their ages ranging from four to seventeen. As they sat down to breakfast on a Thursday morning, the 6 April, two German army trucks and a car carrying Gestapo officers from Lyon pulled up in front of the house.

They burst into the house and arrested all the children along with the seven Jewish adults who were their carers and teachers. Two of the children managed to escape to a nearby farm and watched in horror as the German soldiers and the Gestapo brutally manhandled the children into the back of the trucks.

Their destination was Lyon, the Gestapo prison at Fort Montluc.

Doctor Hubert and Marcel had been brought to Fort Montluc on the evening of Wednesday 22 March. They'd been separated but placed in cells with other prisoners and the doctor had ended up crammed in with half a dozen others.

He knew one of the prisoners by sight, an accountant who was a friend of a friend – enough to be able to trust him. The man moved over to sit on the floor next to the doctor, leaning against the wall. He spoke quickly and quietly.

'I have no idea why you're here and don't tell me, but you should be aware that the Germans never know what to make of doctors they arrest: it is as if they can't bring themselves to believe that a doctor would work for the Resistance. The doctor in Caluire – Dugoujon – where all the Resistance leaders were arrested last year, he was soon released. They believed him when he said it was nothing to do with him. My advice is come up with a credible story and then stick to it.'

Which he did.

His first interrogation was on the Thursday morning and he explained at great length that Madame Madelaine was a patient of his and she had called that morning and asked to see him and he'd said that as he was going to be near Rue Ravat, he'd pop in.

'I arrived much later than I'd planned and when I got there Madame Madelaine came up from the basement and asked if I'd wait and I said of course, then soon after I heard shooting and this commotion and I hurried to the back of the shop and towards the stairs and the next thing I know I'm arrested, which is an outrage!'

The interrogation continued all day. He noticed that the man questioning him was uncomfortable with medical details, so he obliged by talking quite graphically about the gynaecological issues he specialised in and explained that while of course he wouldn't talk about poor Madame Madelaine specifically, the woman did suffer in this respect, as did many women of that age which meant they...

There was a long break after this. Doctor Hubert was locked in the interrogation room but without handcuffs and when the questioning resumed it was a different person asking the questions and he was even more queasy about medical details. At one stage in the afternoon his interrogator became more aggressive, but Dr Hubert remained calm and when the man came particularly close to him, he said he didn't want to worry him, but he couldn't help noticing that the red veins in his eyes were very prominent and had he ever been examined for conjunctivitis?

The man stepped back and asked if that was serious and Dr Hubert replied only in a very small number of cases, such as those which could be classed as toxic conjunctivitis, some cases of which could result in blindness and after that the man was a bag of nerves, clearly anxious to finish as soon as possible so he could go and get his eyes checked out.

By the start of the following week Dr Hubert was sent to work in the prison infirmary. He was still under suspicion and he was still a prisoner, but while investigations continued, he could help look after prisoners.

–

On a hot Monday morning in the third week of April Sophia and Jack received an unexpected visitor: Dr Hubert. The last they'd heard he was a prisoner of the Gestapo. When he told his story it was as if a heavy, dark cloud had descended over the room. He told them that Marcel was still alive and then explained how he'd been sent to the work in the prison infirmary and in his second week there, on a Thursday evening, he'd been called down to the ground floor, to be met with a sight that filled him with sheer terror, and which he knew would haunt him for the remainder of his days.

In a large cell, perhaps seven metres by two, were more than fifty prisoners, most of them were children, some very young, even as young as four. There wasn't enough room for them all to lay down on the cream and terracotta-coloured tiles. A water pipe ran horizontally along the bottom of the wall, above which the three barred windows let in what was left of the light. He was ordered to check them all out and he spent the next hour and a half moving slowly amongst them, the few adults reassuring and calming the younger children, the older ones seemingly aware a terrible fate awaited them. The room was surprisingly quiet: no screaming or shouting, some crying and hushed conversations between the adults. A woman spoke quietly as he bent down examining a child. They were from a Jewish orphanage, she explained. They'd been raided by the Gestapo that morning and Dr Hubert told her not to despair, maybe because there were so many children they'd be released, and she shot him an angry look and leaned close, hissing in his ear that it was precisely because there were so many children that their fate was sealed.

'And that was that,' said the doctor. 'I was told to return to the infirmary. The following morning the children and their carers were gone. A few days later another prisoner told me he'd heard from a guard that the children and the adults had been sent by train from Perrache station to Paris. One of the others in my cell said this meant they'd be sent from there to Poland.

'And then on Saturday – two days ago – I was released. They said there was no evidence against me, that the other person arrested at the same time – that would be Marcel – had insisted he had no idea who I was and they admitted they had no file on me. We waited a day and here we are. I have no sense of having been liberated. I cannot think of anything other than my dead comrades and those poor children.'

'Can I ask, Doctor; did they tell you the name of this orphanage?'

'It was near a place called Izieu, if I remember correctly.'

'No!' Sophia shouted out in shock. Her face had turned bright red and she held her hand to her mouth in disbelief as tears streamed down her face. Jack tried to put his arm round her shoulder but she was rocking to and fro and now sobbing uncontrollably. It was a couple of minutes before she spoke.

'This is all my fault, these poor children!'

They all reassured her that, of course, it wasn't her fault.

'It is, you don't understand. In the last week I was at Avenue Berthelot I came across a Verified Source Report: it was from a source, an informer telling them about the Jewish children being kept at Izieu. I knew it was urgent and I did mention it to Agnes Kléber, but I ought to have done more with the information, maybe told Madame Madelaine myself – but I was so preoccupied with the escape that I just assumed Agnes would deal with it. I ought to have treated it with more urgency. If only we could have sent a warning to them! I did remember about the place when I was here, but by then I'd forgotten the name.'

No one said a word, because they knew Sophia was correct.

They sat in silence for quite a while, mourning.

Chapter 32

Siegfried Schroth knew full well he'd been riding his luck since the 17 February, the day Sophia had intercepted the telex from Gestapo headquarters in Paris alerting Gestapo offices around France that he, along with Sophia and Jack, was an enemy of the Reich: 'wanted for espionage'.

Of course, all three of them were using different names and there was no reason for anyone to link Erhard Schröder with Siegfried Schroth, just as there was no reason for anyone to realise Sophia von Naundorf was Luise Brunner. But the difference was that the Gestapo had a photograph of him, a professional publicity shot taken by the Stadt Theater in Düsseldorf just a few years previously.

They'd managed to keep the photograph out of the hands of the Lyon Gestapo and since 5 March, he'd been in hiding – first in the apartment in Lyon near Parc de la Tête d'Or and since the middle of March in a farm near Annecy.

The plan had been for Emile to organise his escape from there into Switzerland. Emile had visited twice and said he was trying to come up with a plan, but it was very dangerous, which started an argument because Siegfried shouted and told him of course it's dangerous, wasn't that the whole point?

That was in mid-April and it was the last time he saw Emile. By the beginning of August, the farmer said it was too perilous for him to remain there and he'd not received any money for weeks and hoped Siegfried would understand and Siegfried felt he had no choice but to say he did and said he'd move on.

His instinct was to head north towards the Swiss border, but the closest crossing around twenty miles away was too heavily guarded. He'd need to travel further north and cross into Switzerland over the Alps and his chances of doing that successfully without a guide were remote. He decided instead to head into Annecy and hide there until France was liberated, which was now surely just a matter of weeks.

He arrived in Annecy on a bright morning – Tuesday 1 August. The town was dominated by the lake, with beautiful gardens and promenades alongside it, the streets of the ancient but immaculate old town mixed with canals and arcades and covered passageways leading off them. But the war had not passed Annecy by: the small streets teemed with German troops and the atmosphere felt as oppressive as that in Lyon. He found the theatre on Avenue Jacquet where he'd performed many years before and went into a small café next to it, sitting at a quiet table at the rear overlooking the Canal du Vasse. He ordered bread and cheese and a glass of red wine and gathered his thoughts and realised he perhaps needed more of a plan than he'd wandered into the town with.

He had 280 francs, which he hoped would get him a room in Annecy, perhaps one above a café like this where he could also work in the kitchen.

At that moment three SS officers noisily arrived at the table next to his, glaring in his direction at first but then ignoring him. They were worried men: the most senior one spoke in an Austrian accent and said they were being sent to Paris the next day and he wouldn't be surprised if they were fighting within hours of their arrival and one of the others wondered if he'd be able to get back to the Reich and Siegfried was shocked because he thought he heard him say 'ever'. The other two nodded and when they looked round Siegfried was staring at them in a manner that suggested they knew he'd understood what they were saying because the next thing he knew the Austrian asked him what he was looking at and Siegfried said he was very sorry, he wasn't actually looking at anything he was just letting his mind wander.

But for some unaccountable reason, he'd replied in German. After all this time, the actor had forgotten his lines. It was an unforgiveable mistake, which he compounded by standing up a bit too fast and saying goodbye, he must be off and Heil Hitler! But they stopped him and said who on earth was he and what was he doing there, and Siegfried sat down again and said he worked for the Reich in Lyon and muttered something about 'Avenue Berthelot' and when they demanded to see his *kennkarte* he took out the only one he had, that of Erhard Schröder.

The Austrian studied it carefully and nodded as if all was in order and passed it to the others and the one who'd wondered if he'd ever get back to the Reich said something wasn't quite right.

You are to come with me!

Five minutes later he was in the Gestapo office in the Préfecture on Pâquier. He heard the SS officer tell someone in a side office that they were to check this man out and Siegfried was counting on the Gestapo in Annecy having enough on their plate to worry too much about a German whose papers appeared to be in order.

It would require something of a bravura performance, but one he was more than capable of. He'd make up for his fluffed lines of earlier.

He looked up to see the elderly Wehrmacht guard looking at him and at something behind him. When he turned round, he found himself staring at a poster, with the word 'WANTED!' on top, above a photograph of himself.

–

By the middle of August Marcel had been a prisoner of the Gestapo in Montluc for over four months, since the raid on Rue Ravat towards the end of March.

He was amazed he was still alive and unsure why.

He had little memory of the first fortnight after his capture: he was aware he'd been interrogated and tortured but he'd no clear memory of that period and by the time he began to come to his senses it became apparent that the Gestapo had no idea of what to make of him.

He was woken one night in the prison infirmary: a hand gently shaking his shoulder and another over his mouth. In the thin shaft of moonlight, he made out the face of Dr Hubert close to his. The doctor nodded and smiled and then leaned so close that his mouth was pressed against Marcel's ear.

'They've made a point of watching me whenever I'm near you: I tell them I'd never seen you before that day, that I was only there to treat Madame Madelaine: you understand?'

Marcel nodded.

'I've heard them discuss you: they think you're either very clever or completely innocent. My advice is to keep quiet, say nothing other than making up a story of how you came to be in that cellar by mistake. You'll think of something. You're a mechanic, aren't you?'

Marcel nodded.

'This place is a mess, nothing works properly: the Germans hate that. Tell them you can fix anything: make yourself invaluable.'

Doctor Hubert had been released soon after that and then Marcel's interrogations trailed off. Now he was just another prisoner at Montluc, though that was about the most dangerous thing you could be in Lyon as the spring of 1944 turned into summer.

He'd admitted to one of the officers that he was a skilled mechanic and the Germans took the bait and put him to work in the boiler room, where he managed to make a job he could have completed in a couple of days last for weeks.

Not long after the prisoners heard on the grapevine about the Allies landing in Normandy, Marcel had an unexpected visitor. He was working on the boiler when a warder came in and took him to one of the offices at the front of the building, where he was shocked to find himself in the presence of his detested brother-in-law. René Dupont was wearing the blue uniform of the *milice* and seemed to be genuinely pleased to see him.

'How are you, Marcel?'

'I'm a prisoner of your Gestapo, René, and you have the cheek to ask how I am?'

Dupont opened a bag and laid out its contents on the desk between them: a baguette, a portion of Saint-Félicien cheese – his favourite – and a Rosette de Lyon sausage. Marcel stared at the feast in disbelief as his brother-in-law hovered over the desk like a maître d'.

Eat, please.

Marcel's instincts were to tell him to get lost, but the food in the prison was so dreadful he couldn't resist.

'Why are you here: to seek absolution?' He spoke with his mouth full. He was eating as quickly as he could.

'Something like that, yes.'

'Really? I was joking. I always got the impression you didn't believe you'd done anything wrong! I guess that as the Allies are now on French soil you're frightened for your life and you think coming here and giving me this food is going to save you, eh?'

'You were caught red-handed in a meeting of *resistants*, Marcel: haven't you wondered why you're still alive? It's because of me!'

'Don't be ridiculous. I had nothing to do with the Resistance. I—'

'I've had my eyes on you, Marcel, ever since last September when I spotted you going into that shop on Rue Ravat: you led me to them and I was just waiting for the right time. But I'm glad you survived: I told them to spare you.'

Marcel said nothing as he absorbed what Dupont was telling him. He picked at the food; his appetite now gone. What, he asked, did he want?

'For you to return the favour when all this is over: promise me that and I'll continue to use my influence to protect you.'

On the 11 August Marcel had watched in horror as more than five hundred of Montluc's prisoners were assembled in the courtyard of the prison and divided into four groups: men and women; Jews and non-Jews. That evening an orderly was overheard saying he'd seen the prisoners being put on trains at Perrache station, along with dozens of other Jews in detention in the city. Their destination was Drancy, in Paris: the transit camp for Auschwitz.

By now Marcel was working on the prison's antiquated generator. Two days after the deportations he was walking across the courtyard when he was horrified to see a familiar figure walking towards him, handcuffed to guards on either side of him. It was the German, the man they knew as Erhard Schröder. The last Marcel had heard of him was that he was on a Gestapo wanted list.

It now appeared he'd been found.

As he came closer, Erhard spotted Marcel and turned towards him and as he did so the Gestapo officer behind him placed a hand on his shoulder and asked if he knew Marcel. Marcel had paused, not wanting to cross the path of the guards. From the corner of his eye, he watched Erhard's frightened expression as he shook his head.

That evening he passed Erhard on the first-floor landing. 'Don't say a word about me, don't let on you know me: do you understand?' He was surprised how threatening he sounded. Erhard nodded meekly, clearly terrified.

Two days later another rumour swept the prison shortly after the evening roll call: the Allies had now landed a large force on the Côte d'Azur and their armies in the north were close to Paris. Lyon would be liberated by the end of the month, surely.

The mood of elation among the prisoners was tempered by the evident fury of the Germans. Barbie was determined to liquidate all remaining Jews and *resistants* and he'd started the process on 11 August with the deportations from Perrache.

On Thursday 17 August another group of prisoners were taken from Montluc to the nearby military airfield at Bron where they were massacred.

The remaining prisoners were desperate: was there nothing the Resistance could do? The sense of panic about the prison was palpable, both among the prisoners and their guards. On the Thursday afternoon he bumped into Erhard again: the German was in a terrible state, his face was bruised and there was an open wound on his temple.

'They're torturing me! What can I do?'

'Tell them nothing: it's only a matter of time before we're freed, then you'll be safe!'

'They'll take me back to Germany before that, to one of those camps!'

A warder shouted to them to move on. Marcel felt he was smart enough to have a chance of survival and as much as it pained him to admit it, it did seem as if his brother-in-law may indeed be protecting him. His biggest threat was Erhard. If he broke down under interrogation that would be his death sentence too.

There was another round up of prisoners at Montluc on Sunday the 20 August. Marcel watched as more than one hundred of them were lined up in the courtyard. He was ashamed to admit to a sense of relief when he saw Erhard being pushed into line and marched towards the waiting trucks, desperately looking around for someone to save him.

On the Thursday evening – the 24 August – the rumours which spread around the prison were especially fevered: the Resistance had issued an ultimatum to the commandant, Captain Boesche: get out now while you can, leave the prison. Later that night, when the prisoners broke out of their cells, they found the Germans had indeed fled.

Marcel stood on the ground floor of the main cell block. Some prisoners had already left the prison, others were convinced it was a trap and he was inclined to believe them, but then someone said they'd discovered the basement was packed with explosives which were timed to go off at midnight.

Within minutes, the prison emptied, turning Montluc into a ghost ship adrift at sea, a storm gathering on the horizon.

Resistants were outside Montluc, leading prisoners away in small groups. Marcel was led to a convent near la Guillotière. Creeping through the shadows he turned a final time towards the prison.

The flag of Free France flew above it.

Chapter 33

Lyon
September 1944

Lyon was liberated on a glorious Sunday at the beginning of September by units of the Free French and United States Army, along with significant help from the Resistance. Anna had taken part in the battle and once it was evident the Germans were defeated, she headed to Place Bellecour where the crowds had gathered and a festival seemed to be in progress.

She felt strangely deflated, exhausted more than anything else, and was struggling to feel triumphant. A crowd had gathered in one corner of the square to watch a group of women being tarred and feathered and having their hair shaved. A jubilant onlooker told Anna they were collaborators who'd slept with the enemy. Anna wondered how many of those taking part had led blameless lives during the war.

She headed south on the Presqu'île, past Perrache station and in the direction of the Confluence, and without having any definite purpose as to where she was heading, she found herself on Rue Ravat. Madame Madelaine's boutique was empty, the door barred and as far as she could tell by looking through the one window which was not boarded-up, devoid of its contents. In the café next door Madame Faure looked terrified. The place had been ransacked, all the crockery smashed on the floor, the legs of the tables and chairs broken.

She told Anna she'd been the subject of the most terrible rumours, malicious lies about her informing on Madame

Madelaine and nothing could be further from the truth – in fact they were like sisters, and her son Jacques, he was in the Maquis and...

Anna left and continued walking and was on Quai Perrache when she remembered they'd agreed that when – if – the liberation ever occurred then they'd gather in the safe house off Rue Pouteau in the Croix-Rousse.

It was dark as she entered the *traboule* that led to the safe house.

There was no one in the room, so she removed a tricolour from under a floorboard, and hung it in the window and then moved an ugly blue vase from the mantelpiece to the window ledge.

And then she fell asleep.

–

Most of the Germans had scurried away from Lyon in that last week of August when it was obvious to even the most fanatical Nazi that the fall of the city was imminent.

Klaus Barbie was one of those who vanished that week: the last sighting of him was on the last day of August at his apartment on Rue Paul Lintier, close to the vandalised Grand Synagogue on Quai Tilsitt on the Thursday morning. He'd left in a hurry before lunchtime, heading east.

It was less easy for the collaborators, though, for the French men and women who'd so happily aided the Nazis. Few of them had anywhere to hide.

The occupiers had been quick enough to wash their hands of the collaborators: they'd never really respected them, and they'd only been of any use for the duration of the war. Some collaborators were more fortunate than others. They were the ones from other parts of France, who could return there with the possibility of no one knowing what they'd been up to in Lyon. Some of them had even gone to the trouble of establishing back stories to show they'd been sent to Germany as slave labourers, along with tens of thousands of other French men.

This was certainly the case with many of the *malice*, and their headquarters on Rue de la Barr resembled a tourist office in that last week of August.

But for the collaborators who were from Lyon, who'd strutted around the city for the past few years as if they owned it, no such option existed. They could flee the city, but with the country now being liberated, there was nowhere for them to go. Instead, they had to return home, hoping that in the euphoria gripping the city their neighbours, family and erstwhile friends would forget about the dirty business they'd been involved in and if they did remember, hope they'd agree they were only doing their duty.

Let bygones be bygones.

In almost every case that was wishful thinking.

René Dupont had hoped his brother-in-law would show more gratitude than he did when he told him he'd used his influence to protect him. He wondered if he'd made a mistake in admitting that he'd told them to spare him, which on reflection did reveal he'd been the person behind the raid on Rue Ravat. But nonetheless, he'd done what he could, and after all, family was family and hopefully once the war was over, all would be forgotten.

René Dupont was increasingly unwell during August. His stomach was in a terrible state and when he managed to get a private meeting with Barbie and asked him if he could be transferred to Germany the Gestapo chief had laughed in his face and told him to get lost.

After that he decided to base himself with the *milice* at Rue de la Barr, where the rumour was that in the event of the Germans leaving the city the *milice* would be seen as a stabilising force, that its possible excesses would be forgotten in return for it pledging its allegiance to the new regime.

Dupont could see the sense in this, though he wasn't convinced his fellow Lyonnais shared that point of view. However, on the 20 August he was part of the *milice* contingent sent to Saint-Genis-Laval to assist the SS with some prisoners they'd brought there from Montluc.

And after the events of that day – the massacre – he knew no one would forget the *milice*, or forgive it.

He returned home on the Friday, the first day of September and two days before the city's liberation.

No one said a word to him, not his wife, or his children or the various members of her family when they visited. It was as if he wasn't there, a ghost, an uncomfortable presence in his own home where he was no longer welcome. On the Sunday evening there was a party in the garden and when he came downstairs, he was shocked to see Marcel there. He went up to him and speaking loudly in case anyone missed it, said how pleased he was to see him and he put an arm round Marcel's shoulder and announced that Marcel had survived thanks to him and then he began to sing the 'Marseillaise', but to his intense embarrassment no one joined in and Marcel pushed his arm away and said he ought to leave now.

–

They gathered in the silk workshop on Rue Pouteau, like awkward mourners after a funeral, though so soon after the liberation the mood ought to have been more of a festive one.

The habits of the past four years were hard to shake off, so they'd each carefully made their way to the meeting through the *traboules*, still checking all was safe and that they weren't being followed, pausing in doorways and hurrying across courtyards, entering the building one by one.

Anna was already there and she was joined by Marcel and Alain, both arriving around three o'clock that afternoon. They waited, oblivious to the party still going on in the narrow streets of the Croix-Rousse. Just after four, Dr Hubert arrived, along with Sophia and Jack. Despite being the youngest there, Anna had assumed leadership of the group. They should establish what they knew about the others, she said.

Alain spoke first. 'We know that Madame Madelaine, Michel, Maurice and Georges were all killed by the Germans in Rue

Ravat in the raid on twenty-second of March. Gilbert contacted me soon after, he'd been instructed to tell the few of us remaining to go to ground, that Mars was being suspended – is that correct?'

Anna said it was.

'I saw Gilbert a few times after that: he told me he'd joined the FFI. I found out on Saturday that he'd been killed the previous day in fighting around Part-Dieu. Emile I'm less sure about: Gilbert said something about him helping Siegfried escape to the east, but he was certainly back in Lyon in June and joined an FTP unit, he was always a communist, eh? I'm told he may have been captured by the Gestapo late in July and murdered by them, possibly in Dijon.'

'You mentioned Siegfried – what news of him?' It was the first time Sophia had spoken.

'I saw him in Montluc,' said Marcel, 'he arrived there around the middle of August; I can't be sure of the precise date. But he was one of the group of prisoners taken away on Sunday the twentieth of August: I don't know what happened to him, but—'

'I can tell you what happened,' said Alain. 'They were taken from Montluc to Saint-Genis-Laval and—'

'It's part of Lyon,' Anna explained to Sophia and Jack. 'On the left bank of the Saône.'

'More than one hundred of them – some say as many as one hundred and twenty – were taken into a house at Fort de Côte-Lorette and massacred by the SS and also *milice*. There was only one survivor, a Frenchman.'

They all looked down and Sophia clutched Jack's hand.

'Your brother-in-law, Marcel—'

'Dupont?'

'Yes: he was involved, I'm told.'

Marcel nodded.

The gathering ended soon after that: they agreed that Mars had possibly served its purpose, though at a most terrible price. But their work was now done. They would resume their lives. Sophia said they needed to get to Switzerland as soon as possible and Anna asked Marcel if he could help with that?

Marcel said he could find transport, but if someone else could actually take them he'd be grateful. 'I have some family business to attend to.'

–

By the Wednesday after liberation, René Dupont had come to the conclusion that remaining at home – isolated and ignored – was not a good idea. Sooner or later, someone would concoct something against him and he'd be treated as a collaborator. He needed a few days to decide where to go: he could head south and possibly start a new life. Maybe his family would give him some money and help him get some new papers, just to be rid of him.

He was aware of people entering the house and muffled voices downstairs. It was becoming unbearably hot in the room and he was about to leave it when the door opened and his wife Jeanne looked at him pitifully from the corridor and he stood up and smiled and said it was good to see her and it would be good if they could talk and maybe… But she told him to be quiet.

'Why did you return here: don't you think you brought enough shame to this family, eh?'

He started to reply but she told him to shut up. 'You should have disappeared, that would have been best for everyone. But you're so arrogant and stupid that you're incapable of making the right decision.'

'I was going to tell you that I'm leaving, Jeanne, I do so with a heavy heart but I—'

Jeanne had stepped back and it was then that he saw Marcel in the corridor and when he entered the bedroom, two of his wife's cousins were with him. Dupont was cornered against the boxes, aware he was breathing heavily and panicking. One of the cousins was holding a thin rope with a stick tied to it and when they grabbed his arms and tied his hands he began to struggle and shouted out, demanding to know what was going on, and Marcel said what did he expect – for them to forget and to show him mercy? The two cousins had pinned him down and Marcel was struggling to put something round his neck.

'My advice is to keep still: let the garotte do its job and it won't take long; just long enough to think about what you've done.'

Chapter 34

Sophia von Naundorf and Jack Miller arrived in Berne on Thursday 7 September.

Despite their evident exhaustion, Basil Remington-Barber insisted on bringing them into the embassy where he fussed over them in his office until he announced he had some rather unpleasant news to impart, as he put it, which is when he told them about the killing of Barney Allen and the discovery that Noel Moore was a traitor, would you believe it, and how annoying it was that he and that other traitor – Source Armand – had disappeared.

Into thin air.

He sat there shaking his head and muttering about what an unfortunate mess this had all turned out to be.

'So, we've wasted our time, then?'

'What do you mean, Sophia?'

'The mission we've just been on, everything in Lyon, the deaths, what Jack has been through… you think all this has been just a dreadful mess?'

Basil swept his hand through his silvery hair and managed to look contrite. 'No, good heavens, no… I'm sorry if you think that. That isn't what I meant. Your mission was an undoubted success, notwithstanding the casualties along the way, which is the unfortunate but inevitable consequence of any battle. In fact, I was speaking to London only yesterday and they are of the very firm opinion that you helped to keep the Resistance intact and ensured that by the time the Allies landed in Normandy, the Resistance was an effective fighting force. The importance of what you achieved should not be underestimated. There is no doubt you played a vital role in the Liberation of France.'

Sophia started to reply but stopped as Jack tugged at her sleeve and said he really didn't feel terribly well and did the embassy have a doctor he could see?

He deteriorated very quickly after that: he was admitted to the university hospital that evening and the following morning Sophia and Basil were called in to a stuffy office where a doctor told them that Herr Miller was very ill: 'He appears to have damage to his right kidney, which should have been treated some time ago, and he would require an operation but that would only be possible if he pulled through the next twenty-four hours and…'

Sophia remembered breaking down and an embarrassed silence before she composed herself and asked the doctor what were his chances of survival and he said it was impossible to say, but fifty–fifty at best, and Basil asked where was the best place for Jack to have the operation and the doctor asked if there was any chance of him being taken to London?

Basil was most impressive after that: once Jack was stabilised, he was driven by ambulance to Orly airport just outside Paris where the United States Army Air Force flew him to London. That Thursday – exactly one week after Jack and Sophia had arrived in Berne – Jack was propped up in bed in his room at St Mary's Hospital in London, the late morning sun catching his face, and Sophia realising quite how ill he must have been because for the first time in six months she was looking at the Jack she remembered and loved so much: the life now back in his face, the eyes sparkling and the gentle smile lighting up the room. Piers Devereaux was there too, along with a surgeon who was telling them it had been touch and go and how Jack had survived so long without surgery was really most remarkable.

When the surgeon left, Piers told them the plan was for Jack to remain in hospital for another week and then he'd be taken to a convalescent home that the Service used and which was very private and Sophia would be able to stay there too and of course there would need to be a proper debrief, but all in good time.

By the middle of October Jack was much improved, more or less back to normal, and Sophia was asked to come to London for a series of meetings with a team from British Military Intelligence who wanted to question her about Berlin, given that they hoped to be there soon.

She spent a week in London, staying in a hotel in Victoria. She'd been given Swiss papers and instructed not to tell anyone she was German, or anything else for that matter.

It was an exhausting week in a basement room with maps and photographs spread over a large table and she was questioned in minute detail about Berlin.

They finished with her on a crisp Friday at the end of October, the 27, and when Piers Devereaux arrived, she assumed it was to take her back to the convalescent home and when he said he wanted a chat with her first she hoped it was to discuss where they could live until the war was over, which had already been talked about, and she also hoped that he had an answer on the other sensitive matter she and Jack had raised, namely whether they'd be able to get married even though she had no proof as such of her husband's death.

He took her to an upstairs room in whatever building it was they were in, with views over the Thames through the grimy window, which Piers sat in front of. For the first time in years, she felt relaxed: Jack was well and her days operating as a clandestine agent were over.

But Piers looked more uncomfortable than she'd ever seen him, standing up, then sitting straight down, shifting in the chair, fiddling with his watch strap and avoiding looking directly at her. He said that despite what he was about to say, she needed to know that she was held in the very highest regard by the Service and the success of their latest mission just proved that she was indeed one of their top agents… and then he paused, lowered his voice and said she was to listen very carefully because what he had to say was not easy and indeed nothing about the war was easy and it was undoubtedly the case that people behaved differently – unconventionally, if the truth were told – and clearly people were the victims of unfortunate circumstances and she was certainly no exception.

He got up and walked over to Sophia, his arm outstretched, and in his hand was an envelope and he said he'd leave her in private to read it and he'd be back in a while but he was sure she'd want some privacy. He couldn't get out of the room quickly enough.

–

My dear Sophia

This is not an easy letter for me to write and I know it will be an even more difficult one for you to read.

By the time you receive this I will have returned to the United States. An official from the US Embassy came to see me and said if I wished to return home then he could arrange it and the thought of 'home' had a profound effect on me: I realised that despite my feelings for you, my life has been in the United States and I need to return there to understand how I feel about everything. I need to find where my heart is.

It may well be that I will just be there for a few weeks or it could be for much longer, but I do ask that you give me the time to think about the course of my life.

I have promised Piers that I will keep in touch with him.

I hope you understand, Sophia, that whatever happens, I will always love you.

Jack

Chapter 35

Berlin
September 1945

Considering his predicament, Jeffrey Morgan approached Germany's imminent defeat and the end of the war with a surprising degree of equanimity.

He and Noel Moore had arrived in Germany in February the previous year, fleeing Switzerland after disposing of Barney Allen. Their debrief lasted one month and once the Gestapo were satisfied they had all they needed from the two men they put them up in an apartment on Roscher Strasse near Charlottenburg U-Bahn station. They were given jobs translating documents, but it was menial work and the atmosphere in the apartment was tense.

At the end of April 1945 Nicholas left Berlin without telling the bothersome Noel Moore. The order which had so typified the city was beginning to break down and he decided to join the stream of refugees heading west.

He ended up in Marburg, in the area occupied by the Americans, and by the time he got there he'd assumed the identity of Gottfried Schäfer, courtesy of a rotting corpse he'd come across on the journey. No one would be able to connect him with Jeffrey Morgan or Nicholas. Gottfried Schäfer was just one of millions of displaced people in Germany.

He'd got away with murder.

And a whole lot more.

But it was an altogether different matter for Noel Moore. He knew he was a wanted man. Returning to England was out of the question, as was remaining in Germany as an Englishman.

He was relieved when Nicholas disappeared from Berlin: he'd never trusted the man and the fact that he knew his real identity was always something that worried him. He was forced to enlist in the *Volkssturm* – the militia made up of the wounded, old men, boys and anyone else they could press-gang into action, and soon realised it could be his salvation. By now his German was much improved: he wasn't fluent, but his accent was good and he was familiar with the rough Berlin slang. His uniform helped too, not that the *Volkssturm* had much of a uniform, but he had the black *Volkssturm* armband and that meant he looked much like anyone else.

In the last week of April, he was assigned to a battalion in Kreuzberg and they'd come across an abandoned house with the bodies of a dozen fellow *Volkssturm* in one of the rooms. They'd searched the bodies for weapons and that was when he found a *kennkarte* for an Ernst Hauff and assumed the dead man's identity.

In the final days of the battle his *Volkssturm* unit merged with another and then split up again and he was sent with a dozen others to Moabit. On Wednesday 2 May he found himself in the basement of a house on Rostocker Strasse, along with a man in his seventies and a terrified boy of around fourteen. The old man was in no mood for fighting. The war was over, he told them – and it was never his war anyway. *We'll hide here until it's over.*

The building shook the rest of that day and night and Noel Moore had no idea how it didn't collapse on them. At one stage he dozed off and when he awoke it was quiet: the shelling had stopped, and when the boy came back from looking outside, he said there were Russians everywhere and the old man burst into tears of joy and announced he'd always been a communist anyway.

It could have been worse: they'd surrendered to a Red Army unit who'd roughed them up a bit but they'd spotted Ernst Hauff's railwayman's uniform, so he was sent to help clear the railway lines around Friedrichstrasse and although it was hard work, he felt strangely safe: no one suspected him. As far as the Red Army were concerned, Ernst Hauff was just another German and as far as the other Germans were concerned, they weren't especially concerned with him or indeed with anyone else. Everyone kept to themselves and no one talked very much and when they weren't working, they tried to sleep in the rubble of the bombed-out factory where they were garrisoned.

There was a lot of talk about trying to head west, away from the Red Army and towards the British and the Americans, but Ernst Hauff was in no hurry. Living under the Russians was far more preferable than being a prisoner of the British.

The more he thought about it, the more it seemed to be a good idea.

And it was.

Until that fateful Friday.

-

It began as a fine mid-September day.

For the past month Ernst Hauff had been part of a gang repairing the Zoologischer Garten station, known to everyone in the city as Zoo station, and one of the only railway stations in Berlin not completely destroyed. The previous month Berlin had been divided into four sectors: the east controlled by the Soviet Union; the United States in the south of the city; the French in the north; and the British in the west, which included Tiergarten where Noel Moore was working.

At first this had concerned him, but it quickly became apparent that the British occupation forces had far more important matters to worry about than gangs of filthy and broken workmen. And the conditions were better than they had been in the immediate aftermath of the fall of Berlin. His gang were living on the ground floor of an abandoned shop on Ranke Strasse and over a period of weeks they'd made it almost comfortable and they were getting food and it was only a few minutes' walk to and from the station.

And it was on this fine Friday afternoon that Ernst Hauff was returning to Ranke Strasse after a ten-hour shift at the station, which had begun at six that morning and it was now just after four o'clock, and he'd just been told that they were having the following day off and he was feeling quite upbeat. And earlier that day he'd found a pack of Player's Navy Cut cigarettes in the gutter, which must have been dropped by a British soldier. There were eight remaining in the pack, a fortune on the black market.

There was a notable spring to his step as he crossed Kurfür-stendamm. He was heading for a cake shop that had recently re-opened where he'd be able to exchange two cigarettes for a large bun with jam, which didn't taste of sawdust, and a cold lemonade.

He was at the junction with Meineke Strasse when he heard his name and then for some inexplicable reason he paused and when his name was repeated, he turned round.

At which point, his world crumpled.

–

The seven months after Jack Miller had returned to the United States had passed in a strange kind of daze for Sophia. If at any point during that time she'd been asked what she'd been up to the previous day, let alone the previous week, she wouldn't have had a clue.

Which wasn't to say she wasn't functioning. She worked in a unit at the War Office preparing for the occupation of Germany, helping prepare what were called 'Occupation Guides' for each town and city. Once a fortnight Piers Devereaux would stop by her office and suggest they have a chat and though he had little to say she knew it was his way of keeping an eye on her and though they never discussed Jack, he'd always make a point of saying there was 'no news – not yet, at any rate' and sometimes he'd tell her not to despair and who knows what the future holds for any of us?

In April she'd been sent to Münster, which had been in British hands since the start of the month and where some kind of civilian administration was being put together. She'd been there a fortnight when she was told she was being lent to the Americans for a few weeks.

She arrived in Frankfurt late on a Tuesday afternoon and was taken to the US military governor's office on Fürstenbergerstrasse. Five minutes later she was in a comfortable office with sweeping views over the ruins of the city. A young officer had checked her papers and asked her if she'd like a drink and said he'd be back soon and when he returned, she was still looking out over the city and wondering how some buildings had survived intact when she heard a cough and as she turned round a familiar voice said, 'Sophia,' and the soldier standing behind her in an immaculate US Army uniform with tears streaming down his face was Jack.

–

The first thing he said to her was that if she wanted him to leave, he quite understood because he recognised that his behaviour had been unforgiveable and he knew she deserved better than that. She noticed that his German was a bit rusty because he was confusing his tenses and she heard herself correcting him and then his face broke out into that familiar smile, the one that involved every part of his face and he stepped forward and flung his arms around her and now it was her turn to weep.

They talked for hours: when they finished, night had descended over the city, the misshapen landscape as black as the countryside. Jack explained that when he returned to the United States he collapsed and was taken to a hospital and from there to a clinic where they explained to him that he'd had a nervous breakdown and when he explained what he'd been up to these past few years they said they weren't surprised and the only way he'd recover was with complete rest and he was to avoid thinking about his future until his mind was more settled.

'I was given so much medication it was as if I was asleep for months and when they reduced the dosage it took me a few more weeks to feel normal again. It feels as if I lost three, four months of my life. Only then I was able to look at my life with any kind of clarity and that was when I realised it would only have any meaning if it was with you. I want to be wherever you are. I wrote to Piers Devereaux and asked him how you were and whether you'd found anyone and said if you had you deserved that and I'd leave you alone. But he replied and said I should make arrangements to get over here. I'm now an officer in the US Army Military Intelligence – but there's some talk of me being attached to the British once they get into Berlin. Basil had a lead that Moore ended up in Berlin. They regard it as unfinished business, Sophia: they want us to find him together.'

They were driven to a small hotel near the station and given their room keys, Jack's room along the corridor to Sophia's. He waited as she opened her door and wished her a good night and as he turned to head for his room Sophia asked him where he was going and held the door open for him.

—

The British Army arrived in Berlin in early July and only then was it deemed safe enough for Jack and Sophia to return to the city. They arrived at Gatow airfield on a wet Tuesday evening, the 10 July. They were buffeted by the wind as they were led across the apron to a waiting staff car and taken from there to a British Army barracks where they were to spend the night.

The following day they moved to a house on Berliner Strasse which had been requisitioned by the British forces. It had been decided that as few people as possible in MI6 would be aware of the hunt for Noel Moore. They were on their own.

But Piers Devereaux had one lead for them: a British woman working for German radio had been arrested and during her interrogation admitted she'd met Noel Moore and believed he was certainly in the city in April, just before its liberation. As far as she was aware, he'd been conscripted into the *Volkssturm*.

The search continued for the next two months, with a brief interlude in Switzerland at the beginning of August. They combed the city, but there was no sign of Noel Moore. There was no proof he'd remained in the city, or if he had, that he was still alive.

Piers Devereaux agreed they'd give it until the end of September: it was a matter of honour for MI6 to bring to justice the traitor responsible for the death of Barney Allen.

They had to give it their best shot.

By September Sophia had reclaimed her apartment on Potsdamer Strasse, which fortunately was in the British Zone and in reasonable repair, although most of the valuables had been looted, which didn't bother her: they all reminded her of her previous life and she'd have got rid of them anyway. The neighbours were confused at the attractive American who'd replaced her SS officer husband, but knew better than to comment on it.

One Friday afternoon they were on Kurfürstendamm when Sophia found herself gazing at the workman shuffling along in front of them as they approached the junction with Meineke Strasse.

She didn't say anything to Jack because it wouldn't have been the first time she'd stopped a stranger in the street because they looked like Noel Moore or walked like him but there was unquestionably something familiar about this man.

'Noel – Noel Moore!'

And to her disbelief, the man stopped and when he turned round, Noel Moore stared at them in absolute horror, his mouth wide open and his face drained of colour.

He shouted 'no' and then '*nein!*' and turned to run but by then it was too late. Jack had grabbed him by the elbows and pushed him against a wall and Sophia pointed her pistol at him.

Chapter 36

Berne
July 1945

It was a baking hot Monday afternoon at the end of July, two months after the end of the war in Europe, and Basil Remington-Barber's office was so warm he was contemplating removing his tie. Such informality no longer seemed to matter quite as much as it once did: after a lifetime with the Service, he was one day away from a retirement delayed by more than five years.

His successor was a chap called Richards, with little experience of intelligence but evidently he'd had a good war, spoke decent French and German and his father had been at school with Tom Gilbey's father.

Richards wasn't due to start until September, so Basil had been busy writing an extensive handover document and sorting out his office, which meant going through hundreds of files, deciding which ones needed to be kept at the embassy, those which could be sent to London and which ones were to be destroyed.

His secretary brought in what she promised was the final set of files. When she returned minutes later his heart sank: at this rate he'd be here all night.

'There's a foreign gentleman to see you, sir.'

'Where?'

'In the secure waiting area downstairs, sir.' She handed a card to him.

A.I. Stepanov

−

Basil Remington-Barber knew Arkady Stepanov by sight and certainly by reputation. He was the NKVD commissar in Berne – the Soviet Union Intelligence chief in Switzerland – with a reputation for being ruthless and clever. Despite the fact the United Kingdom and the Soviet Union had been allies since June 1941, there had been little contact between the two men and certainly no co-operation.

In fact, there had been a good deal of tension between them, which extended well beyond a professional rivalry. In April 1943 Stepanov had effectively abducted Sophia von Naundorf from the Soviets and kept her captive in a house near Berne, from where Basil had rescued her with the help of the Swiss police. He knew Stepanov was furious about this. He doubted this visit was to bury the hatchet.

Stepanov was very formal, standing up when Basil entered the room and waiting until Basil sat down before doing so himself, and then offering him a cigarette. He told Basil to keep the lighter, a large one with a picture of Stalin on the side. It was a gift, he said.

He spoke very good German. He wanted him to know he was very pleased that the courage of the Red Army along with that of their British counterparts had resulted in the defeat of Nazism.

Basil said indeed and decided not to point out that the Soviet Union and the Nazis had begun the war on the same side.

'I am aware that your agent, Sophia von Naundorf, and her American companion were involved with a Polish scientist, a Jew. We know that you brought him here and he was assisting you.'

Basil said nothing.

'You have your operations and your agents and we have ours but occasionally there is a connection and… our understanding is

313

that the Polish scientist is called Roman Loszynski and he is from Poznań: his wife is called Lea and his children are Raisa and Max. They escaped from the Warsaw ghetto just before the uprising in 1943 and were hiding near the Slovakian border when Loszynski began his journey to Switzerland.'

There was a pause. Basil Remington-Barber had never made the error of underestimating the NKVD but even so, this was impressive. Stepanov knew a lot about Roman Loszynski, though it was notable he was talking about him in the present tense. Perhaps he was unaware the man had blown himself up in Geneva two years ago.

'Let me tell you why I am here, Mr Barber. It's not to interfere in your operations or with your agents. It is what you could call a humanitarian mission. Soon after Loszynski left Poland his wife was captured and taken prisoner by the Gestapo. We understand she perished at Auschwitz in June or July 1943. But his children escaped and hid in a forest and when they emerged at the end of the war they were rescued by the Red Army. A young Jewish officer called Marshak from the 110th Rifle Division took them under his wing and because the Jews all know each other he placed them under the protection of another Jew, a senior colonel in the NKVD, a man called Krupkin. The children told him they intended to travel to Switzerland where their father is waiting for them. Colonel Krupkin persuaded them to remain in Poland until the end of the war – and now the war is over. Yesterday Raisa and Max Loszynski arrived in Berne, accompanied by Leytenant Mikhail Danielovich Marshak! I'm sure the British government would not want to see any delay in reuniting them with their father!'

–

It was a horrendous situation, so much so that Basil Remington-Barber had to remain in Berne for a further week to sort it all out. A.I. Stepanov was shocked at the news that the children's father had died two years before and seemed to be of the opinion that Basil should have told him.

'Had you bothered to check with me first, Arkady, then I could have told you of Loszynski's unfortunate death, but to bring these poor children here like that seems irresponsible and—'

'I had no idea the children were coming: I was just told to expect Leytenant Marshak who was on an important mission on behalf of Colonel Krupkin.'

In the end Basil asked London for permission to bring Sophia and Jack down from Berlin for a couple of days. They'd been the ones who worked closest with Roman Loszynski. Sophia in particular knew him better than anyone else in Switzerland. She'd been the person who'd met him in Vienna and smuggled him across the border.

So, on the 1 August Sophia and Jack arrived in Berne. London had allowed them two days before they returned to continue hunting for Noel Moore.

Inevitably there'd be a row about where they should meet: the Soviets didn't want to bring the children to the British Embassy on Thunstrasse and the British ambassador vetoed any suggestion of them meeting at the Soviet legation and neither side wanted the meeting to take place in Swiss government premises because the Swiss could be so nosey, so there was a rather undignified stand-off before it was decided they'd meet at a hotel, the Beau-Site on Schanzenberg Strasse.

Basil, Sophia and Jack entered a private lounge on the first floor of the hotel where A.I Stepanov and the young Red Army officer were waiting, with the two frightened children sitting on a sofa. There was an awkward silence before Jack asked quite what it was that they were there for.

'The children need to know what happened to their father,' said Stepanov.

'In that case I will speak to them alone.' Sophia walked over to Max and Raisa and asked them if they understood German and they nodded. She turned round and asked everyone else to leave the room.

They hesitated, but Jack understood the situation: he recognised the fear in the children's eyes, the look of abandonment, of being alone in the world at an age when no child should feel like that. He'd seen it on the faces of thousands of children in Berlin.

Once they were alone, Sophia sat down and spoke quietly. She told Raisa and Max that their father had been an exceptionally brave man and they should know that he helped defeat the Germans by inventing a device that helped the British Air Force. And more important than that, she said, he never forgot about his family. It had broken his heart that he was separated from them and their mother. He constantly talked of how he could bring them out of Poland.

The children sat there quietly, tears in their eyes, but very subdued and they politely asked a few questions: had he eaten well, how often did he mention them, how had he died...?

Sophia said he'd died in an accident, but he hadn't suffered at all, and both children nodded and the girl thanked her as if to indicate that they now knew as much as they needed to know.

When the men returned to the room Sophia asked what would happen to the children. Stepanov said they weren't to worry: they would be looked after by the Soviet Union.

'We could take them back to Berlin with us,' Sophia said to A.I. Stepanov.

'Who?'

'Jack and I.'

'That is out of the question: you want to take two Jewish orphans to Berlin? Don't be ridiculous.'

Jack said nothing as Sophia spoke to the Russian. 'I have a large apartment in Berlin: I will bring them up as my own!'

Stepanov looked unsure, as if he was giving what Sophia had said some consideration, but the young lieutenant settled matters.

'I had a telegram from Colonel Krupkin this morning. They will live with his family in Minsk.'

Epilogue

Some people get away with it.

It's an unfortunate and inconvenient fact of history that so many traitors and murderers evade justice. In no period of history is this truer than the Second World War.

–

Source Armand certainly got away with it.

The man originally known as Georges Moreau had enjoyed various other personas over the years, even before the war. After killing Agnes Kléber in March 1944, he disappeared, unwilling to take the risk that anyone may discover he was the traitor, as unlikely as that seemed.

He left Lyon, never to see his mother again.

–

Jeffrey Morgan got away with it too.

He'd got away with the murder of his wife, Dorothy, in England in 1941 and with the many years of being a Nazi agent in Britain and then he'd got away with the murder of Barnaby Allen in Berne in February 1944.

He became Gottfried Schäfer, remaining in Marburg until 1947 when he moved to the Soviet Zone. It was a strange move as most people were heading in the opposite direction, but it was obvious relations between the Soviet Union and the west were deteriorating and he knew he'd be safer in the east, far away from the British.

He eventually settled in Brandenburg, finding work as a janitor in a school, living on his own in a tiny cottage in the grounds. It was a lonely life but in time he came to appreciate the order and certainty in what was to become the German Democratic Republic. It was very much the kind of world he'd imagined would be created in Nazi Germany.

He carried on working until 1953, when he was seventy-five. He died peacefully two years later.

–

But not everyone got away with it.

Noel Moore certainly didn't.

After being caught by Sophia and Jack on Kurfürstendamm on the Friday afternoon he was flown back to Britain and taken to an MI6 safe house deep in the Hampshire countryside.

He'd barely arrived before an almighty row about what should be done with him began. MI5 and Special Branch had both caught wind of Noel Moore's arrest and wanted him tried under the Treachery Act, which was still in force and could result in the death penalty. But Piers Devereux was worried that the evidence against Moore of committing espionage in the United Kingdom was not as strong as it seemed, despite the fact that he'd changed his name from Harold Dickson. He was keen that Moore should be tried and punished for the murder of Barney Allen, but that depended on the co-operation of the Swiss authorities and they were being difficult. They wanted him to stand trial in Berne, which was out of the question.

He was interrogated for the remainder of September and well into October while they decided what to do with him. It had all been rather unsatisfactory: Moore had admitted he'd been foolish but said he'd been tricked by the man he knew as Nicholas but who was in fact Jeffrey Morgan and as far as he was concerned, he had never divulged anything of any importance and when he was asked about betraying the Resistance in Lyon, he denied all knowledge of it.

Tom Gilbey was brought in at one stage and he questioned him about the murder of his close friend, Barney Allen. Moore insisted he had nothing to do with it: he'd been at work that day and when he returned to his apartment Nicholas was waiting for him and was armed and he was forced at gunpoint to go with him to Germany.

In the middle of October Piers Devereux met with Roly Pearson in Downing Street. 'Our legal advisers take the view that notwithstanding the predominance of circumstantial evidence against Moore, there is nonetheless a strong case against him. They are of the view that a prosecution under Section 1 of the Treachery Act would succeed.'

Sir Roly Pearson nodded and said that was his understanding too and then paused and looked carefully at Piers Devereux before asking him if he'd mind making sure the door was closed properly. 'All this assumes of course, Piers, that we believe it is in the interests of the Service for Moore to be put on trial.'

'It is surely in the national interest!'

'The national interest and the interests of the Service are one and the same and there is a view, Piers, that it is in no one's interest for there to be a trial where the evidence would show that an employee of first the Foreign Office and then of MI6 has been an active enemy agent since late 1933 or early 1934, which by his own admission was when he was recruited. For it to be revealed that such a person operated from within the heart of our most sensitive departments for over ten years would raise some very difficult questions. It would harm our reputation and that would not be in the national interest.'

'And what about the involvement of this Jeffrey Morgan? He claims he was with him in Germany as recently as March this year.'

'But there's no evidence to support that claim, is there, Piers? As far as we're concerned, the body of Jeffrey Morgan has been rotting in a pauper's grave in Sussex since September 1941.'

'What do you suggest, Roly – surely Moore should not go unpunished?'

'Good heavens, no!' Roly Pearson shifted his ample bulk slowly from the slumped position he'd been sitting in. 'Absolutely not: apart from anything else, the chap was involved in poor Barney's murder. No, what I am saying is that if Moore were to disappear before the messy business of a trial, then the view around here is that it would be altogether neater, far more convenient to all concerned: very much in keeping with the national interest.'

'And by "disappear", Roly, do you mean…?'

Sir Roly Pearson stood surprisingly quickly and held up a hand to stop his visitor saying any more.

'Tom Gilbey will handle matters, Piers: he has our blessing.'

–

Noel Moore was driven from the safe house in Hampshire on the last Saturday of October, handcuffed before being led into a car with blacked-out rear windows and driven for what was an uncomfortably long time before he became aware of the car turning off a road because the surface became increasingly uneven and the car lurched from side to side and the sound of heavy rain beating against the vehicle became louder. When the car stopped, they were in a clearing in a forest and the light was fading and it took him a while to make out his surroundings. A dozen men were standing around and he began to feel fear rising in him because nothing felt right.

And then a familiar figure approached, one of the men who'd interrogated him, a very well-spoken type who'd mainly questioned him about the death of Barney Allen and who at one point had told him that Barney Allen was his friend.

The man said he was to come with him and before he could say anything he was grabbed by each arm and frog-marched along, deep into the forest.

Noel Moore only saw the grave when they stopped right next to it. It was deathly silent, the trees so dense that their canopy blocked the rain. He stood there, too shocked to say a word, and when he felt his legs buckle, he was held up and then one of the men holding him said, 'You'd better get on with it, sir,' and he was pushed down into a kneeling position and he felt the wet, freshly dug mud seep through the overalls.

His final senses were of something hard being pushed against the back of his neck and then the earth rushing towards him before his world turned black.

–

Franz Boehm – the Lyon Gestapo officer who'd inadvertently been of so much help to Sophia – didn't get away with it either. An inquiry in Berlin decided he'd been unprofessional and had shown a serious lack of judgement but would remain in the Gestapo, though demoted in rank and with a reduction in pay.

He was transferred to Lublin in eastern Poland at the beginning of April 1944 and based at Gestapo headquarters on Uniwersytecka Street. Boehm was there on the 22 June when he was arrested by troops from the Soviet 2nd Tank Army who'd just liberated the city. A few hours later, in a dungeon under the building, he drank from the phial of cyanide which had been sown into his lapel. He'd been told it would take a few seconds to kill him. In the end, it took five minutes of excruciating agony.

–

In one sense, there was nothing for Sophia von Naundorf and Jack Miller to get away with. They were two of the many thousands of unsung heroes from the war whose courage only a handful of people would ever be aware of.

They'd undertaken successful clandestine operations inside Germany and Nazi-occupied France and survived imprisonment and torture by the Gestapo. Both had shown an extraordinary level of bravery and there was no question that their exploits had contributed to the Allied victory.

And yet… and yet… as time went on, their feeling of relief at having survived the war and being reunited with each other was tempered by a sense of guilt that they'd survived when so many others hadn't. It played on their minds, so much so that they could never totally feel at ease. And then there were the memories and the dreadful scenes they'd witnessed, the feelings of terror resurfacing in their minds, the long, sleepless nights when they may as well have been back in a Gestapo prison, terrified at the softest sounds, their every sense alert for something they were unsure of.

So, in one sense, Jack and Sophia did get away with it: they survived the war.

But in another sense, they didn't.

For them, the war never really ended.

They remained victims of it.

But no one would have been aware of this had they met either of them and particularly if they came across them as a couple, which was more likely because everyone who met them was struck at how devoted they were to each other, how inseparable they were.

After they'd found Noel Moore, their roles with British Intelligence finished. It was all very amicable and terribly civilised: after signing something called the Official Secrets Act they agreed never to discuss their wartime work. In return, the British undertook to pay them a generous monthly retainer until 1965.

They remained in Berlin, living in the apartment on Potsdammer Strasse. Jack resumed his work as a journalist and thanks to the British retainer could afford to pick and choose which commissions he accepted. He preferred to write features: sport remained a passion, the war was a subject he avoided.

Sophia came across a home for children orphaned in the war and volunteered there. It remained her lifetime's vocation, caring for the children and doing her best to ensure they were never exposed to any kind of extremism.

The illness which claimed her in 1973 did so with astonishing speed. In some ways, her wartime experiences were to blame as they'd given her a notable degree of physical resilience along with a sense that she'd been through the worst she'd encounter in her life. By the time she visited her doctor there was little they could do.

She was just sixty-three when she died.

Jack was utterly bereft at her death. For a good six months he didn't write a word and barely left the apartment. Occasionally he'd wonder if he should move back to the United States, but he'd soon dismiss such thoughts: for all its faults, Berlin had captured his heart in 1936 and that remained the case.

From time to time, he and Sophia had discussed the idea of writing a book about their wartime experiences but Sophia was reluctant. For all her courage and her hatred of Nazis, she was reluctant to draw attention to herself.

Around 1976 Jack dug out the agreement with the British and the ridiculous Official Secrets Act they'd signed. It did say something about not writing about their experiences in either fiction or non-fiction forms, but Jack took the view that as it was many years since the British had paid the retainer, the agreement had expired and, if necessary, he'd get it published in the United States.

Over the next four years he began the book many times, but always reached a point when he'd come to write something about Sophia and her absence would hit him so hard, he'd stop writing for weeks or months.

Jack Miller finally wrote the book over three months in the late spring of 1980. A bout of pneumonia the previous winter had made him aware of his own mortality.

He completed the book in the early hours of a June morning as the sun began to rise over Berlin, throwing light over his study.

Once he'd written the final words he turned off his desk lamp and sat quietly for a long while, calm and at peace.

He was now the agent who'd finally emerged from the shadows.

Author's Note

Agent in the Shadows is a work of fiction: any similarities between the characters in the book and real people are unintended and should be regarded as purely coincidental.

The most notable exception to this is Klaus Barbie – the head of the Gestapo in Lyon from late 1942 and the man known as 'the Beast of Lyon'. Barbie was involved in the actual events covered in this book (see below), although his involvement in the plot is, of course, fictional. He disappeared from Lyon in September 1944 and then, astonishingly, was protected by the United States, for whom he worked in Europe. When the French authorities discovered this in 1951, they sought his extradition, but rather than hand him over for justice, the US authorities helped him to escape to Bolivia.

He lived there as Klaus Altmann for twenty years, until in 1971 his true identity was exposed by French Nazi hunters and journalists: it wasn't until 1983 that Barbie was extradited to France. When he arrived in Lyon he was taken to Fort Montluc, the former Gestapo prison in the city. And that was where he was incarcerated for the first week of his captivity, in the same wretched place where his Gestapo had imprisoned some 15,000 people and executed nearly one thousand of them and tortured many more. It was from where thousands left on their final journey, where he himself had tortured Jean Moulin in June 1943 and where, on the night of 6/7 April 1944, forty-four terrified children and their carers had, on his orders, been crammed into a cell before their journey to Auschwitz.

He was found guilty of war crimes and crimes against humanity on 4 July 1987 and sentenced to life imprisonment. He died in prison four years later, in September 1991.

Helmut Knochen was the SS commander in Paris, Northern France and Belgium for much of the war. He was twice sentenced to death after the war, but for some reason pardoned by de Gaulle in 1963.

To ensure my books are as accurate and as authentic as possible I do try, where possible, to use locations and buildings that existed in that period – for example towns, government buildings and embassies, hotels and railway stations. As a general rule, if I name the location of somewhere in the book then it is more likely than not to correspond to the actual location during the war. The same applies to military units. In the section that follows I'll highlight some of these places.

Likewise, the plot of *Agent in the Shadows* is substantially based on real events and I refer to some of them here.

The British Union of Fascists (Chapter 2 and thereafter) and the National Socialist League were actual organisations, many of whose leading members were interned during the Second World War.

The Nazi euthanasia programme described in Chapter 5 was known as Aktion T4 and was in reality another of the Nazi's large-scale murder operations against civilians, in this case mostly physically and mentally disabled Germans. It is estimated that between 200,000 and 275,000 people were murdered this way during the war. (Source: www.yadvashem.org.) The reference in Chapter 5 to the denunciation of the euthanasia programme by Clemens von Galen, the Roman Catholic Bishop of Münster, is accurate. These comments were made in a series of sermons in July and August 1941.

The Mars Resistance Network is completely fictional, as are all the people associated with it. There were, however, hundreds of such Resistance groups throughout France during the war, as well as the large networks such as Francs-Tireurs, Combat,

Libération-Sud. Jean Moulin – along with the aliases used in the book – was a real person and was General de Gaulle's emissary to the Resistance, with the ultimately successful task of unifying the Resistance. I've tried to be as accurate as possible with the circumstances of Moulin's capture and death.

By D-Day in June 1944 the French Resistance was a far more cohesive body and played a significant role in the Liberation.

Cardinal Pierre-Marie Gerlier referred to in Chapter 6 was the Archbishop of Lyon and the Primate of Gaul during the war and an outspoken opponent of the Nazis. He died in 1965 at the age of eighty-five and was awarded the title of Righteous Among Nations for his efforts to save Jews during the war.

In Chapter 6 (and thereafter) there are also references to the Parti Populaire Français and the *milice*, both of which René Dupont was a member of. These were actual organisations, as was the Mouvement National Anti-terroriste, the National Anti-Terrorist Movement, referred to in Chapter 10. It is a fact that some thirty members of these organisations worked directly for the Gestapo in Lyon during the war. The Francis André referred to in Chapter 10 was executed in March 1946.

The raid on the Jewish community offices in Rue Sainte-Catherine did occur in February 1943, as described in Chapter 6. Eighty of those arrested on that day were deported, of whom seventy-seven were subsequently murdered.

Likewise, the meeting of Resistance leaders and the Gestapo raid on it led by Barbie did take place on 21 June 1943 at doctor Frédéric Dugoujon's surgery in Caluire-et-Cuire. The question of who betrayed the meeting, leading to the murder of Jean Moulin, is central to the plot of *Agent in the Shadows* and even today, remains a matter of considerable conjecture and controversy in France. It is a subject that arouses a good deal of tension and emotion, raising as it does the fraught topic of collaboration with the Nazis in France during the war. More than once I was warned off writing about this, even in fiction. The character Georges Moreau – Source Armand – is deliberately obscure, so as to reflect the fact that the real traitor's identity has never been established. He is not based on any real person.

Readers of my earlier novels may have spotted that Georg Lange (Chapter 7) was also an Abwehr officer in *The Best of Our Spies* while Madame Ladnier (Chapter 11) featured in *The Swiss Spy*. Rolf Eder, who appears in Chapter 12, is also a main character in *The Swiss Spy* and *Vienna Spies*. All three are fictional characters.

Franz Boehm is also a fictional character, but the massacre of three hundred prisoners at Lublin Castle did take place, under the orders of Obergruppenführer Wilhelm Koppe. Koppe escaped justice after the war: the West German authorities refused to extradite him to Poland and decided not to prosecute him themselves.

Towards the end of *Agent in the Shadows* a series of war crimes and other real events in 1944 are featured. These include: the raid on the Jewish orphanage at Izieu in the April (see following section); the deportation of 600 Jews from Perrache on 11 August; the massacres of prisoners taken from Montluc at Bron (17 August) and St-Genis-Laval (20 August). There were, of course, many other atrocities committed by the Nazis in Lyon in that period and indeed throughout the war.

Two hundred and thirty-five thousand two hundred and sixty-six French civilians were killed during the war as a direct result of the Nazi occupation. (Source: *World War Two Infographics*, Thames & Hudson, 2019 – first published as *Infographie de la seconde guerre mondiale*, Éditions Perrin, Paris 2018.) Of these, 77,000 were Jews (including 15,000 children), from a Jewish population of 350,000 at the start of the war. The vast majority were murdered in the Nazi death camps, primarily Auschwitz, the remainder in occupied France. The Jewish population of the Rhône-Alpes region (which includes Lyon) was 32,000 at the start of the war. Five thousand had been murdered by the time of the Liberation in September 1944, including four hundred children (source: *Centre d'Histoire de la Résistance et de la Déportation*, Lyon), including the children from Izieu. The identity of the person responsible for their betrayal has never been proven. Their names are listed after this Author's Note.

There are estimated to have been half a million members of the Resistance in France during the Second World War, operating clandestinely under conditions of constant and extreme danger. It is thought that some thirty-four thousand *resistants* were killed by the Germans as a result of their Resistance activities.

The inspiration for the title of this book is twofold: on the one hand it is intended to evoke a sense of Lyon during the war, where the dark *traboules* and the narrow streets of the Croix-Rousse played such a key role in the work of the Resistance. It's also intended as something of an *homage* to the French/Russian writer Joseph Kessel, who fought with the Free French in the war and whose 1943 novel *L'Armée des ombres* (*Army of Shadows*) was part set in Lyon. In 1969 it was adapted into a film of the same name, directed by Jean-Pierre Melville.

A word about the currencies referred to in the book. I've worked on the basis that one Reichsmark was worth twenty French francs; that £1 in 1938 is the equivalent of (just under) £69 in 2022 and $1 would be worth $18.55 today. £1 (during the war) was worth around twelve Reichsmarks.

I'd like to express my sincere thanks and appreciation to the many people who've helped bring about the publication of this book. I visited Lyon in early 2022 to carry out research for this book and would like to thank a number of people and institutions who assisted me on that visit: Stéphanie Engelvin at Lyon Tourisme; Lisa Emprin at the Montluc Memorial; Bénédicte Roy, a specialist guide who showed me round the Croix-Rousse and Presqu'île; and finally the staff at the Resistance and Deportation History Centre Lyon (based at the former Gestapo HQ on Avenue Berthelot). I would highly recommend visits to the Avenue Berthelot and Montluc museums. I'm also very grateful to Séverine Fraysse of the Association de la Maison d'Izieu for her assistance with my research regarding the victims of Izieu. The house at Izieu is now a memorial, open to visitors.

I'd especially like to thank my agent, Gordon Wise, and his colleagues at Curtis Brown. Gordon has been enormously supportive over a number of years and I'm delighted to be able to express my appreciation. Likewise, my publishers Canelo, who couldn't have been more impressive with the manner in which they've handled the *Wolf Pack* novels and before that the *Prince* series and the re-issuing of the *Spy Masters* novels. As ever, Michael Bhaskar and the whole team at Canelo have been thoroughly professional, supportive and encouraging throughout the writing and publication process. I'd like to thank Nick Venables for designing the cover of *Agent in the Shadows* – and indeed for all my other books published by Canelo. My thanks too to Jo Gledhill for a skilful copy-edit, and to everyone who helped me with aspects of the book and answered seemingly odd questions as I was writing it.

And finally, to my family – especially my wife, Sonia, my daughters and their partners and my grandsons – for their encouragement, understanding and love.

Alex Gerlis
London
September 2022

Victims of the Gestapo raid on the Jewish orphanage at Izieu, 6 April 1944

Source: *Association de la Maison d'Izieu, mémorial des enfants juifs exterminés*

www.memorializieu.eu/en

Sami Adelsheimer, 5
Hans Ament, 10
Nina Aronowicz, 11
Max-Marcel Balsam, 12
Jean-Paul Balsam, 10
Esther Benassayag, 12
Elie Benassayag, 10
Jacob Benassayag, 8
Jacques Benguigui, 12
Richard Benguigui, 7
Jean-Claude Benguigui, 5
Barouk-Raoul Bentitou, 12
Majer Bulka, 13
Albert Bulka, 4
Lucienne Friedler, 5
Egon Gamiel, 9
Maurice Gerenstein, 13
Liliane Gerenstein, 11
Henri-Chaïm Goldberg, 13
Joseph Goldberg, 12
Mina Halaunbrenner, 8

Claudine Halaunbrenner, 5
Georgy Halpern, 8
Arnold Hirsch, 17
Isidore Kargeman, 10
Renate Krochmal, 8
Liane Krochmal, 6
Max Leiner, 8
Claude Levan-Reifman, 10
Fritz Loebmann, 15
Alice-Jacqueline Luzgart, 10
Paula Mermelstein, 10
Marcel Mermelstein, 7
Theodor Reis, 16
Gilles Sadowski, 8
Martha Spiegel, 10
Senta Spiegel, 9
Sigmund Springer, 8
Sarah Szulklaper, 11
Max Tetelbaum, 12
Herman Tetelbaum, 10
Charles Weltner, 9
Otto Wertheimer, 12
Emile Zucherberg, 5
Lucie Feiger, 49
Mina Friedler, 32
Sarah Levan-Reifman, 36
Eva Reifman, 61
Moïse Reifman, 62
Miron Zlatin, 39
Léa (Laja) Feldblum, 25 (survived Auschwitz)